# DOUBLE LIFE

## BY
# TYRONE WALLACE

Copyright © 2004 by Tyrone Wallace
**Life Changing Books**

Cover and book design: Stacy Luecker, Essex Graphix
Edited by: Clara Anthony
Interior Design by Nancey Flowers

First Double Life  trade paperback printing 2004

For more information, or to contact the contributors, address correspondence to:

**Life Changing Books**
PO Box 423
Brandywine, MD. 20613

Or visit: www.lifechangingbooks.net

ISBN: 0-9741394-1-6

Printed in the United States

# Dedication

This book is dedicated to my grandmother Cleola P. Cooper, the woman that helped me pull through some hard times with her infinite wisdom. And to Rufus T. Denny, my stepfather, you're still #1.

Rest in Peace


Also, to Ms. Patsy: Your kind heart will never be forgotten.

# Acknowledgements

First and foremost I have to thank my higher power. Without *You*, this would not be possible. Ten years ago, if someone would have told me, I would write a book, I would have disregarded their statement and kept it moving. But here I am, a published author! Now you tell me how a ninth grade drop out, who went on to receive his GED is supposed to feel.

I must acknowledge my immediate family: My mom, Carolyn Wallace (a.k.a.) pretty lady, I love you with every bone in my body. You are the true definition of strength. You've displayed your super-woman abilities every since I came out of the wound. To my brother Ben, I love you, Slim. Man, I know that we could have taken our dough, and started a business. To my sister Renee, I love you girl. Although you're an introvert, your characteristics shine brighter than the sun. To my brother Russell (a.k.a.) Rah Rah, I love you Joe, we've been trooping this thing we've got goin' for a minute now. Hopefully it's almost over. Oh Yeah! **I did it!** To my lil sis Alisha, I love you girl. And to my extended family, I love all ya'll. I didn't give shout outs individually because some of ya'll don't deserve it. So I played it safe.

I must give thanks to the many people who have helped to bring this project together. Whether you've proofread, provided publicity, or was there for support, thanks. To my man Divine, outta Queens, NY, thanks for all your help. You kept a brother on his game. To the NOI, thanks for opening up my mind. Lisa Williams, words cannot express my appreciation for your promotions. Keep pounding the pavement! To my test readers, you are all what I call women of excellence: Cheryl, Teresa, Kim, Leslie, Tam, Danielle, Ronnique, Dora, and Schalette; thanks for doing a brotha right, and making sure Double Life is tight. Clara Anthony and Leslie German I can't imagine the hard work you put in. So thank you for your dedication and expertise on editing my work. In a year or so, I can put Four Eyes editorial services to work again. Richard from Sepia, Sand and Sable, thanks for the support. It means a lot. Stacey from Essex Graphix, you did your thang on the cover. Angela Jones and Nancy Flowers thanks for the technical support. You're the best.

I can't go on without thanking my distributors who make it possible for thousands of people to read my work. To the Culture Plus family, A&B, African World Books, and Baker &Taylor your support is greatly appreciated. I wanna personally thank the many bookstores who have promoted and supported this book from the start. I must give a shout out to the #1 vendor in Queens, Masamba. Good lookin' out. A special thanks goes out to the local bookstores near my hometown: Karibu, Sepia, Sand and Sable and Meja Books. Thanks for showing me luv!

To the many authors who have given me hope. Keep doin' your thing. Darren Coleman , you did it when you put out *Do or Die*. You're doin' the damn thing!  Natasha Gale Lewis I wish you much success on *Men Cheat Women Experiment*. Saving the best for last, Azarel author of *A Life to Remember* the Queen B of LCB, no words can really express my gratitude for what you've done. You've opened a new chapter in my life that will enable me to have a better future. You opened your arms and gave a brotha a chance from the gate, without throwing a stone at him. That alone has shown me that you are a person that believes a person can change. I wish you and your family the best that the future has to offer. If you think I should've mentioned your name, don't worry I'll get you on my next joint.


One Love,
*Tyrone Wallace*

# DOUBLE LIFE

## BY
## TYRONE WALLACE

# PROLOGUE

The over populated and most violent unit of Washington D.C.'s city jail was filled with young and old men facing charges from murder to DWI. Unit NW-2 was just one of many that comprised what inmates and citizens called "D.C. Jail". Built for 160 inmates, it mirrored a concentration camp because of all the cruel sentencing guidelines. There were many reasons why tempers would flare in the crowded unit. The place was filled with an abundance of drugs, homosexuality and all the other negative elements of the streets. In some cases, tempers would rise over a man claiming a woman guard was his girl.

A female guard that chose to have sex with an inmate was any man's woman as long as he came up with the right amount of cash she demanded. In jail, that was one of the luxuries of being a "Baller", because the women knew exactly who to fuck for money. But if they liked you for your style, that made you a lucky man. You didn't have to pay. Unique Johnson was definitely one of those lucky men.

The 6 foot, light-skinned, slightly muscular man with short wavy hair, and thick black eyebrows lay nude across the bed. Lying on the small bottom bunk in the two man cell, Unique waited patiently for Ms. Hill to make her once a week appearance. Even though the cell was made for two, Ms. Hill made sure he was the only inmate occupying cell #26.

Tonight was special because it was Unique's last night in jail. Grinning as if he'd won a prize, he waited for Ms. Hill. He thought back to the night that led to his being locked up. That hot July night, six months ago, Unique rode in one of his leased cars with his young runner who he took everywhere with him except to the location of his drug connect. Unique was stopped at a light on Massachusetts Avenue when a police cruiser pulled beside him. The two black officers glanced up with envious looks.

Unique knew the cops were looking his way but he refused to acknowledge them. He didn't want to give them any reason to pull him over and discover the 80 grand he carried in his backpack on the back seat of the black Lexus GS 300. He was on his way to get rid of 28 grams of his last supply of crack cocaine. Before he could reach the Southeast neighborhood, he and his young runner were pulled over by two cops. As soon as Unique pulled over to the curb the runner who already knew his job, jumped out of the car and ran with the crack and a loaded 9mm. Unique had been reluctant to carry a gun since his arrest a while back. The police officers pulled around the Lexus and gave chase after seeing the youngster flee from the car. They called for back-up and gave the license plate and model of Unique's car to the dispatcher.

After watching the cops go after the young passenger, Unique pulled off nonchalantly only to be surrounded by other cops a few blocks away. They held him in the back seat of one of their squad cars until they heard word over the radio that the cops had not caught the other suspect. But the cops that gave chase had recovered the 28 grams that the youngster dropped while being pursued.

One of the cops that heard word over the radio walked over to the squad car Unique sat in and peered through the back passenger window. "Looks like your partner left you in deep shit," the fat cop said. "They found a heap of crack they believe is yours since it came from outta your car."

Luckily, when Unique was tried he had beaten the charges because one of the two officers on his case made a mistake. Although the judge wanted to release Unique on the spot, the court had to wait to see if his probation officer was going to violate him. Even though the final outcome was favorable, Unique enjoyed the moments he spent with Ms. Hill.

Now, the night before his release, he looked at his watch. It was ten minutes after 2 a.m. When Unique walked to his cell door and peered through the small window, he saw Ms. Hill walking from cell to cell flashing her flashlight through the cell windows of the unit. Flicking on his light, Unique quickly spot checked the cell he was warned about on several occasions. Ms. Hill had told him how important a clean room was to her. So he always made sure he had a fresh jail house incense lit as well as two jail house issued blankets tucked nice and neat on both beds.

Flicking off the light, Unique stood in the middle of the floor with his arms folded across his bare chest waiting for her to enter. All he could think about was how good she felt last week when she visited. Since this was his last night, it was going to be better than ever. Ms. Hill had guaranteed that after tonight he would be looking for her in society.

The sound of her key entering the cell door sent a chill of excitement through Unique's body. Although the cell was dark, Ms. Hill knew every square inch of it. She had visited the cell at least twenty times during his six month stay.

"I know I'm a little late," she whispered as she stepped into the cell. "My partner took a long time falling asleep," she explained slowly shutting the sliding door behind her.

Her elderly partner was an overweight, short, man who had been diagnosed with a sleeping disorder. So, for the last six months, Ms. Hill took advantage of his handicap by talking to him until he fell asleep in his chair. Then she would slip out the booth, do her count, and head to cell #26.

"Any of those hot niggas see you come in?" Unique asked.

"I don't think so and it doesn't matter. You leave in the morning," Ms. Hill replied with a big smile on her face.

"I'm just try'na make sure you have a job after I leave."

"Don't worry, I will," she whispered, then began slithering out of her uniform.

Under Ms. Hill's uniform was one of the most stunning bodies a thirty-four year old woman could possess.  She stood five foot six, 135 pounds with long black hair that swept her shoulders.  Her caramel skin matched her light brown eyes perfectly.  Measuring an alluring 36-24-37, Ms. Hill was just what the doctor ordered.

As many times as Unique had sex with the gorgeous woman, he never had the pleasure of seeing her nude.  He had only felt the body that he had grown to love fucking.

"Unique," Ms. Hill whispered, stepping closer to where he stood.  She now stood face to chest with him.  "Put your hands over top of your head."

With both of her manicured hands, she slowly rubbed Unique's muscular chest while kissing it at the same time.  Dropping down to his stomach, she ran her tongue along his six pack. She then came up slowly and pressed her lips against his.

"Why you playin' games?" Unique asked as his swollen dick poked her in her stomach.

"I do what I wanna do," she responded as she grabbed hold of his dick with her left hand, and cupped the back of his neck with her right. She stuck her tongue deep down his throat. After what seemed like an eternity for Unique, she dropped on her knees and pleased him like no other woman had.

"Damn!" Unique sighed, looking down in the direction of his dick and wishing the lights were on so he could watch her gratify him.

Ms. Hill took deep long strokes that just about gobbled his eight inches. She was determined to please him, even if it choked her. After noticing the nerves jump in Unique's dick from the eruption that was about to take place, Ms. Hill withdrew her mouth. She rolled on her back and cocked her legs near her ears, "fuck me!" she murmured as he positioned himself in between her legs.

The blankets that were used for carpet were now sliding along with Unique's vigorous movements.  The pumps that he took were hard and deep.  He kissed her as he dived in and out of her wet womb that had him in heaven.

Ms. Hill's thoughts at that very moment were about her ex-husband who had left her for a young woman the same age as the twenty-five year old man that was now thrusting himself into her. But that wasn't her reason for fucking Unique. She really was attracted to the young thug. The first time she saw him, she knew she wanted him, even though she'd never had sex with any other inmate during her five years working as a Correctional Officer.

"Turn around," Unique whispered, pulling himself out of her.

In three seconds Ms. Hill was perfectly planted on all fours. Face down and ass up, she grunted when he entered her from behind. After plugging Ms. Hill doggy style, Unique had sex with her for at least an hour in every corner of the cell, including the top and bottom bunk. Then their pleasure ended.

"Did you enjoy that?" Unique quizzed, sitting at the edge of the bottom bunk with his head slumped back in a state of exhaustion.

"Yes I did," Ms. Hill quickly replied. While she put her uniform back on, she said, "I just don't give head to anybody you know. I know you're clean because I checked your medical records awhile back. And I know you ain't on no boys for a fact."

"You got that right," Unique shot back springing to his feet and stepping over to the sink that Ms. Hill had already used to clean herself off.

"Well, I gotta get back to the booth before Mr. Brown wakes up," Ms. Hill stated watching Unique intensely.

It was now 3:30 a.m. Ms. Hill didn't leave right away. She watched Unique clean his dick off at the sink. At that moment, she flashed her flashlight on him while he stroked his dick with a washcloth. Wanting to have sex again, she moved slowly. She had to be out of that cell by 4 a.m. before the food service inmates showed up at the entrance of the unit with the unit's food cart.

"I gotta go," Ms. Hill said in what sounded like a painful voice. "But here's my phone number and address. Use it."

"I will," Unique replied while simultaneously pulling his underwear up and reaching for the piece of paper she held out to him.

"Yeah, and by the way, when and if you see me on the streets, don't call me Ms. Hill, call me Kim," she said, looking out the cell door then smoothly slipping out of the cell.

Kim couldn't take her eyes off the monitor for cell #26 as she sat in the control booth with Mr. Brown who sipped a cup of hot coffee. The control booth operated the entire unit and was built near the entrance of the unit so all the officers had to do was look through the thick plexiglass to observe the entire unit. At the particular time, Kim didn't care about the entire unit. All she was thinking about was Unique, and wondered if he'd ever use the number or better yet the address she gave him.

Kim was now sitting in the booth with what she called her life book, her diary. She had been writing in it for over a year, from the onset of her divorce. She kept all her deepest secrets in it including her and Unique's jail house relationship. Kim shielded her diary from Mr. Brown who was standing a foot to the right watching an episode of Perry Mason. She began to write.

*It's January 10th, 2001, Wednesday morning 5 a.m. Today is a good day for me, or maybe a bad day. It all depends on Unique's judgment of a good woman. I know I'm a little older than him but that's good. Maybe I can get him to settle down at a young age. But then again, what would a young, handsome, good dick man like him get outta settling down? Nothing. Anyway, the boy got money. I hope Unique can stay out of jail because from what he told me, this was his second run in with the law. His first charge that got him probation was for a gun. So, if he knew what I know, the system never runs out of bed space. Their gates are wide open just for young black brothers. But I don't think he's coming back. Especially, if he's with me. I can show him how to love and respect a relationship. So, I've done my part. I gave him my phone number as well as my address and some great sex.*

After those last words, Kim shut her diary only to wonder about the moment Unique would walk out a free man. Would he forget her? Would he forget the good sex they shared?

# ONE

It had only been three days since Unique's release and already he was on his way to meet his drug connect. Dressed casually, flexing his red leather Avirex jacket, and a NFL Redskins skullcap, he rode through Georgetown, D.C. in his dark blue, freshly leased Navigator truck. The traffic seemed to move in slow motion through the leftover rubbish of snow that had fallen upon the city.

Like clockwork, on Saturdays at noon, twice a month Unique would re-up on his supply. But since his absence of six months, he had to re-up as soon as possible. The last of his supply, which he was arrested for, was now in an evidence room or maybe on the streets.

Finally reaching Peabody Street in Georgetown, he cruised through the neighborhood admiring the prestigious brownstone houses that were in a row on both sides of the two-way street. Pulling into the same parking space where he'd parked ever since he had his license, he grabbed the backpack out of the passenger seat and stepped out of the truck. As he walked into the four foot high steel black fence that separated the house from the others, he saw someone peep from behind the curtain. He smiled knowing who it was as he walked up the seven steps to reach the front door of the house. One ring of the doorbell and the heavy mahogany door flew open revealing a little girl who looked to be around the age of seven with dark smooth looking skin and long pretty jet black hair. She held on to Unique's right leg yelling, "Daddy! Daddy! My big brotha is here.

A few seconds later a tall man who stood around six foot three came to the door wearing an expensive red silk robe with matching slippers. His full, closely trimmed beard and short afro had streaks of gray. But his body was that of a young man. He looked 30 years old instead of his 48 years of good living.

"Stacy!" Unique shouted, cheerfully reaching down to scoop the girl up with two hands.

"I heard you were in jail for being bad," Stacy stated with a mile long smile on her face that exposed her missing front tooth.

Unique frowned. "Who told you that?" He placed her back on the ground.

"I'm not gonna tell you." She took off running into the house.

Unique turned his attention on the man that stood in the doorway. "What's up young man?"

"You," Dad said, while he looked over Unique's shoulder examining the truck he drove. "I see you took my advice…never drive the same vehicle when you're in the game."

"The older you get, the wiser you get," Unique replied.

"How was that lawyer I got you? Was she on her job or what?" Dad quizzed as he and Unique made their way to the kitchen then down to the basement. The small basement with its two washers, two driers, and a variety of workout equipment had the smell of fresh lemons rather than the smell of sweat and dirty laundry.

"Yeah," Unique responded with a grin as he thought about the young white blond that defended him.

"Yeah, that's who I use when I get in some shit. She specializes in law and business."

"I'm not gonna lie, I don't usually lust off no white girl, 'cause you know, they don't have no ass, but that lawyer you got me got a body like a Black girl. When I first met her at the jail, I couldn't believe how pretty she was with that phat ass."

"Boy, if your father and mother were here to hear you talk like that, they'd correct all that foulness that just came from out of your mouth, especially your mother," Dad said.

Unique's mother and father were dead, leaving Dad, his wife, and Unique's late grandmother to take care of him and his younger sister Glory. Unique's father was one of the biggest low-key drug dealers in D.C. He had flooded the streets with dope from 1970 to 1983. And Bobby, who Unique now called Dad, was his partner. The two men had operated in all four parts of the city, making other drug dealers as well as the local police department envious.

One Friday night while Unique and his sister were at their grandmother's house, the police raided one of three apartments his father rented in Southeast. In the process of the raid, Unique's mother and father were shot and killed. The police department later released a statement stating that both suspects drew guns and that was the reason they both were shot.

Months later, the Washington Post dropped a bomb on the two white cops that were the shooters. The paper reported that the two officers were believed to have shot and killed at least three other couples during so called drug raids, but no evidence of drugs or guns were found in any of the raids. The last murders the two cops committed were Unique's parents. In 1984 an all white jury sentenced the cops to life without parole on eights counts of murder.

"I know you're glad to be out of that funky ass jail," Bobby yelled from the bathroom in the basement.

"Hell yeah! I couldn't wait to get the fuck outta there," Unique shouted while lying under the weight bench pressing 205.

Emerging from the bathroom, Bobby held four ziploc bags filled with already cooked crack cocaine with a street value of 18 to 20 thousand dollars a kilo. "Here are four kilos," he said handing the ziploc bags to Unique.

Sitting upright on the bench, Unique opened his backpack pulling out the cash passing it to Dad.

"How much is this?" Bobby quizzed.

"Eighty g's. Why?" Unique stuffed the backpack with the crack.

"Because I'm giving you a kilo free," Dad replied peeling 20 thousand from the money and handing it back to Unique. "I gotta look out for you sometimes, baby."

Unique didn't utter a word. He just stood up from the bench and stuffed the money into his pants pocket as they walked back upstairs.

As they sat on the expensive burgundy cloth sofa in the living room, they talked about many things as they always did when Unique came over.

"Ain't no sense in you selling this shit for much longer. It won't do nothing but give you a big head and have a thousand of those trigger happy thugs trying to rob you. Besides, the Feds will be on your ass."

"So what about you?" Unique inquired, watching as Dad snatched the remote control off the table.

"What about me?" Dad replied.

"You gotta be selling at least 25 to 50 keys. I don't see you getting robbed or looking out for the Feds."

"I don't have to. I've got two legitimate shoe stores and one ice cream parlor that backs my revenue. And as for me being robbed, I've been dealing with the same people for nineteen years. If anybody tries to rob me, I'll more than likely know who it is."

"Man, you've been giving me four keys for four years now. I wanna step it up," Unique spat, eyeing Dad as he relaxed on the sofa.

"Let me ask you something. How much money do you have saved up?"

"About 400 thousand...I think."

"Where is it?" Dad asked.

"At my crib in my safe."

"You see. That money is supposed to be at a bank accumulating interest. Not in your house where it doesn't have any insurance on it in case something happens," Dad said.

"I don't trust no ban..."

The sound of Unique's two-way pager interrupted his next words.

*Hurry the fuck up Slim.* The words across the small screen of the pager read.

"I gotta go," Unique murmured now standing up looking down on Dad.

"Yeah, take care and be careful. Tell your sister I said I love her and her Mom said call her," Dad said giving Unique the evil eye.

"Oh yeah! Tell Donna I…"

"Mom!" Dad shouted, breaking Unique's sentence. "Don't forget that woman as well as your grandmother raised you and your sister like y'all was her own."

"I know," Unique replied with a slight smile on his face walking out the living room and stopping at the bottom of the stairs in the hall. "Stacy," he yelled, looking up the steps that led to the bedrooms upstairs.

"I'm coming," a distant voice yelled, as Stacy appeared at the top of the stairs.

"I'll see you later," Unique said to Stacy while looking into the living room at Dad who was glued to the TV. "Here," he whispered, tip toeing half way up the steps to pass Stacy a 50 dollar bill.

"Thanks," she whispered.

"We got big trouble on our hands, another Bush steppin' in office," Unique heard Dad say from the living room as he headed out the door waving at Stacy.


**Unique parked his truck in the small parking lot of** the cheap motel off of 295 in Riverdale, Maryland. He sat in the truck, checking the lot out like he always did. When he felt everything was safe, he climbed out of the truck with the backpack over his right shoulder. Already knowing the room he was going to, he strolled through the first floor of the two level motel, then headed up the crooked steps to the second floor. One knock at room number 28 and the door swung open.

"How many times I gotta say the same shit to you PooBear?" Unique fanned his nose as he walked into the clouded room.

"Fuck that shit Slim. It ain't gonna hurt nothin' if I smoke this blunt," PooBear stated shutting the door behind Unique.

"Put that shit out and let's get to work."

The 18 year old had been answering to the name PooBear since his mother named him that after she watched him drink honey from a bottle when he was around two years old. But today he showed no character-istics of that name. PooBear had been in a juvenile center twice before reaching the 8th grade, when he finally dropped out. One of the visits was from a fight he had in school where he stabbed his classmate with a knife over a jacket that the boy claimed PooBear stole from him. The other visit was from stealing a car which later turned out to be Unique's 98 BMW.

After dropping all charges against PooBear, Unique wanted to meet the young thug who stole his ride. So he did, and liked the young fear-less thug. So he took PooBear under his wing, and they've been to-gether for the last two years.

Instead of putting the blunt out, PooBear quickly sucked it into a tiny roach then placed it in an ashtray. Unique placed his backpack on the bed where he sat and watched PooBear take two guns out of his waist and place them next to him.

Unique looked at PooBear wondering how a young nigga like him could be so nonchalant at a time like this. Here they were about to break down four kilos of crack that could put them both in jail for life, and he had this cool look on his face.

It wasn't that PooBear didn't care about getting caught, be-cause he did. The careless look on his face was just natural for him. His cream colored light skin gave his baby like smooth face an angelic glow. His black, curly, short, 'fro made his face look more adorable. His five foot nine inch stocky frame made him appear fat, but that was only when he wore baggy clothes. The extra material hid his muscular build.

Both men sat at the edge of each bed facing each other with razors in one hand, and a block of crack in the other. They broke down one kilo after the other without saying a word. After they weighed and bagged it all, it came out to 32 big eighths, with a street value of $80,000. But that number was far from what they would pull in. Actually they would pull in $160,000 off the four kilos. After counting, the money would be split with Unique always receiving $130,000 and PooBear receiving the remainder, depending on the shorts he took.

Before Unique met PooBear, he was a foot soldier, but gave that up once he saw how fast PooBear could sell out. Unique decided to make PooBear his foot soldier and now thanks to him he would always see his $130,000.

Unique always gave PooBear two eighths at a time. Making sure he brought back no less than $10,000. It didn't take PooBear but two days to get rid of the two eighths. But little did Unique know, *PooBear had a team*. Wop and Darkman had secretly been on PooBear's squad since the first package he got from Unique over two years ago. PooBear wasn't the foot soldier that Unique thought he was. *Wop and Darkman were*. But the money they saw was small compared to the big money PooBear was making.

PooBear, Wop and Darkman had been friends since elementary school, all growing up in the tough neighborhood of Barry Farms. They were a team of car thieves at one point before PooBear met Unique. But after PooBear was introduced to another form of illegal activities, they switched occupations, with PooBear being the leader.

**As they finished cutting and bagging the crack,** Unique walked toward PooBear who was stuffing the two black Glock 9mm's on his waist. "I wanna ask you somethin'. Why you have two guns with you? Why you have on all black? And why you have on baseball battin' gloves?"

PooBear smiled before he answered the questions. "I always wear black." He looked down at his denim jean outfit and his black timberland boots.

"What about the gloves and the extra gun?"

The smile on PooBear's face vanished as he thought of something to say. He didn't want Unique to know the real reason for the extra gun. "I…I just…"

"Listen," Unique snapped. "We don't have time for no bullshit, Joe. We just gotta get this money and don't shit else matter. So if you was 'boutta do some dumb shit, forget about it."

"It's not dumb," PooBear replied, swiping the two eighths from the bed and placing them in his blue backpack along with the scale and other paraphernalia. "I was over this bitch's house the other day and some bamma called and we exchanged a few words."

"Are you in love with the broad?  Or you just fucking her?"

PooBear let out a fake laugh then shouted, "I'm just fucking her.  I 'on love them bitches."

"All right, leave that broad alone then.  I got a broad for you.  She's your age too."

"Damn!  I was hopin' you was talkin' 'bout your sista," PooBear stated in a sarcastic way as they walked towards the front door.  They both had their backpacks hanging from their shoulders.

"Play your cards right and maybe you can get her," Unique said as they walked out the room knowing his sister was too good for a drug dealer.

# TWO

The January cold weather at Reagan National Airport located in Virginia, a few minutes away from Washington D.C., was filled with freezing travelers waiting for cabs. They all stood in what looked like a single file line. Some travelers had luggage that would hold an elephant down, others had luggage as simple as a laptop computer.

But one man stood out amongst all the travelers. He stood in the cold afternoon weather in timberland boots, black denim Sean John jeans, and a white long sleeve Sean John T-shirt holding a silver briefcase. He stood about six feet with light-brown smooth skin, and brown eyes. Noticeable to most he was slim, and possessed a well-built frame, close shaved full beard and neatly braided cornrows that touched his shoulders.

People glimpsed at him because he had no coat in such cold weather. Luckily for the young man a yellow cab pulled in front of him. The cab driver jumped out and quickly opened his trunk. "I don't have nothin' but this briefcase," the coatless young man said to the cabby as he opened the cab's back door leaping into the back seat.

"Where to?" the tall cabby asked in an African accent.

"To any D.C. hotel that's decent," the young man replied taking a deep breath tossing his briefcase to the side.

"I know just the place," the cabby responded as he pulled from the curb.

The two men rode in silence until they were five minutes from entering the city. The cabby had been looking through his rearview mirror at the young man since he left the airport. He wondered what was in the briefcase. He very seldom saw anyone carrying a briefcase dressed the way his passenger was.

"So, what's ya name young man?" the cabby asked, looking straight ahead trying to keep his eyes on the heavy traffic.

Before answering, the young-looking man reached for his briefcase and sat it on his lap. "Supreme," he said with a sharp look at the cabby through the rearview mirror.

"That's a great name," the driver replied with a shake of his head. "That means you are the most high, right?"

"I guess so," Supreme shot back.

"Sure it does my fellow African. Your name has a strong meaning just like mine. My name is Ike, which means power."

Supreme didn't respond after being side-tracked by the upcoming hotels.

"How old are you?"

"Twenty-two. Why?" Supreme snapped.

"That explains why you're running around town without a coat," the cabby smirked, pulling into the parking lot of a Days Inn on New York Avenue in Northeast, D.C.

The hotel parking lot was filled. There were only three or four parking spaces left in the entire lot. Supreme peeled $100 from his pocket and told the cabby to wait while he paid for the hotel room.

"Yo!" Supreme yelled cheerfully, talking to the cab driver after paying for his room. "I don't have any clothes but what I'm wearing. I was hoping you could pick me up tomorrow around noon, and take me to a mall or somethin'."

"I don't think so young man. I have…"

"I'll pay you $200 for a round trip to the mall," Supreme quickly responded before the cabby could finish his sentence.

"You have a deal young man. Now get yourself in that room before you freeze to death. I'll see you at noon."

After watching the cab pull out into the traffic, Supreme strutted into the entrance of the hotel with his briefcase held tightly. As he walked through the lobby, two beautiful women were standing at the check-in desk laughing with the male desk clerk. One of the two women eyed him intensively as he made his way onto the elevator.

"Damn that bitch is bad!" Supreme thought to himself as the elevator door closed.

Stepping off the elevator onto the fourth floor of the hotel, Supreme reached into his pocket for his room key. After walking to the rear of the hall he stopped at room number 418. Before opening the door, he looked down the hall to see if he was being followed.

Once inside, he positioned his body at the foot of the bed with his briefcase placed on his lap. Popping the two locks that sealed the case, Supreme slowly opened it with a big smile on his face. The inside revealed nothing but 50 and 100 dollar bills that totaled seventy-five thousand dollars.

As he sat there captivated by the money, he remembered the events that brought him in contact with it…

*Time was running out for the known stick-up kid named Supreme. Niggas all over Brooklyn were hipp to him and the chrome 9mm that he possessed. He had to complete his last stick up before his flight to D.C., because if he didn't, he would be stuck with only $400 left from his last hold-up. And possibly a one way ticket to a cemetery if he didn't leave New York.*

*The day before, Supreme sat in a black Honda Accord in the Flatbush section of Brooklyn, New York. He sat crouched down behind the steering wheel looking into the window of a restaurant. His eyes barely blinked as he closely watched the short, heavy-set man he'd been plotting to rob for two months.*

Supreme was a professional. He'd been robbing since he carried out his first robbery in the 4th grade at P.S. 135. He held a plastic school knife to a fellow student's throat and demanded his lunch money. That incident triggered a life long thirst for power over the next man. Robberies became his identity.

Living at home with his mother, Supreme stayed in trouble. He despised her for not being able to buy the things he saw other kids with. He always thought his mom spent her government welfare checks on alcohol and the many men he saw her with.

When he was only eight years old, he was beaten up bad by one of his mother's male friends who accused him of stealing $50 out of his wallet while he slept.  But in reality, his mother was the one who took the money.

That incident drew even more hatred towards the woman that was supposed to love him but did nothing as a grown man punched her son repeatedly.  Those were the times when he ran into his small bedroom and hid in his empty closet wishing for the return of his father.  Although Supreme's father vanished when Supreme was only four years old, he still remembered the security he felt when his father was around.  But growing up on the streets of Church Avenue, one of Brooklyn's crime infested areas, Supreme quickly learned how to save himself.

*Supreme recalled how he had become restless after 45 minutes of waiting on his target and wanted to stretch his legs.  He knew in 5 to 15 minutes, a black 4 door SUV would pull up in front of the restaurant and a young clean shaved, well dressed Hispanic man would emerge from it carrying a silver briefcase.  He had watched this same transaction take place for two months now, and from what he saw sitting across the street from the restaurant, the men did an exchange in the restroom.*

*Checking his watch, Supreme counted down the arrival of the SUV. "Seven-thirty," he sighed, watching the car pull up. The Hispanic man stepped out of the car sporting black shades, an all black outfit, and the briefcase.*

*Supreme always tried to figure out who carried the cash and who carried the drugs.  Both men looked liked they were capable of possessing money.  The only reason he even considered robbing the short heavy-set man who went by the name Ben, was because he knew about him through one of his ex women who used to call the 40 something year old "THE MAN."  So every since she told him that, Supreme* watched him almost daily. When he decided to rob the man, he quickly dumped the woman after receiving all the information he needed.

Watching the Hispanic man walk into the restaurant, Supreme sat up to observe what he knew was about to take place. The men greeted each other with hand shakes then they sat down in the semi-crowded restaurant. They talked for about five minutes before the Hispanic man sprang from his chair with his briefcase in hand, walking in the direction of the restroom.

The moment Supreme spotted Ben moving his chair from under the table, he jetted from his Honda with his hands stuffed in his dark blue coat pocket. Dashing through the two-way traffic, he made it to the other side of the street and into the restaurant. The second he walked into the restaurant he came face to face with Ben, who was on his way toward the restroom. To draw no suspicion, Supreme walked in the opposite direction only to turn abruptly around and head straight into the restroom.

Walking into the restroom, he immediately spotted the two men leaning over the sinks washing their hands as they looked into the mirrors. They both had silver briefcases between their legs. After checking all stalls Supreme vanished into the one from which he could get a clear view of the men, then he drew his gun.

Sitting on the toilet, he peered through the crack of the stall's door observing the men. He saw them switching briefcases the moment he peeped through the crack.

"Let's go baby," Supreme whispered to himself taking a deep breath before springing into action.

The stall's door flew open with Supreme yelling, "Don't move mothafuckas and don't talk until I tell you to."

Both men looked into the mirror only to see a chrome 9mm pointing in the direction of their backs.

"Which one of them cases got dough in it?" Supreme asked, waving his gun back and forward between both men.

"The one I have Poppi," the Hispanic man replied, throwing his hands in the air slowly turning around.

Knowing in a couple of hours he wouldn't be in New York, Supreme didn't care about being seen, so he didn't worry about the man's actions.

"Poppi don't do this," the Hispanic man said with his hands still in the air. "I can give you a job working for me. You don't have to rob us."

"Shut the fuck up and pass me the fuckin' case pretty boy."

Without uttering another word the Hispanic man reached down between his legs and grabbed the briefcase handing it to his robber.

"Now you fat boy," Supreme said with one hand holding the briefcase and the other pointing his gun at Ben. "Turn around and open that case so I can see what's in it."

Turning around, the man known as Ben had beads of sweat tumbling down his face. "Hurry the fuck up nigga!" Supreme shouted, making the already nervous man fumble with the case.

"I'm trying," Ben uttered, popping the locks off the case as he kneeled.

"I don't want that shit," Supreme spat after seeing at least four kilos of powder cocaine neatly packaged in the briefcase. "Yo! You niggas can keep that shit."

"Poppi, if you're robbing us you better be on your way outta here before somebody comes to use the restroom. Besides, I know just about everybody in Brooklyn. So, I hope you have somewhere to hide."

"Who the fuck do you think you talkin' to?" Supreme angrily stated, taking a step toward the Hispanic man with his gun pointing in his face. "Son, I don't know if you're just stupid or you just have a lot of heart, but I'm the nigga with the hammer."

Without any warning at all, Supreme cocked his arm back and sent his gun crashing against the Hispanic man's forehead, knocking his shades off and sending his body sprawling to the restroom floor.

"I would put a hot one in ya, but I gotta go," Supreme said, looking down on the bloody man on the floor.

Walking pass Ben who was standing with his back against the sink and his hands still in the air, Supreme quickly dashed out of the restroom, then out of the restaurant to his car.

*It only took a few minutes for Supreme to reach his apartment on Foster Avenue known as Vanderveer Housing in Flatbush. His apartment was a two bedroom that was laid out with top notch furnishings. Everything he owned came at the expense of the people he robbed. As he walked into his apartment building, he felt that something was wrong.*

*When he entered his apartment he scrutinized the entire place, still feeling suspicious, he peeped out of every window. After doing so and coming up with nothing, he took off his coat and flopped down on his living room sofa.*

*With his gun resting on top of his coat on the sofa, Supreme began to open the briefcase when a knock at the door stopped him. Without thinking, he ran to the door with the briefcase in hand and peered through the peephole. Just when he got a good look at the two hooded men, a bullet came crashing through the door just above the door knob. Quickly running back to the sofa he scooped up his gun and ran towards the back room of the apartment. But before he reached the room, another bullet burst through the door whizzing pass his head lodging into the adjacent wall.*

*After safely reaching the bedroom, wasting no time Supreme sprinted like an Olympic runner headed for the window when he heard the front door cave in. Within seconds, the two men had gained on him. Before they could grab him, he jumped from the second floor.*

*Without any other alternative, forty-five minutes later Supreme arrived at LaGuardia Airport in Queens. Not being able to carry his gun to one of the most dangerous cities in America brought a high level of anxiety to him. Worst of all, he didn't know anybody in D.C.*

*Stuffing the gun under the driver's seat of his Honda, Supreme grabbed the briefcase then stepped out of the car only to be met by the cold January air. He knew that in a few days the abandoned car would be towed away, and the gun would be found. He reached back into the car, and using a washcloth he wiped everything down he thought he had touched, then he shut the car door.*

*Walking away from the car, he wondered if there were any way they could connect him to the car and the gun. Then he smiled*

*remembering a year ago when he first purchased the 1995 black Honda
Accord. A neighborhood crackhead had signed for it and wasn't concerned about Supreme's name; as long as he received the $400 he was
promised.*

*The line at the ticket counter took longer than he expected.*

*"May I help you?" a tall white blond woman at the ticket counter
asked Supreme with a welcoming smile on her face.*

*"Can I get a one-way ticket to D.C. please?"*

*"You sure can, but the next flight to D.C. doesn't leave for another
4 hours."*

*"I'll take it," he said checking his surroundings.*

*After paying for the ticket, Supreme walked over to the waiting
area and took a seat with the briefcase on his lap and his hands protecting it. He scrutinized the many people that sat waiting just as he
did. His eyes searched the huge terminal for recognizable faces but
there weren't any. So he..."*

A loud knock at the hotel room door startled Supreme, bringing him
back to the present. The briefcase was on the carpet and money was
scattered everywhere.

"I'll be there in a minute," Supreme yelled out, picking the money up
off the floor and placing it back into the briefcase and quickly sliding it
under the bed. To his surprise, the same woman that eyed him down in
the lobby of the hotel was standing at the door with two champagne
glasses and a bottle of Moet in her hand.

"Yo! What up, Ma?" he yelled, looking out the peep hole.

"I wanna know if you wanna have a drink with me?" she stated,
looking directly at the peep hole.

There was silence on both sides of the door until a minute passed,
then the woman shouted something and walked away. "Fuck it," Supreme said to himself quickly taking the lock off the door. "Where you
goin'?" He had half of his body in the hall, and the other half inside the
room. "I had to put my pants on," he lied with a smile on his face as she
walked pass him into the room. But before he went back into the room
he looked both ways down the corridor, then shut the door.

"I know you're wondering who I am, and what I'm doin' askin' you to drink with me," the woman said the moment Supreme appeared by the bed where she stood.

Supreme didn't answer her. He just stood there mesmerized by the beauty that stood before him. The woman was a dime, he thought as his eyes traveled up and down her body.

Her thick hips bulged from beneath her skirt showcasing her best asset. Although her ass was the way most black men preferred, her waist and breast were small making her a prime candidate for other races of men. Her face was golden brown and could easily be 'Jet's' beauty of the week. Her black, sleek, short hairstyle gave her round face an elegant glow. Her black leather designer high heel boots and skirt went well with the white Chanel turtleneck sweater she wore. With her boots on she stood five foot seven, but with them off she was an even five foot four.

"So, what's your name?" she inquired, breaking Supreme's observance of her.

"First, who are you? And who gave you my room number, Ma?"

"First of all, I got your room number from the front desk. I thought you'd be alone since I didn't see you get on the elevator with anybody. And my name is Booty; at least that's what all the men that come to my job call me."

Supreme caught on right away. "So you're a stripper?" He looked down at her form fitting black leather skirt and smiled.

"Nah, I'm a dancer," she responded as she walked over to the dresser to place the two glasses and the bottle of Moet on it.

"What's your real name, Ma?"

"Glory. Is that all?" she spat sarcastically.

Supreme stood with the back of his legs against the foot of the bed. His feet were in the exact spot where he slid the briefcase. His thoughts raced quickly through all the women he could remember. Then he suddenly thought to himself, "Nobody even knew he was there. So how could anyone send this broad after him?"

"Where you from?" he spontaneously asked Glory, breaking his own thoughts.

"I'm from D.C. Why?"

All the tension that took over his body the second he heard the knock at the door had now been released. Those were the exact words he'd hoped for. A smile appeared on his face as he walked over towards her. "What up with dat drink?" He reached around Glory as her ass rested against the dresser. He grabbed the Moet bottle and the two champagne glasses.

After 30 minutes of their watching the Soprano's, the Moet bottle was damn near empty. Supreme and Glory sat at the foot of the bed staring into the TV, but talking at the same time.

"You said you were from New York, right?" Glory asked.

"Yeah."

"So where all that platinum iced-out jewelry y'all be wearin'?" Glory asked, glancing at him with a sexy drunken look.

"Not every nigga in New York wears that shit," he snapped.

"Yeah, just the niggas that got money huh?" She smiled and two dimples exploded onto her face.

Taking a long swig of his drink, Supreme was quiet for five seconds then he bluntly said, "I don't have to buy that shit. People give me thangs," he grinned.

For some reason after hearing his words, Glory felt a sudden chill jolt through her body. A feeling of pleasure, an attraction, or maybe it was just the Moet taking its toll. She looked at him and suddenly remembered the reason why she wanted to have a drink with him.

Leaping off the bed Glory stood sternly in front of the TV. "Look, I want you to go down to my room with me. I wanna show you somethin'."

Without even the slightest thought Supreme looked up from the bed at her and agreed. She grabbed his hand and pulled him off the bed hauling him toward the door.

The moment they stepped onto the elevator, Glory threw herself at Supreme. She stood face to face with him while rubbing his chest with one hand, and rubbing the inner portion of his thigh with her other hand. She whispered that earlier when she first saw him she noticed how fine he was. But what she had in store for him was something she wanted him to find out for himself. Either he'd go along with it like a smart man would, or maybe he'd decline and miss out like a dumb man.

Once the elevator door opened they walked out looking more intoxicated than they did before they walked in it. After reaching room number 306, Glory reached into the small front pocket of her skirt and pulled out her room key.

Entering the room, a cloud of smoke slammed into their faces. Immediately, Supreme distinguished the smell even though he was drunk.

The room was set up the same way Supreme's was, the only difference were the twin beds.

"Damn! What took you so long?" a chocolate woman asked leaping from the bed.

"I thought you went up there and got drunk...and you know the rest."

"Ya know I wouldn't leave you out of no action," Glory stated accepting the blunt of weed the woman held out to her.

Supreme stood there watching the chocolate woman, remembering seeing her in the lobby with Glory. He looked at her in pure lust as he thought back to the moment he first laid eyes on both women.

"So what's your name?" the chocolate woman inquired.

"Supreme. What's yours, Ma?"

"Body," she replied by spinning around in a 360 degree turn displaying her huge ass and double D breasts.

Body stood five foot six with long black braids that draped down her back. Her face was evidence that somebody in her family had sexual contact with a Native American. Her high cheekbones made her face look narrow, but pretty. She wore tight blue Parasuco jeans and a black sleeveless DKNY turtleneck sweater that matched her black high heel Gucci boots.

"No, what's your real name?" Supreme inquired.

"Pam," she said, looking him up and down. "I like your hair." Pam walked up to Supreme and ran her hand over his cornrows.

After taking several pulls from the blunt, Glory walked up to Supreme and gave him the blunt while Pam stood behind him still rubbing her hand over his cornrows. A moment later, Glory was standing in front of Supreme raising his shirt over his head.

Supreme was now as high, as he was drunk.  But he knew what was going to take place and he didn't protest.  He watched the two women take his clothes off piece by piece until he stood in nothing but his gray boxers.  After they stripped him down they began to take their clothes off displaying beautiful bodies.  Pushing him onto one of the twin beds they walked over to the other one and climbed on it.  What Supreme saw next was something he had never witnessed before.  The two ladies french kissed like a man and woman would.  Then he saw Pam lay Glory on her back placing her head between Glory's legs.  After 3 or 4 minutes of watching Glory's facial expressions from being ate out, Supreme's dick stood up like a knife through the slit of his boxers.

"Can I join y'all?" he asked, already walking over to the bed to join the women for a ménage 'a trois.

"Yeah, slide your dick right in there," Pam stated, pointing to Glory's vagina that was already lubricated.

Supreme did just that by plunging into Glory's woman-hood while she lay on her back with her legs thrown in the air.  She sighed when he entered her.

Pam watched as Supreme dived in and out of her knowing she'd be next to feel the same pleasure her friend and lover felt.

Pushing Supreme from out of her, Glory signaled Pam that it was her turn to enjoy what she had.  She rolled off her back and let Pam occupy her former space.  Pam got on all four's and allowed Supreme to enter her from behind.  She grunted when he entered her.

The three-some went on for several more minutes before it came to a halt. After the sexual escapade, each lay stretched out and cramped in the same bed together passing more weed around.  Supreme didn't have to ask any questions.  Both women told him all he needed to know at the moment.  He knew that they worked at the same strip club a few blocks from the hotel.  They'd been coming to the Days Inn for a year now after every Friday night show.  He also knew that they liked women just as much as men.  They also told him that they had never done what they had done tonight with anybody but him; that usually they just enjoyed each other.  It was just something about him that made them do it with him. They also revealed that Pam was 22, and Glory was 21. They claimed to have only worked as strippers to pay for college. But now, neither one of them was enrolled in school.

After a night of weed smoking, alcohol drinking and vigorous sex, they all fell asleep. Supreme was the first to wake up the next morning only to realize he left the money in his room unprotected from the house-keeper. Moving as fast as he could, Supreme quickly put his clothes on but woke Glory up in the process.

"Where you going?" she mumbled with her eyes partially closed.

"I'll be right back," Supreme hollered already on his way out the door.

The moment Supreme walked out the door, Glory called to check on Pam. Pam had gone to where she always had to be on Saturday mornings at 11:00 a.m. - making sure her 70 year old grandmother woke up to a nice breakfast. Pam's mother died when she was only two weeks from her 10th birthday. So her grandmother practically raised her. Pam's mother had been murdered by a gang of men who committed every sexual act imaginable against her. Then they cut her throat and left her lifeless body prone beside a trash dumpster two blocks from where her and her only child lived. Thanks to the police department who relentlessly sought after the men, all six of the men were caught, tried, found guilty and sentenced to life without the possibility of parole.

"I told ya I'd be back," Supreme announced as he walked into the room after Glory opened the door for him. "Where's Pam?" he asked.

"She left early this morning. You do know you took about 20 minutes right?"

"No doubt, Ma," he replied, noticing Glory looking at the briefcase he held.

"Damn! You have that much loot that you need a briefcase," Glory stated while she fastened her belt to the form fitting jeans she now wore.

Supreme and Glory were on their way out the hotel lobby when Supreme looked at his watch and remembered the cabby. "Hold on," he said to Glory as they both stopped a foot short of the glass sliding doors at the entrance of the hotel. "I'll be right back."

Supreme peeled $50 from his pocket and passed it to the young

black man that stood behind the check-in counter. "The fifty is for the
cab driver that might stop by lookin' for a man by the name of Supreme."

As Glory led the way to her car in the hotel's parking lot, Supreme
smiled as he thought about the $50 the cabby might never see.

"Damn!" he said after seeing Glory's black 323 BMW. "I know ya
do more than strip for a whip like this."

"Yeah, I told 'cha I had a day job at the court buildin'. But my
brotha copped this fa me. Didn't ya hear me tell you that last night?
Were you too tore up ta hear me?" Glory pulled her car keys from her
Christian Dior bag, opened the doors and they climbed in.

"I like ya whip," Supreme said, looking around in the car.

"Thanks." Glory watched him as he scrutinized her ride. "Where
ya coat?" she asked, just realizing he didn't have one on.

"Somebody stole it at the airport," he lied with a straight face.

Glory smiled. "I'll pick ya up one," she said starting her car engine,
and then pulling off.

# THREE

Supreme walked out of the bathroom with just the hotel's white towel wrapped around his lower body. The hours of shopping with Glory had taken their toll on him. He looked tired. Standing in front of the king size bed he looked down at all the shopping bags. There were bags from just about every hip clothing store in the D.C. area. He looked down at his two fake ID's both registered in New York, Brooklyn and the Bronx. He carried these ID's for emergencies.

Glancing at his watch he began to take some of the clothes out of the shopping bags. He didn't want to be late arriving at the show. Glory and Pam were performing at 11:00 p.m. like they did every Saturday night. Glory told him to make sure he showed up at the club no later than 10:45 p.m.

After dressing he stuffed $500.00 from one of the stacks of money into his pocket and placed the remaining $54,500 in the bottom of the shopping bag under his clothes. He snatched the two ID's and the car keys from the bed and left the room.

The smell of the newly purchased used Acura brought a smirk to Supreme's face. He cut the inside light on to examine himself before pulling out of the hotel's parking lot. "Damn I'ma good lookin' mothafucka," he mumbled while looking into the rear view mirror examining the sharp shape up of his trimmed full beard.

Pulling into the club's parking lot, Supreme looked at the big red and white sign *Welcome to Club Jubilee* above the entrance illuminating the entire lot.  He parked between a row of cars then looked in the backseat at the briefcase that lay across the seat.  He grabbed the briefcase and tossed it under the driver's seat.

The entrance of the club was empty.  Supreme looked around the lot to see every parking space filled but wondered why there wasn't a line outside standing behind the velvet rope.  The moment he walked in, he quickly understood why there wasn't a soul outside.  The club was packed with young and old men.  Two men, one white and one black, stood side by side about three feet into the club.

"That will be ten dollars," the tall white man said with his hand out towards Supreme.

Supreme looked at both of the identically dressed men. They wore black jeans with tight black body shirts showing off their muscular physiques.

"I thought it was free ta get in here?" Supreme said.

"Look!" the tall black man shouted over the loud music that began to play in the background.  "Either pay the ten bucks or miss out on the great show that's about to start."

Supreme quickly reached in his pocket and peeled off a ten.

"Enjoy yourself," the white man said patting Supreme down then stepping to the side.

As he entered the club, Supreme's nostrils immediately caught the scent of sweaty pussy with a mixture of perfume and cologne.  His eyes were met with flashing red, blue, green and purple lights. His attention was aroused after seeing two beautiful women in red bikinis serving drinks behind the bar.

"Let me get a glass of Mo," Supreme yelled over the music as he slid onto one of the ten stools in front of the bar.  He watched the caramel, thick legged bar attendant walk over to a small refrigerator pulling out a fresh bottle of Moet.

The young bar attendant batted her eyes at Supreme as she reached under the bar pulling out a tiny glass.  "Dis yo first time here?" she quizzed while pouring the drink.

"Yeah."

"Well you gon' love the show that's 'bout to take place."

"I hope so," he replied, grabbing his drink.

He looked around the large club. Men were lined up in front of the T shaped stage with money already dangling from their hands. Supreme smiled thinking of what Glory and Pam might do. He had already seen some of their wild side that most of the men there would never see. The colorful lights that flashed throughout the club went out and one bright light focused on the stage.

"Noooww!" sounded the DJ's voice. "The moment you've all been waiting for is here. So, let's get this shit started."

Smoke rose from the stage making it difficult to see. Suddenly, Glory and Pam could be seen standing approximately 6 feet apart from each other. They dressed identical, two yellow pom-poms, burgundy, yellow and white cheerleader skirts with matching tops, and all white classic Reebok sneakers with thick slouch socks and a patch of gold glitter on their cheeks.

"Y'all wanna seeee." They began reciting simultaneously with stomps of their feet and shakes of their pom-poms. "This thang shakeeee, then let us hearrr, y'all yell make it shake!"

"Make it shake! Make it shake! Make it shake!" the crowd of shouting men yelled with their hands in the air waving money. Mystikal's song Danger came blasting through the club's speakers sending the men into an uproar.

Glory and Pam did all types of moves that had the men shouting at the top of their lungs. Some men even tried to climb aboard the four foot high stage, but were quickly subdued by two of the six burly bouncers that protected the girls.

Mesmerized by Booty and Body, Supreme slammed his now empty glass on the bar then smoothly slid off the stool leaving the bar attendant staring at the back of his jacket.

The walk through the tables were like a maze as Supreme maneuvered his way to the stage. Money was being placed around the red garter ribbons that were wrapped around Pam and Glory's thighs. They stood side by side until the hot song "Shake Your Ass" blasted through the speakers signaling them to tear off their outfits. Now their pom-poms as well as their cheerleader outfits were tossed to the side of the stage leaving them both in nothing but gold glitter around their areolas, gold glittered thong panties and their white Reebok sneakers.

Once the first verse of the song began, Pam and Glory turned around with their backs facing the crowd. Then they placed both of their hands on their knees and slightly bent their legs. With small movements of their legs their butts began shaking with thunderous claps that almost emulated the loud music.

Before Pam and Glory left the stage, they spotted Supreme in the crowd, but only Glory acknowledged him with a wink of her eye. Supreme stood alone in front of the stage still in a trance. The way both women moved their bodies played repeatedly in his head. Then he snapped out of it when the DJ yelled, "I see there's still a loyal fan of Booty and Body still standing in front of the stage. I guess he wants to see more."

Supreme turned around and saw all the men that were shouting in front of the stage now laughing while sitting at the small round tables that he dodged to reach the stage. A little embarrassed, he waved his hand in the air with a slight smile as the DJ shone the spotlight on him while he walked to an empty table.

After the DJ took the spotlight off of him, Supreme had an opportunity to study the club.

Damn! Supreme thought scanning the club's customers. "I know that piece alone is worth at least $50,000 dollars," he said eyeballing a young dudes iced-out platinum chain seated at a table a few feet away.

"Shit!" Supreme lightly blurted out, now seeing more men draped in diamond Rolex watches. "These niggas are luckier than a mothafucka. I'd rob the shit out of them…"

"Can I give you a lap dance?" a woman's voice whispered in Supreme's ear from behind him.

"Yeah," he replied, thinking it was either Glory or Pam standing behind him.

The woman stepped in front of him with her hands on her hips. It was neither Pam nor Glory. "You like what you see?" she asked, now rubbing her flat stomach with both of her hands.

Supreme looked at her and immediately his dick began to rise in slow motion in his pants. If it weren't for her ass the lady could easily be mistaken for a white woman. She wore a plastic shiny looking red raincoat that was opened slightly showing off her red thong panties and Double D's. Her face was beautiful, along with her light brown eyes and long black, silky hair.

The raincoat slipped to the floor leaving nothing to Supreme's imagination. His tongue nearly fell out his mouth when the stripper turned around in a wide legged stand and began to shake her big red ass in his face. Then she turned around shaking her tits in his face.

Just then, Glory walked up on Supreme placing her arm around him like they were a couple.

"Damn! This your first time at the club and you're already making yourself at home," Glory chuckled.

"Naw, it ain't like that."

"Yeah, sure. You and Big Red seem to be enjoying yourselves," Glory said walking towards the door. "That bitch is a stone cold freak."

"Yo! Y'all can dance like a mothafucka," Supreme said fleeing from Big Red and following the girls outside. " I see y'all stars in there," Supreme said looking down at Glory's outfit. "What happened to that shit I seen you in on the stage?"

"Right here," she stated, patting the designer bag she held in her hand. "I can't leave none of my shit in there or it'll be gone."

"Yo! What up for the rest of the night?" Supreme asked.

"As you can see," Pam took a step back and placed her arms above her head in order to display her Gucci foil denim pantsuit with a pair of striking high heel sandals with rhinestone straps that matched her rhinestone Chanel bag, "I'm going out after I drop Glory off."

"Girl go 'head and have you a good time. Supreme can take me home, right?" Glory tapped Supreme out of his observance of Pam.

"No doubt," he responded, then complimented Pam. "You got some pretty toes, Ma."

"Thanks, but if I don't get out this cold, my toes goin' freeze. I'll see y'all later."

Glory and Supreme watched Pam run between cars until she reached her red Maxima. Then they started walking in the direction of Supreme's car.

"So you left your car at home huh?" Supreme inquired as they walked through the parking lot.

"I didn't feel like driving tonight," she lied, knowing the real reason she didn't drive was because she wanted him to come over her crib. Not only did she know that, Pam did also. They planned for things to go just the way they were.

"You gotta show me the way to your crib," Supreme said as they reached his Acura. Supreme opened the passenger door for Glory, but while doing so, he took a quick look at her ass before he shut the door behind her. "Them jeans huggin' that ass. Damn she got a phat ass," he mumbled walking around to the driver's side. He wondered if she was going to reach over to unlock his door. She did. Supreme smiled as he entered the car.

"You thought I wasn't gon' open your door huh?"

"Naw, I wasn't even thinking about that."

"Yes ya were."

Supreme started to turn the car radio on, but Glory stopped him.

"I gotta ask ya some questions," she said.

"Shoot."

"You're not a murderer that's on the run or nothin' are you?"

"Naw." Supreme shook his head while smiling.

"O.K. then, it's only one more thing me and Pam wanna know…You don't have no AIDS or nothin' do you?" She held her breath waiting for him to answer.

He looked at her and grinned. "Naw, I had a check up a few months ago." He lied straight faced.

"Thank god." She blew out a sigh of relief. "Me and Pam was talking about that all night. We was so fucked up we forgot to put a condom on ya dick last night."

"O-Shit! I left my clothes and money in my hotel room," Supreme blurted out as they drove past the Days Inn on New York Avenue.

"So," Glory replied, knowing what was on Supreme's mind. "It's not like you won't be back there tonight."

"Oh, so I can't sleep at your crib tonight."

"If you want to," she responded by turning the car radio on then peering out her window.

Supreme made a u-turn going back in the direction of the Days Inn. After stopping at the hotel to grab his belongings they drove to Glory's Southeast apartment. The quiet neighborhood shocked Supreme. He expected something more inferior than what he saw.

The apartment off of Alabama Avenue was quaint. Glory's crib was laid out. Once you walked in, you knew she had paper. Supreme, impressed by her arsenal of books, admired her even more.

Supreme sat on the sofa watching a movie Glory had placed into the DVD player, before heading straight for the shower. Fifteen minutes later she reappeared in the living room prancing around with a pink towel on her head and a long pink t-shirt on with nothing underneath. Her petite well pedicured toes slid across the expensive white wool carpet that covered her apartment.

"I'll whip us up something to eat," Glory said looking at Supreme seductively. "I got some bubbly to go with the food since we can't smoke in my crib."

"Why?" Supreme asked suspiciously.

"My brotha can't stand the smell."

"Your brotha don't live here do he?"

"In this one bedroom…hell no! But he does have a set of keys."

Twenty minutes later Glory returned to the living room with a bottle of Cristal and the food she had cooked.

After all their food and half of the bottle of the champagne was gone, everything seemed funny. They watched a Spring Break video and laughed at just about every student that appeared on the TV. Feeling more relaxed, Supreme eyed Glory.

"Let me ask you this?" Supreme inquired, breaking up the laughter. "Do those niggas that was in the club tonight be there every Friday and Saturday when y'all dance?"

"Not all of them. Why?"

"I just asked because I seen some niggas wearing one hundred thousand dollar watches and fifty thousand dollar chains around their necks. I figured at least one of them gotta be interested in you."

"They all are, but if that's ya way of askin' me do I have a man, ya answer is no.  I have friends though."

Supreme smiled.  He just killed two birds with one stone.  He found out just what he needed to know.  He was sure that her brother was involved in some illegal activities.  The BMW Glory told him her brother brought for her assured him of that.

"I ain't try'na be in your personal business but what type of money y'all make for dancing for two nights?"

"About $500 from the customers each night, and $1,500 from the manager.  The club makes its money from the door fee.  Me and Pam always pack the club on the weekends.  That means the club might pull in 10 to 15 g's each night that we dance, not including the money they make at the bar."

Supreme sat secretly calculating Glory's earnings while she cleaned up their mess. After drinking the other half of the Cristal, Supreme was the first to make eye contact in their intoxicated state.  Glory felt the pair of lustful eyes staring at the side of her face.  She looked at him and, simultaneously, they both sat up on the sofa.  He reached for the towel that was wrapped around her head and unwrapped it, then placed it on the back of the sofa.  At that very moment Supreme realized that Glory was unspeakably beautiful.

Glory's hair was still a little damp from the shower. Supreme grabbed the back of her head with his right hand pulling her towards him, and in an instant, their lips met.  They took turns sucking each other's lips until Supreme made his way down to her neck.  Little murmurs escaped Glory's mouth, and before she knew it, she was raising her pink t-shirt up over her own hips.  Not really realizing his own movements, Supreme pushed her upper body against the arm of the sofa then parted her legs in a wide V.  Wasting no time, he dived face first into Glory's wet vagina.

Glory let out loud yells when she reached an orgasm, but quickly pushed Supreme's head away from her love box after fully releasing herself. "Get up!" she ordered him in a sassy tone of voice, springing to her feet, her legs buckling slightly.

She grabbed Supreme's hand escorting him to her bedroom. Supreme stopped in his tracks to observe the spacious bedroom. His eyes were drawn to the all white canopy bed that was draped by a chandelier. "Come on!" Glory said, yanking Supreme's arm, and making him stand.

With the back of his legs pressed against the foot of the bed, Glory peeled her t-shirt off then began stripping him until he stood nude with an erect dick. She dropped to her knees in front of him then reached out and grabbed his dick with both of her small hands. She looked at the swollen rock hard muscle, then she placed her lips on the head of it, nipping at it. When Supreme looked down to see what she was doing, he saw her take him deep into her mouth. Oooh's and aaah's escaped his mouth while his head rotated from side to side. The sensations he received had his entire body feeling like each part was separately being attended to.

Actually feeling her pussy getting wet all over again, Glory pushed her face as far as she could down Supreme's thick shaft, held it there, then slowly slid her mouth off it making a smacking sound.

On her way to her feet, she pushed him onto her crisp white expensive quilt then mounted him. She rode him like a stallion. She slowly moved up and down his dick with her hands planted on his chest, and her head tilted backwards. "Aaaah!" was the sound that escaped her lips. "Aaaah!"

Supreme examined the beautiful body that brought so much gratification to him. Glory's body was perfect. Her tits were perfectly round and perky, just enough for a handful. She had a small waist and a flat stomach. And when she turned around to ride him with her back facing him, he saw a huge plump ass with thick hips and thighs looking out at him.

Without warning, Glory jumped off Supreme and landed on all fours. "Come get this," she murmured softly, using her left hand to smack her own ass causing it to shake in a wave.

Supreme pulled up behind her and plunged deep into her making her flinch and sigh at the fulfillment of her vagina. Five minutes later, he was long stroking her missionary style with both of her ankles tightly enthralled in each of his hands.

"Take it out or leave it in?" Supreme barely spat the words out through tightly clenched teeth as he looked down into Glory's beautiful face.

"Leave it in," she loudly yelled. "I won't get pregnant. I'm 'bout ta come too." They both reached their orgasms simultaneously. Moments later, they both were on their backs staring up at the chandelier.

"I haven't been fucked like that in I 'on know how long," Glory beamed, rolling off the bed. "Ya comin' to the shower wit' me?" She didn't wait for him to answer. She sashayed out the bedroom.

"Damn!" Supreme said, smiling as he sat on the edge of the bed. "I've only been here two fuckin' days and I've already copped just the type of bitch I like. She's intelligent, got a lot of style, a laid out crib, and a little dough... and last, but not least..." An even bigger smile emanated his face, "some bomb pussy with outrageously potent brain."

# FOUR

Noon the next day, Supreme was awakened by a sudden urge to use the bathroom. To his surprise, the woman that fell asleep next to him wasn't there. After relieving himself, and standing at the sink to wash his hands, he saw a note on the mirror that read: *Sorry I'm not here to fix you breakfast, but I can't go one more day without my hair done. If you're hungry, the frig is all yours. Around noon my landlord should be knocking at my door to leave a newspaper that he gives me every Sunday. So accept it.*

*And last, if my brotha comes by or calls, tell him I'm at the salon. He knows which one. And if he ask who you are, tell 'em we've known each other for a year. We just decided to kick it. Ah yeah! One more thing. I've got your car keys. [Smile]*

A knock at the front door startled Supreme. With the note Glory wrote to him still in his hands, he put one eye to the peep hole then opened the door.

"As-Salaam Alaikum!" A slim man, five foot six with a shaved head and face, and wearing a black suit smiled and said, "Hi, I'm Brother Hetep Muhammad. Is Glory in?"

"She's home but she told me you had a newspaper for her."

"Yes I do." Hetep handed the paper to Supreme and walked off.

Immediately after closing the door Supreme flipped the newspaper open reading the title *The Final Call*. Walking back to the bedroom, Supreme threw the newspaper on the dresser. Feeling curious, he checked the pockets of the jeans that he tossed on the floor last night. The keys were gone just like Glory had said.  He started searching the bedroom for her closet but didn't find it.  He walked out the bedroom into the hall and that's when he saw the closet that he hadn't noticed before.

"Damn!" Supreme spat using both of his hands to slide the sliding doors of the closet open. The spacious walk-in closet, almost large as a bedroom, was nearly filled to capacity with expensive name brand clothes. Supreme's eyes lit up when he unzipped a black garment bag that revealed two stunning fur coats.  One was a multi-colored bolero and the other was a natural white fox fur.

"I see why she took my car keys," he mumbled, grinning while zipping the bag back up.  "She wasn't sure if she could trust me with all this expensive shit around."

"You move I'ma put one of these hot balls in your ass…" A serious looking PooBear stood in the doorway of the closet with his black Glock 9mm drawn.  "Now put your hands in the air nigga."

Supreme stood with his hands in the air with his back facing PooBear. "Yo don't shoot, Son!" he pleaded.

"Hey Unique! Get off the phone and come check this shit out," PooBear yelled, but still pointed his gun at Supreme. "Turna 'round, Joe."

"My name ain't Joe," Supreme stated angrily.

"Nigga I know, I call er'ybody Joe."

"What the fuck you doin' in my sista's closet?"   Unique asked standing beside PooBear.

"Wait a minute.  I'm Glory's boyfriend," Supreme quickly answered now facing both men.

"That still don't answer my question.  What ya doin' in my people's closet? And with nothin' but boxers on ya ass."

"Son, can I put my fuckin' hands down now?" Supreme boldly asked realizing he wasn't going to be shot.

"Yeah go 'head."

As Supreme walked towards them, their iced-out platinum chains caught his attention. He eyed both of them down before saying another word. Unique's medallion read *DC's Finest*. Every word was fully diamond encrusted just like the cross PooBear wore.

"Talk nigga, say somethin'," PooBear ordered with his gun two feet away from Supreme's face.

"I ain't sayin' shit until ya get that burner out of my face."

PooBear dropped the gun to his side.

"All right Slim, go put some clothes on then come in the livin' room," Unique roared, stepping to the side to let Supreme pass.

"Sit down," Unique ordered after Supreme returned to the living room.

"Yo! I'm good." Supreme protested, looking at the Glock that rested on PooBear's lap.

"How ya meet my sista?" Unique questioned.

"I met her about a year ago at..." Supreme hesitated, thinking about his pre-meditated lie. "A store downtown," he finally said.

"You sure you didn't meet her at that funky ass club she works at?"

Surprised, Supreme quickly replied, "Naw, she told me she dance at a club but that's not where we met."

"Where you from, Joe?" PooBear asked.

"New York."

Just then Glory walked in the front door. She tossed the few bags she held in her hands onto the glass dining table.

"Hi baby!" Glory threw her arms around Unique's neck leaning over the back of the sofa. "I'm glad you out."

"Where's my hug and my kiss?" PooBear asked grinning devilishly at Supreme.

"You get one too," she said in a joking way, throwing her arms around PooBear's neck. Glory gave him a light kiss on his cheek not knowing she was enhancing the invisible war PooBear and Supreme had going on.

"Lil'sis' let me holla at 'cha." Unique leaped from the sofa heading towards the back room.

"Who been in my closet?" Glory asked once she entered her bedroom behind her brother.

"Ask that nigga in your livin' room."

Glory instantly knew what happened so she quickly played it off. "Oh yeah, I asked Supreme to pick out what he wanted me to wear tonight. So what's up bro?" She smiled showing her dimples.

"You know what's up. Who the fuck is that bamma?"

"Boy don't be cursing at me like that," Glory said.

"Ok, I'm sorry. Now who is that nigga?"

"I would say my man but we've only known each other for a year. So technically he's just my male friend, boyfriend or whatever you wanna call it."

"Stop playing Glory," Unique ordered quickly realizing she was being sarcastic.

"He's my man Ok," Glory shouted walking over to her computer punching a key on the keypad. "You've got mail! You've got mail!" the computer repeated over and over.

"Why you didn't tell me about him a year ago?"

"Do I have to tell you everything?" Glory asked while reading her e-mail message.

"You been telling me everything."

"Ok!" she said, tapping a key on the keypad deleting the message on the screen. I met him. We've been kicking it on the phone. He's been here four times over the last year. He's from New York. I like him, and I fucked him only twice. Is that all?"

"Does he have a job? Does he have a business? Or does he sell drugs?"

Relieved he didn't ask where they'd met, Glory said, "I don't know. I think he used to sell drugs but he stopped."

"Shit!" Unique cursed walking toward the room's door then back toward his sister. "I don't want you to fuck with no nigga that's in the game. I told 'cha that."

"What's wrong with a nigga in the game? You in the game. Anyway, it's not like I'ma marry him or anything."

"I just thought you was goin' to college and hook up with one of them future doctors or lawyers." He paused frowning, "I thought you said you was gonna stop dancing at that club after you get enough money. You could've easily got money from me or Dad if you really wanted to go to college. But naaaw 'I wanna do it by myself,' you said on that independent woman bullshit. I think you like shakin' your ass for bammas, you and…what's that black bitch name?"

"Pam. And you didn't call her a bitch when you stuck your dirty dick in her," Glory said with her lips poked out.

"I know," Unique replied smiling, showing his white teeth thinking of Pam.

"Yeah, but when you gonna stop dancing at that club and enroll in college?"

"Soon, Unique, soon," Glory said walking over to her dresser picking up *The Final Call Newspaper*.

"Your landlord still giving you those Muslim papers?"

"Yeah, and what's wrong with that?"

"I think whatever his name is likes you and wouldn't mind gettin' his righteous dick wet."

"Hetep's a real Muslim. He never tried to hit on me one time since I've known him." She flipped through pages of the newspaper.

"Me and Bear 'bout ta go play some ball. I'm a take…"

"Supreme," Glory added.

"Yeah something ain't right with Supreme. I need ta get ta know him a lil' better."

"I don't think he has any basketball gear."

"We'll stop at a store and cop some then."

"Yeah, and make sure none of them bitches try to talk to my man."

"That's up to him," Unique muttered walking out the bedroom.

"Glory!" Supreme called out with his jacket on, now standing in the bedroom doorway. "I'ma go with your brotha ta play some ball."

"Your car keys," Glory said, reaching into her sweat pants pocket pulling out Supreme's keys then tossing them to him.

"Oh yeah, I overheard you tell your brotha I was your man."

"To tell you the truth I said a lot of shit in order to convince my brotha we've been kicking it for a year. You fucked me good but not that good that I'm hooked and jealous in three days."

"You will be," Supreme replied pushing her hand away from his crotch. "You will be."

"Let's go," PooBear yelled from the living room.

Supreme was wide-eyed when they walked towards a brand new pearl white Escalade truck with 22 inch chrome Adonis rims and rugged Dunlop tires parked directly behind his Acura in front of Glory's apartment.

Supreme took a quick glance at his car to make sure nobody had tried to pry into it where all his clothes and all the money rested. PooBear climbed in the driver's seat, Unique in the passenger seat, and Supreme sat on the second row. The truck was loaded with two 6 inch TV monitors in each headrest. And to give the truck that street look, it had jet black limo tint. Supreme's mind wandered while admiring the plush interior of the truck.

He thought about Glory and the two hot heads sitting in the front seat. He wondered if Glory had ever fucked PooBear. If so, he knew trouble was near. Supreme's wildest thought focused on the cars, money, and jewels being flashed by Glory's circle of people. It was just a matter of time before he found out just how much money they had and how he could profit from them.

# FIVE

See y'all Monday," Kim said, waving at her co-workers as she walked out of the jail to her car. She quickly jumped into her Infiniti I-30 to escape the cold February chill. After placing her Gucci tote bag into the passenger seat, she started the car up and peeled off her dark blue correctional jacket.

For the last month, Kim found herself deviating from her after work routine. Instead of going straight home, she would find herself cruising through some of the worse neighborhoods in D.C. looking for Unique.

Kim had grown up in a quiet neighborhood in Prince Georges County. Her father was a bus driver, and her mother, a nurse. That enabled Kim not to worry about where her next meal was coming from. Her parents had purchased a small suburban house a few months after she was born, making sure she would have an opportunity to do or become anything she wanted.

But things changed for her when she graduated from high school. She hung out with a rough crowd and started to become a little aggressive, but never ran into any trouble with the law. When she was nineteen she met Jay, her ex-husband, who convinced her they should try out for the police force. He passed the exam, but she failed. That killed her motivation and she decided to pursue her childhood dream of becoming a bus driver just like her father.  She drove buses for seven years until her 29th birthday.  Then she switched to a career in corrections.

Jay was in uniform during his early years on the force.  He was eventually promoted to a street crimes unit team wearing civilian clothes. They were together on and off for six years before they became really involved with each other.  And after 8 years of knowing each other they got married.

After riding through a few neighborhoods without any luck of stumbling across Unique, Kim headed home.  That was her 19th time cruising around hoping to spot him after work.  Parking her car on a quiet block of row houses off of Georgia Avenue in Northwest, Kim grabbed her things and made her way into her two story brick house.

Her place was lavish for an annual salary of $43,000.  But the house she loved didn't cost her anything until Jay moved out.  He was the one who put the down payment on the house and paid all the bills. Kim only paid for her car and various gadgets that she brought for the house.  But now with Jay not around, she paid for everything.  He'd offered to finish paying the mortgage balance off but she declined. Kim didn't want him to think he still had the right to show up anytime he wanted to. But he thought differently.

Once he showed up at her door with that beautiful smile that had always been close to her heart.  She was completely caught off guard. Opening the front door wearing her satin lace gown and the matching white bedroom slippers, Kim thought about shutting the door in his face. Before she could react, out came a dozen red roses from behind his back.  After smelling them, Kim casually waved him in.

The moment he sauntered pass her wearing his signature cologne, she knew what was up.  He was having problems with his young bitch again. The only time he wore that cologne was when he wanted something and he did.  Scheming on how to get a hug out of Kim, Jay finally gave up and confessed how he'd missed her over the last year. Although Kim knew he was lying, she still found him to be handsome.

Kim also knew his relationship wasn't going well.  If it were, he would have never showed up at her doorstep.  After twenty minutes of lying he finally told the truth.  Obviously, his young girl had run out on him. Kim silently laughed in his face. She was so happy to hear that someone gave him a taste of his own medicine.

After reminiscing, Kim got upset. *Fuck that! I'm done thinking about him, she thought.* Kim was still perplexed about not seeing Unique, or hearing from him. She'd been dreaming about her young, handsome thug since they released him. *I'm sure he didn't forget about me, not the way I fucked and sucked him before he was released. I know something has to be wrong. I know what it is...he lost my phone number...naw, he lost my address. Maybe he just forgot about me.*


**The shower water ran smoothly over Kim's body.** Music from the small radio that hung from her showerhead played a sultry song by R&B soul lady Jill Scott. She ran her washcloth over her body while her head was tilted upwards letting the water beat softly on her neck. She closed her light brown eyes and fell into deep thought while allowing the washcloth to travel down her flat stomach and thick thighs. Before she even knew what she was doing, the soapy washcloth was gently caressing her vagina.

Kim hadn't had sex since that last night with Unique. And she wasn't about to just have sex with anybody. In fact, in all her years of having sex, she had only been with two men. Jay and Unique. Breaking out of her trance, she stopped herself before she reached an orgasm. After showering, she stood in front of the body size mirror that was mounted on the closet door. She let the towel she wore around her body fall to the carpet. Turning around checking her plump butt, free of dimples and cellulite, she lightly tapped it looking for anything unusual. It was perfect. *The gym had really paid off she thought as she prepared for bed.*

Thirty minutes later she was in her bed sleeping like a baby.

Bringgg!...Bringgg!...Bringgg! The phone that sat next to Kim's bed rang waking her out her sleep.

"Hello," she murmured into the receiver, propped up on her elbows with her eyes still closed.

"Hi, can I speak to Ms. Hill...I mean Kim, sorry."

Immediately Kim's eyes popped open as she recognized the male voice.

"Who's callin…?" Kim asked barely getting her words out.

"Is this Kim?"

"Yeah," she responded, with her heart pounding like it was going to rip through her chest.

"I didn't wake you up, did I?"

"No and yeah," she nervously replied now sitting on the side of her bed. "It depends on who this is."

"Who you want it to be?"

"I don't know," she lied. She knew that voice anywhere, but she still wasn't 100 percent sure.

"What 'cha doin' sleepin' at 4 o'clock in the afternoon?"

Kim looked at the time on her phone clock and lost all hope of the caller being who she thought it was. *If it was him he would've known I've been working, so it can't be him*, she thought.

"Hello," the man on the other end of the phone uttered.

"Look, who is this?" Kim snapped, becoming angry. Her hope of the caller being who she wanted it to be began to fade.

"Look out 'cha window."

Kim got off her bed and walked to her window pulling her satin, royal blue curtains back. "Oh my god!" She placed both of her hands over her mouth in excitement, not noticing she only wore a red cotton bra and thong panties standing in plain view of the window.

Unique had just come back from getting a fresh haircut. His waves were spinning uncontrollably, and his goatee was crisply sharp just like his hair line. The afternoon sun slammed against his handsome face making him resemble a model. His body leaned up against the driver's side door of his Navigator. He still held his cell phone in his hand waving it at Kim to say hi. Still with her hands over her mouth she was exposing herself to anybody who looked at her window.

"Come downstairs." Unique pointed at her front door.

"What?" she gestured with her hands now on the bottom of her window as if she was getting ready to raise it.

Unique quickly locked the doors to his truck and walked across the street towards Kim's house.

*What was he saying? Kim asked herself watching Unique approach her house.* "Shit!" she yelled, jumping back from the window after realizing her nakedness. She quickly ran to her closet and slid on a red pullover sleep shirt. She pinned her hair up into a ponytail then ran out her room. "Okay, act like it's no big deal that he's here," she told herself while running down her steps heading to her front door.

"What's up Kim?" Unique said with a big smile when Kim opened her door.

'Nothin'," she exclaimed with a slight smirk while opening the door wider meaning for him to walk in.

Unique's thoughts immediately shot back to the jail as he walked into Kim's living room. He smiled at the cleanliness of her house and thought about how Ms.Hill always made sure he kept a clean cell.

"So, how you doin'?" Unique pointed to the sofa as if to ask for permission to sit down.

"I'm doing great… now sit down, you don't have to ask to have a seat."

"I 'on know," Unique replied while taking a seat. "You might not want me to stay long."

*Kim thought to herself, Oh yes I do! As long as I've been looking for your ass you can stay as long as you want.*

"You're welcomed here anytime, that's why I gave you my address," she told Unique, still trying not to show her excitement.

"Yeah, I would've called or stopped by sooner but I had a few financial things I had to deal with first. You know how it is when a nigga get out." He smiled up at Kim.

Unique took his jacket off and placed it next to him. He then got up from the sofa and strolled through the living room.

"That's Jay, my ex-husband," Kim uttered, walking over to Unique while he held a picture of her ex-husband posing in his police uniform.

"So this your hero huh?" Unique murmured admiring Kim.

Kim didn't respond, instead she commented on Unique. "Damn you got a little taller since the jail. What? You six one, six two or…"

"I'm still six feet. You just short with no shoes on your feet," Unique exclaimed, moving his eyes from Kim's face down to her pretty polished red toes. But before he reached her feet he couldn't help but notice the cleavage she showed from the V-neck sleep shirt she wore. *Damn she looks good to be 34, he thought.*

"So, what made you show up today?" Kim questioned, walking over to the living room's window.

"To tell you the truth…" Unique had his arms crossed smiling as he stared at Kim's ass wondering what kind of panties she wore under her sleep shirt. "I know you like sports so I said I hope you'd go to the NBA All Star Game with me tomorrow at the M.C.I. Center."

"What time?" she asked, knowing she had nowhere else to be tomorrow. But she still wanted him to think so.

"It starts around 8 o'clock, but I wanna get there at seven."

"OK." Kim turned around, catching Unique's eyes fixed on her ass. "You like what you see?" she inquired, more out of wanting to know if her body was as attractive as she believed it was.

"I'll like it even more if you came over here and let me take a closer look," Unique seductively responded by licking his lips.

Kim slowly walked over towards him but told herself she wouldn't do anything to arouse Unique. She wanted him to wait like she had. "What did you say?" she quizzed, already knowing what he said.

"Don't act like you didn't hear me," Unique snapped as Kim faced him.

"I didn't hear you," she murmured in a sexy tone of voice that sent a tingle through Unique's body. She gazed up into his face and immediately felt her pussy thump. She crossed her legs in an attempt to change the feeling that surged through her body. "I'm for real. I didn't hear you," she protested now with her hands planted against his chest. She smiled at him with a cute look on her face.

"Why you have your legs crossed like that? What? You gotta use the bathroom or somethin'?"

Kim now had Unique's sweater balled up in her hands with her knuckles pressed against the middle of his chest. She tried to hold herself together but her hormones were racing faster than a race car doing 100 mph. She knew if she had sex with him now he might not show up again. She rationalized her dilemma then said the hell with it. I'll just fuck him good to make sure he wants to show up again.

"What's up?" Unique frowned at the grip Kim held him in.

She didn't respond, instead she released the grip on his sweater and pulled his head down to meet hers. They kissed like two lost lovers who had just reunited from years of separation. Unique slid his hands down Kim's back then onto her ass. He smoothly raised her sleep shirt inch by inch until he felt her bare ass. Unique scooped Kim up and carried her over to the sofa. The moment he placed her on it, the cell phone that was in his jacket pocket rang.

"Don't answer it," Kim said, pulling Unique down towards her.

"I have to," he said, pecking at her lips but still pulling away from her.

"No you don't," Kim snapped as Unique sat on the sofa beside her with his phone in his hand.

"Hello." He reluctantly spoke into his phone.

"I'm ready." A woman's voice said through Unique's cell phone.

"Oh shit!" he exclaimed, looking at his Rolex watch that read 5:05. "I'm on my way." Unique stood up from the sofa and looked down on Kim while placing his phone into his pocket. "I'm sorry I gotta go. My step-father invited me and my sista over for dinner and ain't no way we can miss that."

"Don't worry about it. I'll see you again right?" Kim gave Unique a seductive stare, biting down on her bottom lip.

"Yeah," Unique replied, grabbing his jacket from off the sofa slipping it on. "We're going to the All Star Game tomorrow right? Or, I can come back over tonight and we leave for the game from here tomorrow?"

"I don't know," Kim replied knowing her answer was yeah, hell yeah.

"What? You have somebody coming over tonight?" Unique threw his arms around Kim hugging her.

"Naw, nobody's coming over."

"I'm comin' over." Unique let her go and headed towards the front door.

Kim was enjoying everything that just happened. She was happy that he was coming back. In fact, she was hoping for something like that to happen. She knew for sure now that she'd see him again and she'd get the dick she wanted for a month now. Kim smiled as she watched Unique walk out to his truck. She shut her front door and ran upstairs like a teenage girl who was getting prepared for her first date.

# SIX

Glory was waiting by her BMW when Unique pulled up. She was involved in a deep conversation with Brother Hetep Muhammad.

"You rushed me, and now you out here talkin'," Unique said the moment he rolled his window down.

"She's coming Brother. We're just finishing our conversation," Hetep said smiling.

"Yeah I'm comin'," Glory stated, knowing how her brother viewed Hetep.

Unique cut his blinkers on and sat staring at his sister and the man he considered a fake. Even though he had never talked to Hetep, he just knew he wasn't the man Glory said he was, and if he could ever prove it, he would. Watching the brother intensely, Unique noticed Hetep's gray suit and bowtie, and expensive looking gray wool overcoat. Hetep waved at Unique as Glory walked away smiling. She ran around to the truck. Unique reluctantly gave Hetep a nod and a lazy wave of his hand.

"You got me parked in the middle of the street while you talk to your pimp pastor," Unique uttered with a smirk as Glory climbed into the truck.

"Boy I know you didn't just call Hetep a pimp," she replied.

"That's what he looks like," Unique snapped, pulling off. "A short pimp."

"So if he's a pimp and I was talkin' to him then, what am I? His whore?"

"I ain't say all that. What was you and Hetee talkin' 'bout anyway?" Unique asked

Glory pushed Unique's shoulder. "His name is Hetep. Anyway, if ya must know Mr. Nosey, he was telling me about how years ago there used ta be drug dealers right here where I live, until he brought some of the buildings and renovated them. In doing so, he and his Muslim brothers ran the dealers out of the neighborhood."

"How did he pull that off?" Unique asked suspiciously.

"He said by teaching truth about how the Black man can do bigger things than just sell drugs to his own people."

"How you gon' run bammas off by saying that?"

"He said more than that. I'm just saying what I remember. But whatever he told them, it worked because he said some of them same drug dealers are Muslims now," Glory said proudly.

"I 'on know why they did that, ain't no money in being a Muslim."

"Why you say that? Hetep owns three buildings with twelve units in each buildin'and rent averages $525 a month. Some of them are two bedrooms and cost more. That's money in the bank."

"Damn, you take up for that nigga quick. I hope you take up for me like that when somebody talkin' 'bout me."

They rode without talking as the CD player pushed out soft tunes. Unique couldn't help but glance over at his sister, appreciating her beauty. Glory wore a lime, Dolce & Gabbana leather pants suit with black leather ankle boots that matched her black knit sweater, and she was styling a three hundred dollar pair of small framed glasses. Her hair was in another sleek short style that enhanced her brown, flawless skin.

Unique couldn't help but notice how Glory resembled their mother. He was only seven when their parents died, but he remembered his mom being smart and business oriented. She and Donna had gone to Howard University together and had plans of going into business together.

The thought of college struck a nerve in Unique. "Glory, you been outta high school for three years now, and you haven't enrolled in college yet. But you've been shakin' your ass at that club for a year," Unique said.

Glory gave her brother an unpleasant stare. "What about you? Why didn't you go to college after you finished high school? Don't say ya needed money," Glory snapped before he could respond. "You could've gone ta Dad fa money just like ya told me. I want my own shit just like you."

"You could have your own shit. All you gotta do is ask me or Dad, and it's yours. Like when you wanted a car, I copped the Beamer with no problem."

Glory was smiling looking at the sincerity in her brother's face. She knew he didn't like the idea of her stripping. And she respected that, but she was addicted to the quick money. She had told herself she was going to stop, but she didn't know when. "You really want me to stop dancin' don't you? Ok, I'ma stop this year."

They rode in silence until Unique ordered his sister, "Open the glove compartment. This is fa you."

"Thanks," she said flipping the thick bundle of money through her hand and grinning from ear to ear.

"Yeah, where that nigga Supreme at?" Unique asked as they stepped out of the truck in front of Dad's house.

"I 'on know, he left my place right before I called you," Glory said, placing the money Unique gave her into her Prada bag.

"Well tell him he owe me for that 5 g's you just slid into your bag."

"I thought 'cha gave this to me?"

"I did," Unique grinned as he and his sister stood on the porch of Dad's house. "But since you have a man now who got some doe, he can pay back whatever you get from me."

Glory wanted to yell out "that's not my man. I'm just fuckin' him." Instead, she knocked on Dad's door.

A woman, who stood five foot six with light skin, and a natural pretty face framed with a short boy-like curly jet black afro, answered the door. The smile on her face proved that she was more than happy to see the two young people that stood before her.

"My babies!" The lady Unique and Glory called Donna or sometimes Mom, hugged them both before grabbing Glory's hand and pulling her into the house, straight toward the kitchen.

After closing and locking the door, Unique walked into the living room only to find it empty. Walking towards the sliding glass doors separating the living room and dining room, he discovered Dad punching keys on his laptop computer.

"What's up Dad?" Unique asked.

"Nothin', just finishing up a little work," Dad replied without looking up.

"That food smellin' good. What Donna fixin'?"

Dad stopped typing and glanced at Unique through the small framed glasses he wore. "What I tell you about that? You just…"

"Sorry," Unique quickly murmured placing his jacket on the back of a chair at the table. "I'ma try my best to call her Mom from now on." He smiled and sat down across from Dad.

"Bobby, you have that computer off my table yet?" Donna yelled from the kitchen.

"Yeah baby," Dad answered, closing the laptop and signaling Unique to head toward the kitchen.

"Mom, you lookin' good," Glory said, sitting on a stool watching Donna dip her cooking spoon in pots as she prepared the food.

"I know, I gotta keep up with all you young girls out there."

"What 'cha doin' to stay lookin' that young at your age…not that you're old or anything."

Donna turned from the pots and said, "Girl you don't have to sugar-coat it. I am getting older. I'll be 46 next month, but look…" Donna lifted her apron showing off her petite figure. "I could still get any young man I wanted if I didn't love and respect Bobby."

"You damn sure could because you look goooo…d."

"Child don't play with me like that. Do I look that good?" Donna smiled from ear to ear.

"Yeah," Glory replied leaping off the stool. "That hair cut you rockin' makes you look like you in college or somethin'."

They started laughing then jumped on another topic while Donna put the finishing touch on the food. Unique and Bobby joined the women at the table for dinner. They all laughed, talked, and helped themselves to lots of filet mignon, cajun rice, and mashed potatoes with gravy.

After everyone had finished their food, Donna and Glory took the empty plates into the kitchen. They returned with bowls of strawberry ice cream and a delicious looking cheesecake Donna made from scratch.

"Unique, have you put your money into a bank yet?" Dad quizzed, while digging into his dessert.

"Not yet."

"What's taking you so long?"

"I don't know.  I guess I just don't trust banks with…"

"You said that before.  I didn't put you on my payroll as an employee at my shoe store for nothing.  I did that so you could have a legitimate alibi to make a deposit at a bank and to show your P.O. you have a job."

"I told him that a long time ago." Glory intervened, rolling her eyes at her brother.

"Even if I do open up an account, I can't just walk up to the teller with the kind of money I got.  They'll arrest me on the spot."

"That's why you put in a little at a time," Donna added.

"How much your workers get paid?" Unique quizzed Dad with his lips in a sneer.

"I have you down as manager.  So, let's just say around $17.00 an hour.  So that would be…" Dad tilted his head back thinking.  "$136.00 a day, $680.00 a week, $2,720.00 a month, and $32,640.00 a year."

"Ooo….h! My baby can aaadd," Donna drawled with a smile.

"I gotta open the account with a check, right?"

"No, but if you would stop procrastinating all you have to do is stop by the shoe store every Friday and pick up a check that would be made out to you for that week.  All you have to do then is get money orders with the amount you saw on that first check. I just remembered, at my office I have checks made out to you that are six months old.  You can open your account with them.  I won't charge you for those 24 checks, but any checks after those you'll have to pay me back."

"All right, I'll do it, but I'll just open it with the checks you got for me now, then put my own money in after that."

"Just make sure you keep me updated on how much you have in the bank so I can keep your pay stubs in order. Remember, you get paid $680 a week. So don't deposit too much at one time."

"Are y'all finished?" Donna inquired being sarcastic. "Bobby, did you tell them the good news?"

"Baby I am," Dad said, nodding at his wife.

"What good news?" Glory asked excited.

Unique knew that if Dad had good news it would be something really big because that's how he rolled.

"In a few months I'm opening a club in Largo, Maryland," Dad revealed smiling at his announcement. "A hip hop type club."

"All right do it baby!" Unique shouted grinning in excitement.

"Also, also..." Dad waited for Unique's excitement to subside. "I'll be getting out of the game in a few months."

Unique's grin quickly turned into a frown at the sound of that announcement. The threat of his only connection being cut off was definitely detrimental to him because Dad was the only person he'd dealt with the five years he'd been in the game. He felt comfortable dealing with the man he considered his father. In fact, the reason Unique got into the game was because Dad got tired of giving him money without him having to work for it. Since Unique was already hanging in drug infested neighborhoods, Dad gave him his first kilo of crack.

"Ain't that good news?" Donna said while picking up the empty ice cream bowls and carrying them into the kitchen.

"Yeah," Glory agreed smiling in Dad's direction. "You have all the money you need. Go legit." She smiled in her brother's direction.

"I don't," Unique snapped. But he did have enough money. He just wanted more.

"Tell 'em the other good news," Donna pressed coming back into the dining room and taking a seat at the table.

"The ice cream parlor is now Donna's. She's the official owner. My name isn't on any documents pertaining to ownership or anything else in that matter."

Glory and Donna jumped out of their chairs and embraced each other screaming like they'd just won a prize.

"Donna!" Dad shouted over the screaming women. "Tell Glory what you told me."

"Ok." Donna held Glory by her hands. "I want you to quit your job and help me run the shop. You'll be manager."

"I'll be glad to, but you know I dance Friday and Saturdays."

"You'll be off on weekends," Donna assured.

"Oh yeah," Dad murmured as the women sat back down. "That's a good move. I'm sure you've made more than enough to pay for college by now," he smiled at Glory.

Glory didn't respond. She didn't want the college thing to escalate.

Ringgg! Ringgg! Unique's cell phone was ringing. He reached into his jacket pocket for it. "Yeah," he muttered into the phone, said a few words, then hung up. "I gotta go," he announced after putting his phone back into his jacket pocket.

"Yeah, I gotta dance tonight," Glory said.

"Call me tomorrow," Donna said to her step-daughter as they hugged each other while walking out to the truck.

"So what's up Dad?" Unique whispered as they stood on the porch watching the two women talking beside the door of the truck.

"It's that time, Baby. I have to get out of the game while I don't have any indictments. Everything is going great for me now, and I don't want anything to get in my way. Besides, I've made millions already. Now I'll invest my money in all legit shit. It's over for me. I'm getting older, and I can't take chances anymore."

"So, what about me?" Unique inquired, looking at Dad with a desperate look in his eyes.

"If you can afford 20 kilos or better, I'll hook you up with my people."

Unique's face lit up. "I can afford it," he quickly replied, thinking of meeting the connection Dad had dealt with for over 19 years.

"All right, I'll let you know when it's time to make that move. And, make sure your money is right. If it's not right, when it's that time to cop, your drug future is dead."

"My money is right," Unique bragged, walking down the porch steps and out to his truck.

"Make sure you put that money in the bank," Donna said to Unique as she hugged him.

The ride to Glory's apartment was short. Unique's next destination after dropping Glory off was to respond to the phone call he received at Dad's house. He parked in front of an apartment complex off of Wheeler Road located in Southeast. Upon stepping out of his truck, Unique was met by two men with broad smiles on their faces who shook his hands.

"What's up, Slim?"

"Ain't shit!" Unique replied as they walked in the cold.

Apartment 10 was jammed packed with at least 15 to 20 men and women. The only furniture in the two bedroom apartment were two king size beds, and a large table in the living room with a radio. There were two sets of gambling groups in a huddle in the living room. Men and women were in both groups. Unique walked over to the huddle that was the loudest. That's when he saw PooBear, shirtless, shaking dice in one hand, and holding a stack of money in the other. He smiled looking at his youngster who wore a big smile on his face that said he was winning.

"One minute," PooBear stated looking up at Unique while kneeling. "Six, baby, six." He rolled the dice out and they landed on his number. "Yeah, niggas!" He snatched the money up that he'd won. He stood up and went over to Unique.

"How much is this?" Unique asked accepting the bundle of money from PooBear. "Ten g's exact," PooBear replied as he and Unique walked back into the living room. "Listen, we've got some big things that's 'boutta go down real soon."

"What's that?" PooBear quizzed, not ever hearing those words before.

"I'll let 'cha know soon, but for now, keep your eyes open for some young'uns you like. We might need them. See you later, Slim." Unique opened the door and walked out.

PooBear stood with his back against the front door. Thoughts scrambled through his head about what Unique had said. He smiled. Unique copping more drugs was worth smiling about. If that was indeed what Unique was talking about, that meant more money for him.

**Unique's trip home didn't take long. Not too far**
from the gambling spot Dad purchased him his first home. At first, Unique
didn't like it because it was so close to some of the worst neighborhoods in Southeast. But Dad didn't feel that way. "If you don't fuck
with the neighborhoods, they won't fuck with you," he told Unique.
Come to find out, that statement was true. In the four years Unique
lived there he hadn't had any problems from neighbors.

The only problem he encountered was when he allowed one of his
women to stay overnight. She turned one night into a week. When Unique
told her she had to leave, she threw a tantrum. And from that day on, he
took his women to hotels or stayed at their cribs. They weren't allowed
at his house, nor were any of his associates, except for PooBear. If you
weren't a part of his family, you didn't even know where he lived.

Entering his house, Unique went straight upstairs to his bedroom.
He turned his room light on revealing a well kept bachelor pad. Rushing
to the back of his closet he triggered the combination to his safe and
removed a counting machine.

Money nearly covered his entire bed. He placed 100's, 50's, 20's,
10's, 5's, and dollar bills in separate stacks. But all was placed through
the machine. It had been a while since he'd counted his money. He
wasn't planning on doing anything big with it since he felt he had everything he wanted. He just wanted to make sure he never had to ask Dad
for anything. That meant a lot to him because Dad had given him and
Glory everything they wanted. But now that he'd been taking care of
himself since he was twenty, he wanted to keep it that way. And having
money secured that.

Unique smiled broadly when he saw the number on the machine.
After all the money was placed through the machine, it came to a total
of $440,000, not including the 10 g's PooBear gave him earlier that was
still in his pocket. He had more money than he told Dad he had a month
ago. The thought of more soldiers working for him flashed in his mind.
He knew he definitely needed more than PooBear.

He put the money machine and his money back into the safe. Unique
was on his way out the house when a thought came to him. He grabbed

the camcorder and jetted to his car. After arriving at Kim's place, his plan went into effect. He placed his cell phone in the glove compartment so he wouldn't be disturbed. Climbing out of his truck with his camcorder in hand he noticed that all of the lights were off in the house. He walked up several steps to the porch. One knock on the door and it jerked open. From that moment on, Unique knew it was a game, and he didn't mind playing it.

It was totally dark inside the house when he entered. Kim had taped all of the light switches prohibiting Unique from turning on any lights.

"I like this." Unique quickly cut the camcorder on and started filming. "If she likes to play games, I'm sure she don't mind me filming this."

He checked the living room, dining room, kitchen, the two bedrooms upstairs, and the bathroom seeing no sign of Kim. A little upset now, he walked back downstairs and checked everything again, with no luck. He went in the living room and sat on the sofa. "Kim?" he shouted. "I give up." After he shouted, he heard a noise that sounded like it came from under his feet.

"How could I forget the basement?" he mumbled leaping from the sofa heading towards the kitchen. The door to the basement was wide open, something he didn't notice the two times he checked the kitchen.

As he walked down the basement steps, the smell of Kim's perfume filled the air assuring him that she was down there. He smiled taking in the smell as he made his way through the basement. The basement was as dark as the rest of the house, but Unique continued to use the camcorder as his vision.

"What do we have here?" he whispered, touching a knob to a door. Slightly turning the doorknob, he slowly pushed the door open only to find an unfinished bathroom.

He continued to walk through the basement until a bright light caught his attention. Following the light, he walked up to the door and pushed it open. The first thing he saw was Kim sprawled out on her back on the king sized bed. Her arms were extended as if she were strapped down. Her legs were lying straight out with the right one slightly arched. She wore a white crotchless teddy that matched the white sheets she laid on.

Unique moved through the room with the camcorder as if he was a professional camera man. He slowly walked along the edge of the bed filming from Kim's feet up to her face. He knew she didn't mind because she had a big smile on her face, and she started to pose in model like postures.

"So you don't mind me filming you?"

"Why should I?" Kim was still posing in various poses. "That tape is for me and your eyes only, right?"

"Yeah." Unique was already planning on showing PooBear, which he did whenever he recorded his sexual encounters. Noticing the ceiling that was all mirror, he aimed the camera at the ceiling reflecting Kim's beautiful body that was now crawling across the bed towards him.

"Put this down," she said, taking the camera from Unique and sliding off the bed. She walked over to the blue recliner that sat in the corner of the room and placed the camera at the edge of it making sure it was pointing directly at the bed so it could record the action that would take place on it. "This thing is still on, right?"

"Yeah," Unique replied, staring at Kim as if she was the last woman on earth.

After Kim ripped Unique's clothes off, she ordered him onto the bed. He lay on his back with his head propped on the pillow. Kim climbed up on the bed and stood above him with his body stationed between her legs. Unique looked up at her remembering not being able to see her body when he was incarcerated. Now the lights were on, and this was no cell. Her waist was small, her ass, round and plump, and she had big tits. *And her face and long black hair were beautiful.*

"How do you want it?" Kim teased Unique squatting down gripping his hard penis with one hand.

"However you wanna give it to me," he replied, looking at her from the ceilings mirror.

Kim let go of his stiffness and jumped down off the bed. When she returned to the bed she held a can of whipped cream she retrieved from behind the recliner. And in an instant she was spraying it all over Unique's body.

Unique exploded the moment Kim begun licking the whipped cream from his body. She made love to his body with her tongue, and when she reached his rock hard penis, she gave it extra pleasure. In a way that would keep him around for a long time.

"Damn!" Unique moaned, now propped on his elbows looking at Kim, while she orally satisfied him. She lay in between his legs.

Kim didn't take her eyes off him and continued to assault his penis. This was the weapon she thought she'd use to assure their togetherness. Feeling the eruption that was about to explode from Unique's penis, Kim withdrew her mouth and mounted him. She rode him with cruel intent, making sure to work every muscle in her vagina. *There was no way she was going to lose him, she thought.* A second later, they reached orgasms simultaneously.

# SEVEN

April showers poured on the black Acura Vigor that sat parked on a Southwest block lined with small houses. The darkness of the sky almost overshadowed the dim lamp poles that were supposed to illuminate the street. That enabled Supreme who sat in the Acura to go unnoticed, not just tonight, but for the last three months. He was at it again, doing what he did best. He sat crouched down behind the steering wheel of his Acura dressed in all black. A black Desert Eagle 44 sat in his lap, along with a black stun gun.

His motivation was simple. *Money.* He only had 10 g's of the $75,000 he had when he arrived in D.C. The money seemed to vanish into thin air especially since he'd been hangin' with Unique. Supreme found himself spending more money than he wanted to. He had paid almost $8,000 for the hotel room that he'd been staying in for the last ninety days, he also brought more clothes that put huge dents in his pockets. Sometimes he found himself buying Glory the same costly outfits he would buy himself. He secretly hoped that Glory would ask him to move in with her. But she hadn't asked yet, although, he was still optimistic about it.

Supreme looked at his watch and casually slid the black bandanna up over his mouth and nose as he saw his victim pull up in a Ford Expedition. He had gotten his lead at the strip club the first time he went to see Glory and Pam dance. When Supreme saw the costly iced-out chain that hung from his new victim's neck, he was on his trail immediately. Supreme visited the club on some days that Pam and Glory didn't dance and would see him. For the last three months he had followed the man on occasion clocking his route, knowing where he was going before he got there.

The house he was going in tonight was without a doubt the place where the man kept a large portion of his money. And the place where he slept at least three times a week. Now, Supreme watched the truck that was parked five cars in front of him. He took a hard look at his gun that he copped a month ago from gun dealer named Bullet, who threw the stun gun in for free. It would definitely come in handy due to his profession.

He quickly put the stun gun in his jean pocket then slid the 44 Desert Eagle into the pouch of the hooded sweater he wore. A little nervous due to it being his first stick-up in D.C., Supreme took two deep breaths. Closely watching the truck through his front windshield, Supreme saw the truck's inside light cut on. When he saw the light cut off, he slid the hood to his sweater over his head so the only thing you saw of his face was his brown eyes and the lightness of his forehead.

Supreme knew that the pouring rain would cause the man to jump out of the truck and make a run for his house. Knowing that, Supreme stepped out of the car and went to his trunk, not caring that in a minute he would be soaked. Pretending to open the trunk, he watched as the truck door swung open. Seeing that, Supreme hopped on the sidewalk and walked with his head down, eyes up, still looking at the truck. As the man rushed around the front of his truck with two bags in each arm, Supreme had his hand in his hoodie's pouch pulling out his gun. The man didn't even notice the man in all black until he heard splashing footsteps behind him as he walked up the steps that led to the porch of his house.

"Keep your hands on those bags and don't turn around," Supreme ordered in a harsh tone. "Who in the house?" He had the gun pressed into the man's back.

"Shit!" was the only response the man gave.

"I'm gonna ask you one more time. Who in the house?" Supreme already knew who was in the house. He just wanted to confirm what he knew.

"My girl," the man mumbled.

"Where your keys to the house?"

"In my front pocket."

Supreme reached into the man's front pocket and pulled out his keys. With the gun in his left hand, he pushed the man's body against the frame of the house. With his right hand he stuck the key into the door, unlocked it, and pushed it open. Supreme grabbed the back collar to the ski vest the man wore and walked him into the house.

"Call your girl," Supreme shouted, standing over his victim. His hands were still gripping the bags like he was told.

"Hey Poo!" the man yelled, watching his robber place his gun against the side of his left leg.

"Be down in a minute," a woman upstairs replied.

Supreme took a step back from the sofa to distance himself. If the man wanted to play hero and leap at him, all he had to do was draw his gun from his side and let off numerous shots.

"Look, take whatever you want, just don't hurt my girl," the man said. "I think she's pregnant."

"Call your girl again," Supreme snapped.

"Hey, Poo I need to see you down here."

"I'm comin' I just got out of the shower, boy."

"What's your name?" Supreme asked already knowing his victim's name.

"Ray"

"Boy you callin' me like you got somethin' for me." Ray's woman walked down the steps heading to the living room wearing a pair of cut off jean shorts and a small white t-shirt. Her skin was a pretty tan color, and her hair was long and wavy.

"Who is this?" she asked, frowning, walking toward her man.

Before she could say another word, Supreme drew his gun and pointed it at her. She yelled, turned around and ran back towards the steps, but she only reached the first step. Supreme grabbed her hair and dragged her across the carpet. "III…III!" she screamed.

"Get what the fuck you want man and get out!" Ray was now standing up. His snarled lips expressed his anger.

"If you don't sit 'cha punk ass down I'ma lay your ass down permanently…" Supreme had his gun in his left hand pointing it at Ray, and in his right a handful of hair. Ray's girl sat on the floor clutching Supreme's hand trying to relieve some of the pressure on her hair. "I'ma let 'cha get up and sit with ya man, bitch!"

Immediately after Supreme freed her hair she sprang to her feet and ran into her man's arms who was still standing.

"Both of y'all sit the fuck down!" Supreme waved his gun at them both and they sat down.

"What you want, nigga?" Ray asked, with his girl crying in his arms.

"Every fuckin' dime you have!" Supreme replied.

"Take it all," Ray said, kicking the two shopping bags with his feet. He looked at his robber with malice in his eyes as Supreme stepped over to the sofa and picked up both bags. Backing into the middle of the living room, he crouched down and scrambled through the bags while keeping his eyes and gun on his victims

"How much money in these bags?" Supreme roared dumping all the money into one bag and finding a .357 in the other.

"About 25 g's," Ray replied.

"Where the rest of the money at?"

"That's it right there!"

"Son, don't fuckin' play with me…" Supreme walked to the sofa, stuck his Desert Eagle up against Ray's head.

"Just give him everything," Ray's girl yelled, with tears streaming down her face.

"I ain't got shit else."

"Nigga let me help you remember where the rest of ya money at." Supreme pulled his stun gun and zapped Ray.

Ray's girl screamed, leaped off the sofa, and ran towards the steps again. She made it halfway up the before Supreme gripped her hair. He pulled her hair so hard she fell down several steps before coming to a painful stop at the base of the stairs.

Supreme leaped over the woman's body and over to the sofa where Ray sat, incoherent and paralyzed.

"I...I...I told you I think she's pregnant," Ray muttered, the effect of the stun gun wearing off slightly. He managed to raise his 280 pound load, gazing across the living room at his girl's sprawled body. "Is she dead?" Water built up in his eyes and a single tear rolled down his face. "I don't know and I don't give a fuck nigga...now stand ya ass up." Supreme grabbed Ray by his arm and struggled to pull him to his feet. With his gun pressed into Ray's back, Supreme walked him over to his girl's body. They looked down and knew she wasn't dead. Her slightly protruded belly moved up and down with every breath she took.

"Yo, I'ma ask you again, and if you don't say what I wanna hear I'ma put one in your back and one in your girl's stomach. Now, where the rest of the dough at?"

'Up...upstairs," Ray reluctantly responded looking down at his girl.

Ray walked Supreme into an empty room upstairs then into a spacious closet where a small safe sat on the floor. Ray picked the safe up from the floor and walked out the closet placing it on the floor. Supreme ordered him to stand by the wall and asked for the combination of the safe. Ray told him the numbers, and Supreme found at least 70 g's in it. He grabbed what could fit in his pockets and stuffed them. The rest he gave to Ray to carry to the living room. On their way back downstairs, they noticed Ray's girl body was gone. The front door to the house was wide open.

"Where'd that bitch go?" Supreme hollered, running over to the door and kicking it shut.

"I don't know," Ray stated as his eyes grew the size of two quarters.

As Supreme reached for the bag of money Ray was carrying, he swiftly swung the gun across Ray's head hitting him on the temple, and knocking him to the floor. When Supreme saw that Ray wasn't unconscious, he pulled his stun gun out, and zapped him. Peering out the front door as he slowly opened it; Supreme didn't see any signs of police or anyone who would block his escape.

Later, blocks away from the house, he reached into his pocket and pulled out Ray's house keys and threw them out the car window. As he headed to the hotel, he wondered where Ray's girl had gone. He smiled while snatching off the hood to his sweater, and pulling the bandanna from his face. *The bitch was fakin' when she fell down those steps, he thought.* He couldn't stop thinking about the woman and why she didn't grab the bag of money that he threw on the floor before she jetted.

Supreme's hotel room was cluttered with new clothes along with several shoe boxes. He tossed his Desert Eagle and his new .357 on the bed. Smiling, he dumped onto the table all the stolen money. Sitting down, he began counting. Thirty minutes later he was done. The total of $130,000 had him laughing out loud. This was the biggest stick up he'd ever pulled off. Never had he gotten this much money in one hold up, usually it took him five to ten capers to reach that amount.

After placing all his money…except a thousand dollars into a shopping bag, Supreme shoved the bag under the bed and headed for the shower. As he showered he credited himself on the robbery. After showering, he dressed casually and headed for the club.

As soon as Supreme entered the club he went in search of Unique. A short, light-skinned woman, thick in all the right places stepped in his path.

"Who you wit?" the woman asked.

"I ain't here wit' nobody Ma," he replied, bending down towards her ear.

"Dance with me then," she said smiling, pulling Supreme to a designated area. But before they could start dancing they were interrupted by a dude wearing all black.

"Nigga stop bein' greedy…you gotta girl," PooBear smiled as he cut in between Supreme and the woman.

Supreme laughed. He was getting used to PooBear's insults. At first he believed he envied him because he was fucking Glory, but lately he'd been feeling the resentment was over more than just some ass. Maybe it was because Unique and him were getting closer.

Tapping PooBear on his shoulder, Supreme asked, "Where Unique at?"

"I 'on know nigga. I ain't his girl."

Supreme stepped off grinning when he noticed Unique talking to two women with his back up against the wall.

"What's up, Son?" Supreme blubbered, now standing beside Unique and the two women.

"What's up, Joe?" Unique said embracing Supreme. "I thought you wasn't comin'."

"I had to take care of somethin' first," Supreme said.

"Excuse us. We are *still* here," one of the two women said.

"Oh, my bad ladies. This my man Supreme right here. Y'all go downstairs and wait for me," Unique said.

"So what's up?" Supreme asked Unique taking a seat at the bar.

"You, I'm try'na find out what 'cha doin' out here," Unique said, sipping on his drink.

"What 'cha mean?" Supreme responded, knowing what Unique meant.

"You know…" They looked at each other. "How you makin' a livin' and shit."

"I'm still livin' off the money I brought down here with me, Son."

"You brought a mill down here with you or somethin'?"

"Naw Dog, I ain't got that type of cream."

"I 'on know," Unique replied. "You been buyin' up some shit lately."

"So, this why you told me to meet 'cha at the club so we can talk about what I got?"

"Yes and no," Unique said plainly. "Nigga, are you Fedz?" He looked Supreme dead in his eyes.

"I know you ain't ask me no shit like that," Supreme said.

"Why wouldn't I? To me, you came from out of nowhere. You might of known my sista for a minute but that don't mean shit. The Fedz sneaky like that. They don't send old mothafuckers to get young niggas; they send young'uns like you."

"Naw Dog, I ain't Fedz. But what made you think that?"

"You got money, no job, don't hustle, and livin' at a hotel."

"I'm at a hotel 'cause your sista didn't ask me ta move in yet," Supreme joked.

"Nigga get your own crib. You don't wanna be living with no girl. Shit, my sista on that independent woman bullshit anyway, so you can forget about her asking you to move in."

"Yeah you right." Supreme said as he thought to himself. *I've been laying pipe to this bitch, and she ain't said shit yet.*

"So when you run outta dough what'cha gon' do?" Unique inquired.

"The same way PooBear gettin' his money, that's how I'll get mine."

Supreme spoke those words but he knew he'd never sell drugs. His forte was stick-ups which he started doing when he was a kid to buy the things his alcoholic mother claimed she couldn't afford. But now, he did it because he was addicted to robbing. He loved it, and robberies were his only income.

"You don't know nobody yet, niggas ain't gon' let 'cha just come and set up shop, especially with you being from New York."

"Yeah, but that's where you come in. You got respect."

Supreme and Unique turned around to find PooBear grinning with his right arm around the neck of the woman that asked Supreme to dance earlier.

"I'ma holla at 'cha tomorrow, Joe." PooBear shook Unique's hand but gave Supreme a slight nod of his head with a sinister stare before stepping off.

At that very moment Supreme hated PooBear. He wanted to slide right off of his stool, get his.357 and murder the hater. But Supreme wasn't a vicious killer, he only did what he had to do to make a living.

"Shit! I just remembered them bitches waitin' for me downstairs. Unique slid off his stool. "I take one, you take one."

"I'ma chill. Go 'head, I'm tired," Supreme replied.

"I can't believe you turning down some pussy."

After watching Unique walk off, Supreme looked around the club for a few minutes then headed out to his car. Several minutes later he was pulling up to Wendy's drive-thru. Supreme turned his music down and placed his gun in the pocket of his sweatpants.

"Can somebody take my order?" he yelled impatiently.

"Yeah, if you give me a chance," the voice replied and took his order.

Supreme pulled up to the drive-thru window waiting for the cashier to face him. He sat there for a minute knowing he had heard that voice somewhere before. When the lady turned around his suspicion was confirmed.

"That's six twenty…" She had a hand out for Supreme's money. Supreme grinned when he saw the lady at the window was Big Red who he hadn't seen since Glory interrupted his lap dance.

"What? You don't make enough dough dancin'?" Supreme quizzed, handing her a ten dollar bill.

"Yeah, but there's always room for more money. Where you comin' from anyway?" Big Red asked smiling.

"DC Live," Supreme answered, checking his rearview mirror to make sure no one was behind him.

"So, are you ready to pick up where we left off? I'm 'boutta get off. What's up with you?"

Supreme didn't think he heard her right. He looked at her with a frown on his face. "What 'cha mean?"

"You know what I'm talkin' 'bout boy don't play dumb." Big Red had a wicked grin on her face.

His mind drifted back to how fast his dick rose when she stood in front of him at the club. I ain't turning down this ass, he thought.

"I'ma pull around front. How long you gon' be?"

"Five minutes," she said, ducking her head back inside the drive-thru window.

In the restaurant parking lot, Supreme stood against the side of his Acura waiting for Big Red.

"So, where are we going?" Big Red questioned walking toward Supreme. She wore a pair of skin tight black Guess jeans, and a white shirt with a quarter length black rain jacket over it. Her fairly long hair was braided and pulled back into a ponytail.

"Let's go to this hotel room I got," Supreme said opening the passenger side door for her letting her slide into the car. Then he walked around the car and hopped into the driver's seat.

"Hold on, I hope you don't think I'm free," Big Red said after Supreme started the car.

Supreme had no problem with giving women anything. A matter of fact, he had been generous to women all his life. He pulled out his money and gave Red two hundred dollars, then pulled off. It wasn't his first time paying for some ass. He knew that it was either pay now, or pay later, but you would pay in some way. *All men did.*

"So what made you come out of the blue and ask me what's up?"

Supreme questioned his eyes on the road, but also looking at the thickness of Big Red's thighs.

"I'm gonna keep it real," Red replied, turning around in her seat to face Supreme. "I overheard Body talkin' to Booty about how good you can fuck and how nasty you are with a nice size dick. Where are you from anyway?" She smiled at him.

He thought about it for a second then responded, "New Jersey."

Supreme knew Big Red's reputation. Red was the type of woman that fucked every dick there was. She'd been with so many men that when niggas wanted to know where their enemy resided, she would be the person they would go to. Money was her God and Supreme knew that telling her he was from New York might be detrimental to him in some way down the line.

They pulled into the front parking lot of the hotel. Supreme parked, they got out of the car and walked towards the entrance of the hotel. Suddenly, Supreme saw two black shadows emerge from Red's left side. As the two shadows became more visible, he could now see two men with guns in their hands. Before Supreme could warn Red, the men had already begun firing.

Several shots hit Big Red. Because Supreme was on the right of Red, he had sufficient time to get his gun from his pocket. He let off four shots while sprawled on the asphalt. The two men were now running back to their car with their backs turned.

Supreme let off one shot while scrambling to his feet. The taller of the two men fell to one knee, but his partner was right there to snatch him up by his armpit while letting off two shots. Supreme let off his last shot before running into the hotel's lobby. The sound of spinning tires stopped him before he ran pass the empty check-in desk. He looked through the entrance glass doors and saw the uninjured man that shot at him jump out of their car and walk over to his Acura.

Powww! Powwww! Powww! He shot up Supreme's car.

While the man shot his car up, Supreme paid attention to the driver of the car. He couldn't believe who he saw behind the wheel of the black Honda Accord. Poo, Ray's girl. The man he robbed earlier. Now he noticed the man that was now climbing back into the Honda. It was Ray.

"That bitch followed me," Supreme fussed, running towards an open elevator hopping on it, and taking it to the 4th floor.

When he entered his room, the first thing he grabbed was the bag of money that was under the bed, then the Desert Eagle from under the pillow. Without a thought, he went out the door then down the fire exit and out the back door of the hotel.

Five minutes later he was flagging a cab down. "Damn I left my stun gun," he mumbled. A yellow cab quickly pulled up in front of him. He told the cabby Glory's address then slouched down with relief into the back seat. Arriving in front of Glory's building, Supreme pushed number seven on the intercom buzzer. Thirty seconds later Glory's voice came blasting over the intercom. "Who is dis buzzing at my door at two something in the morning?"

Supreme smiled. He knew she couldn't have been sleep with a voice sounding as live as that. "It's me Preme."

"Boy, you know you wrong. It's too late for you to be buzzin' shit…how you know if I was sleep or not? I do have to work tomorrow."

"Are you gon' let me in or not?"

"No!"

He waited for a minute thinking she was just playing. But when another minute passed without a word from her, he pushed number seven again.

"You ain't gone yet?" she snapped.

He smiled. He knew she was still standing next to her intercom the entire time there was silence on both sides. She responded to his buzz too quick. "No, I'm try'na come in."

"You better get back in ya car and head back to that hotel. Better yet, go where ya been for the last three days 'cause I did drop by your hotel room and you wasn't there!"

"Ma, you sound vexed." Supreme said sarcastically.

"Are you gon' roll out or what?" she asked.

"Ma, all jokes aside. I just crashed my car, it's totaled."

"Boy stop playing."

"That's my word, Ma. I ain't playin'."

"You hurt?" Glory asked with concern.

'Nah."

Supreme smiled at the sound of the building door unlocking. When he entered the apartment, Glory was now sitting in the corner of a dark yellow leather sofa, reading Men Cheat, Women Experiment by Natosha Gale Lewis.

"Why you up readin' this late if you gotta work in the mornin'? Supreme asked as he locked the front door.

"I 'on go to work until noon…" Glory slightly rose up from the sofa to look Supreme over. She glanced down at his boots. "Wasn't it rainin' earlier?"

"Yeah," Supreme hoped that Glory didn't see any blood on his clothes resulting from the shooting.

"Boy, don't you dare walk on my white carpet with those boots on."

Supreme took his boots off and sat them on the black floor mat in front of the door. He placed his bag of money and his two guns in a chair, then slid the chair under the table.

"Why you lookin' me over like that?" Glory asked, slamming her book closed and sucking her teeth.

Supreme shook his head and grinned. "You bad, Ma. You look like that gospel singer CeCe Winans. But, you look better, that's my word."

Glory blushed. "How ya crash your car boy?"

'You wouldn't believe me if I told 'cha."

"Try me."

"Rushing over here to see you."

"You right, *I don't believe you*." Glory twisted up her lips. "You wasn't in that much of a rush, I ain't seen you in three days."

"You miss me?" He leaned forward and tried to plant a kiss on her lips.

"No." She placed her hand out in front of her, stopping him. "What 'cha gon' do, cop another ride?"

"Yeah. I'ma call your brotha tomorrow and see if he gon' take me to that car lot he be leasin' his cars from."

"How much money you bring from New York with you? And don't lie." Glory's face had a no nonsense look on it.

"Enough."

"What's enough?" she quickly fired back.

"Enough to buy whatever I want."

"I hope you didn't rob no bank or nothin'."

"Nah, I ain't rob no bank. I just saved a lot of money."

"What kind of car you…"

The sound of Glory's phone ringing cut off her words.

"Who the hell is callin' this late?" She reached for the cordless phone. "Hello."

"Glory!" Pam's voice shouted on the other end of Glory's phone.

"Girl, it's almost 3 in the…"

"I just got a call from Lexus and she said Big Red is dead!"

Glory threw her book on the floor and placed her hand over her mouth. "Mmmmm, stop playin' girl."

"I ain't playin'. They said she got shot in the parkin' lot of a hotel about an hour ago. Matter fact, up the street from the club…I think it's the same hotel Supreme stayin' in."

"How long ago you left your hotel?" Glory asked Supreme. She held the phone away from her ear.

"Around midnight, why?"

"Dis Pam on the phone. She said Big Red got shot in the parkin' lot of the hotel you stayin' in."

"Damn." Supreme tried to look as surprised as he could. "That's fucked up."

Glory put the phone back to her ear. "Yeah."

"Who that you talkin' to?" Pam bawled.

"That's Supreme."

"Mmmmm y'all gettin' tight ain't ch'all."

"Girl it ain't even that type of party," Glory said as she rose from the sofa.

"Girl I 'on know, that's the second girl that got killed that worked at the club," Pam said.

"Like I told 'cha yesterday, that was my last day dancin'," Glory uttered. She stood in front of Supreme while he sat slouched down into the sofa. Supreme's eyes widened. He was shocked by what he just heard.

"I might quit too," Pam announced.

"Girl you should've heard my brotha when I told him yesterday that I quit dancin'. He was happy. But you know what he asked me after I told 'em with his ungrateful ass?"

"When you gon' enroll in college."

"Yep, he always stressin' that college shit like without goin' there, you ain't gon' be shit. If he really thought that was true, he would have taken his ass to college when he graduated from high school."

"Shit, I guess he feels he doesn't have to go to college when he's makin' money all ready. Most people go to college to make sure they get a good job so they can make that money. But anyway, what 'cha gon' do? Just work at your mom's ice cream shop?" Pam quizzed.

"I could. I get paid enough," Glory replied.

"If I stop dancin' I'ma just do private parties or somethin'…them sugar daddies still e-mailing you trying to get a private dance?" Pam asked.

"Yeah."

"If I stop dancin' you gon' get me a job at the shop? That way both of us can work at the shop and do private joints on the side."

"We should just keep dancin' at the club if we gon' do that…that's ass backwards girl. Plus it's still dangerous just like dancin' at the club. But at least at the club we have a little protection," Glory said.

"You said most of the men that e-mailed you were old timers," Pam gabbed. "We can handle them."

"Yeah but it's still dangerous…look, I'll holler at you later. I'm goin' to bed."

"Yeah right," Pam snapped. "You gon' get you some dick first."

"Even if I wanted some, I couldn't get it," Glory replied looking down on a now sound asleep Supreme. "This nigga knocked out cold."

"So! Wake his ass up and get you some of that good dick girl…shit, I want some of his dick right about now."

Without warning Glory's body shook like a chill had jolted through her. It was a feeling she had never experienced before but she knew what was causing it. *Jealousy*. Hearing Pam say she wanted some of

Supreme's dick struck something in her. Her face tightened up a little. She bit down on her bottom lip. She took a deep breath, inhaled then exhaled.

"Glory! You still there?" Pam shouted.

"Yeah, yeah, I'll call you tomorrow." Glory hung the phone up then grabbed Supreme's ankles spreading his body along the sofa. She looked down at his face. "How the fuck can I be jealous and both of us fuckin' him? Maybe it's because I'm spending more time with him."

Glory walked away from the sofa and turned the living room light off then headed to her bedroom.

The next morning Supreme walked towards the bathroom, upon entering the bathroom he noticed a small piece of paper taped to the cabinet mirror above the sink.

The piece of paper read: *Like always help yourself to the fridge, but clean up behind yourself. Look on the washcloth rack...the cream colored washcloth and towel are for you. Look at the toothbrush rack...the blue one is for you. Don't let my hospitality go to your head. I'm just a clean bitch. Oh yeah! Don't get lost 'cause I want some dick tonight. And by the way, when you go buy that car...buy yourself a 2 way pager or a cell phone or somethin'. Not that I wanna keep in touch with you or anything, but I might want you.*

Laughing, Supreme balled the paper up and threw it into the wastebasket. He grabbed one of the razors Glory purchased just for him to shave his beard. When he finished the only hair left on his face was his newly pencil thin goatee. It gave him a suave look. Now he really looked his young 22 years of age.

After cleaning the sink out and placing the razor back in the cabinet, he headed back into the living room.

Stopping at the dining table, Supreme grabbed his bag out of the chair and placed it on top of the glass table. Looking through his bag, he saw that everything was still in the same order. Nothing had been moved or taken out, not even the blood stained white headband he placed into the bag after stepping out the cab last night. He smiled as he removed the headband. Walking back towards the bathroom, he thought about how he liked the fact that Glory wasn't inquisitive. Only one time had she gone into his things.

He dropped the headband into the toilet and flushed it. The sound of Glory's phone ringing caused Supreme to run into the living room to answer it. "Hello."

"What's up Dawg?" Unique said cheerfully.

"Ain't shit. I'm fucked up right now."

"You should be. You missed out on some good pussy last night." Unique bragged.

"How you know the pussy was good? You didn't hit them bitches."

"Nigga I hit both of 'em."

"You bullshittin', Son."

"Nigga I got proof," Unique shouted.

"What kind'a proof?"

"Video proof !"

"Word, them bitches let 'cha tape them? I 'on believe you."

"Why not nigga? I 'on do no lyin' on my dick."

"Look, I don't wanna change the subject on you, but I need a favor from you," Supreme revealed.

"What's the favor?"

"I'm try'na go to that lot you be gettin' your whips from."

"What happen? You tired of drivin' that outta date Acura Vigor." Unique teased.

"Nah, I totaled that shit last night."

"You fucked up?" Unique asked.

"Nah I was wearin' my seatbelt, Son."

They both laughed.

"So you gon' come pick me up and take me to the car lot?"

"Damn, you crashed your whip and the first place you ran to was my sistah. You in love, Slim."

"I doubt that," Supreme quickly replied.

"I'll be over in a few minutes," Unique said.

Twenty minutes later Unique walked into his sister's apartment.

"What 'cha jumpin' for nigga?"

"Damn, I forgot you had keys." Supreme was looking at Unique from the sofa.

Unique locked the front door and walked over to the sofa.

"Why you cut your beard?"

"New look Son, new look, that's all," Supreme replied.

Unique flopped down on the sofa next to Supreme.

"You ready?" Supreme asked while grabbing his bag of money that sat on the floor in between his legs.

"Yeah," Unique responded looking Supreme over. "Why you got on the same gear from last night?"

"All my clothes was in the trunk of my car," he lied with a straight face.

"Slim, while we out…we gon' find you an apartment. You livin' like a homeless nigga with your clothes in your car and shit. I got somebody I know can sign for an apartment for you."

"I'm with that." Supreme stood up with his bag of money in hand. It was only 50 g's in it. The other 79 g's was in the kitchen in the food cabinet, hidden behind canned goods. The two guns were right under the sofa. The 50 g's was for a car and new clothes. Unique stood up from the sofa and he and Supreme walked out the door. On their way to the truck, Supreme struck up a conversation.

"So your sista stop dancin' at that club, huh?"

"Yeah that's what she told me, but I gotta see if she for real. You know how addictive that money is for them broads. That strippin' money for a bitch is just like that drug money for a nigga. Oh yeah! I ran into that nigga Bullet last night at the club. He told me you copped a heater from him," Unique said changing the subject.

"Yeah, I 'on wanna get in no shit and can't back myself up."

"What kinda joint is it?"

"Uh, Desert Eagle 44. It's black."

"That's big boy shit, Slim. I got knocked carryin' one of them. Matter fact, I forgot to tell you, before we go to the lot I gotta go see my P.O. I only have 6 more months on that shit, then I'm off. You got that on ya?"

"Nah, it's in ya sista's crib."

"Go get that shit, Slim." Unique took Glory's keys and passed them to Supreme. He then started the truck.

When Supreme stepped out of the truck, Unique smiled. He wanted to give Supreme a job carrying a piece. Knowing in a few months or so he might be a little more known, and niggas might try their hands at trying to get some of his dough, he wanted someone to be seen with him who packed a gun. Not that he looked at himself as a punk and he couldn't carry one himself, because he wasn't a punk, at least that's what he thought. But he never had to prove to himself or anyone else that he wasn't.

However, he didn't know that when he used to be on the block, niggas used to say he was soft. But they never had a reason to test his thuggism. Unique wanted a gun man down with him. PooBear would have been sufficient for that role, but Unique wanted him to stick with selling drugs. His thoughts were interrupted by the sound of Brother Hetep Muhammad tapping on the truck's window.

Unique looked at Hetep then at his camcorder that was sitting on the dashboard. It was playing his last night's ménage a trois. His first reaction was to leave brother Hetep standing out there, but then he thought about how he wanted to prove Hetep's unrighteousness. He grabbed the camcorder and turned it toward Hetep, then lowered the window from his control panel.

"As-Salaam Alaikum brother." Hetep's brown, hairless, youthful face had that smile that seemed to be glued on.

"Yeah what's up?" Unique replied with an exasperated look.

"Nothing much Brother. I just saw you sitting here so I decided to come to talk to you. Your sister has been living around here for some time now, and I've been talking to her but I never got the chance to chat with you."

"Chat with me about what?" Unique was staring Hetep dead in his face. He anticipated the moment Hetep's round bubble eyes would slide over in the direction of the camcorder.

"Nothing in general. I just thought since me and your sister get along great, we should at least say something to each other."

"Yeah, watch your back. Somebody behind you."

When Hetep turned around he smiled at Supreme who was standing behind him. They shook hands.

"What's up Brotha Hetep? What's the word today?"

Supreme and Hetep had talked to each other on several occasions.

A couple of times on Sundays, Supreme would be the one who opened the door to Glory's apartment in order to accept the newspaper he brought for her. Somehow Hetep would lure Supreme out into the hallway and they would have a twenty, or thirty minute conversation.

"The word today brother is '*discipline*'." Does the Black man have enough discipline to control his lower desires?"

Unique was looking at both men. Not being able to hear their conversation completely from where he sat in the driver's seat, he leaned over a little to listen in.

"Unique," Supreme called. "You hear what he just asked?"

"Nah. What he say?"

Supreme opened the door and climbed into the truck shutting the door behind him. Brother Hetep stood in front of the door on the curb, looking into the truck at the two men.

"Tell 'em what you said Hetep." Supreme leaned back into the soft leather seat smiling.

"I asked does the Black man have enough discipline to control his lower desires?"

"What lower desires?" Unique quizzed.

"The lower desires that you're displaying with young sisters. It's morally incorrect. A man should be with one woman. A man should be married and in a monogamous relationship with the woman he's married to," Hetep said.

"I ain't married. So I don't have to be with one woman," Unique shot back.

"Brother by nature you know you're supposed to be with one woman."

"So you tellin' me you been with one woman all your life?"

"No, I'm not saying that. I'm saying, find the woman you want to be with, and marry her."

"I will. I gotta run through a couple first." Unique giggled. "Then I can choose which one I'm gon' be with."

"All right Brother," Hetep said smiling. "You got that."

"What kind of Muslim are you anyway?"

"What kind of Muslim do I look like?"

"I 'on know," Unique replied. Although his sister had already con-firmed, the crisp suits and bow ties Hetep wore verified what type of Muslim he was.

"Brother, I'm with the Nation of Islam."

*Unique looked at Hetep and thought to himself. Hetep wasn't so bad. Still, he believed Hetep wasn't as righteous as Glory thought he was. But, for now, he couldn't prove it.*

"Brother, your sister told me your name but I forgot it." Hetep extended his hand through the window reaching over Supreme.

Unique extended his hand also, revealing his name, and they shook hands.

"Unique, both of you brothers have righteous names. Are you all doing righteous things?" Hetep asked.

Neither Supreme nor Unique replied.

"Silence from both of you. I take that as a no. Let me say this, then. Don't wait too late to do the right thing. Do it now. Oh Yeah! Do you Brothers play any basketball?"

"Yeah!" they both replied in unison.

"One day I'll show you all how a five foot six, 40 year old man can regulate the court."

"We ballin' this Sunday coming', what's up?" Unique inquired.

"I can't ball this Sunday, but I'll catch you all next Sunday. All right, Brothers." Hetep turned around sharply, and briskly strutted up the block like a soldier.

"I like that lil dude," Supreme exclaimed. "He on some righteous shit, but he cool."

Unique grinned. "I 'on know, I think he fakin'."

"Why you say that, Son?"

"I 'on know. I just ain't seen too many righteous niggas in my life time."

"Well you might've just met one."

# EIGHT

PooBear stood in the mirror checking out the ripeness of his arms and stomach. He was thick and muscular, just like his father, whom he had never seen, not even a picture of him. PooBear made his way to his bedroom to dress. He slid on his black jeans, black on white Nike sneakers, a white long sleeve T-shirt, and his iced-out platinum chain.

"Yeah what's up?" PooBear said answering the knock at his door with an irritated look on his face, before he saw the big butt, thick, pretty woman. She stormed into his room, wiggled her cream colored skirt up over her butt and got on all fours on his bed. She didn't have to worry about pulling her panties down because she didn't have any on.

"How much time do we have?" PooBear quizzed, his pants were already tossed to the floor. He climbed up on the bed behind the lady he'd been calling Mrs. Peaches since he was 10 years old. She was the same age as his mother, a young forty.

"About 5 minutes," she replied, with her deck of cards still in one of her hands.

Most Fridays for a year and a half now, PooBear and Mrs. Peaches used the same scheme to get her upstairs for their quickie. He would play his music loud to disturb their card game knowing his mother would send Peaches or another one of her card buddies upstairs to tell him to cut it down. But Mrs. Peaches wasn't the only one trying to throw her pussy at him when they found out PooBear was the reason for him and his mother moving from their old neighborhood into the nice new two bedroom house. He was the one paying all the bills, and had bought his mother a silver Acura 2.3 CL Coupe. Mrs. Peaches was just the only one he'd chosen.

He'd been lusting for her since he was a kid. Now at eighteen years old, he had her, even though he had to wait many years to get her. And all she asked in return for the pussy she was setting out, was a little money once in a while.

Four minutes into it PooBear was pounding Mrs. Peaches from behind. "I'm 'boutta come!" he yelled, pumping hard and fast while palming each of her ass cheeks.

"Come then baby." Mrs. Peaches groaned.

"Ahhhhh!" PooBear screamed as his body jerked for several seconds.

As usual, it was satisfying for both parties. After Mrs. Peaches cut PooBear's stereo off, she cleaned herself, and ran back downstairs. PooBear went into the bathroom, washed himself off, and slid his pants back on.

Triggering the combination to his three foot high, black steel safe that sat deep in the back of his walk-in closet, PooBear inspected the guns and stacks of money that were the only things in his safe. Each of the potential killer guns were purchased by Unique. But PooBear was the one who kept them all. He took the .380 from the safe, and tucked it into his pants, then he moved his hand over the stacks of cash wrapped in rubber-bands. He felt good. Just two years ago when he was sixteen, he would have never thought he'd be looking at over one-hundred grand of his own money.

PooBear stepped onto the porch of his house. It was the first week of May, the sky was dark, and 70 degree weather was just right. When he reached his pearl white Escalade, under the windshield wipers he saw a yellow piece of paper that read: *I'm tired of these Friday night quickies. I want your young ass to feel the full effect of a woman. No more five minute quickies! I'm gonna find another way to get away from my husband other than playing cards. Tear this paper up!*

"I ain't got no problem with that," PooBear mumbled, ripping the paper up, letting it float to the ground.

PooBear jumped into his truck and drove straight to a drug infested neighborhood in S.E. He parked in front of a bay brick building, got out and walked to LaLa's apartment. The door was opened for him by a brown skinned petite woman. The smell of marijuana, and the sound of Go-Go music escaped the apartment. "Bling, Baby," the petite woman exclaimed shutting the apartment door behind PooBear.

"Where Wop at?"

"I 'on know," Toya replied, walking over to the sofa and sitting next to PooBear. "You know his lil short ass be lunchin'. He talkin' 'bout he ain't lettin' me smoke if I don't give him no ass."

PooBear burst into laughter.

"What's up Dawg?" Wop asked as he walked into the living room. Wearing a Sean John muscle shirt revealing his tattoo that read *untouchable,* Wop swiftly walked past Toya. A cloud of smoke followed him as his right hand held a cigar size blunt to his mouth. After sucking enough weed into his lungs, he reached over Toya to pass the blunt to PooBear. Smiling at Toya beads of sweat began to appear on his bald-head.

"Boy, why you ain't pass it to me?" Toya asked.

"I already told 'cha I ain't lettin' you smoke if you ain't tryin' give up no ass." Wop said.

"I ain't fuckin' nobody for no weed," Toya said. She stared down on PooBear and Wop with a grin on her face. "But I will fuck for some money. *Five hundred dollars to be exact."*

"I know you will," PooBear and Wop said laughing.

PooBear leaned over to Wop and whispered, "How long Darkman and LaLa been in that room?"

"About twenty minutes or so."

"Let's jump up and run in the back and burst in the room on Darkman."

"Don't do that y'all!" Toya yelled, jumping up from her seat. Her cry was in vain because the sound of LaLa's bedroom door being kicked opened exploded.

"Young un' that nigga had her pinned up against the wall," Wop said giggling. They were seated back on the sofa in the living room when Darkman appeared.

"What's up?" Darkman announced walking into the living room, a big macho grin planted on his chocolate face. He stood off to the side of the sofa looking down on Wop, Toya and PooBear while fastening the buttons to the brown plaid shirt he wore.

There was one thing that stood out physically about Darkman that was almost extraordinary, especially since he was a dark-skinned brother. He had light gray eyes that were spooky to some people but appealing to others.

"What 'cha mean what's up nigga?" Wop stated. "We out here smokin' and waitin' for you ta get 'cha nut off so we can bounce from outta here."

"Let's go," PooBear announced, leaping up from the sofa. Suddenly, LaLa appeared, stopping everyone in their tracks. Although she was a white girl, her body looked like a black woman.

"Ya'll broke my damn lock," she hissed, folding her arms across her chest and maintaining a black girl stance.

PooBear pulled a roll of money from his pocket and peeled off a $100, placing it on the cocktail table. "Take care of your door snowbunny," he joked and walked out the door.

"What's up with that nigga Unique? We ain't had no shit in a week. We gon' lose our clientele," Wop asked.

"I talked to him yesterday," PooBear replied. "He said if he don't get nothin' in three weeks he gon' cop from somebody until his peeps come through."

"Shit! He better do somethin' 'cause crack heads don't wait," Wop snapped.

"So, what 'cha think that nigga gon' be giving us?" Wop questioned PooBear.

"I 'on know, Joe. He ain't said shit to me yet."

"I'm sayin', he was givin' you two eighths at a time. So he might give me and Darkman two at a time."

"Yeah, he might," PooBear replied reluctantly.

"You 'on sound too happy about that. What? You'on want us to see no real paper like you?"

"Come on nigga. I ain't selfish," PooBear fired back.

"I can't tell, Slim. Me and Darkman been sellin' the shit and you makin' the most money."

"You right Dawg, but I was just tryin' to put some money in y'all pockets. I could've just sold the shit by myself and been pulling in 9 g's off every two eighths he gives me. I'm the one losing out," PooBear said. But he was lying.

After asking PooBear to recruit more workers for their team, Unique finally met Wop and Darkman over two weeks ago. Now, since they were no longer a secret, PooBear knew he'd have to put in work.

"He's right," Darkman acceded.

"Nigga get off his dick and stop bein' a yes man. You supposed to be rollin' with me on this," Wop scolded.

"You ain't gonna do nothin' with more money but buy weed and trick with it," Darkman fired back.

"Yeah, and the first bitch I'ma trick with is LaLa's white ass."

The truck fell silent. PooBear and Wop were waiting to hear how Darkman would respond. They both felt Darkman had strong feelings for LaLa because every chance he got he was at her crib.

Darkman looked over at PooBear then in the back seat at Wop who was slouched into the buttersoft white leather seat. "Stop waitin' for me to say somethin', 'cause I'm not. But I will let y'all know I ain't sweatin' that cracker." Darkman lied.

Wop burst out laughing. "I bet you won't tell her that to her face. Nigga, you on that cracker so stop fakin'," Wop said snickering. "Hey PooBear! What's up with Unique's sista? The one you always talkin' bout."

'Nothin', she just a bad bitch…Oh yeah! She stopped strippin' 'bout a few weeks ago."

"She dealing with some bamma from New York right?" Darkman asked.

"Yeah."

Wop scooted back up between the driver and passenger seats. "That New York bamma is the reason you 'on hang out with Unique as much as you used to. How much money you think he holdin'?" Wop questioned with a devilish grin on his face.

"I 'on know, but he stacked."

"What about that New York nigga? Do he hustle?"

"You know what? I 'on know what that nigga do. But he got some dough 'cause he just copped a dark green Lexus GS 300 and just a month ago he was pushin' an Acura Vigor."

"You think him and Unique doin' somethin' on the side?" Wop continued to question.

"Nah young un, that nigga Unique is one of those low key mothafuckas. He don't like to fuck with too many dudes. The only reason he gon' fuck with y'all is because I said y'all my dawgs, and he gon' be coppin' more shit than he used to. But, as far as fuckin' with that nigga Supreme on some drug shit, I 'on think so. If anything he might just be Unique's gun man, 'cause Unique don't wanna tote no gun since he got locked up for one."

"Where we headin' to PooBear?"

"To the gambling spot."

"Man, take me back to La La's," Darkman complained.

Wop pushed the back of Darkman's head. "Nigga you just wanna be under that cracker. You on that devil hard."

"Don't push my head no more." Darkman was turned around in his seat looking back at Wop with a cold look in his eyes.

"Nigga what 'cha gon' do?" Wop said challenging Darkman.

"Break that shit up Joe," PooBear acceded. "Both of y'all actin' like bitches."

"That's that nigga," Wop quickly stated. "He wanna be under a bitch all day. *A white bitch at that*."

"Look! I'm droppin' both of you niggas off and I'ma go make me some money."

# NINE

*T*oday is May 26, 2001 Saturday 10:08 am. Kim began writing while sitting at her dining room table. An empty breakfast plate sat next to her diary.

*"I feel so good today. I've been feeling this way for quite some time now. I would say for the last three months. I know what's bringing about this wonderful feeling. It's Unique that's making me feel so alive. It's Unique. I'm sure it's him because it wasn't until he showed up at my door that my life was revolutionized. He makes me feel so good, and young, and full of life. I am young, what am I talking about, I'm only in my 30's, but he makes me feel like I'm 21 again; not only from the exhilarating sex we have, but from the other things we do together.*

*I'm not going to lie. There is only one thing that bothers me a little; Unique hasn't taken me over to his place yet. I wanna say something to him about it, but I don't wanna seem too pushy. I know he's seeing other women, but I know they don't visit his place, because he's been over my place a lot lately. Listen to me, I sound so young and naïve. How can I assume no women visit his place? He's not with me 24/7. Well let me say this then. I know he'd rather take me to his place than one of those stank lil hoes he dealing with…"*

*"I have to go, I hear my girl Mona blowing her horn for me. We about to head to the gym. Let me say this last thing before I go, I'm not 100 percent sure yet, but I think I'm in love."*

Kim closed her diary and ran into her living room grabbing her gym bag from her sofa and in a flash she was out the door.

"What's up girl?" Mona bawled with a big smile on her pretty face as Kim stepped into her black Camry. Mona was a year older than Kim with a petite body that some women would kill for.

"Nothing, I'm ready to get my sweat on girl," Kim replied after they embraced each other with feminine hugs and a light kiss on the cheek.

"Let's go then," Mona said excitedly, pulling away from the curb.

"What's been going on with you lately?" Mona asked.

"Work. Nothing new, just more criminals coming in and out. And they get younger and younger by the day."

"You know what my next question is, don't you?" Mona smiled at Kim who had been her friend for 13 years now.

Kim blushed like a little girl. "No, I don't know your next question."

"It's one word. Unique. Who is he?"

"I have five words." He makes me feel gooddddd," Kim laughed.

"Well enlightened me about this doctor feel good man."

"There ain't much to tell you but he's young, handsome and can put out my fire."

"Ok, let me run down what you should be telling me. You should be telling me his age, what he does for a living, if he has kids, and where you met him since you only told me his name so far. And you told me that three months ago."

"OK", Kim exclaimed, taking a deep breath. "I'm not going to lie to you. He's only 25 years old with no dependents and he works as a manager at a shoe store."

Mona was silent for a moment, then she said, "Damn girl you robbing the cradle…" She looked over at Kim. "You forgot something."

"I met him while he was in jail," Kim muttered quickly, she looked away from Mona and stared out the passenger window.

"I know you didn't… I heard what you just said, but who am I to judge."

Kim swung her head in Mona's direction with a smile on her face. "I knew you'd understand."

"Yeah but what was he in jail for?"

"Selling drugs. But he beat the charges because it wasn't his drugs."

"That's what he told you?" Mona quizzed.

"Yeah, he told me it wasn't his drugs.  It was a friend of his."

"OK. Girl, just watch out for him being that he's young and all 'cause you know those young boyz like to play the field."

Mona parked in the lot of World Gym.  The friends stepped out of the Camry with their gym bags and headed for the women's locker room that Kim had been going into for the past two years.  This was the gym where she and her ex-husband Jay had a membership, but for the past year and few months, Kim had gone with Mona rather than Jay.

"You're gonna hit the heavy bag with me right?"

Mona looked at Kim as if she was crazy.  "Girl please, I'll leave that to your aggressive ass."

"Girl you don't know what you're missing.  That's a workout that will have you fit for life, and it builds your punching power.  You never know when you may have to beat a man down instead of him beating you down."

Mona rolled her eyes at Kim.  "You better punch that bag because you never know when one of those criminals may attack you on your job."

Kim was already five minutes into punching the heavy bag, and she had begun to work up a sweat.  Her EVERLAST boxing gloves rhythmically smacked forcefully against the heavy bag.  She was moving just like a pro boxer would. Kim was in her zone.  She was dancing around the bag, when suddenly out of nowhere, two massive hands gripped her waist.  She spun around aiming her right hook at the head of the person holding her waist.  Luckily for the man, he ducked the face crushing punch.

"Hold on baby it's me," Kim's ex-husband Jay announced, taking a step back to avoid any more punches being thrown at him.

"I see you still like to be touchy, touchy," Kim snapped sarcastically, turning her attention back to the bag.

Jay walked around the bag and hugged it while staring directly at Kim.  He held the bag like a trainer.  "I never knew how good you looked working out in spandex," Jay said. "Your body is thick and toned just right. Black spandex. *Good choice*."

"Thanks but I looked like this under that sweat suit that you insisted that I wear when we used to come here together."

"Well, you know, I didn't want everybody eye balling my woman."

"It really shouldn't have mattered because I *was* all yours," Kim said rolling her eyes.

"You really didn't have to say it like that."

"Oh my bad. I thought you didn't hear me the first time I said it." She punched the bag again, but this time harder.

"I see you walking around her with no shirt on. What? Your young girl vanished so now you wanna pick up another young girl?" Kim grinned.

Jay smiled broadly. "I'm well taken care of. But what's going on with your love life?"

"Why?" she snapped.

"Just curious."

"I'm seeing someone," Kim revealed.

Anger immediately shot over Jay's face. His mind quickly envisioned Kim in bed next to another man after sex. Veins could be seen on his forehead.

"Are you all right?" Kim asked, staring into Jay's face. She had struck something in him. Anger was written all over his dark face.

"Why you ask that?" He tried to straighten his face up.

"I thought I saw an angry look on your face," Kim said.

"Angry for what? You're entitled to see someone. We're divorced."

"You got that right." Kim threw a right jab at the bag.

"So who is he?"

Kim stopped. "None of your business."

"I hope you didn't belittle yourself and hook up with a guy that's beneath you."

"And what's your idea of 'beneath me'? Not being a cop?"

"Yeah." Jay laughed. "No I'm just playing. I'm talking about a guy that makes less money than you, doesn't respect you, and won't stand up for you. Most of all, a guy that makes his living by engaging in illegal activities." He smiled.

Kim's heart suddenly started racing.  She thought about Unique. She believed he was involved in illegal activities, although he still hadn't told her.  If Jay found out about Unique, he wouldn't think twice about investigating him and locking him up if he found out anything that involved dealing drugs.

"No he's a good man," Kim managed to say.

"How old is he and what does he look like?"

Kim smiled and had a look on her face as if she was actually thinking about Unique. "Well he's young like the girl you're seeing…" She looked at Jay's muscular body. "He's got muscles like you, but he's slimmer than you; and he's six feet and handsome like a model."

Jay drew a fake grin. "Yeah he's a lil guy compared to this." He stepped to the side and posed like he was in a competition. Then stepping closer he said, "Can I kiss you on the cheek for old time's sake?"

Kim thought about it for a split second. "No. Get out of here." She threw punches at his body making him run away.

After Jay left, Kim went to find Mona so they could leave. They talked the entire ride to Kim's house. Kim told Mona about the encounter she had with Jay.  She told her that seeing Jay made her angry, but also happy. She had mixed feelings because he left her, but she was happy that Jay, now noticed her. Before their separation, he wasn't attentive to her. Now, it seemed as if when they did cross each other's paths, it was all about her.

When Mona turned onto Kim's block, she was the first to notice the man that sat on Kim's front porch. "Girl, who is that sittin' on your porch?"

"I don't see nobody," Kim said trying to block the sunlight.

"He's sittin' right on your porch," Mona pressed.

"Oh, I see him now. Girl that's my baby Unique," Kim replied, happily.

As the Camry stopped at Kim's house, Unique stood.

"I'll call him to the car." Kim's face still lit up with a big smile. She reached over and signaled for Unique to come to the car. He walked down the steps of the porch toward them.

"Damn! You wasn't lying; he is handsome," Mona said just before Unique approached the car.

He stuck his head into the passenger side window and before Kim could say a word, he locked lips with her.

"Mmmmmmm!" Kim hummed, placing her right hand on Unique's chin, pulling their lips apart.

Kim and Mona smiled at each other quickly. They both smiled for different reasons. Mona smiled because she saw the felicity in her friend's face. Kim's smile said, *see, that's one of the reasons why I said he makes me feel good.*

"Unique, I want you to meet my closest friend Mona."

"Please to meet 'cha Mona." Unique reached over Kim to give Mona a handshake.

"Please to meet you, too." Mona replied, still shaking Unique's hand.

"So, did y'all work up a good sweat today?" Unique asked.

"Kim did, but I didn't. I'm not as advanced yet. It's gonna take some time for that," Mona expressed.

"I'ma be on the porch," Unique told Kim, then walked away.

"Girrrrrl….., I can tell you happy," Mona snapped, smiling from ear to ear. "He ain't even at the car no more and you still smilin'."

"To be honest with you, I am happy. I haven't been this happy since the beginning of me and Jay's relationship. And that was when I was nineteen."

"Come here, girl." Mona hugged Kim. "I'm happy for you."

"Tell Big Mike and Lil Mike I said hi," Kim said as she was exiting the car with her gym bag in hand

When Kim walked up to her porch, Unique had an up to no good smirk on his face.

"Why you lookin' like that?" she quizzed, standing a step down from where Unique sat on the porch steps.

Unique remained silent for a bit, then finally said, "You look good with that sweat suit on. You got that sweaty look like I be havin' after I finish ballin'."

"Boy, let me pass," Kim giggled. She stepped around him with her keys out, and walked to her front door. When she got the door opened, Unique rushed her from behind and bear hugged her. Kim exploded with laughter while being tugged into the house. "I gotta go get in the shower."

"OK. I'ma chill out." He stood up straight with just his right hand on the doorknob smiling.

**Time passed and they were ready to go out.  They**
went roller-skating, to the movies, then out for ice cream, and lastly to a
club called "Zanzibar".  They danced on the second floor of the facility
first, working up an appetite. Then they headed down to the first floor and
enjoyed a satisfying meal. They didn't make it home until a little after 2 am,
but when they did, they fell straight to sleep after taking a shower together.

The next morning, Unique was awakened by the sound of his cell
phone ringing.  He rolled over and snatched it off the nightstand. "Hello,"
he spoke into the phone.

"This is Dad. It's that time Baby. You home right?"

"Nah, nah."  Unique sat up and tossed his legs off the side of the
bed.  "I'm over my woman's crib."

Kim was on her side, her eyes wide open staring at Unique's back
while he talked on the phone.  She smiled. "I'm over my woman's crib"
rang repeatedly in her head.  That was something she enjoyed hearing
because Unique hadn't yet expressed his feelings to her.  And for that
matter, she hadn't expressed her feelings to him.

"What do you mean your woman's crib?" Dad inquired.  "Don't
you mean girl? Because you ain't sleeping with nothing but young girls."
Dad giggled.  "It's that time.  I need you to go home and put on something casual, and I'll meet you there. By the way, is that straight?" Dad
asked with in a serious tone of voice.

"Yeah."

After Dad said he'd see him in 45 minutes, Unique put the phone
back on the nightstand, and smiled.  Dad telling him that it was that time
was something he'd been waiting on for three months now.

"Kim! Kim!" Unique uttered, nudging her out of what he thought was
her beauty sleep.  But she'd been awake since he answered his cell phone.

"Uh huh," she mumbled playing it off.

"I gotta go," Unique said, picking up his jumpsuit.

"You want me to fix you some breakfast before you go?"  She sat
up in the bed exposing her caramel colored 36 D's.  "I like to cook
breakfast on Sundays, you know that."

"I know," he replied, staring at Kim's chest.  "How long you been
working out?"

"About 10 years. Why you asking me something like that?"

Kim grabbed the white sheets on the bed and covered her chest.

"Nah, I'm just sayin' you look good...Especially since you'll be 35 soon."

"Boy, don't joke about my age." She smiled.

Unique grinned. Now how fast can you fix me an omelet?"

"Fast."

Unique looked at his watch. "I got like 30 minutes."

"I can fix it in 10 minutes." Kim kissed his lips again then stepped around him to head downstairs. Unique followed her; and in 30 minutes he had eaten.

"I'll see you tonight," Unique said while he gazed at Kim as he stood on her front porch. She stood behind her open front door, her face the only thing exposed.

"You know I go to work tonight right?"

"Damn! I forgot. Okay, I'll see you at 12 o'clock tomorrow then. And yeah, that omelet was good." He stepped off.

Unique slid into his truck, and drove off grinning. He thought about Kim the entire ride to his house. Things between them were getting serious he thought. But that was only because he allowed it to get serious. He could have eradicated that dilemma by just fucking her and leaving like he'd done so many women in the past. But Kim was different. She sparked something in him that no other woman was able to. And he wasn't mad at all.

Unique parked his truck in front of his house and quickly ran inside to change. He stood in front of his dresser fastening the buttons to the white linen shirt he wore that matched his linen pants. He slid a pair of Gucci shades on his face to enhance the casual look Dad asked for. The sound of Unique's doorbell ringing stopped him in his tracks.

"Damn!" Unique answered, giving Dad the once over. Dad wore a white on navy blue, custom, pinstriped Armani suit. His close shaved beard made his dark face look model-like. "You sharp." They gave each other a handshake then bumped shoulders while still hand in hand. Dad broke their embrace to shut the front door.

"You don't look too bad yourself," Dad said.

"Dressing in all white looking just like your father used to. Where's that pool table at?" Dad headed towards the dining room. He took a pool stick from a rack up against the wall. "Rack the balls up young buck. We have enough time to play a couple of games. I know I'm gonna win. "

"What's the deal?" Unique asked leaning over the pool table. "The deal with the connect."

"We'll be meeting up with him at 3 o'clock at Union Station." Dad stepped up to the table after Unique missed his shot.

"What's it gon' be?" Unique quizzed, watching Dad set up his winning shot. "Do I take money with me or what?"

"No first you're gonna talk to him, then he'll let you know when to bring money and where." Dad took his shot knocking the 8-ball into the side pocket. "I told you I'd win." Dad smiled arrogantly. "So, how long you plan on staying in the game?" Dad inquired, breaking the rack.

"I 'on know. How long do you think I should?"

I think you should stop now before you buy the 20 kilos." Dad stared at Unique while preparing to take his shot.

"I knew you was gon' say that. I'ma cop 5 or 6 times then I might quit. I 'on know yet, I gotta see what's it like to push 20 keys first." Unique smiled. "So it's official? You're out the game?"

"Without a doubt." Dad knocked in two balls.

"What really made you get out the game?"

"Two things. One is the Feds and the tactics that they're using. That conspiracy shit will put your ass in jail for life. They can have just the testimony of two or more people to say you're the man and you're fucked. Secondly, I came to realize that I make more money with no risk being a legit businessman. By the way, my club's grand opening is June first this Friday. I named it, *The Spot*." Dad grinned.

"Oh yeah! I got off the phone with Glory not too long ago and she said something about Mom said you've been acting strange lately."

Dad smiled wide. "I know, I was a little stressed out about something. If you don't remember, today is me and Donna's 20th anniversary. I have a big surprise for her today, and I mean big." He smacked the white ball into the 8-ball and the game was over.

"That's it," Unique said, relinquishing. "You win."

Dad looked at his watch. "Yeah, it's time for us to go. He put up his stick and they walked towards the front door.

"You ready?" Dad questioned.

"Yeah, let's roll."

Dad walked up to a brand new Aston Martin DB 7 Volante. The sun struck the sky blue car giving it a heavenly glow.

"This your whip?" Unique quizzed with a surprised look on his face. He placed his face up against the passenger side window, gazing at the white leather interior.

"Yeah, I just got it last Friday." Dad stood on the driver's side sticking his key into the door. They hopped in the costly car and sped away. Twenty minutes later, Dad was parking in Union Station's Parking garage. His cell phone rang as he stepped out of the car.

"Mommy told me you were comin' to pick us up at five thirty," Stacy whined in the receiver.

Dad smiled. He knew his wife had something to do with the call. "I have to go baby, but I'll see you in a few. Tell your mother that's standing beside you I'll be picking you up and not her."

"Okay, I'll tell her."

"Bye baby." Dad placed his phone back into his suit jacket.

"What's funny?" Unique asked.

"Donna wants to know what's going on. She knows something isn't right, but she can't put her hand on it."

"I can't either. What's up? What's the surprise?"

"I'll show you after we finish handling this," Dad exclaimed.

They rode the escalator down to the floor where the movie theater was located. Dad scanned the huge food court and spotted who they were looking for. They walked towards two men who stood up when they saw Dad and Unique coming.

"Good to see you." A thick built brown skinned man who stood around five foot ten shook hands with Dad.

"Good to see you too," Dad replied.

"What's up Bob? Good to see you man." The other man that was standing shook hands with Dad.

"And who is this young brother you have with you?" Chris asked, already knowing who Unique was.  In fact he knew Unique when he was a toddler.  Unique just didn't know him.

"This is big Unique's son," Dad spoke up with a smile.

"I should have known…"  The man extended his hand to Unique. "You look just like your father."  He was looking Unique over while they shook hands.  "I like you already.  Let's sit down."

"If Bob didn't tell you, my name is Chris.  And this is the man who solves my problems," Chris said pointing to the bulky man in the black suit.  "Did Bob ever tell you why your father named himself Unique and you too?"

Unique glanced over at Dad then shook his head 'no'.

"From what he told me, that's one of the many proper names for the black man.  You know what?  Even though ya pops was involved in illegal things, he still was a man with a vast amount of knowledge.  He was studying the teachings of the Nation of Islam. Okay, enough of the small talk.  So, you think you can handle 20 fish without going to prison for life?"  Chris quizzed Unique.

"Yeah without a doubt," Unique replied.

"Okay, here's the deal.  You won't be dealing with me.  I'm out the game like Bob is.  You'll be dealing with my son."  He dialed a number, spoke into his cell phone, and then hung up.  "Twenty fish costs 400 g's, but you'll only be paying 250 g's since I have love for your father and Bob."

"You playin' right?" Unique asked smiling, looking at Dad.

"No, I'm not.  I already told my son what you'll be paying.  OK, I have to be going."  Chris stood up, followed by everyone else.  "My son should be walking up in a few minutes."

"Thanks," Unique said joyfully, shaking Chris' hand.

"Nah, you should thank Bob.  You just make sure you think smart and trust no one.  So Bob, I'll see you when I get back."

"Yeah," Dad replied, shaking Chris' hand.

"Maybe when I get back we can take a cruise on my yacht with the wives."

"Yeah, we can do that.  I'll be opening my club on June first; and my two shoe stores are doing good. As you know, my wife owns the ice-cream parlor. It's doing good too."

"I see why you're out the game; you're a successful business man now." Chris smiled.

"I'm still not anywhere close to you," Bobby responded.

"Yeah, but you're on your way. Don't stay in the game too long," Chris said directing his comment to Unique. "You never know when your luck will run out. All of us have a different lucky stick. You may have a short stick or a long stick. Who knows? Don't wait too late."

"I'll remember that," Unique said.

"OK I'll get in touch with you later," Chris said while he and the man in the black suit walked off.

As soon as the two men walked off, two young men walked up. The taller of the two walked with a slight limp popping bubble gum in his mouth.

"What's up Mr. Bob?" Chris' son shook Dad's hand.

"How are you doing Raymond?" Dad said smiling.

"Come on man. Why you gotta say my full name when you see me? Like I'm still a kid. I'm 24 now."

"OK," Dad giggled. "It's Ray from now on."

"I'd appreciate that. What's up?" Ray said turning to Unique. The 2 carat diamond he wore in his ear caught Unique's attention immediately.

"You," Unique said.

"Damn! What am I doing?" Ray said to himself. "This is my man Sean."

"Let's get this out the way so we all can get out of here," Dad murmured.

"Okay," Ray agreed. "I know you already know the deal, so it ain't nothing to really talk about. I'll call you later on tonight with the twenty and you have your two-fifty ready. Give me your number and I'll let you know where we're gonna meet."

"All right," Unique responded perplexed. He had no idea it would be this easy. He watched his 280 pound, out of shape supplier closely. His calm demeanor put Unique at ease. Something told him that they'd have a good business relationship for years to come.

Ray rose from the table. "I'll see you tonight. And, don't bring no more than one nigga with you," he ordered.

They shook hands and departed.

Dad and Unique pulled out of Union station at 4:30 pm. Dad rushed through the downtown streets like a mad man. He shot around cars as if he were racing.

"We gon' get pulled over," Unique warned Dad. He smiled like a little kid riding along with his father for the first time.

"I am 100 percent out the game now," Dad grinned.

Twenty minutes later Dad was driving through a prestigious neighborhood in Silver Spring, Maryland. He stopped in front of a beautiful brick house. His facial expression said it all.

"Hell nah man!" Unique shouted, looking at the big house. "I know you didn't cop this." A sign could be seen above the front door that read 'Happy Anniversary Donna'.

"You been in there right?" Unique quizzed.

"Of course I have. I paid 600,000 for it. The house has a three car garage, four bedrooms, and five full baths.  And it's all ready fully furnished. This is what Donna has wanted for years. She picked this house and don't even know it. This is why I've been acting strange for the past two weeks. The furniture wasn't delivered until yesterday. So I was a little stressed out."

Unique looked at his watch realizing he needed to get home quick. Dad knew the importance as well. He got Unique home within twenty-five minutes.

"I'll call you later," Dad told Unique. "Be careful tonight."

"I will," Unique uttered, closing the door. Dad pulled off. Unique ran into his living room and dialed a number.

"What's up nigga? This Unique."

"What's up Slim? I hope you callin' with some good news."

"I am. It's time to shine."

"I'll be over in a few."

Unique hung up and thought about calling Supreme. Then he remembered what Ray said about bringing only one nigga. Anyway, he and Supreme weren't that tight yet to take him along to meet his connect. In fact, this would be PooBear's first. *He ran up stairs to bag 250 g's.*

# TEN

"Grandma!" Pam yelled while she and Glory stood in front of the door of Pam's house. They were heading out the door. "Grandma!" she yelled again.

"Child I'm coming. Don't rush an old lady in a wheelchair."

Pam's grandmother came cruising from around a corner in her powered wheelchair. The colorful sweater she'd been knitting sat across her lap. She was a heavy-set woman resembling her granddaughter.

"Grandma, I'll see you later tonight," Pam stated as her grandmother pulled in front of her and Glory.

"Y'all not going to shake y'all tails in that club are you?"

"No Ms. Cleo. We stopped dancin' at that club two months ago," Glory uttered looking over at Pam only to roll her eyes at her. "We work at my mom's ice cream parlor. Pam didn't tell you?"

"Yes she did, but y'all sho'nuff dressed like y'all going to shake y'all butts." She ran her eyes over Glory and Pam. "But I'm glad y'all have real jobs now. Y'all don't need to be shakin' y'all tails for no men in the nude. It's bad enough the young men these days don't respect y'all. And seeing you all in the nude ain't gon' motivate them to respect you any faster."

Pam giggled. "Grandma, we don't have on anything provocative. We just have on jeans."

"Yeah, but they tight," Ms. Cleo snickered.

"Grandma, stop it." Pam and Glory both landed a kiss on her cheek.

"Bye Ms. Cleo," Glory said as her and Pam made their way out the door.

"Be careful." Glory heard Ms. Cleo say after she closed the door behind her and Pam.

"We will," Glory replied with her face near the door so Ms. Cleo could hear her.

"Your grandmother is a trip," Glory said to Pam as they hopped into Pam's car.

"I know girl, she be lunchin' but I love her to death."

"I know you do," Glory agreed. "I love her too."

Pam started her car and pulled from the curb.

"So what 'cha plan on doing for the 4th of July?" Pam asked Glory.

"Girl, let me find out you losing your memory."

"What?" Pam snapped.

"Well ah since you don't remember. I'm going to Dad's club on the 4th."

"Damn, I forgot all about that shit.  I 'on know how I forgot that when that club is off the hook.  Plus we get in free."

"Dad's club only been open since the first of this month, but it's already the place to be.  He picked a good spot to open a club; although it be a lot of Maryland bammas in there."

"You ain't lyin'," Pam agreed, hissing.

"OK, enough of the bullshit!" Glory snapped out of nowhere.

Pam looked over at her as if she were crazy.  "What 'cha talkin' 'bout Glory?"

"You know what I'm talkin' bout.  I'm talkin' 'bout you and your manipulating ass ways."

Pam bursts into laughter.

"What 'cha laughin' for?  I'm dead serious."

"Girl you trippin'," Pam bawled.

"First you got me to dance at the club.  Secondly you convinced me to fuck some nigga we both didn't know. And now you convinced me to do these private dances for some old men when we both agreed to stop strippin'!"

"Girl, I didn't put a gun to your head and make you do anything," Pam snapped. "Anyway, it took you two months since I asked you to agree. You agreed on your own. I didn't manipulate you."

"Bitch you make me sick," Glory said with a smile, looking over at Pam. She shoved Pam's right shoulder.

"Don't get mad at me bitch 'cause you like shakin' ya ass."

They both laughed.

"Nah...but this is gon' be easy money," Pam assured Glory. "All we gotta do is dance for these old heads for 25 to 30 minutes, then we out with their money."

"We need some protection like the club used to have for us."

"Don't worry I got that covered," Pam stated. "Remember my bamma cousin BamBam?"

"Yeah I remember his big black ass."

"Well we on our way to pick him up. He gon' be our protection. Just in case."

"Nooooo," Glory pleaded. "He's always talkin' freaky to me. Plus I don't want him to see me half naked. I hate when I see him."

"Bitch please. He already seen you half naked at the club."

"I never saw him at the club."

"Yeah, well he saw you 'cause he calls me from time to time askin' me where CeCe Winans at."

"Why didn't you tell me that before?"

" 'Cause it wasn't essential for me to tell you."

"It's essential to me. What if he'd planned on stalking me or some crazy shit like that?"

"Glory, my cousin is not like that."

"You never know, he might not be that person you think you know."

"You know what? He might not be," Pam stared with her eyes on the road. "Girl, I wanna ask you somethin'. Yesterday at the hotel with Supreme you were acting kind of funny." Pam cut her eyes over at Glory.

Glory turned her face toward the window. She gazed out the window with an expression on her face that said she knew exactly where Pam was going with their conversation. "What 'cha mean I was actin' funny?" Glory swung her head around to look at Pam.

"I'ma be blunt with you.  You was hoggin' the dick yesterday.  Like you wanted it all to yourself."

Glory burst into a fake laugh.  She placed her face into her hands. "I can't believe you bitch," she exclaimed. She dropped her hands from her face and looked at Pam. "I wasn't try'na hog no dick.  Girl I can't believe you just said that."

"Yes you was and you know it," Pam pressed, smiling while driving.

Glory knew her friend was telling the truth but she insisted on denying the accusation.

"I ain't never see you burn his dick up like you did last night.    I ain't blind girl!"

"Yes you are." Glory snickered.

"So, what's up?  Are you feelin' him like that?"  Pam inquired.

"Yeah," Glory said plainly.

"Keepin' it real, I figured you was feelin' him for about two months now.  I just wondered when you was gonna throw shade on the dick. But at least you've been letting me get some of that good dick."

"You my dog," Glory muttered.  "I didn't wanna say anything."

"Yeah, you just gonna hog the dick up and have me in the room butt ass naked with y'all waiting for some dick that you didn't plan on sharing."

They both laughed.

"So, let me ask you this.  What about me and you?  Are we still gon' get our freak on with each other?" Pam quizzed.

"I 'on see why not," Glory replied.

"Okay, now it's clarified," Pam stated.  "Anyway I'm gettin' enough dick already.  I can let one of my dick supplies go," she giggled.

"And I'm not getting' enough dick already?" Glory questioned, smiling at Pam.

"If fuckin' one nigga is sufficient for you, then you getting' enough dick."

"How you know I ain't fuckin' nobody else?" Glory spat.

"I be around you enough to know you don't be givin' your pussy out like that. You conservative with ya shit." Pam snickered.

Glory didn't respond. She knew Pam was 100 percent right. She was never the type to spread her legs to every man she met. On the other hand Pam was. She gave out charity pussy at will, but only if there was a fair exchange. *Pussy for money.*

"What time did you tell them we'd be there?" Pam questioned.

"I told 'em around 9:30," Glory said.

"You e-mailed them back and told them how much we charge, right?"

"Yeah, $300 a piece. So we better be good for only 30 minutes of dancin'."

"Look!" Pam said in an enthusiastic tone. "All we gotta do tonight is dance good for these sugar daddies and they can become our regular customers. We gon' take the price up to $400 if they want us to dance for them again after tonight. We can make a small business out of this shit like everybody else is doin' through the internet."

Glory had a look on her face as if she smelled something foul. "Who gon' be ya partner? Not me."

Pam didn't reply. She didn't want to say the wrong thing and make Glory stay firm with the decision she'd already made. Pam would get Glory to change her mind in due time. She had been doing that since they met in high school. Manipulation, without a doubt was her forte.

"What's really up with Supreme?" Pam inquired, changing the conversation. She wanted to get off the subject of stripping privately. She knew Glory would agree in a week or two, if that long.

"What 'cha mean what's up with Supreme?"

"You know, like how come he ballin' out of control? Where the hell is he getting his money from?"

Glory thought for a second then replied, "The last time I asked him something about his money, he told me he just saved when he was in New York."

"Yeah, but damn! He must have brought a million dollars down here or somethin'. He crashed one car and copped another one a day later. He copped an apartment and furnished it like bammm!"

'You know he be hangin' with my brotha.  Maybe he doin' somethin' for him and getting' paid," Glory expressed.

"Look, you already takin' up for your new man, and you know he copped the Lexus and his apartment before him and your brotha started hangin' tight like they are now,"

Glory sat quietly.  She knew Pam had a good point.  She'd wondered just how deep Supreme's pockets really were.  She knew something wasn't right, but she rationalized it by saying maybe he did save a lot of money before coming to D.C.

"You think he robbed a bank in New York or killed somebody for their money who had money?" Pam questioned.  She glanced at Glory out of the corner of her eye, and then focused her attention back on the road.

"You know, I asked him that already."

"It ain't like he gon' tell you."

"Yeah, you right, I know," Glory agreed.

"I know he told us his mother died but I know he has some family back in New York.  Why hasn't he been back up there to see them?"

"I 'on know and I 'on wanna talk about him right now," Glory exclaimed, reaching to cut the radio on.

"Hold on, hold on."  Pam said.

"What girl?  I gotta enjoy myself before your crazy ass cousin get in the car fuckin' with me," Glory said, pouting.

"You gon' dance tonight like you'd dance if we was still at the club right?"

"Yeah.  Why?" Glory looked at Pam curiously.

"I just asked," Pam exclaimed, letting Glory's hand go.  She lied, she asked because she knew if Glory performed the way she would if they were still stripping at the club, they would definitely be asked to perform again by the sugar daddies.

A few minutes later, Pam was parking in front of a brick building on K Street Southeast.

"Why it's so dark out here?" Glory asked, looking at the neighborhood.

"I 'on know.  One of them dirty ass niggas probably burst the light in one of the street lamp poles," Pam uttered.  "You see."  She pointed to a pole that wasn't illuminated.

"I see it," Glory replied. "Where your cousin at?" Glory asked cutting the radio down.

A few seconds later, Pam's cousin BamBam's head emerged from a third floor window of the four story building. "I'll be down in a minute," BamBam yelled, sticking his head back into the window.

"How much you paying him?" Glory asked Pam.

Pam gazed at Glory with an 'are you serious' expression on her face. "You playin' right?"

"No. How much you payin' him?" Glory glared at Pam.

"You mean how much we payin' him," Pam corrected. "We payin' him $25 a piece. And before you say anything, don't forget you're the one who suggested we get protection."

Glory didn't respond.

"Girl, stop actin' like you beat for money. You got more money than me and my cousin put together. We gon' make more than $300 a piece tonight anyway…watch," Pam snapped sucking her teeth.

Glory reached for the radio, turning it up when she saw BamBam coming out of his building wearing all black.

"What's up cuzz?" BamBam said excitingly, shutting the car door after climbing his six foot three, 240 lb. dark skinned frame into the back seat of the car. "What's up CeCe Winans with your sexy ass?"

"I knew he was gonna start that shit," Glory said turning the volume up even louder.

"Don't act like that," BamBam pleaded, scooting his body up between the driver and passenger seats as Pam drove off. "I'm just complimentin' you CeCe." He had a big smile on his face.

"Boy!" Glory shouted. "You know my name, stop callin' me CeCe."

"Okay then Booty," he said snickering.

"It's Glory, black ass! Ms. Glory to you."

"Okay Ms…" He paused, thinking for a second.

"BamBam stop playin' so damn much!" Pam yelled.

It was 9:30 when Pam pulled up in front of a white painted wooden house. Scrambling through her bag, Glory pulled out a piece of paper with an address written on it.

"This the right house?"

Clack! Clack! Was the sound of BamBam loading his P226 black 9mm.

"Boy!" Pam yelled, staring into the back seat at BamBam.  Glory was doing the same.  "Why you bring that?"

"What 'cha mean why I bring this?  I'm here to protect y'all right?"

"Yeah, but damn!  It ain't nothing but some sugar daddies in there. You big enough to scare them with your size alone," Pam stated.

"Let's just go get this over with," Glory said, opening her door to step out the car.

They went up to the porch and BamBam rang the door bell.

A short man swung the door open with a smile that quickly turned into a frown when he saw BamBam.

"Hi, we're the dancers," Glory said with a bright smile, extending her hand out to shake the man's hand.

The man took Glory's hand, but his eyes were on BamBam.  "We're all straight here," he uttered, a nervous expression on his nearing old face.  "We only want women to dance for us."

Pam, BamBam and Glory burst into laughter.

"I'm not a dancer Slim.  I'm here with the ladies as protection," BamBam said.

"Oh, I'm sorry about that," the man smiled and waved them in.

"Now which one of you young ladies is Booty?" the man asked as they stood in the living room of the house.

"That's me," Glory replied stepping forward.

The man looked Glory over. "Mmmm Mmmm."

"So you're the one who I've been talking to on my computer," Glory commented.

"Yep.  I'm Carlos and this is my house."

"So where is the rest of your crew?"

"They're all downstairs in the basement waiting.  They're gonna be surprised to see how beautiful you girls are."  Carlos reached into his gray slacks pulling out money.  "That's $300 a piece right?"

"Yep," Glory responded accepting the $600 Carlos handed her. "Now is there a bathroom downstairs where we can change?"

"Yep, and it's clean."

Glory peeled $300 from the money she was given and handed it to Pam.

Glory asked, "y'all have a CD player down here right?'

"Yep, we sure do. Follow me."

Carlos led them to the kitchen then down to the basement.

"Yeaaah!" About seven middle aged men shouted with beers in their hands when they saw Glory and Pam. The basement looked to have been already set up for the event. A big empty space was directly in front of the sofas. Enough room for Glory and Pam to shake what their mommas gave them.

After showing Pam and Glory to the bathroom, Carlos joined his buddies on one of the sofas.

"Boy stop playin'," Glory snapped, pushing BamBam out of the bathroom. "Stand in front of the door and make sure none of them men try to come in here."

They both put on the same outfits but different colors. Pam wore black and Glory wore red high heel, thigh high, shiny boots, leather hot pants, leather bra-like tops and long shiny trench coats. They both wore thong panties under their hot pants.

"We ain't takin' shit off but our coats; until them mothafuckers set out some money. We gon' leave here with at least $600 a piece. No lap dancing until you see $50 or better in your hand."

"You ready?" Pam asked with Missy Elliott's latest CD in her hand.

A lanky man jumped up from one of the sofas when his entertainment came out of the bathroom. "Let's get this party started!" he slurred, and then did a little dance causing all of his buddies to roar with laughter.

"Man, sit your drunk ass down. You in my way," one of the tall man's cronies said.

BamBam stood between both sofas with his arms folded across his large chest, playing his part. He looked down to his right seeing four men on that sofa. He looked down to his left seeing four men on that sofa also.

"I love me a dark skinned sista," one man uttered, referring to Pam. Especially, when she has big tits and a huge ass. Lord have mercy on me."

"I love me a golden brown skinned sista," another man said, not to be out done.

"Shut the hell up and let me and my girl dance for y'all," Pam shouted after placing the CD into the stereo that sat off to the side.

"I love a young aggressive bitch," one man shouted, springing to his feet, digging into his pocket, pulling out a stack of money.

Glory and Pam stood side by side dancing five or six feet from the sofa. Pam glanced at Glory and smiled, simultaneously they slid their trench coats to the floor. Together they kicked their right legs up in the air, holding them with one hand beside their faces, then dancing on one leg, and turning around in a circle. All the men were now on their feet hooting and hollering and digging into their pockets for whatever money was in there. After placing their legs down, the women turned around with their backs facing the men. The leather hot pants they wore hugged their huge asses.

Like they'd practiced this routine before, they both unbuttoned their shorts inching them down just enough to expose the thong panties they wore.

"Yeah, take 'em off!" all the men shouted, including BamBam.

Pam and Glory quickly turned around facing the men. They shook their heads 'no' then placed their hands out in front of them signaling for money. In a stampede, all the men ran up to their entertainment, placing money in the hand of which ever one of the two they enjoyed the most.

As soon as they stuffed five, ten, even twenty dollar bills into the open space at the top of their boots, they both turned back around with their backs facing the men. Slowly they inched their hot pants down, then off, tossing them to the side.

"Lord help us!" one man yelled with his eyes glued to both phenomenal asses.

"Man the thongs are gone," another man said. "Where is the piece that is supposed to be between the cracks of their asses?"

"Man we dealin' with black women here. Ain't no white girls in here. Their thongs are hidden between those big ass cheeks they have."

In one quick drop to the floor, Glory and Pam both were in a cheerleader's split. Half an hour later, the girls were finished their dancing. After they got dressed, Carlos walked them to the door and said, "I was hoping you ladies wouldn't mind coming back to dance for us soon. Maybe staying a little longer next time. Money is no problem." He smiled. "We're livin' off our 401K's and pensions."

Glory glanced at Pam then responded, "Just e-mail me and I'll let you know what's up."

Pam smiled, she knew if Glory didn't plan on dancing again for the sugar daddies, she would have told Carlos straight out, "No. We won't be back and don't e-mail me."

"Where is my motherfuckin' money?" BamBam asked when Pam parked her car in front of his apartment building.

Glory and Pam both peeled $25 from the money they had just made and passed it back to BamBam.

"Hell naw!" BamBam bawled after counting $50.

"Hell naw, what? I told 'cha $50 from the jump," Pam gabbed.

"Yeah, but y'all pulled in more than $300. Hit me the fuck off and stop bein' so damn cheap towards your only security."

They both peeled another $25 from their thirty minute dancing money.

"Boyyyy y'all tight!" BamBam said, then opened the back door and got out of the car.

"I told you we was gon' make more than $300," Pam exclaimed. "How much you make?"

They both sat counting their money.

"I got $780," Glory revealed. "Plus the $50 I gave BamBam."

"Damn they must have liked you more because I 'on have nothing but $700 including the $50 I gave my cousin."

"Nah it wasn't that. It's just that the men that handed you money was cheap."

"Yeah right bitch, you know you like that."

As Glory stepped out of the car Pam reached out and smacked her on her ass. "My cousin was right. You do have a big-O-ass on ya." She chuckled.

"You do too," Glory replied, shutting the car door.

"Call me tomorrow before you go get 'cha hair done," Pam said to Glory. "I might go with you 'cause it's 'bout time for me to put some new braids in."

"All right," Glory agreed, walking from the car with her black tote bag in hand.

Glory stood on her porch watching as Pam turned off her block. She looked at her watch that read 10:30pm and ran to her car.

Around 10:55pm, Glory had parked her BMW in front of a bay brick building that looked well managed on Buena Vista Terrace in Southeast; not too far from where she lived. She killed her engine and gracefully slid out of her car and headed into the building. After walking up a flight of stairs, she stood in front of apartment #4. The moment she raised her hand to knock on the door it was opening.

"Damn girl!" Supreme stepped back with his right hand in route reaching for the .357 snug nose that was tucked in his waist. "You scared the shit out of me."

"Why you scared? Somebody looking for you or something?" Glory replied.

"Nah," Supreme shot back with confidence. But in reality he wasn't sure, although there wasn't any evidence that anyone was after him. "I was opening my door to go out, but when I did, I saw you standing there with your arms up getting ready to knock on my door."

Glory rolled her eyes at him. "Where you going? You on your way to get one of those bitches my brotha probably hooked you up with."

Supreme squinted. "Where'd all that come from? But nah, I'm going to take care of somethin' real quick. You came here to see me right?"

"Yeah."

"Well, come in and I'll be back in no more than an hour or so."

"Where you going to take care of somethin' at 11 o'clock at night?"

"Damn, Ma. You nosey. You in everything but a casket." Supreme laughed at his own joke.

"Boy," Glory said, pushing him to the side and walking into his apartment. "Go 'head and hurry back," she said pushing him into the corridor

"Yo, hold on, where you comin' from anyway? Me and your brotha stopped by your crib earlier and you wasn't there. Matter fact, your brotha just left here about ten minutes before you showed up."

"I was with Pam."

Supreme smiled. "I know she said something to you about yesterday."

"Like what?" Glory snapped. She knew what he was talking about. She just wanted him to say it in order to see if he and Pam were on the same page about yesterday's event.

"You hoggin' the dick."

"Yeah, she said exactly that."

"And what 'cha say?"

"Let's put it like this. You won't be fuckin' us together anymore. And if you fuck her behind my back, I'ma cut 'cha dick off and flush it down the toilet so the doctors can't sew it back on." Glory snickered.

"Yo that shit ain't funny girl." Supreme grabbed his crotch.

"Yeah, well don't do it then."

A grin spread over Supreme's face. "Remember that day in your bedroom when you said I didn't fuck you good enough for you to be hooked and jealous in three days?"

"Yeah I remember that," Glory mumbled. She knew what he was insinuating.

"Now you're hooked and jealous just like I said you would be." Supreme smiled.

Glory sucked her teeth. "Boy go 'head where you goin' and come back quick."

Before Supreme could get out the building, Glory yelled his name, "Supreme!"

"Yo!" he shouted, standing in front of the door.

"You have your cell phone on you?"

"Yeah."

"If you take longer than an hour, I'ma call you."

"Damn she must want some dick," he mumbled to himself. "All right," he shouted.

Supreme stepped into his car and twenty minutes later turned onto

Unique's old stomping grounds.  To his surprise, there were plenty of people outside.  He glanced at his watch that read 11:26 pm.

"Damn" he mumbled, slowly cruising through the block.  "It's a lot of mothafuckas out here."

The block was crowded with drug dealers, crack addicts and just plain old hood rats that were either selling drugs or waiting for their drug dealing boyfriends to sell their last bit of poison so they could go to hotels and get their freak on.

"Yo," Supreme said after rolling his window down.  He stopped his Lexus in front of two men that were leaning up against the driver's door of a black Ford Explorer.

"Yeah what's up Slim?" one of the men responded.

"Y'all know Bullet?"

"Nah" the other man quickly said, looking over at his friend who spoke up first.

Supreme's cell phone started ringing.  "Yo," he said into the phone, his eyes on the two men that he thought viewed him as a crack head.

"Yeah, this Bullet.  Look straight ahead."

Supreme took his eyes off the two men and looked straight ahead.  Up ahead in the middle of the street stood Bullet waving his right hand in the air while holding his cell phone to his ear with his left.

Supreme pulled off driving almost to the end of the block.

"What's up N.Y.?"  Bullet stood next to the driver's side door of Supreme's Lexus.  He reached into the car and shook Supreme's hand.

"Ain't shit, Son.  Looking for you."

"I know I told 'cha 9 o'clock but I had to take care of somethin'."

"Don't worry about that 'cause I didn't come at nine anyway."

"So you still want that right?"

"That's why I'm here nigga." Supreme stuck his hand out the window for another handshake.

"I feel you, Slim." Bullet shook Supreme's hand then told him to park his car.

Supreme parked, pulled his .357 out, checked to see if it had all six rounds in it, and then placed it back on his waist. He looked out his rearview mirror and saw Bullet leaning against his pearl white GS300 Lexus.

Supreme stepped out of his car and walked toward Bullet.

"Yo, Son. It's a lot of mothafuckas out here for it to be almost midnight," Supreme said as his eyes roved the block.

"Yeah, it's always like this," Bullet replied. "Some of these niggas grind all day and night."

"You know Unique used to be out here grinding like most of these niggas are now until he met that young'un PooBear. Now that nigga on some low key shit. The only time I really see him is at a club, at the court on Sundays, or when he comes around to gamble. That nigga PooBear must be sellin' a lot of shit for that nigga."

Supreme started to respond, but before he could, a slightly tinted black Jeep Cherokee pulled up in front of them.

"That's 5.0," Bullet softly whispered to Supreme. "Don't say nothin'. Let me do all the talkin'."

"What's up boys?" a dark-skinned, bald headed cop with a goatee asked. He sat in the passenger seat of the jeep. His right arm was hanging out the window. The jeep was so close to Supreme and Bullet that if the cop wanted to reach out and grab one of them, he could. The other cops were in the jeep, all of them grinning as if they were up to something. Wearing civilian clothes you could see badges hanging from their necks by a silver chain. The Black driver leaned low in his seat like most young men did while behind the wheel.

"Ain't shit," Bullet said, raising his voice.

"What are you up to tonight Bullet? You ain't out here floodin' the streets with guns are you?"

"Nah man I don't have nothin' to do with no guns. I ain't had a gun since the last time you caught me with one," Bullet answered the cop who sat in the front of the jeep.

"Looks like we have a new kid on the block," the cop said, looking Supreme over. "Who's your new friend Bullet?"

"Oh, this my cousin from Maryland."

"Get the fuck out of here. I've seen one of your so called cousins before, and the nigga was as black as you," the cop teased. "What's your name?" he asked Supreme, looking at him with a watchful eye.

"Preme."

Supreme's cell phone started ringing.

"Don't even think about answering your phone," the cop said, watching Supreme's hand move. His Glock 9mm was sticking out of the jeep's window, one foot away from Supreme's face.

"Come on, Man. What the fuck you doin'?" Bullet snapped, taking a step away from Supreme.

"Yo what's up?" Supreme stated his hands now in the air. Fear leaped into his eyes.

"If you had touched that phone, I would've shot your ass. All I had to say was I thought you was reachin' for a gun," the cop said laughing as he pulled off.

"Damn Son, what the fuck was up with that nigga?" Supreme dropped his hands. He stared at the jeep as it vanished from the block.

"That's that crooked ass cop "Jay the Snake" and his flunkies. They be on some bullshit."

"Son, let me get that so I can bounce," Supreme expressed.

"Come on," Bullet ordered, leading the way around his Lexus and into a white painted brick building. He knocked on the door. Next, the sound of the door's chain being removed could be heard. Bullet entered and walked with his normal thuggish swagger toward the two back rooms with Supreme on his heels. Removing a big blue suitcase from the closet in the smallest bedroom, Bullet unzipped the suitcase.

"Damn!" Supreme exclaimed, looking at the merchandise.

"I told you I have it all," Bullet said proudly.

Supreme reached into the suitcase and grabbed one of the two bullet proof vests and placed it up against his chest.

"That's the T-shirt bullet proof vest. That's you, Joe. You could wear that joint like a T-shirt outside and the average mothafucka wouldn't know it's a vest."

Bullet reached into the suitcase and pulled the blue vest from it. "This the standard vest the police wear, it's steel but it can even stop a Black Talon bullet. The T-shirt joint you have on can stop anything between a 22 Caliber handgun and a 44 Magnum at point blank range."

"You know your shit, Kid." Supreme stated, grabbing the vest out of Bullet's hand.

"This what I specialize in. I 'on sell drugs, I sell protection."

"How old are you, Son?"

Bullet smiled. "I'm 31."

"I thought your short ass was like 25. The baseball cap and your clean shaved face makes you look young. That's $600 for the T-shirt vest, right?"

"Yeah," Bullet replied putting the suitcase in the closet. He came back out of the closet with a white shopping bag in hand. "You said you needed another stun gun right?"

"Yeah," Supreme nodded.

"It's in the bag free of charge." Bullet gave Supreme the shopping bag, and Supreme passed him the $600 he pulled from his pocket.

"Let me ask you something else. Are you fuckin' Unique's sista Glory?"

"Why you ask me that?" Supreme frowned.

"'Cause I seen her out there at the courts cheering you on last week like you was her man."

Supreme pondered for a second. Why was Bullet really asking if he was fucking Glory? Did he want to fuck her or was he fucking her?

"Nah," Supreme answered. "I ain't fuckin' her."

"Joe, that bitch is a dime hands down."

"Why you ask? What's up? You try'na hit that?"

"Hell yeah!" Bullet bawled. "I been tryna get at her for two years now. I offered her a thousand dollars to fuck me. She told me hell no. I asked her was I ugly or somethin' and she said naw. She just don't fuck for money. You know she used to be a stripper right?"

"Yeah I know." Supreme smiled. He had a new found respect for Glory.

"You know that broad, Pam, she be with?"

"Yeah."

"I fucked that bitch for $500. She a bad bitch too but she ain't fine as

Glory. She let me titty fuck her and she sucked the shit outta my dick."

Supreme grinned. He thought about Pam. He knew Bullet was telling the truth about her. But he wondered could he fuck her up the ass for free. Then he thought about Glory's words. *'If you try to fuck her behind my back, I'ma cut your dick off and flush it down the toilet.'*

"What's up, Dawg? You ready to go?"

"Yeah, yeah," Supreme answered with the shopping bag in hand.

"I'll holla at 'cha, Joe." Bullet and Supreme shook hands and bumped shoulders as they stood in front of Bullet's Lexus.

Supreme pulled from the curb. He dialed the number to his apartment, hoping Glory didn't get mad and leave because he didn't answer his phone.

"Hello," Glory answered.

"Yeah, this me." He hoped Glory wouldn't start bitching.

"You on ya way, right?"

"No doubt, Ma."

"I got something for you," she said in a low sexy voice that she'd never used before.

"Yeah. What is it?"

"If you not here in fifteen minutes, you won't get it!" She hung up in his ear.

Supreme smiled while speeding up. He thought about how good things were going for him in D.C. Everything had turned out quite different from what he'd expected. Coming to D.C. was now the best decision he'd ever made. Not only was he pushing a Lexus after only being in D.C. for five months, but he had an apartment, a stash of about $75,000, and a whole new wardrobe. On the first of the month he would receive 10 g's from Unique as payment for carrying a gun while they were together. But his most premium possession was Glory. He knew if it wasn't for her, he wouldn't have been in the position he was in. Fucking one of the most gorgeous women he'd seen was without a doubt something to boast about.

Supreme pulled up behind Glory's BMW and parked. He looked to his right at his building hoping she wouldn't emerge from it. He was two minutes late.

"Should I take this shit with me or not?" He wondered if he should take the bullet proof vest and stun gun he had in the shopping bag into the house. He decided to take it into the house. He snatched his .357 from his waist and placed it into the bag with the vest and stun gun.

He stepped out of his car and swiftly walked into his building. He stuck his key into the lock. Remembering what Glory said about having a surprise for him, he slowly opened the door and was met with brightly lit apartment. It seemed like Glory had all the lights on in his crib. When the door was fully opened, Glory stood butt naked with her legs apart like a cowboy preparing for a quick draw showdown. The only piece of clothing she wore were red, thigh high boots.

"Damn Ma," Supreme said shutting the door.

"Stay right there," Glory ordered.

"Oh shit!" Supreme muttered, now noticing what he should have noticed the second he saw her. Glory's entire body was covered with 'body glitter'. It made her body sparkle like a decorated Christmas tree.

"Throw that bag on the floor and take off all ya clothes, right now," she snapped.

Supreme didn't hesitate. He placed the shopping bag down beside him slowly; making sure the gun that was in the bag wouldn't thump against the hard wood floor. Next, he took off all his clothes and placed them on top of the bag. Now he stood nude in front of the door.

Glory extended her right arm out pointing the remote control she held at the stereo system. The stereo came to life with Lil Mo's hit single "Super Woman" featuring rapper Fabolous rumbling though the stereo. Glory began to dance seductively. She twisted her body all type of ways, never taking her eyes off Supreme and his little soldier that was now beginning to slowly rise to attention. It seemed to have a mind of its own. Glory turned around with her back facing Supreme. She easily made her legs and huge ass cheeks move simultaneously in wave like motion.

'Ma you killin' me!" Supreme yelled blood rushing to his face making it red. He was overly excited.

Glory quickly dropped down into a squatting position only to leap back to her feet and continue to make her legs and ass cheeks dance. She looked over her left shoulder at Supreme and ceased her movement.

"Why you stoppin'?" He whined like a kid with his rock hard dick sticking straight forward.  Pre-cum made its way from his pee hole that he didn't notice, but Glory did.

"Boy you ain't 'bout ta nut are you?" She asked with a chuckle.

"Nah.  Keep dancin'," he replied over the music.

She did just that, by placing her hands on her knees and slightly bending her legs.  And in less than a second her ass began jumping, opening and closing like butterfly wings, and he could see her vagina doing the same.

"That's enough," Glory said after dancing for another five minutes after Supreme asked her to.  "I'm hurting you.  You can't take me dancing for you…" She was walking up to him.  "I still have a surprise for you." She kissed him on his lips then roughly grabbed his still rock hard dick with her right hand.

"Ohh girrrrl," Supreme muttered joyously with a smile.

"Come on," Glory ordered, pulling him by his dick.  She walked him over to the tan cloth sofa.  She sat on the edge of it while he stood between her legs with his stiff dick aimin' at her face.

"Yo, this what I'm talkin' about,"  Supreme said to himself.

"What 'cha want me to do to you?" Glory asked.

"Do whatever you want," Supreme replied, looking down at Glory. He anticipated her next move.

Glory looked up at Supreme.  "I wasn't talking to you.  I was talking to him." She grabbed his dick and kissed the head.

"Do whatever you want to.  I'm talking for my dick.  It's your show. I'm just a spectator."

"OK."  She reached around palming his ass cheeks with each of her hands.  Pulling him towards her, she opened her mouth and pushed his stiffness inside.

After four minutes of pleasing Supreme, Glory pushed him back and stood up from the sofa.  She grabbed his hand and guided him towards the bedroom.  And as they were walking into the bedroom, Supreme looked down at Glory's ass. It shook like it had a life of its own. Every step she took, it fluctuated like jello. The glitter on it enhanced the joy of observing it.

"Cut the light off." She told him. She slid out a drawer and pulled out two long yellow candles and a book of matches. She placed the candles on top of the dresser.

"Them candles been in here?" Supreme asked. He flicked his bedroom light off.

"Yeah, I put them in your drawer the last time I was over here." She struck a match and lit the two candles.

"So you had this planned?"

"Yeah." She smiled. The glow from the candles made her entire body sparkle.

"That shit you have on your body is crazy, Ma. You sparklin' like shit. That shit is sexy as hell!"

Glory stepped over to the water bed and climbed on it. "Come here." She used her index finger to signal him over. She sat on her knees in the middle of the bed.

When Supreme climbed aboard the bed, Glory laid him on his back. With his head resting on one of the two satin pillows, Glory positioned her naked body between his legs.

Still wearing her red thigh high boots, she gave instructions.

"Look to your right," she told him.

"What?" he snapped, but did as he was told. "Why you want me to look at the wall?"

"Boy you 'on see our shadow on the wall?"

"Oh shit! Yeah, yeah, I see it."

Glory took his now semi soft dick into her hands. "Can you see this?" She stood up and looked at the wall.

"Ma, you buggin'." He laughed.

"Keep your eyes on the wall," she ordered, taking his dick in her mouth.

"Aaaah girrrrll," Supreme growled, feeling his dick growing to its full capacity inside her mouth. Slurping sounds could be heard as Glory pleased him while observing her own work glancing at the shadow.

"You still want that surprise I have for you?" she quizzed after withdrawing her mouth from the massive slab of meat she held in her hands.

"Hell yeah," Supreme replied, gazing at Glory as she slid both of her hands up and down his drenched shaft. She suddenly squeezed it from the base causing the head to swell up.

"Reach under your pillow." She still held his man-hood in a choke hold.

He placed his hand up by his head and slid it under the pillow. When he pulled his hand out from it, he held a small bottle of baby oil and a condom.

A chill of excitement and anticipation shot though Supreme's body. Excited because what he thought was about to go down was something he would have never thought she'd let him do. He anticipated it because this was an opportunity that most men never came across, unless they were dealing with a trick. And in some cases, the woman you were tricking wouldn't allow you the opportunity, especially if you were well endowed.

She rolled the condom slowly down his shaft then squirted baby oil in her right hand. Closing the top to the bottle, she tossed it to the far side of the bed, and moderately massaged the oil onto Supreme's penis that stood straight up. While her right hand placed oil onto Supreme's dick, her left hand was between her legs placing oil along the crack of her ass.

"You ready?" She inquired with a cracked voice.

"Yeah."

Glory moved from between his legs and was now lying on her back with her head resting on the pillow. She slowly raised her thick, toned, and slightly bowed legs up near her ears. Her hands gripped behind each of her calves.

"You sure you wanna do this?" Supreme asked, stationing himself in front of her. He asked that just to try to ease the tension that was now in the air. But in his mind, he was praying his question wouldn't give her a gateway to say no.

"Yeah I'm sure. If I wasn't I wouldn't do it," she snapped in order to boost her confidence. She needed to do this she thought as she watched Supreme take hold of the Anaconda he was getting ready to propel into her virgin anus. Letting him do this would have him on a leash and would assure he wouldn't go behind her back and fuck Pam. She wanted him all to herself. She no longer wanted to see everyone else in love. She wanted someone she could call her own. If she could help it, Supreme would be that someone she could point to and say he's mine.

"I'ma take my time ok," he muttered placing the head of his dick up against her anus.

"Don't laugh at me if I start screamin'. I heard this shit hurt, especially the first time you do it. And to make it worst, you have a big dick."

"I ain't gon' laugh if you scream," he replied, pushing the head in.

Glory grunted and then let out a loud yell, "IIIIIII!" She slammed her legs down hard onto the water bed.

"Supreme! It hurts, *but it feels good*."

# ELEVEN

Unique sat parked in his Navigator as he blew his horn for Supreme to exit the building.

"What's up Dawg?" Supreme uttered as he climbed into the passenger seat.

"What's up, Slim?" Unique replied. "I've been thinking a lot. What 'cha think about them two young'uns I'm fuckin' with?"

"You talkin' 'bout Wop and Darkman right?"

"Yeah, who else nigga? Them the only two young'uns I fuck with besides PooBear. That nigga ain't young no more. He gon' be 19 in two months."

"I 'on know, Kid. I like both of 'em. They both bringin' somethin' to the table."

"Yeah, and what's that?"

"Money nigga," Supreme said laughing.

"Yeah. You right. Everything's been legit with them since I started fuckin' with them. PooBear said their money is always right. But I 'on know. I think in the long run somethin' gon' go down with that young'un Wop; he a wild mothafucka."

"Yeah, but he ain't no wilder than that nigga PooBear."

"You right, but they a lil' different," Unique said.

"I wanna know how in the fuck Darkman hooked up with them two wild niggas. He ain't shit like them," Supreme added.

"You ain't lying. Darkman is from a different breed of niggas. He just graduated a month or two ago. He told me he's thinking about going to college at UDC."

"I know he grew up with them niggas, but he's strange," Supreme said.

"I'm gonna watch all of 'em", Unique announced. "What 'cha think about that club we went to last week on the 4th?"

"The "Spot" right?"

"Yeah."

"I like that joint…it's hot. There was a lot of bad bitches in there." *And a lot of niggas that's ballin' I can rob Supreme thought to himself.*

"Too bad my sista was there cock blockin' you huh," Unique said, cutting his eyes at Supreme.

"Nah, she wasn't cock blockin'. I wasn't looking for no bitches anyway."

"Yeah right nigga. Glory got 'cha pussy whipped." Unique giggled.

"Nigga please" Supreme blew air from his mouth, causing his lips to rattle.

"You fakin', Joe. You ain't hit shit else but my sista since you been in D.C. No, I take that back. You probably fucked that bitch Pam behind my peoples back."

Supreme had a slick grin planted on his face. He looked over at Unique. "No comment."

"Oh, you ain't did nothin' big nigga. I fucked that freak bitch before you came down here," Unique fired back.

Supreme smiled broadly. "I ain't said shit."

"All right nigga, you like to play games." They both laughed a little.

Unique changed the subject. "You remember the dude I was talking to at the club in front of the VIP section?"

"Yeah, I know that's your father. Glory told me that night in the club."

"What else did she tell you?"

"That he's your father and he owned the club. That's it."

"She didn't tell you that he's not our biological father?"

"Nah Son." Supreme's ears were now fully open. He looked over at Unique clinging to his every word. When Glory told him that the dude was their father and he owned the club, the first thought that came to his mind was robbing their father. Then he decided he couldn't hurt Glory's father. He wanted to show some type of discipline and loyalty. But after hearing the truth, his thoughts of robbing the man were back.

"Yeah, he was my real father's best friend," Unique continued. "But to me and Glory, he is our father. We love him. He had us since my Mom and Pops died. I was seven and Glory was three years old when they died."

"I'm sorry to hear that." Supreme sat in deep thought.

"Yeah well, shit happens. Oh yeah, let me tell you now before I forget. I want you to go with me tomorrow mornin' around 9 o'clock to pick up somethin' I ordered," Unique said.

"I 'on give a fuck, I'm gettin' paid to ride around with you totin' a hammah," Supreme said.

"This is an easy job, huh?" Unique asked.

"You damn right it is."

"So if the shit gets hard, you still ain't gon' mind ridin' around with me totin' a hammah on ya?" Unique asked.

"What 'cha getting' at Dawg?"

"You know. If you have to fire that thang at a nigga, the job will be easy for you, right?"

"Yeah," Supreme snapped. "Come on, Son. Me bustin' a nigga is a part of our deal."

Unique smiled. "I'm just makin' sure."

"When the time comes you'll see," Supreme said confidently.

Unique drove slowly through his old stomping grounds. The block was filled with people. Kids were in the street playing in water that shot out of the fire hydrant at the end of the block. Young, fly dressed men exchanged crack for money. Cars were parked with music blasting from some of the trunks.

"What's up?" Unique said after he stopped in front of three men.

"What's up nigga?" One of the men walked up to the Navigator, and shook hands with Unique, then reached over Unique and shook hands with Supreme. "What's up, Slim?"

"So what's up, PeeWee?" Unique spoke.

"Ain't shit. A mothafucka 'boutta melt out this joint'. I see you in this truck with the A/C pumpin'." He stuck his hand into the truck. "It's chill bill."

"Yeah. So how's shit goin' out here?" Unique quizzed.

"Everything is cool. But you need to stop faking; and hit a nigga off like you hittin' that young'un PooBear off."

"Who told 'cha that?"

"C'mon man. The word gets around. So, what's up? Hit a nigga off."

"Nah man, I ain't…"

"It ain't like I want you to front me nothin'. I'm tryin' to buy it."

Unique's cell phone rung. "Hold on," he told PeeWee who waited patiently by his window. "Hello," he said after pulling his phone from his pants pocket.

"Hi Baby," Kim answered.

"Hold on," Unique said to Kim, taking his phone from his ear. "Slim, I gotta go, but I'll holla at 'cha about that later."

"All right, I'm gonna hold you to that."

"I got 'cha." Unique shook hands with PeeWee and drove off.

Unique placed his cell phone back to his ear. "I'm back."

"What are you doing?" Kim inquired, sounding in good spirits.

" Nothin'. So what's up?" Unique asked.

"I called to remind you about tonight."

"I didn't forget, we goin' over my house tonight right?"

"Yeah, because it's been like a month and a half since you said I'm welcome over to your place, but I haven't been there yet."

"I'll pick you up at seven."

"OK."

"Bye old timer," Unique said chuckling.

"Boy what I tell you about playing with my age," Kim laughed.

"Okay, I'll see you at seven." Unique hung up.

"I ain't gotta ask you who that was because there's only one broad you talk to with love in your eyes," Supreme joked.

Changing the subject, Unique said, "We 'boutta pick up some money from my young'uns."

"Yo! I knew it was somethin' I wanted to tell you," Supreme snapped. "I was around where we just left about two weeks ago kickin' it with the nigga Bullet. We was outside standing by his car when this black jeep rolled up on us. That nigga Bullet whispered to me that there was cops in the jeep. The cop that was on the passenger side pulled a gun out on me just because I was reaching, for my cell phone when it rung. Son, the mothafucka had the joint inches from my face."

"The cop was real dark with a bald head? He was a muscle bound bamma right?" Unique questioned.

"Yeah, Son. I guess so."

"I never seen the bamma before, but niggas around the way told me about him and the other three cops he rolls with. They told me the cop is on the take. He wasn't coming around the way when I used to be out there a long time ago. They say he be takin' niggas shit and won't even lock them up. They nicknamed him, but I forgot his name. But the description they gave me sticks in my head."

"Bullet told me his name but I forgot it," Supreme hissed.

"Yeah, I heard he be takin' coke from niggas and goin' to other blocks sellin' the shit to young'uns dirt cheap."

"Damn! I thought the police was supposed to serve and protect. Now that's what 'cha call a dirty cop. And that would be the same cop that will get on the stand on a nigga he locked up and lie. And the jury will believe him."

"You ain't lyin' Joe," Unique agreed, turning onto the block where PooBear, Wop, and Darkman hung.

"What's up New York?" Wop asked, grinning. He wiped the sweat from his face and body with a white T-shirt.

"Ain't shit, Son."

"So what's up PooBear? You got that?" Unique questioned. They all stood in the street beside a parked old school Jetta.

"Nigga you always askin' me that shit when you know I got that. I told 'cha yesterday to come pick that up…."

"So go get that nigga. You always talkin' slick talk out 'cha mouth." Unique had a smirk on his face. "Keep talkin' slick. I'ma pay Wop 10 g's or somethin' to lay hands on your ass."

Everybody laughed except PooBear.

"Let me holla at 'cha Unique," PooBear said, walking around the Jetta and onto the sidewalk with Unique a step behind him.

"Yeah Slim, y'all niggas pushed twenty keys in like a month and a half. Y'all some bad mothafuckas, 'cause y'all pushed that shit in dimes and twenties goin' hand to hand," Unique was saying to PooBear as they stood on the sidewalk.

"We sold fifties too. So when you gon' cop some more shit?" PooBear asked. "We gotta keep our customers happy."

"I'ma hit y'all off Sunday. I'ma stop by ya house around 8 o'clock."

"How much we getting' a piece?"

Unique smiled. "That's a surprise."

As PooBear walked away from Unique to get the money from his Escalade, he smiled, thinking about the money he would receive. As long as it was over 70 g's, he'd be happy. In fact, if it was only 50 g's it wouldn't really bother him because he still wasn't selling the crack. Wop and Darkman were. He was only getting a kilo at a time from Unique and handing it off to his childhood buddies to break down for distribution. Passing the money off to Unique and walking away, PooBear made plans on how to spend his forthcoming loot.


**Unique glanced at his watch as he drove slowly** over speed bumps entering a parking lot of an apartment complex in Hyattsville, Maryland. He grinned as he entered deeper into the well kept community. Not a negative element in sight. No drug dealers, crack addicts, dope fiends, winos, prostitutes, or anything that would be considered degenerate. Beautiful trees embellished the small community. He cruised past mothers pushing their kids in swings at the complex's pleasant looking playground.

The decision to rent the apartment he was about to visit came a day after obtaining the 20 kilos of crack. He figured it would be best if he got a stash house that only he knew about. And if he ever revealed it to anyone it would be Glory. The purpose for this apartment was simple. It would be used to store his drugs and half of his money. There was no sense, he thought, in keeping everything where he lay his head. From now on, there would be no drugs kept at his house, only half of every dime he made, and on occasion he would deposit some of the money into the Money Market Account he'd opened.

He drove through the complex twice before parking in front of the building he was going to. He sat in his truck observing the parked cars, looking to see if anyone occupied them.

An elderly white couple walked past the truck waving to Unique, and smiling. He smiled and waved back, watching them loiter along. When the couple was a few feet from the truck, he stepped out with the brown paper bag in hand and headed to his building.

When he entered his apartment, he could hear the music that played loud enough for any inquisitive neighbor to hear. He made it his business to leave his stereo on before leaving the apartment in order to make his neighbors believe someone was there. He locked the door and walked in the kitchen. Reaching up, he grabbed a few brown paper bags from the cabinet. After turning the stereo off he headed towards the bedroom. Unique flung the empty bags and the bag of money he held onto the sheetless king sized bed, and walked over to the closet. Kneeling down, he triggered the combination to the gray safe. After retrieving the money he rushed to the cabinet under the kitchen sink. Unique slid the cleaning products to the side and placed one hand down on the board that held the items. With a push downward, then a jerk to the right, the board separated revealing a white "Safeway" grocery bag filled with money. Anxiously, he grabbed the bag and his money machine.

Unique dumped the money from the bag, and sat at the edge of the bed unwrapping the rubber bands from each bundle.

Forty five minutes later he was finished. The money came up to almost $800,000. "I can't believe this shit?" he said to himself. Thinking about the $300,000 at home, he shouted "I'ma mothafuckin' millionaire!"

He ran to the living room and looked out the window. Nothing, nobody. He ran to his front door and peeped out the peep-hole. Nothing, nobody. He ran back into the bedroom and started to separate the money he was going to keep in the apartment and the money he was going to give to his workers.

He placed $400,000 back into the "Safeway" bag and took it into the kitchen, placing it back into his stash spot.

Now back in the bedroom he placed $100,000 into four different brown paper bags. He took his money machine and put it back into the safe and locked it. He turned the stereo up as he grabbed the four paper bags and headed out the apartment door.

As he drove to Kim's house, he thought about his money. Was $100,000 too much to give his young'uns? After all, they did push 20 kilo's for him; so, yes they did deserve it. But was he losing out? Did he make back the 250 g's he used to buy the 20 kilo's? *Yes, he thought*. He did double his money. He did make $500,000. Four hundred thousand was with him now inside the four brown paper bags. Yeah, he did make his money back, plus he had $300,000 at his house in his safe. He also had spent $150,000 on the order he was going to pick up tomorrow morning at 9 o'clock.

Unique beeped his horn the moment he pulled up in front of Kim's house. He grabbed one of the four paper bags and placed it into the truck's glove compartment, and pushed the other three under his seat.

"Hi Baby!" Kim said, jumping into the truck, kissing Unique on his cheek. Her face was lit with a kool-aid smile.

Unique sniffed at the sweet scent that entered his truck. "Damn, you smell good girl." He looked Kim over. She wore a form fitting black DKNY halter dress with black open toed high heel sandals. Her long silky black hair fell down her back instead of in its usual ponytail. "That's the dress I copped for you right?"

"Yessssss," Kim replied seductively by throwing her arms in the air and batting her eyes at Unique. "You like?" She turned from side to side in her seat.

"Nah, I love. You look good. Are you planning on stayin' over my house tonight?" Unique inquired, glancing down at the white tote bag that sat by Kim's feet.

"Yeah. Do you have a problem with that?" She looked at him coldly.

"Nah, nah." Unique threw his arms in the air and laughed.

"Okay, let's go," Kim ordered.

"Don't be so mean girl." Unique joked.

As they drove, Kim talked on her cell phone to her mother and Unique thought of the money he was making. He was on big boy status, had three young guys pumpin' for him instead of one. Dad was wrong for the first time. Selling four kilos was nothing like selling twenty. There was a big difference. He didn't know when he'd quit for good. The money was addictive. Plus he was only paying' 250 g's for twenty kilo's, already cooked. Niggas would kill for a deal as sweet as that.

"Unique! Unique!" Kim called out, slicing into his thoughts.

"Yeah. Yeah."

"Boy, don't be daydreaming behind the wheel."

"I wasn't daydreamin'."

"Yes you were. I hope you were daydreaming about me." Kim threw her left leg up on the dashboard showing her pretty toes.

"Don't make me crash this truck lookin' at you." His eyes went from her legs to the road. Giirrll!!" Unique warned, eyeing her legs that were now kicked up on the dash.

Kim glanced out her window. "I thought you told me you lived off M.L.K. We're on Central Avenue."

"I do. I'm goin' to holla at somebody." Unique pulled up in front of PooBear's house. While Kim was looking out her window up at the house they parked in front of, he reached under his seat and grabbed the three brown paper bags. "Give me ten minutes or so," he said stepping out of the truck, but leaving his key in the ignition.

Kim watched Unique walk into the house when the door was opened for him. She wondered who lived there. She knew he wasn't disrespectful, better yet, crazy enough to have her sitting outside while he visited another woman, so she did stop worrying.

In the house, Unique sat at the table in the dining room. Across from him sat PooBear, Wop, and Darkman. The three brown paper bags sat on the table in front of Unique.

"Listen, Joe. The money I'm about to give y'all is in appreciation of the work y'all niggas put in. Don't let this money go to your head. I'm really talking to Wop and Darkman, 'cause I 'on think y'all ever had this amount of money before." He looked at PooBear who sat in the middle of his two cronies. "But PooBear can handle it. It's a hundred gees in each of those bags," Unique said as he pushed the bags across the table.

"You bullshittin'," Darkman snapped, reaching for one of the bags.

PooBear and Wop both stared at Darkman. Hearing him use profanity was something they didn't hear often.

"Damn nigga you must be happy 'cause you don't cuss but once in a year or some shit like that," Wop said.

Darkman quickly pulled five large bundles from his bag. It's twenty gees in each bundle," Unique explained.

"So, there are no attachments to this money?" Darkman asked.

"Nah."

"So if I decided to cut out and just stop selling that's cool with you?"

"Yeah," Unique responded, confused.

"What about if I didn't want to hustle for you anymore and just wanted to start my own thing?"

Unique didn't respond right away. He thought for a second because he never pondered that possibility before. After thinking, he said, "I know you don't want that 'cause you got $100,000." Unique grinned at Darkman, hoping he wouldn't want to go on his own. Unique vowed never to go back selling hand to hand like he had once done.

"Nah man. I just asked," Darkman said. "But I'll let you know if I ever decide to get out the game."

Back in the truck Kim's jaw hung down like she was getting ready to yell. Her mouth was wide open for a good reason. She was staring into the brown paper bag that she retrieved from the glove compartment.

"It has to be at least $75,000 in this bag," she said to herself, quickly glancing up from the bag to look out the window at PooBear's house. She placed the bag back into the glove compartment. I don't need more evidence, she thought. "He's a drug dealer!" She paused for a second to ponder her situation. Then suddenly her emotions tumbled causing both of her light brown eyes to fill with tears.

Back inside Unique continued. "Look, I wanna let y'all know something." Unique had thought about what he was about to say while watching his content employees thumb through their bundles of cash. "I may not give y'all a hundred g's all the time." He paused, looked at the three of them, wanting to see which one of them would protest what he'd just said. They all remained tranquil, something that he didn't expect since he wasn't really serious about what he'd just announced. He just wanted to see if he was indeed in charge, and if what he said would go, no questions asked.

"I don't have a problem with that," PooBear stated, causing Wop and Darkman to look at him with cold stares. PooBear knew exactly why they looked at him that way. They were the ones doing the hard labor.

Unique slid his chair out from the table and stood up giving them all hand shakes with a bump of his shoulder.

"PooBear, I'ma holla at 'cha Sunday with a brick," Unique said. "After we come from playin' ball."

"Okay."

"So, what y'all plan on doin' for the rest of the night?" Unique asked preparing to exit the house.

"We wanted to go out and have some fun with Darkman for his B-day," Wop spat. "But he wanna be with his white girl tonight."

"So you hittin' a snow bunny huh?" Unique smiled at Darkman.

'Yeah, ain't nothin' wrong with that," Darkman replied, looking at Unique to see if he agreed.

"You right, pussy is pussy," Unique said as he opened the door.


**"Have you been crying?" Unique asked Kim while** he drove.

"I'm all right," Kim uttered, looking out the window to avoid eye contact with her man. She didn't want him to see her face. She had been crying because she was in love with Unique and didn't want to lose him to the system.

"I 'on know. From over here it looks like your eyes are a little watery. Did you miss me for the fifteen minutes I was out of the truck?" He grinned looking at the road then back at Kim.

Kim laughed. "Yeah, I love to be around you. When you're gone, I cry like a baby."

"I do, too."

They both giggled.

"So, where are we going now?" Kim quickly wiped her eyes while Unique's attention was on the road.

"I want you to meet my sista."

"That's good because I haven't met any of your family yet. I would like to meet your step Mom and Dad, too. It sounds like you're close to all of them."

"I am, and you'll meet them soon."

Unique pulled up in front of Glory's building and parked.

"She lives in here?" Kim pointed towards Glory's building. "That's a nice looking building. Matter fact…" Kim looked around observing the neighborhood. "This is a nice looking neighborhood."

"Yeah. A Muslim brother owns her building and several others."

"I like Muslims," Kim exclaimed. "I'll bet you before he became the landlord around here this neighborhood wasn't as pleasant as it is now. Muslims know how to revolutionize a neighborhood. Any community they come into they make a positive impact on it. From what I've noticed, at the jail the 'Nation of Islam' Muslims seem to show greater respect for women staff than any other religious group, and they seem to be more disciplined as far as smoking, and stuff like that," Kim added.

Unique simply nodded at Kim's comments as they stood at Glory's front door.

When Unique opened Glory's apartment door, the music attacked Kim's ears. A party was going on with only two people in attendance. Wearing party hats, long white T-shirts draped down to their ankles, and yellow Big Bird bedroom slippers, Glory and her step sister Stacy danced to the music. When Stacy spotted Unique and Kim stepping into the apartment, she stopped and ran over to her big brother and threw her arms around his waist.

"Unique! Unique!" she yelled, her voice barely hovering over the music that Glory had headed towards her bedroom to shut off. "My sista takin' me to "Kings Dominion" tomorrow for my birthday."

"I can't hear you," Unique said, just before the music stopped abruptly. "Now what 'cha say?"

"My sista is takin' me to "Kings Dominion Park" tomorrow for my birthday."

"That's right; your birthday is tomorrow, a day before Glory's. I forgot to get you something." Stacy let go of his waist and stepped back with an '*oh no you didn't*' expression on her face.

"Well, I'll be eight tomorrow, and since you ain't buy me nothing, I'll take cash." She held out her hand.

Kim smiled at the scene. She was right. Unique was close to his family, and she admired that.

"OK. I'ma hit 'cha off as soon as you say hi to this beautiful lady you see standing next to me."

"Hi," Stacy stated, extending her hand out towards Kim, and giving here the third degree. "You be on TV? 'Cause you look like you be on TV."

Kim blushed while shaking Stacy's little hand. "Thanks for the compliment, but I'm far from being a TV star."

Stacy quickly glanced over her shoulder to see if Glory was coming from the back room. She still had her hand in Kim's hand. "You look better than my big sista, but don't tell her I said that 'cause she thinks she's the bomb."

"OK, I won't," Kim whispered letting Stacy's hand go.

"Hi. You must be Kim," Glory said, coming from the back room.

"Yes, I am," Kim replied, smiling and shaking Glory's hand.

"Unique it's about time you brought her by to meet me. Come on Stacy, let's go in the back and find my camera so I can take some pictures of this. I have a feelin' they gon' be together for a long time." Glory and Stacy ran towards the back.

"I like Glory already," Kim told Unique.

"She likes you too," Unique said. But he meant it in a different way.

"I like Stacy, too."

"She likes you, too."

"So, where is her birthday money?" Kim questioned.

"I see you're already on her side." Unique dug into his pocket.

"How much you plan on giving her?"

"$100 from me and $100 from you." Unique peeled two one-hundred dollar bills from his bankroll, handing it to Kim. "You give it to her."

"You don't think this is a little too much money for an eight year old?"

"Nah, not for my lil sis." Unique smiled.

"Go over there and get in the picture with them," Glory told Stacy when they returned to the living room.

"Here is your birthday money." Kim handed Stacy the money. She quickly counted it like she'd done it a million times in her eight years.

"One hundred is from me and the other is from Kim," Unique announced.

"Thank you," Stacy shouted excitedly, stretching her arms up towards Kim, giving her a kiss on the cheek, and then Unique.

"Come on Stacy, let's take the pictures," Glory pressed. "Say cheese," Glory said, then commenced to flicking away.

After chit chatting, Glory sat with Kim and Stacy on the living room sofa flipping through a thick photo album, while Unique sat at the edge of the tub in the bathroom talking on his cell phone.

"If I wanted to cop more than 20 pieces of fish from you, can I?"

"Nah, that's all I'm supposed to give you. No more, no less," Unique's drug connect, Ray, said on the other end of the phone.

"If I want more fish, who do I have to talk to?"

"Your peeps. He's the one who put a budget on you."

Unique knew he was referring to Dad. "Okay, so I'll see you tomorrow."

"Yeah, same time same place."

Sliding his phone into his pocket, Unique went back into the living room.

"I like this picture of you with your Michael Jackson leather jacket and shiny gloves on.  You look so cute," Kim said, looking up from the photo album at Unique who stood next to the front door.

"Sorry to break y'all lil thing up, but we're on our way out.  Come on Kim."

"Why y'all leavin' so faaast," Stacy whined as Kim rose from the sofa.

"We're goin' over my house," Unique replied, watching Kim sashay over towards him, but also watching Glory's eyes glued to Kim's ass. "Glory!" he snapped, breaking her concentration.

"Yeah."  She smiled at her brother, rising from the sofa.

"I'll see you later."

"Bye Stacy," Kim uttered.

"Bye."  Stacy waved from the sofa then flicked the TV on with the remote control she held.

"I want you to take me to that gym you go to," Glory said to Kim.

"I'll take you. I go at least eight times a month."

"OK. OK."  Unique opened the front door.  "We'll see ya later. Bye Stacy."  Unique shut the door behind himself and Kim.

"I really like your sisters.  They're cool.  They didn't treat me bad at all," Kim exclaimed as Unique pulled his Navigator from the curb.

"I'm glad you liked them."

"I didn't want to say this while we were there, but both of your sisters are beautiful.  And your sister Glory looks like...."

"I know.  CeCe Winans," Unique said.

"She must hear that all the time huh?"

Unique pulled up in front of his house and parked.

"You sure you don't wanna go out because you lookin' good.  I can go change and put on somethin' casual.  I won't be out dressed by you."

"No!"  Kim reached by her feet and grabbed her tote bag. "No, I just wanna be with you tonight."  She opened the door and stepped out of the truck.

After grabbing his bag of money from the glove compartment, Unique climbed out and led Kim to his house.

"Make yourself at home," Unique said to Kim when they entered his house.

"Cut some lights on in here," Kim said, standing in front of the front door.

"Find them if you want them on," Unique stated, grinning in the dark as he made his way up the stairs to put his money away.

"Unique where are you going?"

"I'm going to my room for a second. I'll be right back."

"Cut some lights on first. I don't wanna trip over anything and hurt myself."

Unique stopped at the top of the staircase and said, "Take two steps to your left. The switch is on the wall." He laughed, and then headed to his bedroom.

Kim hit the switch on the wall. She admired the soft looking black leather furniture that filled the room. She looked around for the TV that should have been where most people placed theirs. "No TV. Damn! You can tell he doesn't have a family of his own. Nobody lives here but him."

"Isn't this supposed to be your dining room?" Kim asked as Unique reappeared. "Where is your dining table?" Kim asked as she walked around his chromed-out pool table, smiling.

"Why you smilin'?" he asked.

"Because you have your TV in your dining room rather than in your living room... And your pool table is in your dining room."

"Nobody lives here but me."

Kim threw herself down on the beanbag.

"So you like this room huh?" Unique said, smiling down at Kim.

"Yeah, it's cool. I like it. I wonder what your bedroom looks like," she said.

Unique extended his hand down towards Kim, and pulled her up from the bag. "Let's go upstairs and see." Kim grabbed her tote bag from the pool table and followed him up to his bedroom.

"This is so beautiful..." Kim ran over to Unique's aquarium. "These are some beautiful fish. Cut the light off and let me see it in the dark."

Unique cut the room light off causing the tank to illuminate the room with a sapphire glow.

"Oh my God this is so beautiful Baby, and this tank is so big." Kim had her face inches from the tank.  She tapped on the glass to get the fish's attention.  "Hey little babies."

Unique had a big smile on his face.  "You like that, huh?"  He asked, walking up next to Kim.

"Yes, where did you get this idea to use a fish tank as your head-board?"

"Some movie I saw.  I forgot which one."

"Unique."  Kim stepped in front of him.  She grabbed both of his hands and held them in each of hers while staring up into his face.  "I wanna talk to you about something, but I don't wanna talk right here.  I wanna make us a hot bubble bath so we can relax."

"I don't have a problem with that," Unique said joyfully.

"You do have a bottle of bubble bath in your bathroom right?" Kim smiled, but behind her smile she was crying, because there was no doubt in her mind now that Unique was a drug dealer.  She would lose him one day, whether to the system or the streets, it didn't matter.  She would lose him unless he stopped his illegal activities.

"Yeah, I have a bottle in there," Unique replied.

Kim went to the bathroom and prepared their bath.  "Unique come on!" Kim yelled from the bathroom, after getting in the tub full of bubbles.  Bubbles covered her entire body up to her neck.

"Girl, you knew I was comin'.  I heard you callin' me all the way downstairs," Unique said as he walked into the bathroom, butt naked with two champagne glasses in one hand, and a bottle of "Sex on the Beach" in the other.

Kim smiled at the sight of Unique's naked body.  His penis swung back and forth with every step he took.  The muscle in his stomach formed a deeper visual of his six pack when he lifted his leg up to step into the tub.

Kim sat behind Unique with her legs straddled around his waist.  Their glasses sat on the rim of the tub that was filled to the brim.

"Unique," Kim murmured near his right ear.  His back was up against her 36 D's while his head rested on her shoulder.

"Yeah," he replied.

"I'm ready to talk to you about what's on my mind."

"Go 'head. I'm all ears."

"I don't want you to respond until I'm finished what I have to say."

"I'm listening," Unique said.

"Baby, I know you don't really work at your step Dad's shoe store. I believed you when you told me the drugs the police found weren't yours when you got locked up, but I believed you had a part in it. I now know that you are involved in selling drugs. You prove it to me every-day by the expensive clothes you wear, the truck you drive, the costly stuff you buy me, and now, the expensive things you have in your house. I want you to be truthful with me; I wanna hear it from your mouth. Are you a drug dealer?"

Unique could feel Kim's heart racing against his back. He wondered if he should be truthful or lie. He chose the truth.

"Yes," he answered.

"Unique how long have you been doing this?" Kim questioned in the voice of a concerned parent.

"About five years."

"And what are you waiting on to quit," she asked.

"I never really set a goal until tonight."

"And what's your goal?"

He thought for a second. "Five mill."

"Five million!" Kim barked.

"Yeah, five mill," he repeated.

"I'm not trying to be nosey, but how much do you have now? You don't have to tell me if you don't want to."

Unique thought about telling her, but changed his mind.

"I will tell you that it will be a while before I reach five mill."

"Unique baby," Kim wrapped her arms around his neck. Her hands slid up and down his chest. "I hope you understand the consequences of selling drugs…"

"Come on Kim. Of course I know."

"I know you understand some of it, but do you understand all the consequences?"

"Yeah, I don't see how I wouldn't."

"Unique, they are giving out serious time to young black men. Do you know that if you get caught with just 5 grams of crack, you can get a five year sentence? And if you get caught with 50 grams, you can get 10 years?"

"Yeah, I know that," Unique responded.

"So why are you takin' a chance like this?"

"'Cause I'm not the one sellin' it."

"That doesn't mean you can't go down for it," Kim snapped.

"I know," Unique replied by moving out of Kim's arms and standing. "Let's get out of this cold water and go into the room," he said. "You hungry?"

"Yeah, you gon' fix us something to eat." She rose up out of the water.

"The only thing I know how to make is fried chicken and french fries."

Kim smiled. "That's what I want then."

It was close to midnight when Kim and Unique landed in bed. They both were naked, resting on two fluffy pillows.

"Unique" Kim whispered.

"Yeah."

"Do you love me?"

Unique never expected her to ask him that until they were at least a year and a half into their relationship. He hadn't even asked himself if he loved her yet, and now he was being forced to answer something that he hadn't even considered. But he knew he had feelings for her that he'd never felt for any other woman.

"Yeah," he answered. "What about you?"

"What? Do I love you?"

"Hell yeah!"

"I've been loving you for a while now."

Kim rolled off her back and jumped on top of Unique. She sat on his stomach and held both of his wrists, holding his arms down. Slowly she bent down and kissed his lips. He kissed her back. She withdrew and stared into his face.

"Unique."

"Yeah?"

"I really do love you."

"I really love you too."

"I got something to tell you."

"Go 'head, tell me."

"I was sittin' in your truck and…"

He cut her off. "I know. You looked in my glove compartment and saw my bag of money." He grinned.

"How you know?"

"I didn't. I guessed."

"So I told on myself." She frowned.

"Yeah, but I like the fact that you was gon' tell me the truth." They were silent. They looked into each other's faces, barely blinking their eyes. Unique wiggled his wrist free from Kim's grip and reached behind her head to undo the hair pin holding her ponytail. When the pin was removed, her hair fell on each side of her face.

"I love your long hair," he said, taking his hands and brushing her hair back behind each of her earlobes.

"Unique," Kim whispered her voice cracking. "You are only the second man I've been with in my entire life." Her voice started cracking more. "And I…I…I don't want to lose you." Tears rolled down her cheeks and off her face only to land on Unique. He let her tears fall on his face without wiping them off. He was somewhat stunned by her overflow of emotions.

"Don't cry," he whispered, wiping her face with his hands.

"I…I don't wanna lose you Unique. I don't wanna be alone again."

"You won't. I promise."

"Then tell me you'll quit sellin' drugs as soon as you reach your goal."

"I will. I promise you."

"And if you see any sign of danger before you reach your goal, tell me you'll stop before somethin' bad happens."

"I will."

She bent down and kissed him.  He kissed her with the same intensity she used.  She made her way down to his neck, then to his chest, planting soft kisses along the way.  On his chest, she licked and sucked both of his nipples while her right hand clenched his rock-hard dick. She made her way down to his stomach, stopping only for a second, before reaching her intended target.

"Oooooh shit!" Unique sighed, his hands clenching the sheets.  He lifted his head from the pillow in an attempt to witness the great sensation he felt on his dick.  "Damn!" he mumbled.  Because Kim's head was covered by the sheets, he couldn't witness his dick being assaulted.

Early the next morning, Unique was awakened by the sound of at least three or four different voices.  He rolled out of his bed and ran to his window.  There he saw four people jumping into a black BMW. Two little girls and two grown women, and one of the women was Kim. He smiled. He knew what just happened.  Glory, Stacy, and his little cousin Kelly decided to drop by and pick Kim up so she could go with them to the amusement park.

Unique walked away from the window and went into his bathroom to take a shower.  After showering, he got dressed and called Supreme.

"What's up nigga?  You up?" Unique said once Supreme answered his phone.

"Yeah, I'm up.  I went to bed early last night." He lied; he was out most of the night preying on his next victim.

"I'm on my way over."

"Bet"

When Unique pulled up in front of Supreme's building, Supreme was standing out by his Lexus.

"What's up, Son?  Where we goin'?" Supreme asked, climbing into the truck.

"First, we stoppin' at the I-Hop, then we goin' to pick up my order."

"All right.  I'm hungry anyway."

After they ate at I-Hop, they got on the highway and headed to Arlington, Virginia.  There Unique pulled into a huge car lot.

"You gon' trade this joint in?" Supreme asked.

Unique gave him a wicked smile. "You'll see."

Unique pulled up in front of the car lot's business office. As soon as he killed the truck's engine, an Italian looking, short, chubby guy walked out of the business office. He had a big smile on his face and his hands were in the air as if he was reaching for the sky.

"Hey buddy, how are you feelin' on this beautiful Saturday Morning?" the Italian guy said to Unique the moment Unique stepped out of the Navigator. When he reached Unique, he patted him on both shoulders with his pudgy hands while standing in front of him.

"What's up Tony?" Unique said with a smile.

"You, buddy. Let me tell you now. You're gonna fuckin' love her. She so fuckin, beautiful, you might want to literally pull your dick out and fuck her up the gas tank." Tony dropped his hands from Unique's shoulders and chuckled at his own joke.

"Let me see her then." Unique ordered. He looked at Supreme who stood next to him. "You didn't leave nothin' in the truck did 'cha?"

"Nah, why? What's up ?"

Unique took the Navigator keys off his key ring and passed them to Tony.

"Yeah, you won't need these keys after you see her. Follow me," Tony said as he led the way through the car lot.

"There she is. A Benz CL 500. Ain't she a beauty? You've got the newest model. She's all yours." He tossed Unique the keys.

"She loaded with everything I ordered right?" Unique inquired, walking up to the car with Supreme a step behind him.

"Yep. Even the customized exhaust system you wanted that we had hell finding."

"Son, this is hot!" Supreme exclaimed, checking the exterior of the Benz out. "I see you got those 20 inch Lorinser LM5 rims dipped in chrome."

"Yeah. I gotta have the works on my shit if I'ma cop it," Unique replied, smiling from ear to ear while sticking his key into the door. "Let's see what's inside this joint'."

The interior of the Benz was even more mesmerizing. Java leather with chestnut wood throughout. Navigation system, climate control, two 6.8 inch monitors mounted in the headrest operated by a Sony portable DVD player, and a CD player.

"I 'on know, Son, this car might bring a lot of heat on you.  Being that you jive low key with your shit," Supreme stated, sitting in the passenger seat.

"I'ma try not to let that happen.  That's why I'm buyin' a red Ford Mustang to take some of that heat off me.  I'ma drive this only when I'm chillin' with my girl or out at a club and shit like that.  But I'm a push the Mustang when I'm going around hoods and going to cop my coke."

"So when you gon' cop the Mustang?"

"Right now.  That's why I needed you to come along.  You gon' drive the Mustang to my crib."

As soon as Unique said that, Tony pulled in front of the Benz with a red Mustang.

"Go 'head, Joe.  Push that joint home for me."

Supreme stepped out the Benz and walked to the Mustang.  Tony handed him the keys and he hopped into the car.

"So," Tony exclaimed.  He was standing beside the  Benz.  "Is everything straight?"

"Yeah Tony…" Unique stuck his arm out the window for a handshake.  "Everything's straight."

Tony shook Unique's hand.  "Everything's in both glove compartments.  All the paperwork is straight on both cars.  You bring some of your friends by so I can do business with them, OK?  Tell them if they fuck with me, they fuckin' with the best…" Tony stepped back from the car.

Unique signaled Supreme to pull off.  He pulled off tailing behind the Mustang.  When they made it out of the lot and onto the street, Unique took the lead heading back to D.C.  He turned his radio on and grinned as he leaned low in the butter soft leather seat.  Suddenly, he could hear Dad's voice, causing his grin to fade.  '*Never drive the same car when you're not livin' right.*'  Unique thought to himself, "I'm not driving the same car.  I'm pushing two cars.  A Benz and a Mustang."  He turned the music up full blast, rocking his head back and forth.

# TWELVE

All the lights were off throughout the two story brick house. Not a sound could be heard. Then abruptly, the voice of a man whispering sliced through the peacefulness.

"How long you been followin' me?"

"What 'cha mean?"

"You know what I mean," Supreme said.

"No I don't, nigga."

"How many times have you followed me while I've been layin' on this nigga?"

"Let me break it down to you. One day about two weeks ago, I was just chillin' by myself and I saw you pullin' out a laundromat parking lot behind a SUV. I was already wondering how you was really livin, when you wasn't with Unique, so I followed you. About ten minutes into following you I put two and two together and came up with you was preyin' on the nigga. After that day, I just waited until yesterday to approach you about it. So, in reality, I only followed you that day."

"So when you approached me, you didn't really know I was robbin' the nigga, you just pretended like you knew."

"Yeah…. I was hopin' I convinced you to believe that I was hip to you so I could get a piece of the action. You fell for it and admitted you was gon' rob the nigga.   So, here I am, with you getting' ready to rob a nigga."

"You ran big game on me nigga.  I ain't mad though.  I like your lil crazy ass."

Supreme and Wop sat beside each other on the dark green sofa in the living room of the man they waited for.  They both wore all black with guns lying across their laps.  The smell of marijuana lingered in the air from the blunt Wop smoked before they entered the house through an opened window.

"Why you robbin' niggas when you gettin' paid by that nigga Unique? I know he hittin' you off.  You his bodyguard right?" Wop asked.

"Somewhat.  But I love robbin' niggas.  It's in my blood.  It don't matter how much money I'm getting', I'ma still be a stick-up kid."

"You was robbin niggas in New York?"

"Yeah," Supreme boasted.  "We 'boutta rob a nigga, and you need to be on full alert."

"I got this…I got this Slim," Wop assured.

"I hope so Kid, because this nigga is unpredictable.  While I was layin' on him, I seen him pistol whip one of his runners."

"I 'on give a fuck about that shit.  When we get the draw on him, ain't shit he…."

"Shhhhh!" Supreme said in a low tone, "Somebody on the porch. It's him."

They both leaped from the sofa and ran behind it, crouching down on one knee with guns in hand.

"Don't jump until he cut the lights on," Supreme said in a whisper. Then he slid the black bandana he wore around his neck, up over his mouth and nose.  Seeing that, Wop did the same thing with the black bandanna he wore.

"Girl, I'm gonna fuck you until your pussy dry," the man said as he entered his house with his female companion clinging to his right arm.

"That's what I want you to do," the woman replied.

"I am, don't worry."

"Cut some lights on 'cause I want you to see your treat."

"Nah, let's go upstairs to my bedroom." The couple headed upstairs never seeing or hearing the two men that hid behind the sofa.

"This gon' be sweeter than I planned," Supreme whispered to Wop. They both stood up. "This lame ass nigga gon' get caught with his pants down."

"Pussy will do that every time," Wop stated, grinning under the bandanna.

Slowly, they crept upstairs with their guns out. When they reached the top step, the sound of a screaming woman and a headboard banging against the wall could be heard. Supreme stood in front of the closed bedroom door with Wop behind him. He placed his hand on the doorknob and turned it gradually. Behind him he could hear the sound of Wop snickering.

"Shhh!" Supreme glanced over his shoulder at his accomplice.

"Nigga, don't move!" the two stick-up kids yelled in unison, bursting into the bedroom, with their guns pointing at the couple.

The man Supreme had been laying on was on his knees on the bed with his dick still in the woman he was fucking doggy style. The couple was as stiff as a statue. They literally froze in their position the moment Supreme and Wop burst into the room. Wop took it upon himself to walk over to the bed and grab the man from behind in a choke hold with one arm around his neck, pulling him off the bed and onto the floor.

"Don't move nigga!" Wop ordered the man while aiming his gun down at him. "Turn around and lay on ya stomach." Immediately the man did what he was told and Wop reached into his jeans pocket and retrieved a two foot long piece of rope. He passed his gun off to Supreme then bent down and tied the man's hands together behind his back.

Wop left the man on the floor with his hands tied behind his back and stepped over next to the woman. "Oh shit! This bitch got a dick! This nigga fuckin' a nigga!" He laughed as loud as he could.

Both men sat at the foot of the bed beside each other with their hands tied behind their backs. Supreme and Wop stood in front of the naked men.

"Where is the money? And I'm only askin' you one time," Supreme told the man he stood in front of.

"In the basement under the brown sofa," the man answered.

"That nigga said that too fast," Wop snapped. "Something ain't right."

"I ain't tryin' to pull nothin','' the man said, shaking nervously.

"How much bread down there?" Supreme inquired.

"Two hundred thousand."

Wop, Supreme and the he / she looked at the man as if he was lying.

"What's up man? I ain't lyin'."

Supreme stuck his gun against the man's forehead. "Don't lie nigga or you might make the morning paper."

"I ain't. Just go get it!"

"Go 'head down there and I'll keep my eyes on them," Wop told Supreme. "Give me your gun. I might need both of 'em if these niggas try somethin'."

Supreme handed Wop his gun. "If I don't come back up here in five minutes, somethin' ain't right, so shoot both of 'em."

"I got 'cha, Joe." Wop watched Supreme walk out of the bedroom.

In the basement, Supreme stooped in front of the brown sofa in motion to flip it over. He got a good grip on it and easily toppled it. There, in plain view, two black gym bags sat beside each other. He got down on his right knee and unzipped both bags. They were filled with money. After zipping both bags back up, Supreme was shocked to see Wop standing over him.

"Hey Supreme, do you know a dude named Ben?" Wop asked.

"Nah, nigga. Why you askin' me about some nigga at a time like this?"

Wop snatched the bandanna from his face and began grinning. "You sure you 'on know a dude from Brooklyn, New York named Ben?"

"Nah" Supreme snapped, gazing at Wop coldly. "Get back upstairs!"

"Well, let me refresh ya memory. You robbed him and his connect in a restaurant in Flatbush." Wop took two steps back and raised both guns, pointing them at Supreme. "I got family in New York; and Ben is my uncle."

Supreme smiled nervously because he now knew exactly who Wop was talking about. "Come on Wop, stop playin' and let's get the fuck outta here. Stop pointin' those guns at me, Son."

"Nigga, this ain't no game. You 'boutta die," Wop said coldly.

"Come on Wop and stop playin'."

Wop fired the gun! "Ahhhhh! Mothafucka! You hit me in my leg!" Supreme yelled, stumbling backwards and falling to the floor. He squeezed his right leg with both hands, trying to relieve some of the pain.

Wop stepped over to Supreme and stood above him with both guns aiming down at his head.

"That nigga Unique said you was gon' be trouble one day," Supreme said, biting down on his bottom lip, gazing up at the two holes in the barrels of the guns.

"Nigga beg for ya life," Wop exclaimed, grinning from ear to ear.

Supreme shook his head no.

"I'ma punish that hole between Glory's legs while you gone." Wop laughed a wicked laugh then fired away.

POP! POP! BOOM! BOOOOOOM!

The sound of the TV awoke Supreme from his horrible dream. Supreme slouched into his sofa and pondered his dream wondering about Wop and if he really had family in the Big Apple. He wondered if he was following him while he laid on his next victim.

**The following Sunday around 3:30 pm, Supreme, Unique, PooBear,** Wop, Darkman, and Brother Hetep Muhammad all stood around a green wooden park bench off to the side of the basketball court where they'd just finished playing. They all had plastic soft drink bottles in their hands gulping away. Men still played ball on the court in the background while yelling spectators of mixed gender cheered them on at Anacostia Park.

"Brother Hetep. I think you lyin' about 'cha age. Ain't no way you can be scorin' the way you do at the age of 40." Unique said standing beside Hetep.

"Matter of fact brother, I'm 41. My birthday just passed a week ago."

"Hetep wanna brag now y'all," Supreme uttered.

"I'll be right back. I gotta run to my car for a second," Unique announced.

Unique left the huddle and walked to his Benz.  Opening the door, he grabbed his cell phone and dialed his connect.

"Yeah, yeah who dis."

"Unique."

"Man, I'm glad you called me before you came to the spot, cause we can't do that today."

"Why?  What's up Ray?"

"Everything is cool, but I'm gonna have to hit you tomorrow."

"Yeah," Unique murmured, kind of disappointed because it had been three days since his workers had finished their last twenty kilos.

"Man, my girl just had a lil boy, and I need to be with her and the baby all day. Just a few months ago, my girl almost lost our baby when some bamma ass nigga…., let me get off this phone. I get upset just thinkin' about that nigga," Ray griped.

"Congratulations, Dawg.  I didn't know that was your reason.  I can definitely wait till tomorrow for that."

Unique ended his call and walked back over to the huddle.

"I'm not saying you all are drug dealers, but if you are, what I'm about to say applies to you.  Now the economy is weak, and jobs are being lost, which means crack heads don't have as much money," Hetep lectured.

"Man crack heads always gon' find a way to get money.  That's their job when they on that shit," Wop said.

"Yeah, he right," PooBear agreed, grinning.  "Anyway Brotha Hetep, let me ask you something."

"Go ahead, brother."

"Me, Wop, and my man Darkman only been knowing you for three months now, but how long have you been usin' all those big words?  And why you always usin' them?  Talk ghetto sometimes, Dawg?"

Hetep shook his head but smiled while doing so. "First of all brother, I'm not using big words.  They're just words you're not accustomed to.  Secondly, I've been using what you consider big words ever since I was in the belly of the beast from 1984 till 1989."

"You was locked up?"  Darkman asked.  They looked at Hetep, anticipating his reply.

"Yes brother, for 5 long years in a Federal Pen. And that's where I learned most of what I know today."

"You own three buildings right?" Darkman asked.

"Yes I do, and on the inside is where I learned about real estate. So, when I got out, I applied that information and now I own 3 buildings in DC and one in Maryland. And to finish answering your question PooBear…" Hetep swung his eyes towards the young man. "The reason I use what you call big words is because these words are a part of me now. I couldn't stop if I tried."

"What 'cha was in for?" Unique inquired.

"Bank robbery."

"Damn Son, you don't look nothin' like a nigga that used to rob shit," Supreme said, immediately feeling a sense of connection towards the short, slim, intelligent man.

"Brother Supreme, if you would've seen me back then, you wouldn't have made the statement you just made."

"Brotha Hetep, how come you play ball with a couple of thugs and not with your Muslim brothas?" Wop quizzed.

Hetep smiled a broad smile. "To be honest with you brother, I'm hoping I could somehow convince at least one of you brothers to come try Islam. That's one of the reasons why I ball with y'all. And my other reason is I like being around young men. It keeps me in tune my Muslim brothers. Now, which one of you would like to at least go one time with me to Mohammad Mosque number 4 next Sunday and hear the life giving teachings of the most Honorable Elijah Muhammad?"

The huddle of young men was quiet. Everybody cut their eyes at each other, waiting to see who would speak up first.

"Yeah, I'll go. Just to quench my curiosity," Darkman said, grinning and shaking his head.

"I'ma go check it out too," Supreme said.

"I'll let 'cha know this week if I'll go," Unique exclaimed. "But, if you don't hear from me, that means I won't be goin'. Oh yeah, if I do decide to go, I'm bringin' my girl along with me."

"That's even better brother, bringing the sista along," Hetep uttered,

smiling as usual. "Supreme, see if you can bring Glory along with you."
Hetep placed his attention on PooBear and Wop who looked at each
other.

"Nah, I'ma chill," PooBear said while keeping his eyes off Hetep.

"Yeah me too," Wop quickly spat..

"Maybe next time then," Hetep stated, giving both young men a
shame on you stare.

After talking for another ten minutes or so, they all walked over to
their cars.  Supreme, who was riding with Unique, stopped Wop who
was about to step into his new red Acura.

"Son, let me ask you somethin'?"

"What's up, Joe?" Wop stared at Supreme strangely.

Supreme looked down at Wop, first thinking of how he could ask
him what he wanted without him becoming suspicious in any way. *Then
he thought, there's no other way to ask but directly.*

"Son, you have any family in New York?"

"Naw, not that I know of.  Why you ask me that?"

"Nah, I just asked that's all."  Supreme walked off without saying
another word and stepped into Unique's Benz.

"What's up?  You gon' really go to the Mosque next Sunday?"
Unique quizzed Supreme the moment he slid into his Benz passenger
seat.

"Yeah. It won't hurt to try it. *What's the worst thing that could
happen?"*

## Intermission

Several months had passed. Supreme had no problems with Wop and Darkman. Although, it wasn't always that way with PooBear. They got along better now than they did months ago. No longer was PooBear assaulting him verbally as he once was. Now he talked to Supreme like he would anyone else. Still Supreme seemed to get along better with Wop and Darkman. Why? He didn't know. Maybe there was still some form of animosity between them. He couldn't put his hand on what it was. If his hunch was correct, it would have something to do with Glory. Supreme saw how PooBear looked at her when he was in her presence. He couldn't blame PooBear. What man in his right mind wouldn't want Glory? She's a dime. But she definitely wasn't worth losing your life over, *even if love was in the air.* Supreme concentrated more on spending money and enjoying his new Navigator and 300zx. He felt that trading in the Lexus was appropriate since he was getting a new condo.

### Unique's life had changed over the past months.

His outlook on things changed. He became arrogant, flamboyant, and power struck with every accumulating dime he made. No longer was his goal to stay low-key. He didn't really care anymore if he was anonymous or not. Although he never stood and shouted it out, his actions spoke for him.

Unique had abandoned his goal of reaching five million and getting out of the game. He had no intention of forgoing his current life style now that he felt he was the man. He had 2.5 million between his stash apartment and his bank Money Market Account. The only reason he didn't have more money was because of the three bedroom house he bought, and the silver CLK Benz he copped for Kim.

Another thing about Unique also changed. His short commitment as far as being content with just having sex with Kim was gone. He was back to fucking other women without thinking twice. It wasn't that Kim didn't satisfy him, because she did in every way. It was just that his weakness for women overpowered his judgment.

Unique did one smart thing the last few months. He gave Glory a set of keys to his stash apartment, and told her where it was located. If anything should happen to him, everything in the apartment would be hers. He even told her where his money was located.

Glory's life didn't change much. The only significant thing that changed for her was her attachment and love for Supreme. In her mind, she owned him. He was all hers, and if anyone stood in the way of that, she would do whatever she had to do to correct it. Glory still hadn't enrolled in college like she said she would. Instead, she put most of her energy into dancing for the sugar daddies. She had a website built that went by the name of Booty and Body.com to promote her and Pam's new lucrative business. They only danced on weekends when they were off from work from the ice cream parlor. Sometimes, maybe once or twice each week, they would dance for men privately, but they charged twice as much. On their website, were pictures of Glory and Pam, with different outfits on, striking various erotic dancing poses. They even went as far as kissing and fondling each other in some pictures, causing their site to attract lesbians.

Kim's life definitely changed. Her new man was on the opposite side of the law from her ex-husband. So she thought. She now was the girlfriend of a drug dealer instead of a cop. Even though she always dressed nice in the past, now she wore expensive clothes and drove an expensive car because of her new man.

Kim no longer lived in the house she once shared with her ex-husband. She had moved in with Unique at his house in Fort Washington, Maryland; and Unique somehow convinced her to quit her job at the jail and go back to driving Metro buses.

Kim was madly in love with Unique, so much that she would do anything to secure their togetherness. She longed for no other man but him. She hit the gym more in order to make sure her body stayed looking young so Unique wouldn't have an excuse for wanting to leave her.

**Darkman's life had two faces.  He attended the** University of D.C. in the morning, but transformed into a dealer in the evening.  He also attended Muslim services with Brother Hetep often, but not all the time. Darkman bought himself a one year old BMW sports wagon.  He had an apartment in Landover, Maryland where LaLa came to visit.  He had a stash of about $300,000.  He planned on getting out the game as soon as he reached $600,000.  He figured that would be sufficient for him to live off of until after getting his degree.  But for now, he'd drive his smoked gray BMW with a smile and stay in the game a little while longer.

# THIRTEEN

Supreme stepped out of the Southeast barber shop with Unique one foot behind him. The sun light glowed directly on the iced-out platinum chains that hung from both of their necks. They strolled to Unique's Mustang catching the attention of many eyes. Unbothered, Unique started his car en route to his old neighborhood.

People were standing on both sides of the street when the Mustang arrived on the block. Unique watched carefully as crack heads eyeballed his car as he looked around for a parking space.

"This strip is gettin' stronger and stronger. Supreme reach in the glove compartment and hand me that bag," Unique said.

Supreme handed him the small brown paper bag, but before they could exit the car, PeeWee walked up to the driver's window.

"Damn, Slim. You took 30 minutes, but I'm glad you did, cause these crack heads out here bittin'," PeeWee said, grinning.

"You got that on you Slim?" Unique asked.

"Yeah." PeeWee reached into his pocket and pulled out a lump of money. He passed it to Unique through the window.

"This 10 g's right?"

"It always is," PeeWee replied, accepting the brown paper bag. "I don't mean it to be rude, but I gotta go cut this shit up," he said anxious to leave.

Unique smiled. "Be careful out here."

"I am, Joe." PeeWee assured by a nod of his head while backing away from the car.

Other than PooBear, Wop, and Darkman, Pee Wee was the only other person who Unique dealt with. He had given Pee Wee his word months ago that he'd hit him off with a half kilo once his supply was pumping again. Unique vowed to keep his word. He watched Pee Wee's chubby body strut momentarily until his cell phone rang.

"Yeah what's up?" Unique answered.

"This Darkman, I'm out here waitin' on you to come pick that up."

"I'm on my way now. Where them two young crazy niggas?"

"I 'on know. They left about ten minutes ago, and ain't come back yet, but I got that."

"Bet. I'll see you in fifteen minutes or so."

Unique placed his phone on his hip, then glanced out his rear-view mirror. "I 'on think I'm lunchin', but I think it's a black jeep followin' us."

Supreme looked out of his side view mirror. "Son, that's the jeep them cops was in. It's a Jeep Cherokee."

"Slim, it's up to you. What 'cha wanna do. If they try to pull us over, I can either pull over or lose them," Unique said.

"Yeah, cause I ain't really try'na catch no gun charge," Supreme said nervously.

"Slim, you think them mothafuckers watched me give PeeWee that shit?" Unique quizzed, still watching the jeep from his rear-view-mirror.

"I 'on know. Did you see them before you turned off the block?"

"Nah…Slim. It's only one nigga in that jeep," Unique announced. "And he's a Black dude for sure. Don't no cracka lean in his whip like that," Unique said.

When Unique stopped at the light, the jeep pulled up beside them. The bald headed cop smiled at Unique then lifted up a piece of paper with several numbers written on it. Unique read the numbers which were his tag numbers.

"Yeah, that's that cop that pulled that gun out on me," Supreme said, leaning towards Unique to catch a glimpse of the cop.

Unique and the cop locked eyes. Unique's mind searched through its data base of faces and stopped at a man posing in a police uniform. Strangely, he still couldn't place how they'd met. Supreme patted his employer's arm, signaling him to pull off. The cop made a left while Unique kept straight ahead.

"I swear I know that man," Unique uttered, staring straight out the Mustang's front windshield as if he was in a trance.

"That nigga's name just came back to me. They call him Jay the Snake," Supreme exclaimed.

Unique quickly snapped out of his trance and looked at Supreme. "Jay, Jay, Jay," he repeated, trying to register the name with the face he just saw moments ago. "Damn!" He sighed. "I can't pen point that nigga, but I know him. Why the fuck did he write my tag number down?"

Supreme snapped. "He pulled a gun out on me and folks say he be takin' coke from people and goin' to other blocks sellin' the shit!" Supreme pulled his 44 Desert Eagle from his waist. He gripped it tightly in his right hand and shook it. "Yeah, I 'on know what the nigga up to, but they say he be doin' some dirty shit to be a cop. I would like to put some of these life takers in that nigga and treat him like a street thug instead of a cop." As soon as the word left his lips, Supreme immediately knew something in his mind had changed. Ten months ago, he would never have made a statement like the one he just made. He never thought about taking a cop out. It didn't matter if the cop was good or bad. But now he did. He had become vicious. *Willing to kill.*

Unique pulled onto PooBear, Wop and Darkman's block which was packed with people, but not as packed as the one he'd just left. Unique parked directly behind Darkman's BMW. Supreme looked over at Unique as he killed the Mustang's engine. Unique ran his hands over his head. "I gotta keep my shit tight for the bitches."

Supreme blew air from his mouth, making a hissing sound. "Nigga, please. You just really started fuckin' other bitches. Kim had you on a chain for a while."

"Nigga you got a nerve," Unique snapped, grinning. "You ain't fuck no other broads but my sista and Pam since you been in D.C. She don't count, 'cause that bitch a freak, plus you fucked her in my sista's presence which she allowed." Unique laughed while opening the door to step out into the pleasant afternoon weather.

"Yo, what's up Darkman?" Supreme asked when he and Unique approached the sidewalk where Darkman and two, once beautiful, crack head women stood in front of a bay brick building.

"What's up, Joe?" Darkman and Supreme shook hands and then bumped shoulders.

"What's up nigga?" Unique shook hands then bumped shoulders with Darkman. "Those crazy niggas ain't get back yet?"

"Naw," Darkman said.

A crack head woman grunted to get the men's attention.

"Oh yeah!" Darkman said, trying to keep from laughing out. "These ladies didn't believe me when I told them I don't have no more crack."

Unique looked the two decently dressed women over. "Yeah, he ain't got no more shit."

The dark and short one of the two women pouted, then stomped her feet. "Damn!" she stormed off, leaving her friend. She walked up the block toward another group of men.

"Yo, what's up with your friend?" Supreme asked the woman that still stood amongst them.

"Man." The lady shook her head and poked her bottom lip out. "She was looking forward to gettin' somethin' from Darkman or Wop today." The lady stepped off to catch up with her friend who had already copped from the men up the block and was walking off.

"Damn Son, y'all got 'em like that," Supreme stated, grinning at Darkman.

"Yeah, I guess so. We have the best product out here," Darkman replied.

"Yeah, that's why we don't have no more shit now," Unique uttered. "Listen; tell the fellas y'all off until next Monday. I'm not gonna re-up until next Sunday. Have fun for a week," Unique said cheerfully.

**Unique and his crew parked their bikes side by** side in a row in the parking lot of D.C. Live. Before they could slide their helmets off good, three classy, yet ghetto fabulous women stepped in front of their bikes.

"Oooh! These are some pretty bikes," the older woman of the group said. She stepped over toward PooBear's bike. "This my favorite color," she stated showing her interest in PooBear.

"Every last one of you all are fine," another attractive woman uttered. " Don't leave these bikes out here while you all go in that club."

"We ain't going in. We just chillin'," Unique said.

The woman snickered then replied, "in other words, you came out here looking for some pussy."

Unique looked around at his crew with a smirk on his face before responding. "To be honest with you no, but if we come across some, we ain't gon' pass it up."

"What if we said we're lookin' for some dick?" the Hispanic woman boldly said.

"So we want some pussy and y'all want some dick," Unique expressed. "That makes us compatible then."

"Yeah, but it's only three of us and five of you all."

"Yeah, but if y'all want some dick bad enough, five dicks should be plenty," Wop said, grinning.

"So, you all wanna run a train on us?"

All five men looked at each other smiling.

"Hell, yeah!" Wop snapped.

"So, that means y'all are willing to push out some money?"

"Money ain't nothin' but a word," Unique quickly replied, arrogantly.

"What are your names?" Darkman finally spoke.

"Lisa," one woman said.

"Mya," another woman said.

"Kita," the older woman said, keeping an eye on PooBear.

Mya stepped over to Darkman and gazed into his face. She was the tallest of the three women. "Ooooh. You have some pretty eyes. I have never seen a dude as dark as you with light gray eyes."

"I like 'em," Kita exclaimed, smiling. "Those are real, right?" She was directly in Darkman's face staring into his eyes.

"Yeah,"Darkman responded.

"What's up?" Unique spoke. "We'll give y'all a 'g' each if you let us run a train."

Mya, walked from in front of Darkman's bike and over to Unique. "You sound like you the man," she whispered near Unique's ear, makin' sure not to be heard by his crew.

"Yeah, I am the man," Unique replied.

"We with it, but don't try to run no game on us and try to fake on the money. If you all are real niggas that's ballin', pay us before we get inside the hotel room. We are going to a real hotel, right?"

"Yeah, but we choosin' which one." Unique smiled.

"You're not on no bullshit are you?" Mya asked, giving Unique a cold stare.

"Like I told y'all, money ain't nothin', but a word."

"So, you want us to follow y'all?"

"Yeah, but hold on for a second. How you know your girls with it?"

"If I'm with it, they're with it." Mya spun on her high heeled sandals and stepped over to her friends. She pulled them to the side, away from Wop who stood next to Darkman's bike.

"What's up Mya? What were you over there talkin' to that fine ass nigga about?" Kita quizzed.

"Forget all that girl. Them niggas gon' pay us a thousand dollars each just for some pussy," Mya said excitedly.

"Them niggas gotta be ballin'," Lisa said.

"They are," Kita stated.

"What the fuck y'all doin' over there? Plottin' on us or somethin'?" PooBear barked.

The women broke their huddle up and Mya walked back over to Unique. "Y'all ready?" she asked.

"Yeah," Unique replied, placing his helmet on his head, and starting his bike. At that point none of the fellas realized what a wonderful night was in store for them.

**For the remaining seven days off from their nor-**mal operations, they did nothing but have fun and splurge. From clubbing to bike riding, each day was an adventure. From Ocean City to Virginia Beach, and wherever they visited, they attracted women who were down for whatever.

One morning, as soon as all the bikes were started, a black car pulled in front of them, blocking at least three of the bikes from pulling off. Without hesitating, Supreme swiftly snatched his gun from his waist and flaunted it while sitting on his bike. Just before his brain sent the signal to his trigger finger to fire away, a high pitched voice rang out.

"No! No! I know who that is!" PooBear waved his arm to signal Supreme to put his gun away. He cut his engine, kicked down the stand, then stepped off his bike and walked over to the passenger side of the car.

"Get in," the driver of the Jetta shouted at PooBear through the window!

PooBear looked over his shoulder at the four young men on the bikes. "Give me a couple of minutes." He opened the car passenger door and stepped in.

"What's up? I know you read my messages on your two-way," Mrs. Peaches said with a light smile on her face.

"Yeah, I did, but I told you I was gon' chill with my dawgs this week."

"I know, but I wanted to see you," Peaches said in a soft, whining tone. "I kind of missed you Bear." She poked her bottom lip out.

"I missed you too. By Monday, everything will be back to normal." PooBear gazed at the attractive 41 year old woman.

"I'll call you later," he said sensing the peer pressure behind him.

Peaches gave PooBear a seductive stare. "You ain't had none of this in a week and a half and you mean to tell me you don't want none right now. I know you want it. It misses you."

A smile mounted upon PooBear's face. "Damn! You right, I do want some."

"Then tell your boys you will see them later," Peaches said coaching him.

PooBear looked out the window at his boys, then at Peaches whose hand was now on his crotch.

"If you can't make up your mind, I can make it up for you by pulling off in my new car and we head to a hotel. My treat."

"This your car?"

"Yeah. I just bought it yesterday with some of the money you've been giving me. I can do what I wanna do now. You should have seen my husband's face when he saw me in this car. I told him you bought it for me, something he couldn't afford."

"Why you hurt that man's man-hood like that?" PooBear smiled.

"Fuck him! He can't do nothin' for me but eat my pussy. "

"Park the car while I go holla at my dawgs," PooBear said. Once again age paid off for Ms. Peaches. As usual, experience combined with manipulation would always get just what she wanted from PooBear.

# FOURTEEN

Supreme sat in his black 300zx a block from a basketball court in Northeast, where his next victim played ball. He surveyed the entire court, including the players and the spectators. He thought deeply about the Double Life he was now leading. He hated not being able to tell the truth about his occupation. However, he prided himself on not being discovered by the fellas, especially Unique. Being a stick-up kid was going well and was extremely profitable. At this point, if anyone tried to blow his cover, that person would have to be dealt with quick. He didn't want to re-locate to another city, but if necessesary, he would leave without notification. That meant leaving the woman he loved behind. Supreme tried not to give Glory all of his love in case he had to flee. That was his excuse for participating in the orgy with the three women his crew met at D.C. Live. He had to get used to having sex with other women in order to shake off some of that magnetic attraction he had for Glory. What he didn't know was that Lisa, one of the women from the orgy now wanted a special place in his heart too.

The sound of Supreme's cell phone ringing broke into his thoughts. He snatched the phone from his hip. "Yeah."

"How you doin' New York?" a soft voice murmured through the receiver.

"What's up Lisa?"

"How you know it was me?"

"Don't too many people have my cell number."

"Oh. What 'cha doin'?"

"Shit, right now. But later on tonight, I'm goin' over my dawg's house to watch the fight."

"Damn! So ain't no chance we can get together tonight huh?" Lisa inquired.

"Nah, not tonight, but tomorrow is good Ma." Supreme said.

"Okay, I'll catch you tomorrow."

"No doubt, Ma."

Supreme had made it his business to slide Lisa his cell number when they departed from the hotel room that night after the orgy. Lisa made it very clear that she wanted to keep in touch. Supreme placed his stick shift in first gear, and smoothly pulled off. Within seconds, the black sports car was cruising pass the crowded basketball court unnoticed.

Supreme was approaching the high rise parking lot where he secretly stashed his car used for capers. His cell rang.

"Yeah." he answered.

"What's up baaaabyyy?" Glory sang on the other end.

Supreme smiled, "What's up Ma?"

"You, what's up?"

"Yeah. Why you never told me your brotha had a swimmin' pool at his crib?"

"Boy you never asked."

"So, his house big?"

"Hell yeah. It's big for only two people. I told Kim she better have some kids to fill up the house." Glory chuckled.

"So, you bringin' some women with you?" Supreme asked.

"Yeah, Pam and two other broads who work with us at the ice cream shop. I'm on my way over to pick them up now. We going to my brotha's house early to help Kim out with some of the food."

"I'll see you there Ma." Supreme ended.

Supreme parked his car, stepped out, looked around, and locked up.

Walking to his Navigator, he studied the area. After successfully not being seen, he headed to meet the fellas.

Twenty minutes later, he was pulling up in front of PooBear's house. Seeing that nobody was outside, he parked his Navigator directly behind PooBear's Escalade. The second he did, he saw PooBear emerge from his house with Mrs. Peaches a step behind him. Both of them had healthy smiles plastered on their faces. Supreme watched as they hugged and kissed on the porch until Mrs. Peaches headed towards her car.

Seeing PooBear now standing on his porch alone, Supreme stepped out of his truck and walked up to the house.

"You the first one to make it here. Ain't none of them niggas show up yet?" PooBear said grinning.

"That shit must've been good Son, 'cause you been smilin' since you stepped outside," Supreme said.

PooBear laughed.

"I'm curious, Kid, why haven't you moved out of this house?" Supreme asked.

"Why should I?"

"Don't you have enough money?" Supreme asked for clarification.

"Yeah, I got the money. I never thought about bouncin'. Me and my moms tight, plus I pay all the bills. But, what's up with you, nigga. I heard you livin' in a condo out Oxon Hill." PooBear said.

"True." Supreme replied.

"Unique must be payin' you good." PooBear said looking Supreme up and down as if he were sizing him up.

"Yeah, he payin' me all right, but not as good as he payin' you."

"There go Wop and Darkman pulling up now," PooBear stated.

"What's up?" Wop asked, exiting his car with Darkman. "Unique ain't show up yet?"

At that moment Unique pulled up in front of the four young men with his music pumping loudly. He asked, "ya'll ready?"

"Did your sista bring them broads over yet?" Wop asked excitedly.

"Yeah, Man."

"How they look?" PooBear asked.

"You know how Pam looks already, but the other two broads are dimes." Unique glanced at Darkman and grinned.

"What's up? What's up?" Darkman pressed, seeing the look Unique was giving him. "Why you grinnin' at me?"

"'Cause you gon' like one of them broads." Unique said. "Did everybody remember to bring swimming trunks?" After seeing heads nod, Unique gave the order. "Follow me," he said.

Unique's Benz pulled into a two car garage of a tan brick house. Supreme, Wop, PooBear, and Darkman all parked their vehicles on the street in front of Unique's house. They stepped out of their cars and walked up to Unique's driveway.

"Damn!" Wop yelled, looking at the house.

"Damn!" PooBear echoed, staring into Unique's garage. "You ain't tell me you bought two Benz's," Poo Bear hollered, giving Unique some dap and a bump of the shoulder.

"I copped that CLK for Kim."

Unique lowered the garage door and they all went inside. "Listen, y'all my mothafuckin' dawgs and y'all can do what the fuck y'all want. But, don't smoke no weed in my house. Smoke that shit out by the pool. All right let's go out back," Unique ordered, leading the way across the marble tiled floor of his living room en route to his kitchen.

Once they were in the kitchen, they could hear the women yelling. When they reached the family room that led out to the pool, their eyes lit up. Unique led the way through the open glass sliding door that led out to the stone patio surrounding the kidney shaped swimming pool.

As soon as Supreme stepped onto the patio, he saw Glory and Kim sitting at the glass table next to two ice buckets. In the pool, Supreme saw Pam and two other women, one white, tossing a colorful beach ball at each other, and yelling at the top of their lungs.

"Oh, that's what you was talkin' 'bout," Darkman said to Unique, smiling. "I'ma like one of them 'cause one of them white."

Two minutes later, Darkman, PooBear and Wop were in the pool with the three women, while Supreme and Unique sat on the two patio chairs they placed next to the table where Kim and Glory were sitting.

"What did y'all tell them boys?" Kim quizzed. "They must think they're gonna get some pussy tonight huh?"

Unique looked at Kim. "Why you say that?"

"Because they didn't even come over here to introduce themselves. They jumped straight into the pool after their prey."

The three women climbed out of the pool first, and when they did, Darkman, PooBear and Wop saw that all three women wore thong bikinis. Wop's jaw dropped when he saw the size of Pam's ass. The white girl named Chrissy and the brown skinned girl named Tina weren't short in the ass department either. Supreme and Unique looked down the patio observing the three women who wiped themselves down with towels.

"Look but don't touch," Kim joked.

Glory laughed, too, but was dead serious. "Yeah, look but don't touch." She rolled her eyes at Supreme when he looked her way.

"What are they down there doin?" Glory questioned, looking at the six people at the other end of the patio.

"Smokin' weed," Supreme answered.

"What's up Darkman? Too much smokin' down there for you, Dawg?" Unique inquired when Darkman reached him and Kim.

"Yeah, Slim."

Darkman turned around to head over to the table, but he suddenly remembered his manners and turned towards Kim saying, "I'm sorry. I'm Darkman." He smiled while extending his hand for Kim to shake.

Kim took his hand. "I'm Kim," she said politely.

Darkman looked Kim over. He immediately knew why Unique didn't want his crew eyeballing her. She was beautiful, and when looking at her no man could resist lustful thoughts. "I'm goin' to be honest with you," Darkman began, "Your man told us not to eyeball you. So that's why we didn't come over to greet you when we first arrived."

Unique broke into laughter. "Slim, you ain't supposed to tell her that. Now she knows I don't want nobody lookin' at her."

"Baby please," Kim started, blushing. "I already know how jealous you really are." While joking with Kim and Darkman, out of the corner of his eye Supreme saw Chrissy staring at him. Chrissy's sky blue eyes were locked on his face.

Supreme glanced around quickly at the other five people, but no one else seemed to notice Chrissy staring at him. He decided to ignore her stares, and turned his attention to his woman. He figured the white girl was checkin' out his dick print.

Meanwhile, Chrissy was mumbling to herself. "That face. That face, I know that face."

As she suddenly remembered fear clouded her eyes.

"He the nigg…." She stopped herself, took her eyes off Supreme to look at the people around her. She quickly thought back to the last time she used the word nigga. All she could remember was six black fists pounding on her almost unconscious body that was balled up in a fetal position. She snapped out of her thoughts momentarily and looked back at Supreme.

Supreme cut his eyes at his admirer again. "Damn!" he thought, she must like what she see, 'cause she can't take her eyes off a nigga.

Unfortunately for Supreme, Chrissy wasn't admiring him. She had remembered where she saw him. Supreme was the last person she'd seen with Big Red. On the night of her death he had pulled up at the drive-thru window while Chrissy and Big Red were shouting at each other.

Reminiscing more and more, Chrissy looked harder at Supreme. She noticed that he didn't have the same close shaved beard that he wore that night, but his long cornrows stuck in her mind. Suddenly, Chrissy remembered what the detective on the case told her. Scrambling through her purse she searched for the detective's number. She stood up from the chair she shared with Pam, but just as she stood, she sat again. "I can't give up my boss' boyfriend," she mumbled to herself.

"Chrissy! Chrissy!" Pam called out, shoving the marijuana into her coworker's hand. Chrissy took two pulls from the blunt then passed it.

"I have to use the bathroom," Chissy said standing up.

"Girrrrl," Glory giggled. "Be careful before you hurt yourself."

"I'm fine. I'm just a lil high that's all." Chrissy wrapped her towel around her waist and headed into the house. She tried to remain calm while peeping over her shoulder at Supreme.

Supreme watched the white girl walk awkwardly into the house.

His mind wouldn't rest. He wondered why Chrissy stared at him so long. He had come to the conclusion that she wasn't watching his body. She was doing something else, and he intended to find out. "Glory!" He shouted.

"Huh," she replied drowsily, looking up at her man.

"I'll be right back. I gotta go take a leak."

"Hurry back before the fight starts. 'Cause you know how fast Tyson can knock a nigga out," Glory said.

Supreme headed into the house to find out why those blue eyes were on him so long. Standing outside the bathroom he listened.

"I can't tell you who he is, but I can tell you he was the last person she was with before she died," Chrissy murmured into her cell phone while standing in the bathroom.

On the other side of the door, Supreme listened carefully.

"Should I do the right thing and call that detective?" Chrissy asked the person on the other end of the line. "I don't know. I should just stay out of it," she said after hearing the advice. "The Detective, Alex Brown from 5th District's Homicide Unit gave me his card." Chrissy listened a while longer before responding. "They don't really know who killed her." Chrissy looked at the card again. "They just told me to call if I ever saw the man in the black Acura Vigor, Big Red left with. And this is definitely the guy!"

Supreme was filled with rage. He knew why the white girl had watched him so closely. She was trying to place his face with the man Big Red left with the night of her murder. Now, he also remembered Chrissy's face as much as she recognized his. She was the white girl Big Red was shouting at when he pulled up to the drive-thru window of Wendy's restaurant. He saw her standing over Big Red's shoulder when she was handing him his order.

"I'll call you back after I make that call," Chrissy said. "On second thought, it's too late. I'll call tomorrow. Bye," Chrissy said ending the call.

With his ear against the door, Supreme mumbled, "Bitch you ain't gon' call nobody tomorrow. I'm not gon' let 'cha fuck shit up for me!"

Chrissy placed her cell phone and the detective's card back into her purse, took a quick leak, and reached for the bathroom door.

"Bitch!" Supreme yelled as soon as the bathroom door swung fully open. His right arm encircled Chrissy's neck as she stumbled backwards in shock. Before she could scream, Supreme had a tight grip on her neck. With his face now inches away from hers, he gritted his teeth while staring coldly into her face. Her purse fell to the floor as she threw her two small hands around his wrist tugging at it.

"Plea...Plea...Pleeease," Chrissy managed to say.

"Please what cracka. You thinkin' 'bout tellin' on me right, bitch...right?"

Chrissy managed to shake her head slightly. "No...nooooo," she murmured.

"No what? You gon' call that detective on me tomorrow right?" Supreme growled.

Chrissy dropped her right hand down from Supreme's wrist and pointed down at her purse. "Myyyy....purse."

Supreme abruptly let go of her neck and watched her body slump to the floor. "What about your purse?" he spat angrily, looking down at Chrissy while she rubbed her freed neck.

"My...," she paused to catch her breath. "My purse has the detective's card in it. Take it out and flush it down the toilet. I don't have another card."

Supreme did just that, then cruelly grabbed her by her damp, blond hair, raising her to her feet. Both of their faces stared into the mirror above the bathroom sink.

"Bitch I'ma tell you this one time. Forget about everything includin' this." Supreme angrily stated.

"I will. I will. I promise," Chrissy pleaded, crying.

"If you don't, I can easily get your address from Glory and pay you a visit."

"I understand. I understand. Please don't hurt me."

Supreme grabbed her chin. "You see your pretty face. Look at it bitch!" he ordered.

She looked into the mirror.

"This face won't be on this earth if you open ya mouth to anybody."

"I understand." Chrissy stared at Supreme through the mirror. She saw the seriousness in his eyes, and at that moment she knew she'd do exactly what he said. She'd forget everything and keep her mouth shut.

"By the way, I didn't kill Big Red. Some niggas that was shootin' at me killed her. I just wanted some pussy from her. Now, I want 'cha to go back out to the pool and act like nothin' happened. And stop fuckin' eye-ballin' me," Supreme ordered.

"All right." Chrissy said.

Supreme walked out of the bathroom as if nothing happened and was by the pool within seconds.


**At 4:30 am, Supreme walked out the bedroom he** and Glory slept in. He walked a couple of feet to the next bedroom where Darkman and Chrissy had fallen asleep. Slowly opening the bedroom door, he peeped in looking for a body next to Darkman. Supreme wondered where Chrissy could've gone. He searched the entire house without a trace of Chrissy. He went back into the bedroom with Glory, stripped, and climbed in bed.

"Glory!" Supreme nudged.

"Yeah," Glory replied, half asleep.

"You drove Chrissy over here, right?"

"Yeah."

"She didn't have a way home but through you right?"

"Right. Now let me go back to sleep Baby."

"Fuck!" Supreme cursed under his breath. "That bitch is up to somethin'. I'ma get that bitch's address and put her to sleep," Supreme mumbled.

"Who you talkin' to?" Glory asked.

"Nobody. Go back to sleep Ma."

"I know you ain't still mad about Tyson winning that fight."

"Nah, I'm all right." Supreme said, sliding up behind Glory.

"You want some?" Glory asked.

Supreme thought about it for a second. Maybe going another round with Glory would ease his anger.

After making love for several hours, Glory fell asleep fantasizing about their wedding day and the happy ending she very much wanted. Unfortunately, Supreme only dreamed about murdering Chrissy.

# FIFTEEN

The plastic, black Glock 9mm was held firmly in the grip of a big black hand. The muzzle of the Glock was pressed under the chin of a chubby face.

"Motherfucka, this is my block! I own this block! I let you motherfuckas sell that bullshit out here! I allow young motherfuckas to drive nice cars! I'm the motherfuckin' law!"

"All right, Jay. You got it. You got it," Pee Wee yelled.

"Then where is my money nigga?" Jay asked.

With his back glued to the wall, PeeWee dug into his pocket and pulled out a bundle of cash. Fearlessly, he held it up to Jay's face which was an inch or so in front of his. "Man all I got is $900 right now. I only owe you a 'g'."

Jay drew a smile, snatched the money out of PeeWee's hand, and removed his gun from under the young man's chin. "This is all I ask for baby…" He kissed the bundle of cash then placed it into his pocket. "I'm a nice guy PeeWee. I just want a piece of the American dream just like everybody else. Remember, when I come around each month, have my thousand dollars ready." Jay snapped.

"All right, let me get out the hallway before niggas outside think I'm givin' up info or somethin'." PeeWee motioned to walk off, but was stopped by Jay's hand hitting his chest.

"Next month I'll be looking for $1,100," Jay said walking out the door.

Jay walked out of the building into the dark, humid air. As he headed to his ride, all eyes were on him. Someone said, "I hope somebody kills that big black nigga." Other stares said the same, but in a different manner. "One day, they gon' find that crooked ass cop floatin' in a river."

Jay got into his Jeep Cherokee and started the engine. He pulled from the curb with a sly smirk on his face.

"What's the smile for Jay?" his Black partner quizzed. Jay's two white partners, who were a part of the four man Street Crimes Team, had the day off; and he was glad they did. The $5,000 in his pocket only had to be split two ways, not four.

"I know, don't tell me. You glad the white boys ain't here since we picked up from two different blocks tonight," Rufus said.

"You damn right I'm glad. That means more money for the black man instead of the other man." Jay laughed.

After parking in Greater Southeast Community Hospital's parking lot, Jay and his partner re-counted the money they had extorted. The money came up to $4,900. Jay placed $2,500 of the money into his pocket and Rufus placed $2,400 into his pocket.

"You know what Rufus?" Jay said. "I almost forgot to tell you how lucky we are." Jay reached over into the glove compartment and re-trieved a piece of paper.

"What's that boss man?"

"A tag number." Jay smiled.

"Who's tag number?"

"I don't know yet. I pulled behind a red Mustang that was turning off the block we just left about three weeks ago. I think I saw PeeWee walk away from the car, but I'm not sure. Whoever it was walked away from the car with a brown paper bag in his hand. So, I followed the Mustang and wrote the tag number down."

"So," Rufus snapped.

"So, I'm thinkin' that's who PeeWee's gettin' his coke from. The nigga in the red Mustang," Jay said sarcastically.

" Sooo…," Rufus said dryly.

"So, I'm thinkin' you dumb nigga!" Jay scolded gazing at Rufus. "We can find out who this nigga is by running his tag number. If he is supplyin' PeeWee, me and you can start taxin' the nigga for sellin' shit on my block."

Rufus nodded his head. "Yeah. I get it." Rufus smiled.

After acquiring the information they needed from the dispatcher at the station, they drove to the address near Martin Luther King Avenue and parked in front of the house they intended to visit.

"Jay you sure this couldn't wait until tomorrow?" Rufus asked. "It's 10:15. You don't know if the dude is crooked or not."

"The nigga crooked," Jay snapped. "We all are in some way."

"Didn't the dispatcher give you a woman's name?"

"Yeah. The car might be registered in his girl's name."

"Did you get a good look at the dude?" Rufus questioned.

"Yeah." He's a young nigga with one of those pretty boy faces and short cut wavy hair." Jay answered.

"So didn't the dispatcher tell you the lady whose name the car is registered in was born in 1950?"

"Yeah. So. The young punk likes older women. Her name is Anna Smith." Jay replied.

Rufus chuckled. "That name even sounds old."

"Come on let's get this over with," Jay said, getting out of the car. "I'm gonna ask for Anna Smith and if it's her at the door…I'll just ask if anybody in the house drives a red Mustang," Jay said coolly.

"Man," Rufus shouted as they walked through the small gray fence heading to the house. "I swear, every since you stopped by your ex-wife's vacant crib, you've been super crazy."

Jay ignored Rufus and pounded loudly on the door. A minute or so later, a middle aged black man swung the door open.

"I see those badges around y'all necks, but is it necessary to bang on my door so hard?" the man asked.

"We're sorry about that sir," Jay said. "I'm Detective Harris from the 7th District, and this is my partner Denny."

Rufus reached out giving the man a hand shake with a smile. Jay followed.

"So, how may I help you boys?" the man said.

"We would like to speak to a Mrs. Anna Smith," Jay said.

"Sorry to disappoint you boys, but I don't know anyone by that name. My wife's name is Renee Wilson."

"So, you've never heard of Anna Smith," Jay asked disappointed.

"No Sir," the man responded.

"Sorry for disturbing you," Jay said, beginning to walk off.

"Now what?" Rufus quizzed climbing in the jeep.

"Nothing," Jay replied. "We're going to the club, then I'm gon' drop this Jeep off at the station and we'll get in our personal rides to go the fuck home."

"Okay, but what about the guy in the Mustang?"

Jay smiled wickedly. "I'll catch up with him. You can take that to the bank. He probably moved out a couple of months ago," Jay remarked.

"What makes you say that?" Rufus asked.

"I peeped inside the house while the old man had the door open and saw boxes still on the floor. The old man must have just moved in with his wife," Jay said.

"How long ago you think?"

"I don't know," Jay responded. But nobody will have a good night's rest until I find out.

# SIXTEEN

S itting inside the Florida Avenue Grill restaurant, Supreme and Brother Hetep Muhammad chowed down on soul food.

"Brother, I believe without a doubt that the black woman is the most elegant cook in the world." Hetep dipped his fork into his macaroni and cheese. "Ahhhh man!" he said, after sliding the fork from this mouth.

"I agree with you Brotha Hetep. Black women can cook." Supreme looked across the table at Hetep. "But not all of them," he said biting into his corn bread.

"Yeah." Hetep smiled. "Not all of them, but enough of them can in order to keep the black man mobilized. I was surprised when you phoned me last night saying that you wanted to go with me to the Mosque on this beautiful Sunday evening. I would have thought you would be spending your time with Glory."

Supreme looked Hetep dead in his face. "I wanted to talk to you about somethin'. Plus I just felt like hearing the minister."

"What is it Brother?" Hetep looked concerned. "Are you thinking about becoming a member of the Nation?"

Supreme shook his head. "Nah, I ain't ready for nothin' like that."

"Then what's up Brother?"

"I just wanted to ask you about your past. You know, about some of the things you used to do," Supreme said.

"All right, Brother." Hetep nodded his head. Then as if he was a seasoned actor, his facial expression hardened. He coldly stared into Supreme's eyes. "Brother don't take this personal. I'm from the old school, but I also know what's up with the new school. I know there are CI's out here working for the Feds, and…"

"Yo! Hold on Brotha Hetep. I know you ain't sayin' what I think you sayin'?" Supreme asked taking offense.

"Brother, just hear me out first."

"Okay." Supreme gave his undivided attention.

"Brother, first and foremost, I'm not accusing you of anything. All I am saying is, if I go into what I used to engage in, I wanna make sure you're a good man. I'm living a great life now and I don't want what I've done in the past to bite me on my ass just from me telling you old things I've done. Now, are you a policeman?" Hetep's smile was back on his face.

Supreme was amused. He couldn't blame the brother. . "Nah, nah. I'm not the police," Supreme said sharply.

"Okay then, Brother. What specifically do you want to know?" Hetep questioned.

Supreme leaned forward across the table and whispered, "You said you did a bid for bank robbery, right?"

"Yes." Hetep nodded.

"Was that the only bank you robbed?"

Hetep looked around the restaurant, then back at Supreme.

"No. It wasn't."

"So, you robbed more than once?" Supreme whispered leaning across the table.

"Sit back, Brother," Hetep said with a light chuckle. "Yeah, I robbed more than once. I robbed from the age of fourteen to twenty-seven."

"Would you say you were addicted to robbin'?" Supreme asked.

Hetep cocked his bald head up toward the ceiling as if he were contemplating. After five seconds, he dropped his head back down and looked directly at Supreme. "Yes. I was addicted to it back then just as much as you are now," Hetep said.

The smile Supreme had on his face disappeared like magic, from Hetep's last words. The sounds of other people dining in the restaurant were lost. All he heard were Hetep's last words. He hadn't told the brother anything about him being addicted to robbing.

"What 'cha....What 'cha mean just as much as I am?" Supreme managed to utter after coming out of his trance.

"Just like I said Brother," Hetep spoke clearly and slowly as he leaned his body forward with his eyes locked on Supreme. "You gave yourself away by asking the questions you were asking me. I see the same pleasure in your eyes now that I saw months ago when I first told you I was incarcerated for bank robbery. You love robbing people," Hetep concluded.

Supreme was at a loss for words.

"Brother, what you should ask me is how you can get over your addiction. The only way to get over your love for robbing is to replace that love with another love," Hetep said.

"What 'cha mean?" Supreme inquired.

"I will tell you exactly what I mean. For example, I replaced my love for robbing with a love for real estate. I learned to love the art of buying a building, renovating it, then moving people into them. So, what I'm saying is that an old habit can only be replaced by a new one. Brother, I robbed for the money. Why do you do it?"

"Brotha Hetep, I got money. A whole lot of money. I'm not sure why I still do it," Supreme said sadly.

"May I ask if you plan on investing that money into something legitimate?"Hetep asked.

"Nah, I'm not plannin' on investing in nothin' the way you would, but I plan on investing in myself. I'm securing my future so I can live swell," Supreme boasted.

"Well Brother, you have a big problem," Hetep stated. "The only thing that will stop you then is incarceration. Have you ever been in?"

"As a juvenile, but not as an adult," Supreme answered.

"Well Brother, do you really want to stop?"

Supreme had to think about that. "Yes, I do. I'm tired of living two lives." Supreme decided that if the man he robbed tonight had over $300,000 he'd go cold turkey.

"So, you are going to stop?" Hetep asked again.

"Yeah." Supreme nodded. "Yeah!"

"Good. Stop now while things aren't so bad. You can make money without hurting people my brother. I own five buildings. My annual…" Hetep stopped himself then shook his head. "Brother, let me just put it like this. I have enough money to feed the homeless every night of the week. And I'm legit. I haven't committed a crime in over eighteen years," Hetep proudly boasted.

After an insightful meeting, Supreme had a lot to consider as he drove home. He found out a lot about Brother Hetep and his righteousness. He also realized that everyone can change. *Even him.*


**At exactly 9:30 pm, Supreme was in a position he** didn't want to be in. He was negotiating with one of the two people he had hog tied on the living room floor of a house in Capital Heights, Maryland. He walked in circles around the two bodies holding a tight grip on his .357 and his 44 Desert Eagle.

"I'm so…rry Mr. Washington," the woman on the floor cried. I thought you knew him. You know I would have never opened that door for him if I knew he wasn't one of your friends.

"I know Mrs. Newton," the man on the floor said. "Don't worry. Everything gon' be all right."

"That nigga lyin' to you bitch!" Supreme snapped, still walking around the two hog tied bodies. "If he don't tell me where his money at, I'm gon' kill both of y'all and whoever you attending to upstairs."

The nurse burst into a louder sob, more for the crippled man upstairs that she'd been taking care of for two years, than for herself. "Mr. Washing…ton, you…you not gonna let him do anything to your brother are you?"

Supreme dropped down on his hands and knees in front of the man's face and said, "tell me where the money at so I can get the fuck out of here. So what's up nigga? Your life or your money?" Supreme roared.

"You want it? You find it," Tyrell Washington said.

"Nigga!" Supreme shouted, bringing his Desert Eagle's barrel up against the man's forehead. "You wanna die over some money you can make again?" Supreme tapped the gun against his forehead.

"Okay, it's upstairs," Tyrell replied.

"Upstairs where nigga?" Supreme yelled.

"Fuck that! You find it nig…"

Tyrell didn't get the rest of his words out before Supreme's Timberland boot crashed into his mouth, knocking out a few of his teeth. Blood was everywhere, including on the face of the nurse who cried out uncontrollably.

"Bitch ass nigga!" Supreme shouted placing his boot on top of the man's head, pushing his chin into the carpet. "I've been following you for months. This house is where you keep your money."

A faint yell that came from upstairs stopped Supreme's next words. "Nurse Newton! Nurse Newton!"

"Andre is calling me," the nurse stated. "He just woke up. I gotta go attend to him, please."

"Nah, stay here. I'll be back." Supreme walked off heading up the staircase.

Stepping into the bedroom where Andre still called out, Supreme saw a motionless man lying flat on his back. He glanced around the room filled with medication and spotted a powered wheel chair parked right next to the bed.

"Who that?" Andre asked. He watched as Supreme approached the right side of his bed. "Where is Mrs. Newton? Where is my brother? And why do you have that bandanna on your face?"

"Do you know where your brotha money at?" Supreme quizzed, hoping the paralyzed man would answer yes.

"Yeah, but did you hurt my brotha or Mrs. Newton?" Andre asked. "They're all I have," he sobbed. "They're the only people who love me although I'm like this."

"OK, just tell me where the money at and I'll be out of here," Supreme said pleasantly.

"You gotta lean down here and let me whisper it in your ear. I don't want my brotha to overhear me tellin' you where the money is."

As soon as Supreme's face was an inch from his, Andre opened his mouth as wide as he could, jerked his head forward, and locked onto Supreme's right cheek with the grip of a pit bull. As the pain detonated inside Supreme, he yelled louder than he ever did before.

"I got your mothafucka," Andre growled like a dog while his teeth were still inside of Supreme's face.

Out of nowhere, Supreme's mind sent a signal to his right hand which held the chrome .357, and with a blunt force, he slammed the gun repeatedly against Andre's head until his face was free.

"I still go hard to the end just like my brotha nigga. Just because I'm cripple, don't mean I'm soft," Andre snapped. His eyes were blood shot red like he'd been drinking liquor all day. Pieces of thread from Supreme's black bandanna hung from Andre's lips.

"I'ma start counting. Before I get to ten, you better tell me where the money at," Supreme said wiping the blood that dripped from his face. He aimed his Desert Eagle at Andre as he approached the side of the bed. With the gun pressed against the cripple man's temple, Supreme started counting. "One…Two…Where the money at? Three…."

"This is what I want anyway," Andre said. "I've been livin' like this for two years. I wanna be put out of my misery. I'm glad you came!"

"You gon' get ya wish nigga. Five…six…seven…eight…" Supreme slid his bandanna back up on his face.

"Hey! What's going on up there?" Mrs. Newton yelled from downstairs.

"Nine…ten." Supreme cocked his gun, but as soon as he did, he realized the paralyzed man with the smile on his face wasn't going to tell him where the money was.

"Where you going?" Andre yelled, watching Supreme leave.

Minutes later, Supreme walked back into the bedroom with the back of Mrs. Newton's neck tightly in his left hand while his right hand held the Desert Eagle to her head. Her hands were still tied behind her back.

Watching Supreme walk his nurse toward the bed, Andre uttered, "Don't hurt her.  She's a good woman."

"You should have thought about that shit when I asked you for the money," Supreme snapped.

Supreme knew the cripple man may not have cared about his own life, but he knew he was concerned about the lady who took care of him.  He could tell that Andre loved her.

"Now, I'ma ask you one more time.  Where is the money?" Supreme cocked his gun, pressing it harder against Mrs. Newton's head.

Andre looked into the face of the woman he cherished.  Tears were falling and her body shivered.  "It's under the bed," he said.

"Don't play games with me," Supreme snapped pushing the gun against the nurse's head, causing her to yell.

"I'm not.  It's in between the mattress.  You gotta place me in my arm chair," André said.

"Oh yeah."  Supreme cocked the gun's hammer back into position, and tucked it into his waist.  Without warning he pushed the nurse to the floor then quickly grabbed each of Andre's dead ankles and tossed him off the bed onto the floor.  Immediately, Mrs. Newton crawled to Andre's side.

Supreme vigorously flipped the mattress over.  "Bingo!" he said, glancing back at the two people on the floor.  Andre was obviously unconscious from the sound of Mrs. Newton's cries.

"Bitch you been cryin' since I came in this house," Supreme said tossing the bundles of money into a white shopping bag.  Two minutes later, he was back down stairs in the living room hovering over Tyrell who was still hog tied, but unconscious now.  Supreme knew it was time for him to leave.


**Forty minutes later, he walked into his condo.  As** soon as he locked his front door, his phone rang.  Snatching the cordless phone from its rack, he sat down on the sofa with his new money next to him.

"Yo."

"Hiii…Baby," Glory sang on the other end of the phone.

"What's up Ma?" Supreme said happily.

"You. What 'cha doin?"

"Nothin' right now. But your brotha supposed to be pickin' me up at midnight."

"Where y'all goin'?" Glory questioned like an over protective parent.

"I think to a club," Supreme replied.

"Don't go. Come over here and keep me company."

"Nah, you know I gotta go with ya brotha."

"No you don't," Glory snapped. "He can get PooBear to be his body guard tonight."

"Yeah he can, but that's my job. Your brotha just started payin' me $15,000 a month, so I got to go with him." Supreme stressed every word. He didn't want Glory to see the bite mark on his face. She would instantly think the bite was from a woman who liked rough sex. "I'll make it up to you," he said.

"How?" Glory hissed.

"It's a surprise."

After talking to Glory, Supreme rushed up to his bedroom and began to count his money with the help of the money machine Unique hipped him to.

"Three hundred and eighty-five mothafuckin' g's," Supreme said, after placing the last bundle of cash through the machine. "I guess I won't be robbin' no more," he said to himself. Then out of nowhere, someone came to his mind. Chrissy.

Supreme grabbed the phone and called Glory. "This me Ma," he said.

"You changed your mind huh?" Glory said seductively.

"Nah," Supreme said, trying not to sound anxious.

"What 'cha want then?" Glory hissed.

"You ever hear anything from that white girl?" He held his breath.

"What white girl?"

"Chrissy. The one that works with you." Supreme asked.

"This is your second time askin' me 'bout her. You like her?" Glory questioned.

"Nah…" Supreme paused, thinking of an excuse. "Darkman asked me to ask you about her. He wanna see her again."

Glory paused. "I see her at work all the time. I'll give Darkman her number."

Supreme got excited. He knew Chrissy couldn't have ratted him out and showed up at work.  Besides, the detective wouldn't have allowed her to go back to work knowing she worked under the suspect's girlfriend.

"I'ma call Darkman and tell him now.  Give me her phone number."

"Give me just a second," Glory said. After giving Supreme the number, she thought about what she had done. "You better not let me find out this number is for you.  Do you want her address too?"

"No doubt, Ma," Supreme said excitedly.

Immediately after Glory gave him Chrissy's address, and phone number he hung up.  Supreme smiled while placing the piece of paper with Chrissy's info on it into a dresser drawer. That was all the insurance he needed.

# SEVENTEEN

Unique pulled into the huge parking lot of Iverson Mall in Maryland. While driving his Mustang slowly through the lot, he heard his cell phone ring.

"I see you made it on time," a man on the other end said.

"Yeah, I gotta take care of business," Unique replied.

"I'm parked near the entrance in a blue Dodge Viper. I saw you ride pass me. Drive toward the entrance. Park, then jump in with me. You can't miss this joint'," Ray said.

Finding a parking space, Unique parked and grabbed the black gym bag that was next to him. Stepping out of the car, he maneuvered his way through the parked cars over to the Viper.

"What's up?" Ray asked, dressed in all black linen.

"You," Unique replied, placing his gym bag between his feet. "Slim, it ain't like you to be by yourself," Unique said.

Ray smiled. "Dawg, you right. It ain't like me to be by myself. That's why if you look behind us and in front of us, you'll see I got my men with me."

Unique hadn't even noticed the two men that sat in the white Lexus in front of them. Nor had he noticed the two men that sat in a black PT Cruiser behind them.

"I should've known. You're never alone" Unique said.

"I like it like that. Now let's get down to business," Ray said, reaching for his bag. "There are 30 kilos in here." He patted the bag smiling.

Unique didn't think he heard Ray correctly. "Did you say 30 keys? I only brought 250 g's with me."

"Don't worry about that. When you cop again, just make sure you bring the 450 if you want 30 more keys," Ray said casually.

"Deal Slim," Unique said while they switched bags. "So you talked to Dad about givin' me more shit huh?"

"Nah," Ray said plainly. "Bob and my pops don't have nothin' to do with this game any more. They're both completely out of the game now. So we ain't gotta ask them shit. Let's leave them out of our business."

"I'm with that," Unique replied.

"All right man, I gotta go. I'm proposing to my girl tonight."

"I'm thinkin' about marryin' my girl too, but I'm gon' wait until I get out the game first," Unique revealed.

Ray looked over at Unique. "Tomorrow ain't promised. You know in this game a nigga could wipe you out with the steel, or the feds can pick you up at any moment. That's why I'm not gonna prolong making my commitment to my girl," Ray said sincerely.

"Ray!" Unique exclaimed. "Remember about ten or eleven months ago when I was talkin' to you on the phone and you was tellin' me somethin' about some nigga. I know you said somethin' like your girl almost lost her baby."

Abruptly Ray looked serious. "Yeah, I remember," he said.

"Around April last year, I was…" The sound of Ray's cell phone interrupted them. "Yeah," Ray smiled as he talked on his cell phone.

"Slim I gotta go," Ray announced after closing his phone.

"All right, I'll holla at 'cha."

"I'll tell you about that some other time, but I can tell you that if I ever see that nigga that did that shit to me, I'm gon' take him out and whoever he down with. I don't care if the chump down with the mafia, I'm going at him."

"Damn, you want that nigga's blood," Unique said watching Ray's face.

"You would too if a nigga did to you what he did to me in the presence of your girl," Ray said unlocking the doors.

Unique understood the signal. "We'll talk later," Unique said hopping out of the Viper.

**Pedestrians walking up and down the sidewalks** on 8<sup>th</sup> and H street watched the Navigator cruise along the street as if it was the only vehicle riding the asphalt. They stared in admiration as Supreme pulled in front of Lisa's house. The red bone, petite woman walked from her porch towards his truck. He admired the dark blue micro mini skirt she wore. He also liked the braids in her hair.

"Damn this truck smells good," Lisa purred, stepping into the truck. She looked over at Supreme. "What's up? That's your new look or somethin'?" She was referring to the closely shaved, full beard Supreme had grown to hide his bite mark.

He rubbed his right hand over his beard replying, "Ma, this how I was wearin' it before my goatee."

Lisa reached over and ran her left hand over his beard. "You look good rockin' it like this. It's smooth, I like it." She turned her attention out the passenger window. "We still goin' to the movies right?" Lisa quizzed.

"Yeah."

"What are you listening to in your CD player?" Lisa quizzed.

"Push the play button," Supreme said, focusing on the road.

Lisa pushed the play button on the CD player causing the sounds of singer Brian McKnight's soulful voice to invade the truck. "Ooo, I like Brian McKnight."

"Oh yeah," Supreme replied glancing at Lisa.

Lisa turned the volume up and gazed over at Supreme.

"You know slow cuts make me horny right?" She put on her most seductive look, biting down on her bottom lip.

"Slow cuts make you horny huh?" Supreme nodded.

"Yeeeeeeah," she said softly.

Before Supreme could utter another word Lisa had her head in his lap pleasing him proficiently. Supreme could barely keep his eyes on the road. Pulling into the lot of the theater Lisa's head continued to bob up and down. Suddenly, she felt Supreme's juices flowing. Aaaahhhhh......! Supreme moaned.

"You liked that didn't you?" Lisa asked.

"No doubt, Ma."

Supreme looked closely at Lisa. He knew he wouldn't always get oral sex for free. The dollar signs flashed in Lisa's eyes. It cost to be with her, but he was willing to pay.

"So, what's up Ma?  Do you really wanna go inside?" Supreme asked. He had something else in mind.

"Whatever.  It's Friday night."

"You know I wanna take ya lil' sexy ass to a hotel."

The sound of Supreme's cell phone ringing broke his next thought.

"This Unique, Slim. I need 'cha over here now!  I'm at the gamblin' spot," Unique said with a slight chuckle.

"Yo, I thought 'cha told me you was gon' chill at home with Kim tonight," Supreme said.

"I was until PeeWee called me and told me niggas gamblin' big around the way.  And that nigga wasn't lyin. I'm up 50 g's and some nigga I 'on know won't take his eyes off me.  I think I broke him for 20 of the 50 I won," Unique said. "I think he got fire on 'em."

"You 'on have nothin' on you?" Supreme asked.

"Nigga, you know PooBear got all my heaters."

"Damn, Son.  You know you ain't supposed to go to that spot without me," Supreme fussed.

"Well I'm here now, so hurry up nigga." Unique hung up.

"I know, you ain't gotta tell me," Lisa said. "You gotta drop me off right?"  Lisa folded her arms over her chest and shook her head.

"Let me make it up to you."  Supreme peeled five, one-hundred dollar bills from his bank roll and passed it to Lisa.

"Thank you," Lisa said. "How much is this?"

"Five hundred. That's for having to drop you off so early and plus I might need 'cha to do me a favor one day.  Who knows," he said.

"If that day comes, I'll do it 'cause you do know how to set that money out." She planted a kiss on Supreme's right cheek.

"Maybe we can go out tomorrow. I'll pay for everything," Lisa stated.

"Nah, Ma. You ain't gotta do that."

"I want to."

"All right. We'll see tomorrow."

"Bye," Lisa said stepping out of the truck as soon as Supreme pulled in front of her house.


**Supreme parked his truck behind Unique's Mus-**tang in the Southeast neighborhood. Walking into the gambling spot, he was surprised to see only seven men on their knees in a huddle. One of those men was Unique.

Supreme swiftly scanned the abandoned apartment. All together there were nine men occupying the unit with only six of them actually gambling. One stood next to the door playing the part of the door man and another man stood off to the side scowling.

*That must be the nigga he was talkin' 'bout*, Supreme thought to himself as he strolled over to the huddle making sure Unique noticed his presence.

A couple of the men gambling knew who Supreme was, so each of them acknowledged him with, "What's up N.Y.?"

"I ain't leavin' till I break all you niggas," Unique said at the top of his voice, shaking a pair of white dice. "My point if four. When I hit this four, y'all niggas gon' wish I never came through that door!"

"Roll the dice nigga and stop tryin' to rhyme," one of the men snarled.

"You sure you want me to do that?" Unique joked, grinning up at the man who spoke.

"Fuck yeah. If you hit, I hit. I'm rollin' with you."

"Good choice Slim." Unique threw the dice out and they tumbled until they landed on four.

"Give me my mothafuckin' money niggaaaaaas!" The man that bet with Unique shouted.

"I'm outta here," one man said, walking away from the huddle. "I lost 10 g's tonight. That's enough for me."

"Yeah," the three other men echoed.

"It's only four of us left," Unique announced, now standing with a pile of money in both hands. "What y'all try'na do?" He teased arrogantly.

All three men uttered almost simultaneously, "I'm out."

With only the doorman, Supreme, Unique and the man that stood off to the side left in the apartment, Supreme took it upon himself to approach the man, with his gun drawn.

"What's up, Dawg?" The man said stepping back.

Supreme stood in front of the man searching him with his left hand while his right held the Desert Eagle. "You, what's goin' on Kid? You eye ballin' my man like you wanna do somethin'." Supreme stepped back from the man after not finding a gun on him.

The door man and Unique walked over to Supreme.

"He's all right," Unique jumped in. "I didn't know he was with Russ. I ain't never seen him before."

"That's because you ain't around like you used to be," Russ fired back. "This is my man Tye," he said.

Tye shook his head. "I wasn't thinkin' about tryin' no shit. I was just mad I loss all that money."

"How much?" Unique asked.

"So much that I'm not gon' be able to re-up," Tye said.

"Joe, you know you ain't supposed to gamble with your last," Unique preached.

"I know."

"So you dead broke?"

"Yeah, kind of. I got a lil' somethin' at my crib," Tye revealed.

"Nigga's don't do what I'm about to do." Unique reached into the brown paper bag he put his gambling earnings in. "That should be 10 g's," he said as he passed Tye a bundle of money.

"Never gamble with your last," Unique preached as he walked out.

Outside, Unique and Supreme rushed to their vehicles. "I like how you approached Tye. You drew on him quick," Unique said.

"That's my job to take care of shit like that," Supreme boasted.

"I gotta get home to my lady," Unique said giving Supreme some dap.

"Want me to drive behind ya?" Supreme asked.

"Nah Slim, go do your thing. Where you goin' anyway?"

"I 'on know. I'll make my mind up while I'm drivin'."

"All right, I'm out." Unique said as he stepped into his Mustang.

Immediately, Supreme called Glory. "I tried to get in touch with you earlier today," Supreme told Glory speaking into the phone. "Where you been." He questioned.

"Baby, you know I told 'cha I had to dance for three different clients," Glory said.

"You know what, Ma? You need to hire some girls to dance in your place."

"Why?" Glory whined.

"'Cause."

"I'm not playin'. Why should I hire some girls to dance in my place when I can do that myself?"

"'Cause I'm in love with you, and I don't like you dancin' for niggas any more."

"Yesssss!" Glory shouted on the other end of the phone. "I've been wantin' to hear you say that for months now."

"Well, I said it and I mean it. So, what 'cha gon' do about that?" Supreme asked.

"I'm gonna hire another girl to dance in my spot when men want me to dance for them. But when women want me to, I'ma dance for them. Is that Okay?" she asked.

"Yeah, I 'on mind that. Where you at Ma? I'm on my way over."

"I just got out the shower and I'm layin' on my bed waitin' for you. You better hurry up before I go to sleep. Bye," Glory said hanging up the phone.

As soon as Supreme ended his call his phone rang. Hearing the tone of Unique's voice worried him.

"Did you see anybody following me tonight?" Unique asked nervously.

"Nah. Why? What's up?"

"When I got close to my neighborhood, I happened to glance in my rearview and I could have sworn I saw that black Cherokee behind me. I took my eyes off the mirror for one second, looked up again, and the car was gone," Unique explained.

Supreme made a u-turn in the middle of the street. "I was on my way to ya sista's crib, but I 'm coming to check on you," he said.

"I'm all right. I'm in the garage now. Plus, I know you in loveeeeeee," Unique said laughing. "But good looking out," he said ending the conversation.

# EIGHTEEN

"Man, we've been sittin' out here for an hour," officer Rufus Denny complained to his partner. "I don't think he's comin' out. Matter of fact, do you think we're at the right place?"

Jay looked over at Rufus and grinned. "Man, I told you already, I followed the young nigga to his neighborhood a month ago. Besides, the Mustang he drives is parked right up the block. Be cool man, he should be comin' out any moment."

Jay glanced at his watch. "If he don't step out in fifteen minutes, we'll come back tonight around nine."

"Look, we're not even on the clock until 8 o'clock tonight and we out here laying on somebody. If it wasn't for you comin' to get me, I wouldn't be out here," Rufus snickered.

"Man you should have stayed home, then. I didn't drag you from your crib. You came alone because you know it's money involved. You just didn't think it'd be this long." Jay snapped.

"Jay, I just was wondering if your ex-wife knows you're a dirty cop. I mean after you bought that house, was paying the bills and buying her nice things on a cop's salary... She didn't have a clue about you?"

"Nah, not that I knew of. She never said anything to me that would have told me that she knew anything."

Both men were silent staring out the jeep's windshield waiting for a sign of the man they waited for. Rufus broke the silence. "Man these are some nice houses.  I always wanted to live out here.  How much you think these bad boys would run you?"

"I would say around one hundred to three hundred thousand."

"You think the dude's money that long?" Rufus asked.

"Longer.  The day I followed him here from Southeast, I was told that he was only around that day because he was gambling and left the gambling spot with 50 g's. He used to be on the block before we started working it.  They say he only give coke to one young'un around there."

"Let me guess.  PeeWee."

"Bingo. They say that PeeWee be coppin' from him."

"Did they say what his name is?"

"I can't remember, but it sounds like a righteous name."

Rufus glanced at the house that Jay said the man lived in. "If he drivin' the Mustang parked out here, what's in that garage?"

"I don't know, but I bet it's somethin' nice," Jay replied.

"Maybe one car his and the other his girl's," Rufus said.

"Naawww," Jay drawled, while shaking his head no. "A nigga like him probably owns both cars in that garage.  If one of them cars is his girl's, he either loves her to death or it's his wife."

"Jay.  You think he looked out and saw us parked out here?" Rufus quizzed. "Shit, we're sittin' across the street from his pad."

"Nah, Man," Jay replied grinning. "He wouldn't think we'd be out here in a million years.  He don't even know we're on to him, but he will know.  Starting today, he's gonna have to pay a monthly fee for sellin' on the block like everybody else."

"He don't be out there sellin," Rufus said, as if he was talking up for the young man.

"But he's supplyin' somebody that do sell.  I'm gonna tax him ten g's a month for that, since I know he got money,"

"If he tells you to go to hell, what then?"

"If he tells me that, then his ass is gonna be doin' ten to twenty years in the Feds.  I'll put my word on that.  Everybody pays me. "

Rufus smiled. He knew the words his partner spoke were true. At least ten drug dealers who wanted to play hard were now doing hard time in prison for not paying up. Jay gave a vicious ass whipping to them before he hauled them off to the precinct to start the process of heading to the big house.

"Look!" Jay said excitedly, pointing to the garage door that was slowly rising. "We got action!"

"Yeah, but I don't see but one car in that garage and it's not backing out."

"Yeah, I see," Jay muttered, wondering why the garage opened and the black Benz didn't back out. He looked out his sideview mirror and spotted a silver convertible Benz coming slowly down the block. "This might be him that's comin'," Jay said, watching the convertible coming toward them.

Both men sat up and looked toward the left to observe the car when it drove pass them. Although they didn't get a good look at her, they noticed a beautiful woman with long black hair and caramel complexion behind the wheel. She drove into the garage.

"That must be his girl," Rufus exclaimed.

Jay looked over at the garage and saw the woman who had just pulled in, walking backwards with a purse under her right arm and her left arm pointing her car keys to lower the garage door.

"That's a DC bus driver's uniform she has on," Rufus stated. "I wish she would turn around and face us. Damn, man, she looks good even in that uniform. She got a nice ass too."

Jay sat in the driver's seat of the jeep with his heart in his mouth. The woman didn't have to turn around. He knew that figure anywhere. It was Kim, his ex-wife. As she pulled into the big house where a drug dealer lived, he clenched the steering wheel so tight his knuckles were beginning to turn white.

"Jay!" Rufus snapped after noticing how his partner gripped the steering wheel. His yell fell on deaf ears because Jay still held the wheel like his life depended on it.

Just as the woman turned around, Jay uttered, "That's Kim, my ex-wife." Rufus looked at the woman who was now standing on her front lawn inspecting the blooming flower bed. "Damn man, that is Kim. What the hell is she doin' here?"

Jay stared at Rufus and gave him a look that could kill. "What the fuck it look like. She pulled into that garage, she lives here."

"Damn Jay. I'm sorry man."

"Sorry about what? That my ex-wife dating a drug dealer. A young nigga that brought her a fifty, sixty thousand dollar car."

"Now hold on, we jumping to conclusions. We don't know if that's her car, nor do we know if she's fuckin'…sorry, I mean dating the young man."

"Fuck!" Jay shouted, thrusting his head down and banging it up against the steering wheel. "The last time I saw her at the gym, she told me she was seeing a young kid, just like the girl I'm seeing. This must be him?" Jay took a deep breath.

"Be cool," Rufus said, pointing at the house. "The dude just stepped onto the front porch. Don't do nothin' stupid man."

They watched as Kim walked from the lawn up to the  porch into the young dude's arms.  The cops watched them passionately kiss as the young dude's hands palmed each of Kim's ass cheeks.

"So, she went back to driving buses. Her mother has gotta be happy because she used to always ask me to make Kim stop working at that jail. Damn, I wonder if she stopped on her own, or if this youngster persuaded her. I couldn't get her to. She used to say, "You lock'em up, and I'll make sure they stay locked up.""

"I bet she doesn't want you to lock her man up," Rufus said.

Jay glared at Rufus, wanting to slam him in the face for what he said. "Of course she doesn't want me to lock her man up. I remember his name now. It's Unique."

"What we gon' do? You wanna keep your ex- wife believing you a good cop, but if you're gonna extort him, you know it's probable that she'll find out."

"You right. I wouldn't want that. She has a lot of respect for me as a cop. I always acted as if I was against anything illegal. But I need the money. My young tender thing gotta be draped in the best," Jay said with a smirk.

"Mannn!" Rufus began, "the way you gripped that steering wheel and banged your forehead, I swore you was going nuts."

"Nah man. I'm not gon' lie though, I was hot at first, but she didn't leave me. I left her."

"So everything's still as planned?"

"Yeah. We gon' pull him over. I'm gon get him to step out the car. Then I'm gon' tell him my demands."

"You think he knows you are his woman's ex-husband?"

"I doubt it."

"If he does allow you...us to extort him, you think he can keep it from Kim?"

"I don't think no man really wants to tell his woman he's being extorted."

"We'll soon know. He stepped out the house," Rufus said.

Minutes later the black Cherokee was a car behind the red Mustang. A few minutes after that the Cherokee was behind the Mustang with red lights flashing and the siren wailing noisily.

When Jay reached the door of the Mustang, he noticed a hand already dangling out the window with a driver's license and piece of paper that must have been the Mustang's registration. He immediately noticed the look Unique gave him.

"Ain't y'all out of y'all jurisdiction?" Unique said, looking to his right, noticing Rufus standing by the passenger door.

"Since you know we're out of our jurisdiction, you know who I am and that I don't wanna see that shit you have in your hands," Jay said.

"What's up then? Why y'all pull me over?" Unique asked.

Jay stepped back from the driver's door. "Get out the car."

"What?" Unique snapped, sensing something was up.

Jay snatched his 9mm from his holster. "Get the fuck out the car nigga!" He held the gun against the side of his leg.

When Unique stepped out, Jay ordered him to stand at the rear of the car. While Jay and Unique talked, Rufus opened the passenger door of the car to begin his search.

"I hope you don't have nothin' in there," Jay uttered to Unique, standing in front of him.

"Even if I did, y'all out y'all jurisdiction. I'll beat that in court," Unique smiled.

*I'd like to knock his pretty boy ass the fuck out right now*, Jay thought to himself. He stared into Unique's face with a cold look in his eyes. He hated Unique now, because he seemed arrogant, and was his ex-wife's man. "You sure about that?"

"Nah," Unique swiftly shot back. "But I bet my paid lawyer will be sure about that."

"How old are you?" Jay asked Unique.

"Twenty-six."

Jay placed his gun back into his holster. As he was doing so, he picked up on the look Unique gave him. "What's that look you giving me all about?"

Unique had a look on his face as if he was putting two and two together. "About a month and a half ago, you followed me to my crib from Southeast, right?"

"Yeah," Jay answered plainly.

"So, what's up? What 'cha want, Dawg?" With his arms folded across his chest Unique stood up against the rear of the Mustang.

"OK, here's the deal," Jay began. "I don't know if you know it or not, but everybody that's selling coke around the way in Southeast is paying me a fee every month. They do that to stay out of jail. You don't stand out there and sell, but you supplyin' somebody that does sell there; so you must pay a monthly fee."

"How much?"

"Ten g's a month. I know you can handle that." Jay cracked a smile. He knew Unique was going to buck, he could feel it, and in a way he wanted him to so he could send him to the Feds for ten or twenty years. Plus it would ruin his relationship with Kim if he had to do time in prison.

Unique smiled while digging into his jean pocket. Just as he did, Rufus was shutting the passenger door of the Mustang and walking to the rear of the car, joining his partner. "You said ten g's right?" Pulling his hands out of his pocket, Unique held two small bundles of cash. He tossed one to Jay, and the other in his pocket.

"What's this?" Jay quizzed with a perplexed expression.

"That's ten g's," Unique said.

Jay twirled the money in his hand. A smile crept onto his face. He glanced over at Rufus who had a silly grin on his face. "Smart move. Now you can have a pass to sell to whoever you want to on our block. If you ever run into trouble with the law, I might be there to give you a hand." Jay extended his hand to Unique for a shake.

Unique reluctantly took his hand then said, "I don't have to worry about you ever showing up in front of my house right?"

"I'm a man of my word, I'll never show up at your place."

Jay and Rufus sat in the jeep and watched as Unique pulled from the curb.

"I guess he don't know you're his girlfriend's ex-husband huh?" Rufus exclaimed.

"Nah he doesn't know and I like that," Jay said smiling.

# NINETEEN

The summer was almost over and September was approaching. Supreme stuck to his pledge of retiring as a stick-up kid. Spending most of his time taking luxurious vacations with Glory and chillin' with Lisa on occasions, Supreme was spending a large portion of his savings. Splurging on Lisa had become an investment. He knew she'd be down for the cause if he ever needed her. But his spending habits and his love for Glory increased daily. So much, in fact, that he found himself often telling her he loved her. Supreme made sure he copped Glory nothing but the best. He even purchased his and hers white mink coats and matching platinum diamond bracelets. But contrary to showing his love financially, he would still remind himself that if his life were in danger, he would leave DC and Glory behind without looking back.

Supreme shocked everyone when he and Glory moved in together. Initially, he thought Glory would continue to protest his invitation to live with him. But she didn't. They were actually starting to live a normal life. Supreme's first step in his retirement was to trade in his 300zx. It felt good not to have to hide his new Impala. He had the luxury of parking it right in front of his condo, along with his Navigator and Honda CBR 600. He made it his business to show off the Impala whenever the opportunity presented itself. No one drove it but him. Supreme's life had taken a turn for the best until Unique revealed his situation with Jay.

"Can you believe this shit?" Unique asked Supreme as he drove his Benz up Vermont Avenue, heading to "Club Daedelus." "I'm being extorted by Kim's ex-husband. I knew I recognized that nigga's face. Kim had an old picture of him posing in a police uniform," Unique explained.

"I bet 'cha she doesn't know the nigga is a dirty cop," Supreme said, slouched down into the passenger seat of the Benz.

"Nah, she didn't know then and she don't know now, I ain't gon' tell her. I don't want her to know I know the chump."

"So, Son, what 'cha gon' do? I know you ain't gon' let this mothafucka keep extortin' you," Supreme replied, frowning.

"Nah, that's why I wanted us to chill tonight. I wanna talk to you about dealin' with this bamma."

"Give me seventy-five g's and I'll take care of him plain and simple," Supreme said seriously.

"Deal nigga." Unique stuck his hand out toward Supreme. "You got that," Unique replied.

"Yeah, nobody gon' miss a dirty cop anyway. I owe that nigga one for pullin' that gun out on me," Supreme added.

"Damn!" Unique exclaimed, slamming the palm of his hand down on the steering wheel.

Supreme gazed over at Unique. "What's up, Son?"

"I just thought about somethin'. The day that Jay pulled me over, he had to be waitin' for me to come out of my house. That means he saw Kim pull into my garage because she walked out of the garage and onto the front lawn," Unique said with uncertainty.

"So he know you fuckin' his ex, then." Supreme stated.

"Yeah, and knowing how dirty he is, he might be up to somethin' 'cause he didn't say shit about it."

Supreme grinned. "Don't worry about it Kid, I'ma take care of that nigga. But first you gotta rock him to sleep. In a few days in October you're supposed to pay him right. So pay him then. Let him think everything is sweet. Then I'll make my move when he least suspects it," Supreme said.

"What about his partner?" Unique asked.

"He can get it, too. But take my word for it, by the time you have to pay him in November, his partner won't be with him. A cop like him is greedy. You said it was just him and one other cop right?"

"Yeah, just him and another Black cop," Unique said.

"You see, both of them cut the two white boys off when it came to dealin' with you. I bet 'cha that dirty mothafucka Jay will cut his Black partner off after you pay him this time," Supreme said.

As they approached the club, Unique slowed his Benz down because of all the women that sashayed along the sidewalk heading in the direction of the club. All the vehicles in front of him were moving slowly too.

"Damn, Son," Supreme said, staring out the window at all the women flagging them down.

"Nigga stop looking!" Unique cracked with a light chuckle. "You ain't gon' fuck nothing that you see. You in love with my sista. I been seein' that shit in your eyes for a long time," Unique joked. "You only fuckin' my sista and that lil bitch Lisa."

Supreme smiled. "You right. I am in love with your sista. To be honest with you, I ain't really gotta fuck with that bitch Lisa. Your sista is all a nigga really need. "

" You pussy whipped nigga. She's puttin' that dyke love on your ass," Unique grinned.

"Nah nigga, your sista don't be fucking with no girls no more," Supreme said defending Glory.

"Nigga picture that," Unique fired back. "My sista been fuckin' with girls since she was fourteen. Don't think you just gon' come along and make her stop likin' the taste of pussy." Unique laughed.

It was close to midnight by the time Supreme and Unique stepped into the crowded club. The dimness made it hard to see every single person's face clearly. The two men saw bodies grinding up against each other.

"Now this what I'm talkin' 'bout," Unique shouted over the loud music.

Supreme didn't respond. On his job, he scanned the club. With a stone look on his face his body language insinuated that he was packing heat. Supreme watched Unique closely as he guzzled down several bottles of Cristal with two beautiful women sitting in his booth.

"I haven't seen you crack a smile yet," one of the women said to Supreme."

"Don't worry, Ma. I'm all right," Supreme responded.

"Okay. If you say so, with your fineeeeee... ass." The woman batted her eyes at Supreme.

Supreme ignored the advance. "Check this out Kid, I'm gonna run to the bathroom for a minute. I'll be back."

"Go handle ya business," Unique responded. "I'm straight."

Supreme slipped out of the booth and headed toward the restroom. He walked slowly through the crowded club, slightly bumping against people. Every man he bumped he automatically looked him over from head to toe. He grinned because he started to observe people as if he were still a stick- up kid.

Immediately after using the restroom, Supreme was on his way back to the booth, when he noticed something that didn't look right. In front of the booth where he and Unique sat two men stood as if they were protecting someone or something. As he got closer, he saw a man sitting with Unique, but he wasn't able to distinguish who the man was. Fearing something was happening or had happened to Unique, he walked faster. Supreme slowed down when he was a couple of feet from the booth. And for some reason something told him to glance over the guards and peep into the booth. He did, and saw Unique and someone he thought he'd never have to lay his eyes on again.

As soon as the two men in front of the booth spotted him, they took a step forward and one said, "Who the fuck is this comin' our way through the crowd. I can't see his face 'cause it's too dark in here."

Simultaneously both men glanced back at the two drunk men who sat in the booth laughing hardily with expensive drinks dangling from their hands. Not forgetting the matter at hand, the two guards turned around, zoomed in on the approaching man and braced themselves for a fight, preparing to punish the man who they still couldn't see clearly. As they balled their hands into fists, the man they were preparing for, abruptly stopped and made a U-turn onto the crowded dance floor.

Supreme cursed as he stood in the middle of the dance floor with his eyes fixed on the booth. Dancing club goers bumped him without moving him an inch. He was almost in a trance. He was perplexed.

"I can't believe this shit! This can't be happenin'. How the fuck…"

Supreme's words were cut short by a sudden sharp blow to his side. He frantically swung his head from left to right observing the dance floor. Someone had slammed his elbow into his side, but he didn't know who. Lucky for them, because if he knew who the perpetrator was, he would have wasted no time slamming his fist into their face. The blow to his side didn't hurt him, but a surge of anger was already swelling within him.

Supreme focused his attention back on the booth. Nothing had changed. The two men were still guarding the booth. "What the fuck! This nigga got bodyguards now? He didn't have none when I ran across him. He must've got big over the year and some change since we bumped heads. Shit! I might have to get some of his new money. Make a nigga come out of retirement." Supreme grinned. "But damn! What the fuck that nigga doin' talkin' to Unique? I hope they don't even know each other, they just hit it off in the club while I was in the bathroom. Shit! Two niggas ballin' see eye to eye. I…."

Supreme walked closer to the booth. But noticed there was no one in or around it. "Shit!" He cursed, pushing his way through the crowded dance floor and over to the booth he once occupied. He stood in front of it looking through the club, as soon as he thought he spotted Unique, dancers started yelling, shouting and waving arms from the sound of a hit song. Now there was no way he could distinguish if who he saw was indeed Unique. Now he would have to wait until the song ended and the crowd settled.

Finally, the song ended and the crowd settled. And that's when he looked over where he thought he had spotted Unique. Yep, the man he thought he saw was indeed Unique. He sat at a table with a woman who looked to be enjoying his company. Supreme made his way through the crowd and over to the table

"If this is your friend, the woman began, you need to take him home 'cause he's tore down. He's over here tellin' me he's a millionaire and something about a cop tryin' to extort him."

"What's up, Dawg?" Unique slurred, looking up at Supreme. "Dammmnn! You just comin' back from the bathroom?"

"Please take him home," the woman said with a pleasant smile. "He is too tore up."

"Come on Son, let's roll out." Supreme turned towards the woman while reaching into his pocket. He pulled out a roll of money, peeled big faces from it and placed them into the woman's hand.

"What's this for?" she asked.

"That's for not takin' advantage of my man when you could have. He rockin' at least $100,000 worth of jewelry." Supreme thanked the woman and exited the club.

After placing Unique into the passenger seat of the Benz, Supreme shut the door and hopped into the driver's seat.      "Damn, Dawg you fucked up!" Supreme said wasting no time starting a conversation. He needed Unique to stay awake. He wanted to know what he was doing talking to the dude in the booth.

" I'm twisssssssted." Unique slurred.

"I see nigga."

Daaamn, I'm supposed ta be goin' to the mo-mo with a bitch right about now," Unique said. "But I guess I gotta go home to my baaabbyy."

"Did you have anything else to drink when I went to the bathroom?" Supreme asked trying to place Unique's mind back in the booth.

" Yeah, I had some Moet with my man," Unique said.

"What 'cha talkin' 'bout your man? Me and you came to the club alone," Supreme said, almost yelling. He started to panic, because saying the dude in the booth was his man, meant Unique knew him well.

"Yeah, I ran into my man Ray who I be coppin' my shit from."

Supreme's body suddenly went limp, causing his hands to slide off the steering wheel. The car drifted to the side of the road. He quickly gathered himself and grabbed the wheel guiding the Benz back onto the street.

"Oh yeah, my man is gettin' married. He told me to invite some friends of mine. I told him I'll need four invitations. One for me, you, Glory and Kim."

Supreme thought about the months to come. He knew he'd eventually come face to face with Ray. His identity as the stick-up kid would be exposed, and he didn't want that. Everything he had gained since arriving in the city would be lost. Supreme knew it was just a matter of time before Unique would ask him to tag along while he met up with Ray. He had to do something.

After dropping Unique off Supreme headed home. Supreme started devising his plan immediately. He knew he had to kill Ray. If not sooner, definitely before his wedding day. Killing Ray would be difficult. Supreme knew he was always surrounded by his men. But even if he had to kill each of Ray's men one by one in order to get him, he would. Supreme knew that by killing Ray, Unique would lose his drug connect, and that was his source of income, but it had to be done.

**Rose petals floated around the steamy Jacuzzi as** Supreme and Glory relaxed surrounded by lit candles. Supreme's legs enclosed Glory's waist as his back leaned up against the edge of the Jacuzzi. The back of Glory's head lay up against Supreme's chest. Relaxing in the Jacuzzi had become a ritual for them since Glory moved into Supreme's condo. They would always pick a night out of the week to mellow out and talk about whatever was on their minds. Tonight was different because Supreme was very quiet and Glory did all the talking.

"Do you hear me?" Glory shouted.

"Sure do," Supreme said.

"Well, if you hear me, why you ain't sayin' nothin'?" She complained.

"Go 'head Ma, finish talkin', I'm listenin'."

Seconds after Glory began talking again, Supreme's mind wandered and shut her voice out. Even if he had tried to pay attention, he couldn't have. He was concerned about the cop Jay, and Unique's drug connect, Ray. He had to get rid of them both. But Jay had to be first. Unique had already paid another $10,000 to Jay when he confessed that he knew about Unique and Kim. Unique smelled trouble and wanted Jay dealt with immediately.

Supreme was so deep in thought that he didn't notice Glory sitting up and staring at him. "Supreme!" she shouted, getting his full attention. "You better not be thinkin' about another bitch while you're in this jacuzzi with me." The expression on Glory's face showed that she wasn't playing.

Supreme gave her a weak smile. "Nah, Ma. I ain't thinkin' about no broads."

"Then who you thinkin' about then? 'Cause you've been doing a lot of thinkin' lately. What's up?" Glory asked.

"Glory, stop dramatizin' shit. " He leaned forward and kissed her on the back of her neck.

Although his eyes were on Glory, Supreme still wasn't able to forget about the hits he was about to carry out. Not knowing how his life would end up, he silently hoped for the best.

# TWENTY

Supreme sat parked on a very quiet street. The only sound heard was the hum of his engine. Dressed in all black from head to toe, the skull cap he wore protected him from the November air. Supreme sat anxiously while the .357 with the silencer rested on his lap.

Parked six cars in front of him was a red Ford Mustang. Unique sat inside nervously holding a brown paper bag filled with money, and his cell phone. He snatched his phone from his lap and dialed a number. After two rings, Supreme answered.

"You got 'cha gloves on right?" Unique asked.

"Yeah, Son." Supreme glanced at the time on the car radio. He's supposed to be here at 9:30 right?" Supreme questioned.

"I ain't gon' lie. I'm a lil nervous," Unique said.

"Nigga, I'm the one doin' the poppin'."

"I know, but I'm the one in immediate danger," Unique shouted. "I gotta hand this nigga the bag of money hopin' he trust me enough not to check it. It's only a g in the bag, not ten," he added.

"Don't worry, Kid. I got this. You just do your part and I'll do mine. Put your phone under your seat and leave it on so I can hear what's goin' on in there," Supreme commanded. " If I hear him checkin' the bag, then I'll hit him while he's still in the car. If not, I'll wait to make my move."

"Here he comes. I'm out." Unique ended.

Supreme heard a car door being opened, then closed and the sound of a deep voice.

"What's up?" Jay asked reaching over to pat Unique down. "I think I'm beginning to like you," Jay said with a grin. His eyes zoomed in on the brown bag Unique carried.

"Where your partner?" Unique quizzed, loud enough for Supreme to hear.

"He wasn't with me last time was he?"

Unique shook his head. "Nah. So, you cut him out the deal?" Unique asked.

"Why you askin'? You wearin' a wire?" Jay asked suspiciously.

"Nah Man, I 'on get down like that," Unique replied, smiling inside.

"That's my money in that bag?" Jay grabbed the bag off Unique's lap before Unique could reply.

"Yeah…yeah, that's you," Unique said, looking out of his sideview mirror while Jay peeped into the bag.

Jay looked over at Unique with a cold stare. "Are you all right? You sound a little shaky."

"Na….Nah, I'm cool." Unique barely got his words out.

"How is your relationship goin' with Kim?" Jay asked.

"It's good." Unique stared at Jay's hands hoping he wouldn't go into the bag.

"Yeah," Jay smiled. "I know what you mean. She's a good woman. Well, enough small talk," Jay said. "Let me count this money so I can leave."

Unique's heart skipped a beat. He searched for words that would stop Jay from counting the money. His eyes zoomed in on Jay's hand entering the bag. Everything seemed to move in slow motion. He watched his hand slide out the bag filled with a wad of cash.

Jay felt Unique's eyes glued on him so he turned his head towards him. "What's up?"

"Uh…uh, nothing'," Unique said fearfully.

'Somethin' is up.  You actin' real funny nigga!" Jay snapped his head from left to right, looking outside the car.

Unique started to panic.  He quickly turned around in his seat and looked out of the back windshield.

"What the fu…" Jay said following Unique's eyes.

At that very moment, Unique saw a dark figure standing outside the passenger door.  He knew who it was and he knew what was about to take place.  To defend himself from the bullets that were about to fly, he threw his knees up to his chest and dropped his forehead onto his knee caps while tucking his hands behind his head.

Jay gazed at Unique and knew this was his last day on earth.  He closed his eyes and turned facing the passenger window.  And he was right, a silent .357 bullet burst through the windshield and entered his forehead, killing him instantly.  His body slowly fell forward until what was left of his forehead slammed up against the glove compartment.

"Let's go," Supreme said to Unique, who was still in a cannonball position.  He was peering through the shattered passenger window at Unique.  "Don't forget 'cha cell phone under the seat."

"Damn, you fucked that nigga up!" Unique exclaimed.

Supreme smiled and looked over at Unique.  "How you know?  You was balled up in a knot."

"Yeah, the only reason I tucked myself up like that was because I thought you was gon' bust wildly into the car. Nigga, I was hidin' my most vital organs," Unique joked.

"No doubt," Supreme said, but was thinking differently.  He knew Unique was scared shitless.  He saw the look on his face when he peered through the Mustang's shattered windshield.

"PooBear and Wop stealing that Mustang and this Pontiac will guarantee that we are in the clear.  If somebody did see the tag numbers, they can't be traced back to us," Unique said.

Supreme parked the Pontiac a block from where he used to live, and he and Unique walked a block and hopped into Supreme's Impala.

"Now we in the clear," Supreme bragged, starting the car. He smiled to himself thinking, *one down and five to go*.

# TWENTY-ONE

Supreme sat alone at a table for two in a crowded restaurant in Falls Church, Virginia after tailing a Lexus coupe for two hours. But those hours were worth it, because the man behind the wheel of the Lexus was one of Ray's men. Supreme decided he would kill him first out of the four men on Ray's team. The man seemed to be the easiest target because he was alone more than the others. But tonight he was with his heavyset lady friend who Supreme had seen him with on two occasions. He had followed the man for a week straight before he decided to move in for the kill.

Supreme held the menu up to his face as he peeked to observe the couple sitting across the room. When the waitress came to take his order, Supreme made sure not to look at her. As soon as the waitress left his table, Supreme turned his attention to the couple. He watched as they smiled at each other while enjoying their food. For a second, he wondered if he should go through with what he was about to do. He knew if he killed one of Ray's men; there would be no turning back. He would have to finish what he started by killing all of Ray's men and then Ray.

Supreme thought about walking out of the restaurant and letting fate take its course, although that fate could be detrimental to him. He was sure that if Ray saw him, he would try to kill him.

"Here's your food." The waitress said walking up to Supreme's table with a plate in each hand.

She sat a glass of soda down and handed Supreme his bill. She was getting ready to walk off, but Supreme stopped her to request his check. He reached into his back pocket and passed the waitress a fifty. "Keep the change," he said remembering not to make eye contact.

Supreme wasted no time digging into his meal, but continued his surveillance. Taking his eyes off the couple momentarily, he stared at just about every man and woman trying to determine if any were off duty cops. While he looked from one table to the next, he was caught off guard by a pair of eyes that observed him as he watched other people. Those eyes belonged to the young waitress who waited on him. She smiled at Supreme while batting her eyelashes at him. He smiled back at her and gave her a friendly wave. He watched her for a second, and then turned his attention to his target. Just as he did, he saw Ray's man scoot his chair out from his table and stand up.

Supreme quickly stood up, but was immediately met by his admirer. This time she had the privilege of seeing his entire face.

"You need anything?" she quizzed.

"Nah…Nah," Supreme said. He watched his target walk towards the men's room. "I gotta use the bathroom," he said rubbing his stomach. As he peeped over the waitress' shoulder, he realized his target had already entered the restroom. He started to panic, thinking that what he came to do wasn't going to take place. "Uh…let me get to the bathroom Ma," Supreme said with a fake smile.

Supreme walked into the slightly empty restroom. A pair of feet could be seen in the last stall. He took a step back and entered the stall closest to the target. Wanting to get the drama over with as quickly as possible, Supreme reached into his inside pocket and pulled out a pair of black leather gloves. He slid them on then reached into his pocket pulling out a small piece of paper with something written on it. Then he smoothly slid his chrome .357 from his waist and climbed on top of the toilet bowl. He made sure the silencer was on tightly then planted both of his feet on the toilet bowl for leverage.

Peeping over into the next stall, he saw his target sitting on the toilet with his pants down around his ankles. He let go of the piece of paper, letting it float down into the stall. The paper landed on the man's lap, causing him to do just what Supreme wanted him to. He looked up, and a man with something shiny in his hand was the last thing he saw. The first bullet that hit Ray's stick-man cut his life short hitting him in his right eye and lodging into his brain! Quickly, Supreme removed his gloves and walked out of the restroom.

"There you are," the young waitress stated, standing to the side of the restroom. She scared Supreme. His body flinched. "I didn't scare you did I? I just wanna give you back some of the tip you gave me."

"Yeah you did scare me," he snapped. "I wasn't expectin' you to be standin' in front of the men's room." Avoiding eye contact with her, his eyes scanned the restaurant. "Do you always do shit like this?" he asked easing away from the entrance of the men's restroom. "Don't worry about that tip," Supreme said backing away. "I gave you that from my heart. Maybe I'll stop by here again and give you another tip." As he waved bye to her, he ran head on into the woman who was waiting for the man he just murdered.

"Oh, I'm sorry," she said. "Did you just come from out of the men's room?"

Supreme glanced back over his shoulder to see if the waitress was still standing where he left her. She wasn't. "Nah, I just got off the phone."

Supreme rushed to his Impala and sped out of the parking lot. He dropped low in his seat after seeing several police cars with their sirens wailing, race down the street in the opposite direction. After going unnoticed Supreme took a deep breath. He smiled to himself then mumbled, *Two down and four to go.*


**A day later, four men sat around a table in the** dining room of a house in Northwest. One of the men spoke with indignation in his voice.

"All y'all, except Sean, have been with me for over two years.  Only once have y'all had to put in work for me.  And since then we haven't had beef with nobody." Ray looked across the table at Sean. " I try my best not to get in shit 'cause I'm all about that money and I try to stay low key.  But, we gotta do something about Bud getting' killed." Ray looked around the table at all three of his men.

"I'm fucked up about it," Nut shouted! "I grew up with that nigga. I wanna know who killed him." Nut was unattractive and sat with a pitbull look on his face waiting for Ray's response.

"His moms told me the police said they found a piece of paper next to his body with the words, *won't cheat on me again* written on it," Ray said. "She also said the police told her the camera in the restaurant wasn't working at the time of his murder.  So they didn't see who went in and killed him.  She also said the only finger prints were from Bud and another man they already questioned and don't believe he's the shooter. "

"I think that's bullshit, about the piece of paper that was found next to his body.  The dude that hit 'em probably did that to throw the police off and make like his baby momma or some other bitch had something to do with it.  Or make like it was a chick who put a hit out on him," Sean exclaimed.

"Did anybody talk to that bitch Bud was with the night he was killed?" Ray quizzed.

"Yeah," Nut said projecting his voice. "Her name is Monica."

"You talked to her?"  Ray asked.

"Yeah, she told me she and Bud went to the restaurant and everything was normal.  They ate; Bud got up to use the restroom, but took too long to come back. So she got up to go look for him.  On her way to the restroom, she bumped into this dude.  She asked him if he had just come out of the men's room and he said no; so she walked off and went back to the table." Nut paused as he stroked his hair bringing attention to his receding hair line. "Five or six minutes later, she heard commotion," he added. "When she ran toward the noise she noticed two men blockin' the entrance of the bathroom.  A lady that she stood next to told her they said a man was found in the bathroom dead."

"You know what?" Ray asked with his face showing anger. "She walked pass the nigga that did it. The bamma she bumped into. Did she tell you what he looked like?"

"Yeah. She said he was about six feet with a tannish complexion. He had cornrows in his head and a close shaved full beard. Almost shadow-like."

Ray snapped, "That bitch don't know what she's talkin' 'bout. I want all y'all to keep y'all eyes and ears open, especially for the nigga with the braids." Standing up from the table he continued, "I'm goin' home. I'll see y'all tomorrow. We gotta go make a drop off of fifteen keys to lil Bird in Maryland."

"Oh yeah, Bud's girl said he sounded like he had an accent too, but she couldn't place it," Nut added. He stood up from the table followed by Sean and Pappy.

"Ok, we'll look out for that too. Let's go," Ray said, leading the way out of the house.

# TWENTY-TWO

"Where'd you eat Thanksgiving dinner at today?" Lisa asked Supreme.

"At my girl's mom's crib," he answered.

Lisa gave Supreme a sinister stare. "You 'on have no problem with sayin' that huh?"

"Nah, why should I? You know what's up already."

"I know, but I got some feelings for you."

"I got feelings for you too," Supreme quickly responded.

"Yeah right. The only thing you got feelings for is this pussy."

"Keepin' it real, you right." Supreme smiled.

"I know nigga." Lisa grabbed a pillow from the sofa and hit Supreme with it.

"Anyway, you have a man." Supreme exclaimed.

"I know but he ain't here. He's got ten years. But, he'll be home in about three more years. "

'That's good, Ma. Most broads do niggas dirty when they locked up."

Lisa shook her head to emphasize what she was about to say. "I can't do Nick like that, because he did a lot for me when he was on the streets. I'm down for my man."

Supreme grinned. "He know you fuckin'?"

"Yeah, he know, he's the one who told me to get some dick because if he was out and I was in, he'd be getting' some pussy. He told me just make sure I don't get pregnant."

"Yo! That's why I fucks with you. You're a real broad," Supreme nodded.

"Yeah, and that's why I'm gon' do what I'm doing for you....oh yeah…" She smiled at Supreme. "And I'm doing it for the money too, not just because I fucks with you. Now, where is my half?" She stuck her hand out towards him.

Supreme reached into his pocket. "Here's five g's now and you'll get the other five when your job is complete."

"I want six more g's after my job is done," Lisa demanded.

"No problem. You got that, Ma. The job you gon' do is worth it. Now what's the deal?"

"He'll be here to pick me up tonight around 8:00 pm," Lisa bragged.

"Which guy?" Supreme asked.

Supreme had concocted a story for Lisa about a vendetta he had with four men that were from DC that killed his brother back in New York. He had told her he wanted revenge but needed her help. When she agreed to do so, he told her where they would be and showed her what they looked like from pictures he had taken while tailing them. He also promised her 10 g's if she could get just one of them alone so he could put in work.

"The chubby one is Pappy," Lisa said. I followed him to the club last night. I played it off by bumpin' into him and you know how y'all niggas are. He struck a conversation with me immediately. I gave him my cell phone number. He called today and asked if he could pick me up tonight. I told him yeah, but for a price," Lisa said.

Supreme's face lit up with a huge smile. "You on point huh, Ma?"

"Yeah, I know how we gon' do this," Lisa said taking charge. "Show up here tonight around seven and sit in your car about a block away. Follow us until we reach a hotel. While me and him in the room, I'm gon' tell him I'm gonna go to the ice machine and I'll be back. I'll leave and come straight to your car and pass you the keys to the room. You take the keys and do ya thing," Lisa said proudly.

"Damn, Ma! You got it all mapped out. Are you sure you ain't do this before?" Supreme asked.

"Actually, I did something similar for Nick before. But I set the nigga up to get robbed, not killed," Lisa said sarcastically.

"So, I'll call you around six. Don't get cold feet on me," Supreme said, walking to the front door.

"Boy Pleeeease!" Lisa hissed, as Supreme walked out.


**That evening, Supreme called Lisa.**

"What's up, Ma?" Supreme stated the moment he heard Lisa's voice.

"Damn! You wanna do this huh?"

"Yeah, so what's up?" Supreme asked.

"Everything is in motion. I talked to him already and he'll be at my house at eight. So get over here," Lisa said anxiously.

"Sounds good, Ma. Sounds good."

Supreme hung the phone up then grabbed the black baseball hat and his .357 from off his bed. He stood up and tucked the gun on his waist then threw the hat over his cornrows. He made sure the hat was tilted down below his eyes.

It was 7 o'clock when Supreme parked his Impala half a block from Lisa's house. After waiting for what seemed like an eternity, Supreme saw a green Range Rover pull up in front of Lisa's house.

After hearing a horn blow, Lisa stepped out of her house wearing a black, hip hugging J.Lo. halter dress with a black baby mink jacket over it.

"Damn, you lookin' good girl," Pappy said to Lisa who gracefully stepped into his Range Rover. Smiling, his chubby face acknowledged his approval of Lisa's looks.

"Oh, thank you," she replied, looking Pappy over. "You look good too," Lisa said glancing at the iced out chain around his neck. "So what's up? You know what I'm tryin' to do," Pappy said. His eyes shot down to Lisa's partially exposed thighs. Pappy grinned as he turned onto 8th Street.

"It's whatever," Lisa expressed sassily, rolling her neck.

"You wanna go to hotel downtown?"

Lisa thought for a second then decided not to go downtown. "Naw, we can go to a room on New York Avenue. You 'on need to spend all that money on a room 'cause you ain't gonna' last that long," she laughed. Then she smiled at Pappy.

Twenty minutes later Lisa and Pappy were walking into room number 220 at the Super 8. The moment Pappy opened the door, Lisa remembered to avoid touching anything in the room. She stood by the foot of the bed looking at Pappy. "If you wanna fuck on the first night, you gotta pay me 'cause I may never see you again after tonight," Lisa said sticking her hand out.

Pappy grinned then reached into his pocket. "How much you want?" he said pulling out a thick bundle of money.

"How much do I look like I'm worth?" Lisa said spinning around in a circle.

"You look worth more than I have in my hand," Pappy said, while his eyes traveled from Lisa's feet up to her face. "I love petite red bone broads," Pappy screamed.

"Well if I'm worth more than you have in your hand, give me all of it and you owe me every time you see me." She smiled down at him.

Pappy chuckled then said, "I like that. That was slick." He placed the entire bundle into her hand. "That's two g's. You can have that."

Lisa unzipped her purse and tossed the money into it. "Now stand up," she ordered.

Pappy stood up. He stared at the top of her head then gazed down towards her hands which had already started to unfasten his belt

"You don't have no problem with wearing a condom do you?" Lisa asked watching his pants fall to his ankles. His dick stood stiffly at least 10 inches out of the slit of his boxers. "You might not fit a condom," she chuckled, taking a hold of his dick with both hands. She stroked it back and forth.

Pappy smiled at Lisa's last words. He reached into his leather jacket pocket and pulled out a condom. "I got a magnum. This for niggas that's hung," he boasted.

"Lisa snatched the condom from Pappy and placed it on the nightstand next to her purse. She roughly pushed Pappy down on the bed. She smiled seductively at him while dropping to her knees. She took his shoes off then removed his pants from around his ankles, tossing them next to his other attire.

Pappy watched as she grabbed his stiff dick with her right hand. Lisa stuck her tongue out and ran it from his testicles all the way up to the head of his enlarged dick.

"Whoa!" he sighed as a tingle shot through his body.

"You like that?" Lisa asked.

"Yes!" Pappy screeched.

Lisa quickly stood up. "I just thought of something."

"What?" Pappy spat, showing disappointment.

"You like ice?" Lisa asked hoping he'd say yes.

"Yeah."

Lisa grabbed her purse, throwing the condom Pappy gave her into it. She didn't want to leave any fingerprints. "I'm gonna get some ice so I can put it in my mouth and suck your dick," Lisa said trying to sound sexy.

Pappy smiled. "Why you takin' your purse with you? You tryin' to run game on me? Are you gonna leave out and not come back," he asked sitting up on the bed.

"Nah, anyway, it ain't like you don't know where I live. Now give me the keys to the room and let me go so I can hurry back."

"Check my pants pocket," he said.

Lisa grabbed the room key out of Pappy's pants pocket and headed for the door. She lifted the bottom portion of her dress to touch the doorknob. She succeeded in her attempt to leave no fingerprints. The moment she stepped out of the room, she blew a sigh of relief. She hurried down the corridor and stopped in front of the elevator. Looking up toward the room she left, she cracked a wide smile. Once the elevator door opened, she stepped onto it.

"Mission accomplished," she mumbled to herself.

She slithered through the hotel's parking lot in search of Supreme's

Impala. When her eyes didn't spot it, she started to panic, then she saw set of flashing headlights. Lisa smiled then hurried in the direction of the flashing lights.

"What's he doin' in there?" Supreme asked the moment Lisa slid into the passenger seat.

Lisa passed Supreme the hotel room key. "He's in the room naked with a stiff dick. Room number 220," Lisa added.

"Does he have a gun on him?" Supreme asked.

"Not that I could see."

"I'll be back," Supreme uttered, stepping out the car into the chilled night air.

It took him less than two minutes to reach room number 220. He placed his ear to the door listening for anything out of the ordinary. When he heard nothing, he slid his black baseball batting gloves on and opened the door.

"That you!" Pappy yelled. "I hope you brung a lot of ice, 'cause Im'a put some in my mouth while I eat your pussy," he yelled.

Supreme had his back pressed against the wall peeping from around it at the naked man that laid on his back across the king sized bed. He pulled his .357 from his waist and walked out from behind the wall with his gun extended.

"What the fuck!" Pappy shouted, seeing Supreme with a gun in his hand. He sat up on the side of the bed with fear in his eyes.

"Son, don't move another inch," Supreme said while standing two feet away from Pappy.

"What's up? What I do?" Pappy quizzed. "If that broad sent you in here because she thought I was gonna take my money back after we fucked, I wasn't. I swear."

Supreme ignored Pappy's words. "You're Ray's man right?"

Pappy looked up at Supreme with a perplexed look on his face. "Yeah," he said.

"Well you should know why I'm here." Supreme balled up the piece of paper he'd pulled from his pocket and threw it at Pappy. "Read that," he said.

Pappy grabbed the paper from his lap and unraveled it. "*Won't cheat on me again*." Pappy's eyes grew large after he read the note. He looked at the black leather gloves Supreme wore and the silencer on the face of the chrome .357 and he knew he was going to die. "You killed Bud," he shouted!

Supreme took off his baseball hat to show his cornrows. "I know that bitch your man was with the night I killed him in that restaurant told y'all how I looked." He placed his hat back on his head. "But I bet Ray didn't know it's the same nigga that robbed him last year. He probably forgot all about me," Supreme revealed.

Pappy sat on the side of the bed contemplating on what to do. He eyed Supreme sizing him up. Suddenly, he yelled at the top of his voice leaping off the bed with his arms open wide as if he were going to bear hug Supreme.

From reflexes alone, Supreme took a giant step back while at the same time, letting two rounds off that hit Pappy in his stomach and chest, sending him face first to the carpet right at the feet of his assassin. Seeing the man's body twitching, he squeezed his trigger two more times and watched as two bullets consecutively ripped into Pappy's back. Supreme stepped to the side to examine the body. Pappy was lifeless. Supreme walked out of the room with Pappy's white leather jacket over his black leather jacket. He held his head down low until he reached his Impala.

"Oh no you didn't take his jacket," Lisa said, smiling when Supreme entered the car.

"That was just to throw nosey people off," Supreme said looking over at Lisa. He noticed the small chrome gun resting on her lap with her right hand on it. "Ma, what's up with that .25 you got in your lap?" Supreme asked.

"Don't take offense to this, but I been in the streets all my life and I know how shit goes. When you do shit like what I think you just did, you' on wanna leave no witnesses. I gotta be on the safe side," Lisa said with concern.

Supreme grinned and started the Impala's engine. It rose from off the ground.

"What are you smilin' about?" Lisa quizzed.

"You. You a gangsta bitch," he laughed.

"If you wanna call me that, go 'head, but I'm just a product of my environment." Lisa smiled.

"Yeah, me too," Supreme nodded while pulling out the parking space.

"You gonna' get the rest of 'em?" Lisa asked.

"Nah, I just needed to sleep one of them," Supreme lied. *Three down and three to go, he thought to himself.*

# TWENTY-THREE

Ray, Sean and Nut sat around the glass dining table in the meeting spot. Ray spat angrily, "It's no doubt in my motherfuckin' mind now somebody is tryin' to take us out one by one. When Bud was hit, I thought that was an isolated incident," he added. "But now Pappy got hit. I 'on know who or why? But let's make sure it doesn't happen again."

"I 'on know," Sean said, looking unsure. "We' on know who the chump is, so how can we defend ourselves? The nigga could be somebody we know."

"Nah, fuck nah!" Nut snapped. "Ain't no nigga we know doin'no shit like this." Nut looked across the table at Ray. "Your father got men who will kill an entire family in one day!"

"Ain't no sense in callin' him yet. Let's try to handle this on our own first," Ray said.

"So, what we gonna' do?" Nut asked. "I not try'na let this bamma get me."

"OK, we know the nigga that killed Bud is the same nigga that killed Pappy, because the note found had the identical message. So what we gotta do first is scope the niggas out we know to eliminate them. Then we gonna' follow all the niggas I sell coke to. We lookin' for anybody who looks close to what that bitch described to us," Ray said giving orders like a captain. "Y'all got two and a half weeks to do all this." Ray exploded.

"I pay y'all to watch my back and put in work if it showed its ugly head. It did. I ain't doin' nothin' until y'all come back with results. Spend no more than a day on each nigga... " Ray stopped because suddenly in his mind he saw vividly the face Monica described to them' and it was the same face that robbed him almost two years ago. "Naaaw." Ray shook his head. "This can't be the same nigga," he mumbled.

"Yeah, like I was sayin'," he continued, "If y'all don't see anybody that looks like the nigga that bitch described, move on to the next man. Exclude Unique," he demanded. "My pops and his stepfather are like brothers. I know he ain't got nothin' to do with this shit."

"You 'on know that for sure," Nut said seriously. "So, to be on the safe side if we come up with nothin' from everybody else, we'll check him out too."

"OK. That's fair," Ray said. "Check him out last. But we gotta catch the nigga who did this before I get married next month."

**Nine days later at the meeting spot, Ray, Sean** and Nut sat around the dining table as usual.

"I got good news and I got bad news. I'm gonna tell you the bad news first," Nut said. "I hope you're ready for this. We saw a nigga that fit the description of the chump we lookin' for with your man Unique. That's the bad news." For a split second, the entire house was quiet. Then Ray laughed, as if someone had told a joke.

"What's funny?" Nut spat.

"What you just told me," Ray managed to say in between his laughter.

"I 'on see nothin' funny with what he just said," Sean expressed. "Ray, the nigga with Unique is the bamma we lookin' for," Sean said with a sure look on his face.

"What's the good news?" Ray snapped with his face showing concern.

"The good news is we been followin' him for the last two days and we're hip to him," Sean revealed between the sounds of his gum popping. "We stopped following Unique and started followin' him. We know where he lives and we know who his girl is." Sean paused leaning back in his chair. "You ain't gonna' believe who she is."

Ray placed his attention on Nut. "Who is that nigga's girl?"

"You remember that strip club we used to go to. Well, Booty is that nigga's girl. They live together in Oxon Hill. We're not sure yet, but we think Booty is Unique's sister." Nut grinned devilishly. "I always wanted to fuck that bitch."

Ray dropped his chin against his chest and began shaking his head. Ray lifted his head up. "We have to be sure about this."

"We are," Nut quickly spat! "While we was followin' the chump, he had the nerve to cruise by Sean's crib slowly like he was lookin' for somethin'. We're sure it's him!"

"Damn! That nigga Unique been try'na kill us off. Why though?" Ray asked. "I ain't did shit to him."

Ray needed time to decide what to do next. He was angry about the information he'd just received, and he knew this was a dilemma he'd have to solve carefully. If it weren't Unique, he wouldn't have to ponder. He would just give the word and bodies would drop.

"Ray!" Nut barked, getting Ray's attention. "What we gonna' do 'bout this shit?"

Ray stood up. "I just need a few minutes," he said walking. "Let me think on it a lil more. I'll be right back with my answer." Ray peeped over his shoulder as he walked out of the dining room. Nut wanted drama. That was his forte. He didn't care what the consequences were. He was ready for war. And that was the reason Ray put the rugged man on his team in the first place. Sean was more laid back and would step up if called upon.

Ray walked up to the table and looked down at his men. "Them niggas wanna play games. They placed notes on Bud and Pappy's bodies knowing killing them had nothing to do with them cheatin' on no bitches. OK, this is not gonna be a one-way game anymore," Ray roared walking in circles. "Unique is supposed to cop from me in two days. I'm gonna sell my shit to him and act like ain't shit going on. Y'all with it?" he asked.

"Hell yeah," Nut snapped. "We get to play like they playin' right?" Nut rubbed the long scar on his face as he often did when he was ready for battle.

"Yeah." Ray looked at Sean. "You with it?"

"I take my orders from you. I'm with it," Sean answered strangely.

# TWENTY-FOUR

S upreme! Supreme!" Glory shook him fully awake. "Wake up baby. It's Christmas!" She shook him forcefully while standing above him smiling from ear to ear.

Supreme lay on his back looking up at an excited Glory through his partially opened eyes. The look on his face said it all; he wanted to sleep. "Damn Ma! Why you shakin' me all hard talkin' 'bout it's Christmas? I know that."

Supreme rolled out of bed tiredly sliding on some shorts and a t-shirt. He walked over to the dresser and grabbed the camcorder. "I wanna record your reaction when you open your gifts," he said devilishly.

"Let me put on some clothes." He placed the camcorder back on top of the dresser and then ran over to the walk-in closet and grabbed some clothes. He slid the clothes on, and put on Timberland boots. He snatched the camcorder off the dresser. "You ready to go open your presents?" he asked.

"Yeah," Glory replied, smiling.

"Ma, open the gifts I tell you to open first," Supreme said while filming Glory who had already made her way in front of the beautifully decorated Christmas tree.

"Why?" She pouted. She held a gift in her hand.

"Because, Ma. Just do what I ask," Supreme said pointing to an all red wrapped gift. "Open that one," he said.

Supreme zoomed the camera in on her face.

"Why, I 'on hear nothin'?" She shook the gift then looked perplexed.

"Just open it," Supreme snapped.

She tore at the gift only taking three seconds to tear all the red wrapping paper from it.

Supreme burst into laughter after witnessing the look on Glory's face. He laughed so hard he dropped to his knees. Glory looked at him with fire in her eyes. "I know you didn't wrap this Tampon box and try to give it to me as a gift? Boy!" Glory threw the box at him hitting him on his head. "That ain't funny," she said.

Glory grabbed another gift and immediately tore at it. Frowning, she asked, "Why is this gift so light?"

"I 'on know," Supreme said grinning.

"Supreme what is goin' on?" Glory yelled, angry as hell. The gift she'd just opened was an empty shoebox. She threw the box at him and stood up.

"Look how mad she is audience," Supreme joked. He stood up and got a close up of Glory's face.

"Are all those gifts under that tree full of shit like you?" She pushed Supreme causing him to stumble backwards.

"Oh man! Did y'all see that? An angry actress has just assaulted her director," he said continuing to play around.

"Supreme I'm not playin' with you. Where are my gifts?" Glory asked angrily.

Supreme stepped around Glory and walked to the tree. He reached down and grabbed a green wrapped gift the size of a shoebox. He handed the gift to Glory.

"Supreme, if ain't nothin' in this box, we gonna' fight up in here. Im'a show you what I be doin' at the gym," she said.

"Take the gift." He shoved it into her stomach.

Glory smiled immediately when she felt the weight of the gift. She tore at it at the speed of light. "Baby you bought me some baby blue

Manolo boots." She threw her left arm around Supreme's neck and kissed him for her new $700 boots. Glory took one of the costly boots out the box, which happened to be the boot Supreme wanted her to retrieve. Glory shook the boot and heard a rattle.

"What's that noise?" she asked.

"Reach inside the boot," he demanded.

She placed the box with the other boot in it on the floor, and then reached into the boot she held. She retrieved a set of keys that had BMW engraved on them.

"Supreme, are these what I think they for?" Glory quizzed excitedly.

"Yeah, they go to your new BMW X5 SUV that's parked outside."

"Ahhhhh!" Glory screamed, jumping up and down, dropping the boot she held but holding on tightly to her new set of car keys. She ran out the front door before Supreme could place the camcorder on her.

"Baby I love it," She bawled, running up to Supreme and throwing her arms around his neck.

"I knew you'd like it," he said smiling at his woman.

"I love it." In three seconds she had climbed into her new ride and behind the wheel.

"Wait for me, Ma." Supreme ran up to the SUV and hopped into the passenger seat.

"You like ya new ride huh?" Supreme asked.

"No. I love it." Glory looked directly into the camcorder. "And I love you too." She kissed the lens of the camera.

"I love you too Ma," Supreme said leaning toward Glory.

The ringing of Supreme's phone interrupted the kiss he'd planned on landing on Glory's cheek.

"Merry Christmas, Son," Supreme answered.

"Man, I got bad news. I received a call from Bullet and he told me PeeWee got killed last night around my old stompin' grounds."

"Oh shit…that's your word, Kid?"

"Yeah. He said the word is two niggas walked up to him and his boys last night and out of nowhere both of the bammas drew their guns. They told PeeWee and the other two niggas that stood next to him if they ran, they'd feel some lead. PeeWee and the two niggas he was with put their hands in the air. They said the tallest dude reached in his pocket and pulled out a piece of paper. Then without warning, the shorter of the two fired one-shot point blank range into PeeWee's face. And when his body hit the concrete, the tallest one threw a piece of paper on top of his body and they both stepped off and jumped into a car at the end of the block."

"Damn, the other two niggas that stood beside PeeWee ain't have no fire on 'em?" Supreme asked with concern.

"Nobody had heat on them at that time."

"What about the piece of paper the nigga threw on PeeWee's body?" Supreme asked curiously.

"Bullet said somebody around the way picked the paper up off PeeWee's body. He said when he finds out who took it, he's gonna' let me know," Unique said. "And get this. Darkman called me and said he out of the game. He wants to focus on school."

"What?" Supreme said astonished.

"Well he out," Unique said. I ain't mad at him though. At least he let me know before I copped. I'ma call my man after I get off the phone with you."

"Speaking of ya man, is he still gettin'married?" Supreme asked holding his breath. He was hoping to hear the word *no* come from Unique's mouth, but he had no such luck.

"Yeah. I got four invitations from Ray when I copped from him last week. It's supposed to go down the end of next month. By the way, you try'na go with me tomorrow to pick that up?" Unique asked.

Supreme's heart sped up instantly.

"Nah, I'll take PooBear with me," Unique said before Supreme could respond. "I'll wait until after the weddin' to start takin' you with me. That way Ray will already have met you."

"So what 'cha plannin' on doing for the rest of the day?" Unique asked.

"Me and Glory are goin' to the Mosque with Brotha Hetep today," Supreme said. "Last week the minister tore the house down with his message," Supreme added proudly.

"You need to take Kim with you," Unique pleaded. "She needs to calm down. Last night when I was talkin' to Bullet she was ear hustlin'. She heard some of the shit I was talkin' 'bout, and all morning she's been askin' me 'bout my phone conversation last night. A while back I promised Kim if I saw any sign of danger before I reached my goal, I'd get out the game before somethin' bad happened. If I tell her about what happened to PeeWee, she's gonna' consider that a sign of danger and expect me to get out the game now, not later," Unique whispered.

"Listen to your woman," Supreme said laughing. "I'm out," he said ending the call.

Supreme glanced at Glory who continued to amuse herself with the gadgets on her new ride. At that moment he thought seriously about how he'd propose to her. If he maneuvered out of his mess he was sure she'd make his life complete.

# TWENTY-FIVE

Unique and PooBear rode in silence as they traveled to meet Ray at Iverson Mall. The mood was somber. Unique thought about the information Bullet had given him in reference to Pee Wee's murder. He was still perplexed about the written message that had been thrown on Pee Wee's body. The message *won't cheat on me again* puzzled Unique. Thinking that one of Pee Wee's women sent some niggas after him was the only justification he could come up with.

Unique's thoughts subsided when he spotted Ray in a PT Cruiser and pulled up beside it. He grabbed the gym bag filled with money from the back seat and rested it on his lap. He glanced at the dark tint on the cruiser while his eyes searched the parking lot for Ray's men. Seeing the driver's side window slowly descending, Unique rolled his window down.

"Step in my car for a minute," Ray said.

"Okay," Unique replied rolling his window back up.

Unique opened his door and stepped out of the Mustang with the gym bag in hand. He watched two men step out of Ray's car and walk away as if they were on their way inside the mall. He saw not a hint of their faces.

"What's up?" Ray asked as soon as Unique slid into the passenger seat.

Ray drew a fake smile, to mask his anger. It had taken Sean and

Nut practically two days to calm him down after they all sat in a car in front of Supreme's condo waiting for him to come out. They weren't there to kill Supreme, they just wanted Ray to get a good look at the man that was killing his men. When Ray saw Supreme, he realized it was the same man Sean had tried to kill in a hotel parking lot after the man robbed Ray.

"Where are your other men at?" Unique asked breaking Ray's concentration.

Ray gazed at Unique wanting to reach in his coat and pull his baby Uzi out. Instead, he calmly said, "Bud and Pappy got killed a couple of weeks back."

"Damn, I'm sorry to hear that, Joe. Y'all know who did it?" Unique questioned with a concerned look on his face.

"Yeah." Ray looked at Unique with a cold look in his eyes. "We gonna' do something big with them niggas," he said. Did you know me before I met you? Ray blurted out.

"Naw," Unique replied, wondering why Ray asked. "My first time knowing who you were was when I met 'cha with your pops. I thought I'd be dealin' with your pops, but he said he was out the game so I'd have to be dealing with you. Why you ask?"

*Damn, this nigga can lie with a straight face, Ray thought.* "I just asked," he said to Unique.

"Ray, the reason I'm only coppin' twenty joint's from you is because one of my young'uns quit the game to focus on school; and another young nigga I was hittin' off got killed. They say two niggas walked up on him and shot him in the face. They threw a note on him saying, *won't cheat on me again*," Unique revealed.

Ray smiled inside. He wasn't there when Nut and Sean took care of their business on Saturday night, but he felt a sense of accomplishment because he had sent them to kill PeeWee after he found out PeeWee was copping from Unique.

"I'm sorry to hear that," Ray said. "Y'all know who did it?"

"Nah. This the streets…shit will come out sooner or later," Unique uttered.

Unique and Ray switched bags and Unique exited the car. Sean and Nut stepped in minutes later. Ray told them Unique had played everything off like he didn't know anything. "We're gonna kill Unique," Ray said abruptly.

"Nah, let's take another one of Unique's young'uns out first," Nut said.

Ray agreed. "They took two of us out, so let's take two of them out before we kill Unique."

Exiting the mall, Nut and Sean told Ray about the plan they'd concocted. Sean revealed the information he had found out about Glory. At that moment, Glory had no idea that her work as a stripper would be helpful to their plan.

# TWENTY-SIX

"Man, you gotta come pick up this money," Wop yelled in Unique's cell phone.

"Why can't you hold on to that until tomorrow?" Unique asked.

"'Cause, maaan. I'm at a party and I 'on know what I might get into tonight. Besides, I'm fuckedd... up." Wop chuckled.

"Where you at?" Unique asked. His face showed his exasperation about the whole situation.

"Man, I'm...." Wop paused as if he had to think about it. "I'm on Pomroy Road in Southeas'."

"All right, be out by ya whip in thirty minutes. Me and Supreme are at Dad's New Years Eve party in Silver Spring."

"I'll be outside in thirty minutes," Wop slurred.

"We got a little problem," Unique said to Supreme. "Wop wants me to come get that 40 g's now 'cause he drunk and he's got the money in his car. He 'on know what he might get into tonight and I gotta go inside this party," Unique said looking for sympathy from Supreme.

"Dad wants me to mingle with some of the business people in there. He calls it networking. He told me that he invited ex-drug dealers who have turned into legit entrepreneurs." Unique looked at Supreme noticing that he wasn't concerned about the invited guest. "He said that when I decide to get out the game and go legit, I'll already know people. Besides, this is important to Kim. She's been really worried about me lately. I've got to get outta the game soon," Unique ended.

"OK. So what's up?" Supreme asked.

"Slim, I need you to go pick that up. I know you 'on really wanna miss the party, but I need that money from Wop's drunk ass tonight."

"Where Wop at?" Supreme questioned.

"You know where Pomroy Road at right?"

"Yeah, I think I know where that's at." Supreme turned and walked to his truck.

"Hold on," Unique ordered, causing Supreme to stop. "He'll be standin' outside by his car. Call me as soon as you get that and you're on your way back here," Unique said as Supreme eased away in his Navigator.

**Wop wasn't lying when he told Unique he was** fucked up. What he should have said was that he was beyond fucked up, he was twisted.

Wop slowly pushed his way through the crowd of young partygoers. Because he was intoxicated, his body swayed back and forth. Just as he had made it to the front door of the house, the music stopped abruptly, and a loud male voice yelled out, "We got five minutes before it's a new year. Everybody that brought weed, can fire that shit up. Put all those drinks away. We gon' create a cloud up in this joint'."

"Damn!" Wop shouted, just as the music started again. He opened the door and stepped out of the house into the chilly night air. As he walked down the concrete walkway, he noticed there wasn't a soul outside. He strutted with a slight stagger down the sidewalk heading to his car that was parked a block away.

POP! POP! BOOM! BOOM! POP! POP!

Although he knew the sound of guns being fired to bring in the new year was normal, he was still startled. Wop looked up and down the sidewalk. His eyes shifted from the sidewalk to the street where he spotted a vehicle slowly moving toward him. That might be Unique, he thought as his eyes focused on the vehicle as it moved closer to where he stood.

When the vehicle stopped, Wop immediately knew it wasn't Unique. The two men that occupied the car locked eyes with him. Not thinking of the men as a threat, Wop continued to walk along the sidewalk. He finally reached his car and pulled his keys from his pocket. After pushing the button that operated his alarm, he opened the door and the fresh smell hit him in the face. He slid into his car, he reached under the seat, and pulled out a medium sized brown paper bag with the 40 g's in it. Seconds later, he stood outside his car leaning up against the door with the paper bag clenched in his right hand. He looked up and down the street for any sign of Unique.

He looked down at his Rolex and wondered what was takin' Unique so long. He wanted to get back to the party. He saw a pair of headlights moving toward him, but couldn't distinguish the car's make because the lights were blinding him. But he was sure it wasn't Unique, who was now late. He stood up and eyed the Maxima that was now two feet away from him.

"What's up, Slim?" the man asked Wop, as the car stopped.

Wop looked at the man as if he were crazy. "Ain't shit, what's up wit 'cha?" Wop placed a hard expression on his face.

"That's your car?"

"Yeah, why?" Wop snapped.

"Oh, ain't shit. I just asked." The man's smile had now turned into a wicked grin. "I see Unique payin' you good." He stared into Wop's face knowing that the mention of Unique's name would get a reaction and it did.

"You know Unique?" Wop quizzed, sounding like his guard was now down. He slowly smiled. Just what the scar faced man wanted because if Wop's guard was up, he knew he wouldn't be able to get the information he was about to get.

"Yeah, I know Unique. I'm who he be getting' his coke from," Nut said.

"He ain't buyin' his shit from you," Wop said in disbelief.

"That's what you think," Nut said. "You be with PooBear right?"

"Yeah, that's my dawg." Wop smiled widely.

"What's the other nigga name that y'all be with? He's got cornrows in his hair."

"Oh, you talkin' 'bout Supreme," Wop revealed.

The passenger glanced over at his partner with a smile then placed his attention back on Wop. "His name Supreme huh?"

"Yeah. He's from New York."

The passenger looked at his partner again. "He's from New York, huh?"

Sean tapped Nut on his arm giving him the signal. Nut extended his arm out of the window with a piece of paper in his hand. "Man, we need you to give this note to Unique for us," he said convincingly.

Wop stepped to the car and took the paper from the man's hand.

"You can read it," the passenger said, seeing the curious look on Wop's face.

Wop unraveled the paper and read, "won't *cheat on me again.*" He frowned. "What the fuck does that mean?"

Nut smiled up into Wop's face. "The bitch ass nigga Supreme will know what it means," Nut said.

After those words, Nut's left hand slid out of the window brandishing a .44 revolver that was a foot away from Wop's stomach. BOOOM!

Wop's body immediately slumped forward from the impact of the .44's bullet that slammed into his mid-section.

"Go finish that nigga off close range and see what's in that bag that flew out his hand," Sean said to Nut who stepped over Wop's limp body.

Wop mustered up enough strength to look up into Nut's face. His eyes were glassy as if he was on the verge of crying. They told a story and asked a question. The story dated back eight years ago when he was ten years old, the day his brother was gunned down. When his brother was killed, Wop had been only a block away playing with his friends when he heard several shots. Instead of running away from the sound of the shots, he and his cronies ran in the direction of the gun blazing and saw a dead man lying on the sidewalk that turned out to be Wop's older and only brother.   From that day, Wop had wondered how his brother felt getting shot and dying, and now eight years later he was about to find out.

The question his eyes were asking was why was he about to be killed?  Why was the man that stood above him about to take his life?  Wop had heard the word *karma* before but he never really knew what it meant, and he didn't ask.  Now one thing was for certain, he was about to find out its meaning.

As if Nut read what was on Wop's mind, he squatted down in front of him. "I know you wonderin' why I'm about to kill you?" Nut began explaining. "Your man Supreme did this to you.  He robbed the nigga I work for and killed two of my dawgs.  But you probably know that already." Nut stood up from his squat and aimed his gun at Wop's face.  BOOOM!

"Get that bag and see what's in it," Sean reminded Nut.

Nut grabbed the bag that flew out of Wop's hand and hopped into the Maxima.

"This was a good night to do this," Sean said as he pulled off popping his gum. He smiled as he listened to the  celebration gunshots being fired in the air.

Nut, who was going into the paper bag, yelled, "There's money in this bag."

"That's good," Sean said. "We can split it 50/50."

"I'm wit it," Nut replied, placing the bundle back into the bag. "I'm hungry; let's go get something to eat."


**Supreme slowly drove Pomroy Road in search of** Wop or his car. Then, about fifty feet ahead of him, he spotted something strange.  Something or someone looked to be sitting on the ground in the street against a car.  As Supreme got closer to the scene, he realized it was a person.  His body was leaning to the side.  Then, only three seconds away from pulling along side the scene, Supreme noticed the car was a candy apple red Nissan 300 Z and the person on the ground was Wop.

Supreme smiled. "I know this nigga wasn't that twisted that he...." Supreme's smile vanished as soon as he reached the Z. His words were cut short, as he stared at Wop's body and knew he was dead. Blood was everywhere.

"Nah Son." Supreme whined, quickly pushing his door open and stepping out of his truck. He ran over to Wop's body, and saw what was left of his face. He paced around the body, and stumbled across the piece of paper Nut gave to Wop before he shot him.

"What is this?" Supreme picked the paper up and read the words *"won't cheat on me again."* His body instantly froze. He leaped out of his comatose state and swung his head in every direction. "Them niggas know!" He ran back around the front of his truck and hopped in. He slid the piece of paper he found into his pocket.

"Fuck! Fuck! Fuck!" Supreme cursed, speeding away. He pulled out his Desert Eagle, and placed it in his lap. "Damn Wop! Damn baby! I'm sorry; I got 'cha killed. Damn maaan!!" Supreme yelled at the top of his lungs. "I should've been finished them niggas off...Damn! Now everythin' fucked up. Damn!" *They might be followin' me, he thought.* He looked out of his rearview mirror. "Dem niggas killed PeeWee too...Damn, I bet that piece of paper found on his body had the same shit written on it. Man what the fuck I'm gonna' do?"

Supreme rode around for another ten minutes talking to himself. "Before I jump the gun, let me call Unique and ask him what was written on that paper that was found on PeeWee's body." Supreme pulled his cell phone from the inside pocket of his black coyote coat and dialed Unique's cell phone number.

"Yeah, hello," Unique answered.

"This Supreme."

"What's up? You on ya way?" Unique asked.

"Yeah, but let me ask you somethin' now 'cause I might forget to ask you later."

"Shoot, Slim."

"What did the nigga Bullet tell you was written on that paper that was found on PeeWee's body?" Supreme held his breath expecting the worse, but hoping for a miracle.

"I think he said some shit like, *you won't cheat on me again* was written on it. Whatever that bullshit means," Unique said undisturbed.

"Fuck!" Supreme murmured with his teeth clenched down tightly.

"What's up, Joe?" Unique quizzed after hearing Supreme curse.

Supreme's mind was racing. He didn't know what his next move would be. But what he did know was that he had to do something. Just that second, he came up with a plan.

"I got somethin' to take care of before I come pick you up. And if Kim want 'cha home by a certain time, you gonna' be late," he said.

"Go 'head and take care of your business. I wear the pants in my house. I bet 'cha this got somethin' to do with that bitch Lisa right?" Unique asked.

"Yeah Dawg, she just called me."

"I'll be here waitin', but if my sista find out 'bout that bitch, she gonna' whip her ass and yours." Unique chuckled then hung up in Supreme's ear.

Twenty minutes later, Supreme was running into his condo. He ran upstairs to his bedroom and swiftly climbed out of his casual attire and put on his all black urban wear. It was 12:50 am, and it would be at least another hour and a half before Glory would come home. Pam and Glory had to do a special private New Year's Eve show for a bunch of lesbians that would pay them $2,000 for only three hours of entertainment.

After ten minutes in the condo, Supreme was on his way back out the door. But now he had a mission that needed to be taken care of tonight in less than an hour and a half. He hopped in his black Impala, and placed his guns in his lap. He reached inside his black leather jacket tugging at his bullet proof vest to make sure it was strapped on tightly. It had saved his life before and he was sure it would again if a bullet came crashing up against it.

Supreme's first stop was Sean's house. He parked a block away. In that split second on the phone with Unique he had devised a plan to kill Ray and his two men tonight at their cribs. If he couldn't get them tonight, he knew he'd leave DC because his life was in danger. Ray and his men were on to him. There was no doubt about it. But being a man of his word, Supreme was set to do what he had promised if his life was in danger. He had told himself a while back that he would kill whoever was trying to kill him. If he couldn't' kill them, he would leave DC and Glory without looking back.

He stepped onto the porch of Sean's house and peeped through the window. As he approached the house, he had noticed the house was dark, but he still pressed on. He walked off the porch and walked around the house, not seeing any signs of light. Now, fiercely, he stormed back to the front of the house and up to the porch where he brandished both of his guns. He kicked at the front door twice before it swung open. He ran into the house with his guns extended out in front of him. If less than three minutes, he had run throughout the house without finding his enemy,

"Fuck! Where the fuck these niggas at?" he spat, climbing back into his Impala.

Supreme made it to Nut's house, not far away from Sean's and came up with the same results. All the lights were off, and neither Nut nor anyone else was there when he kicked in the door and searched the entire residence.

"Where the fuck these niggas at?!" Supreme piped, pulling off from where he was parked. These coward ass niggas are hidin' from me he thought to himself, slamming his hand down on the steering wheel as he drove.

At 1:55 he was sitting at the foot of his bed with his face in his hands. Two big black gym bags filled with his money rested at his feet. If he was gonna' leave, he had to leave now before Glory came in. The only reason he was not at Ray's crib trying to take him out was because he knew the house would be empty just like Sean's and Nut's were. So, he relinquished his mission and ended up at home getting ready to leave DC with nothing but his money, the clothes on his back, including his bullet proof vest, his two guns, his cell phone and his Navigator.

Tears escaped Supremes eyes and fell into his hands.  He quickly wiped them away and sprang to his feet.  "What the fuck I'm doin' cryin'?  This ain't nothin' but a bitch, a piece of pussy."  He bent down and cupped both gym bags by their straps in each of his hands and walked out of the condo.

Twenty-five minutes later, Supreme's Navigator was doing 65 on I-95 North heading to New York.  He had known over four months ago that most, if not all the men that were looking for him were either dead or locked up.  His cousin Mark had told him that when he talked to him last.  So, he knew if that was true, it was safe for him to return to his place of birth.

Supreme forced a smile as he thought of Glory.  He smiled broadly. He did have ten times more money than he did when he left New York two years ago.  And that was an accomplishment in itself.

# TWENTY-SEVEN

Girl, where you think he at? And when was the last time you said you saw him again?" Pam quizzed Glory who sat in the passenger seat of her Maxima.

"I 'on know where he at, but if he with a bitch, he can stay with her ass!" Glory snapped with an attitude.

"When is the last time you saw him though?" Pam pressed.

"On New Year's Eve. The same night Wop got killed. My brotha and PooBear said Supreme killed him and took 40 g's off of him." Glory shook her head.

"Do you believe that?" Pam asked.

"No," Glory answered. "Supreme got money, and he told me that he liked Wop. Unique tried to come take Supreme's bike and his Impala earlier today, but I ain't let 'em take 'em though. I wasn't havin' that," Glory said defensively.

"For real?"

"Yeah, Unique said the night Supreme was supposed to go pick up that 40 g's from Wop, he was killed. And he was supposed to pick up my brotha from my stepfather's party, but he never showed up .That's why they think he did it," Glory explained.

"Glory, I 'on mean to change the subject, but is Supreme being missin' the reason you decided to dance for these niggas tonight?"

"Yeah, that's the only reason I'm doin' this. Plus the fact that these guys are payin' us 5 g's for one hour. Supreme didn't want me to dance for guys anymore, so I didn't," Glory added. "But he's gone and I 'on know if I'm gonna' see him again."

"Maybe he went back up to New York to visit his family and wanted to go by himself. You know how over protective you are.   Anyway, did you check and see if money is still in the condo?" Pam asked. "If it's still there, that mean's he'll be back." Pam placed her right hand on Glory's left thigh, to comfort her. "I know you love him, don't worry girl he'll be back."

"I don't know where he hides his money," Glory said sadly.

Pam's Maxima turned onto 11th Street in Northwest.

"Why you park over here?" Glory asked Pam who parked on the opposite side of the street from the house where they were going. "There's a parking space right in front of the house."

"Girl, it don't matter," Pam replied killing her engine.

"Yes it does," Glory snapped, staring at Pam. "What if we gotta run all the way over here to get away?  It's bad enough we don't have BamBam here to protect us."

Pam sucked her teeth and replied, "Don't' start all that whining' shit. You know BamBam can't be two places at one time. He's watching out for Chrissy and Tina who got two spots to dance at tonight. So they need him more than we do," Pam preached.

"Yeah, I understand all that, but what we gonna' do if these niggas act a fool?" Glory barked.

Pam reached for her backpack that was lying on the back seat. She unzipped her bag and dug through her dancing clothes.

Pam found what she was looking for. She pulled a black .25 automatic from her backpack.

Glory folded her arms across her chest and slid her neck back. "Ooooh girl. Where you get that lil ass gun from?" Glory joked.

"I've had it for like a month now," Pam said proudly.

"You know how to use it?"

Pam gazed at Glory stupidly. "No, but all you have to do is aim and fire right?"

"I guess so," Glory replied, taking her arms down from her chest, and reaching in the back seat for her backpack. "Let's go." They stepped out of the car and walked across the street and up several steps to reach the porch of the house they were going to visit.

"They should have at least cut the porch light on," Glory said. "They knew we were comin'. They got us standin' out in the dark."

"You ain't lyin'," Pam agreed, reaching to open the storm door. When she did, she saw a big piece of paper taped on the door. Pam read from the paper straining her eyes to see. '*Booty and Body the door is open. We're downstairs in the basement*'.

"Come on girl, let's go in there and get this money so we can leave," Glory said.

Glory was the first to walk around the living room and into the kitchen. As soon as she stepped into the kitchen she saw the door that led down into the basement. "At least their kitchen is clean," she said to Pam, who stood behind her.

"How come it's so damn quiet in this house?" Pam questioned.

"I 'on know," Glory responded by walking up to the basement door. "I guess everybody is downstairs."

"We'll see when you open that door," Pam said. "And I hope the bathroom is clean. I don't wanna change my clothes in no dirty ass bathroom." Pam walked up behind Glory.

Glory opened the basement door and a strong breeze of marijuana blew past them. "Girl, you smell that weed?" Glory asked. She figured the guys were getting ready for the show. Glory looked down the stairs that led to the basement floor level. She then looked to her left at the wall that looked as if it were padded. "This wall looks like it has cushion on it right?"

"They probably have a studio down there and they don't want the sound to escape. You see." Pam pointed to the inside of the door. "The inside of the door is padded just like the wall. They call it a sound proof room." She shoved Glory down the first two steps. "Come on, let's go down there," Pam said.

Glory turned around on the steps and faced Pam. She gave her friend an evil eye. "Girl, don't be pushin' me like that. I could've fallen down the steps. What the fuck is wrong with you? " And at that moment, Glory saw a tall dark figure appear behind them. The figure definitely belonged to a man. He wore all black with a black mask over his face. Before Glory could yell out to Pam, the man had pushed Pam down onto her. But luckily she had been going to the gym with Kim and was strong enough to keep them from falling to the bottom of the stairs.

Booooommmm!!!! The basement door slammed shut.

Glory and Pam yelled and kicked at the basement door but the three men on the opposite side of it couldn't hear them. Even if they could, they wouldn't have helped them. The two women were exactly where they wanted to be.

Sean pulled his mask off his face. "That shit was too easy," he said to Nut and Ray.

"I told y'all," Nut uttered, grinning like it was his birthday. "When those bitches seen that $5,000 a piece on their e-mail they couldn't refuse."

"Now, I'ma tell you niggas off the bat. We ain't killin' no girls unless we have to. We doin' this to get the New York bamma here so we can take care of him," Ray said. "If we wanted to just kill that chump, we could have, but that ain't what I wanna do. I wanna get that bamma down in the basement and dog his girl in front of him like he did mine. Then we can take him somewhere and kill him. OK, now, like I told you niggas, I'm not worryin' about doing nothing to Unique any-more. I don't think he knew about this shit. Y'all agree?" Ray asked.

"Yeah," Nut and Sean said in unison.

"I went where Unique used to hang at off of Wheeler Road and got a little bit of information on him from this nigga name Russ I know. He told me the New York nigga ain't been with Unique long. He said he's like Unique's bodyguard. I put two and two together and figured that Supreme robs people behind Unique's back. But the only thing that's fucked up about all of this is that Unique's sista Booty gotta go through this shit we 'boutta put her through," Ray said sympathetically.

"That's all a part of the game," Nut spat. "At least we not gonna' kill her."

"Now we're gonna go downstairs and explain to her why we're doin' this to her and let her know she's gotta call her man and get him here, or she might not live to see her next birthday," Ray said.

"Ray! I know you said you ain't worryin' 'bout doin' nothin' to Unique anymore, but what if he know you had somethin' to do with his two boys gettin' killed and he wanna do somethin' to you," Nut asked. "Don't forget that bitch Booty is his sister, so if we fuck her up bad, we gonna' have to kill her. Unique ain't gonna' let that shit ride if he knows it was us who did it. When the bitch calls the New York nigga and tell him what's up, you know he gonna' tell Unique we have his sister."

"Yeah, I thought about all that," Ray said. "And I don't give a fuck. I was told the nigga Unique is soft for real. So, if he get tough he can go to sleep just like his man Supreme gonna' do."

"What about Unique's father and yours?"

"They don't have nothin' to do with this. My father is rarely in town anyway," Ray replied.



**Tears flowed continuously down Glory's face as if** she'd been reserving them for a special occasion. She stood face to face with Pam engaging in a shouting match in the middle of the basement's black carpeted floor. Glory was terrified and couldn't believe she'd gotten herself into such a bad situation.

"Glory, calm ya ass down girl. I'm just as scared as you are," Pam yelled, lying.

"I can't believe this shit, is happenin'," Glory barked, with her hands balled into tight fists. "You got us in this!"

"Hold on." Pam took a step back, gazing at her friend. "You agreed for us to come, so don't put the blame all on me."

"Bitch! You the one who said we should go 'cause these niggas gonna' set out that bread!" Glory yelled.

Pam took a deep breath, then said, "You know what? I'm not gonna get into it with you. This is not the time nor the place for us to lose our cool."

"Lose our cool….lose our cool," Glory shouted! She walked over to the bottom of the basement steps. She pointed up to the door. "What the fuck you mean lose our cool? It's a nigga upstairs that might kill us or rape us and you talkin' 'bout this ain't the time nor the place to lose our cool!" Glory threw her hands up to her face and cried like a baby.

Pam grabbed her backpack that was on the floor. She unzipped it and reached into it for her .25. When she felt the hard steel, she pulled it out the bag and tossed her back pack back on the floor. She then walked over to Glory. "Glory!...Glory!" Pam reached for Glory's right wrist and pulled her hand down from her face. "Don't forget we got this." She raised the gun up to Glory's face so she could see it.

The black .25 automatic was the only reason Pam wasn't crying relentlessly like Glory was. She had thought about the gun five minutes after they were locked into the basement, and that's what gave her the confidence she had. The gun was their only hope and Pam knew she'd have to conceal it on her body to make it out alive.

"Can you please stop cryin'?" Pam asked Glory in a pleading manner. "He might not try to do nothin' to us. He might just be livin' out one of his fantasies."

Glory looked into Pam's face with a cold stare while tears still made their way down her face. "You playin' right? Anyway, how ya know if it's one dude or not? When you read the e-mail, it sounded like it was gonna be more than one dude in here right?" Glory asked.

"Yeah, you right," Pam agreed.

Glory yanked her wrist from Pam's grip and stepped off walking in the direction of the bathroom. "After this Pam, I ain't dancin' no more. Even if these guys don't do nothin' to us, I'm gonna enroll in school. No more strippin'," Glory exclaimed.

"I'm with you, no more for me either." Pam smiled. "But we can still run our little business. We'll just hire more girls."

Glory gave Pam an evil eye.

Pam wrapped her arms around Glory's neck . She still held the gun in her hand. "I'm sorry for even tellin' you about these dudes when I knew you didn't want to dance for niggas anymore," Pam said near Glory's ear.

"I accept your apology, but can you unwrap your arms from around my neck while you got that gun in your hand. I ain't try'na get shot in my back."

They both laughed. Then, they heard the basement door open. Both of their eyes shot towards the top of the stairs.

"Hide that gun," Glory whispered to Pam. "Don't pull it out unless he looks like he gonna do somethin' to us."

Pam placed the .25 in the front pocket of her jeans.

They saw one pair of legs, then two, and then three as the men stomped down the steps.

"It's three of 'em," Glory muttered. "And they all have on masks. They gonna do somethin' to us."

"Y'all stay calm and everything gon' be all right," the last man that walked down the basement stairs said.

"I thought y'all wanted us to dance for y'all," Glory stated.

Nut walked into the middle of the basement floor with two folding chairs under each of his arms. He placed both chairs down, folded them out, and placed them side-by-side.

"There's been a change of plans. So come over here and sit the fuck down," Nut spat.

Glory and Pam slowly walked over to the chairs and sat down.

"We not gon' tie y'all up or nothin' so just sit still and don't talk unless we tell you to," Nut stated. He could tell that Glory, who he knew as Booty, had been crying. Her eyes were slightly puffy.

Ray and Sean walked over in front of the women and stood above them along side Nut.

"Listen," Ray began with his eyes on Glory. "The only reason y'all in this predicament is because of that bitch ass nigga Supreme." Ray paused, expecting a reaction from Glory, which he instantly got. She looked over at Pam who looked back at her. They both had perplexed expressions on their faces. Ray continued, "That's your man ain't it Booty?"

Glory stared up at Ray. She nodded her head slowly. "Yeah." She wondered who was under the mask.

"Well, I don't' know if you know it or not, but your man is a stick-up kid." Ray waited for a reaction again.

"What 'cha mean he's a stick-up kid?" Glory quizzed.

"He robs niggas for money. He robbed me! That's why we here now, and he killed two of my men," Ray shouted angrily.

Glory gazed at Pam who gazed back at her with the words, *I knew he wasn't right* written on her face.

"Supreme doesn't have to rob people. He got money," Glory yelled.

"Well let me see if you know this," Ray said. "The night I got robbed by your man is the same night Big Red got killed. Well, I killed her by mistake trying to kill your man, because he robbed me!"

Glory immediately put it together. "Are you sayin' Big Red was with Supreme the night she died?" Glory asked surprisingly.

"Yeah," Sean acceded, "You think it was a coincident that she got shot in the parking lot of the same hotel your man was stayin' in? Nah, he was about to walk inside that hotel with Big Red to fuck her."

Pain was in Glory's eyes. She wouldn't have felt the way she was feeling now, if she had been told about this when it occurred. At that particular time she wasn't in love with Supreme, but now she was, and hearing what she just heard hurt her tremendously.

Pam's mind raced. She knew exactly what was going on. The men wanted Supreme. She knew a long time ago that Supreme was doing more than watching Unique's back. His money was too long, too early.

"If it's Supreme y'all want, how come y'all got us here?" Pam asked.

Ray looked at Pam. "Y'all here because we couldn't get to him." He lied.

"Y'all didn't try hard enough because he was in town until New Years Eve," Pam revealed.

All three men looked at each other.

"So you sayin' he ain't in DC no more?" Nut asked.

"We 'on know," Glory answered. "I haven't seen him since New Year's Eve night."

"Well…" Ray reached into his pocket and pulled out his cell phone. "You better hope he's still in DC for y'all sake." He passed the phone to Glory.

"What 'cha want me to do?" Glory asked.

"I want you to call that chump and get his ass to this address. If you don't get in touch with him, I'ma kill both of y'all," Ray snapped.

Glory and Pam instantly became nervous, but Glory's nervousness was apparent. Her hands started to shake and her eyes became watery.

"If…" Glory's voice started to crack. "If…If I get in touch with Supreme and he come here, what 'chall gon' do to him?" She asked.

"Don't worry about that. Just call him like I told you to bitch!" Ray spat.

Somewhere deep inside of Glory, she wanted to fight like hell, but she knew she would be hurt bad or even killed if she did. She knew one of them, if not all of them, had guns tucked on their waists. She loved Supreme with all her heart. She had told herself, a while back, that she would die for him, but the real thing was unfolding in her face, and she wasn't too sure about that statement anymore. She knew if she got in touch with Supreme and he showed up, he would be killed, and if she didn't' get in touch with him, she'd be killed. So, what did she have to lose?

"Did y'all kill Wop?" Glory asked the masked men.

"Yeah," Nut spat!

"I knew Supreme didn't do that!" A ghost of courage leaped into Glory and she let the cell phone drop to the carpet. "I ain't callin' him." She pouted.

The three men didn't have to say a word, Pam was all over it. "Girl have you lost your fuckin' mind? I ain't try'na die for that lyin' ass nigga." Pam bent down and picked up the cell phone. She grabbed Glory's hand and placed the phone into it. "Call him."

Glory let the phone drop to the floor again.

Nut stepped forward and backhanded her viciously across her face, sending her flying out the chair and onto the floor. "Bitch!" He grabbed his 9mm from his waist as he stepped over to where Glory lay. He bent down and placed the gun against her temple. "Do you think this is a game? Bitch, this ain't no fuckin' game!" Nut shouted.

"Pleeeease!" Pam bawled, she burst into tears with her hands up to her mouth. "Don't hurt her. Pleeeease!"

Nut swung his head around and looked at Pam. "Bitch!" He took his gun away from Glory's temple and pointed it at Pam. "Shut the fuck up!"

"Now get the fuck up!" Nut thrust his hand down on Glory's neck gripping it. Pulling her to her feet by her neck, he paid no attention to her clawing at his wrist. Finally, he dumped her down into the chair freeing her neck.

Glory coughed while rubbing her neck and gasping for air.

"Now, you wanna pick up that phone and dial that number?" Ray asked, looking down on Glory. He smiled under his mask.

Finally catching her breath, Glory gazed at Ray and answered him. "No! I'm not callin' him, 'cause you gon' kill him and us anyway." She braced herself for another attack by placing her hands behind her head and bending forward where her elbows touched her thighs.

Nut was in motion to attack again, but was stopped by Ray. "No!" He stepped in front of Glory blocking her. "I got this." He stared down at her and said, "Lift your fuckin' head up. I'm only askin' you one time, and if you don't I'm gon' shoot you in your head."

Glory quickly took her hands from behind her head and sat up in her chair. She glanced over at Pam who earlier showed no signs of crying, but who now had tears rolling down her face.

Ray smoothly lifted his black sweater up and grabbed the chrome .38 revolver from his waist. He extended his right arm out with the gun in his hand and aimed it at Pam who sat to his right. Promptly, Pam's sobs became louder. "I'm gonna shoot Body in her fuckin' face if you don't pick up that phone from the floor and call that nigga! I'm gonna count to three. One…"

The second Ray began his count down; Pam started her plea to Glory. "Pleeeease Glory!" She whined. "Pleeeease don't let him kill meeee!"

By the time the number two left Ray's mouth, Glory had bent down and picked the phone up from the floor. She slowly dialed the number to Supreme's cell phone.

# TWENTY-EIGHT

Supreme sat in the hotel room he'd stayed in since the night he was allegedly leaving D.C. That night while traveling along I-95 North, he realized that he loved Glory too much to leave her. He turned off an exit in Maryland and headed back to D.C., but instead of going back to his condo, he checked into a hotel. There he concocted his next move, and that was to eliminate Ray and his men even if that meant losing his own life. Since Ray and his two men seemed to disappear, he thought if he laid low for a week or so, they'd think he was gone and return to their regular routines. And then he would strike.

He looked at his cell phone intensely as it rang. This was only the second time he'd received a call in the last four days, and just like before, he didn't answer it. He wanted to complete his mission before he contacted Glory and Unique. Strangely, to Supreme his phone rang repeatedly. He began counting the number of rings as he stared at his phone. In his heart he knew it was Glory. He smiled as he grabbed the phone from the table, but didn't push the button in time before it stopped.

A minute passed without his cell phone ringing again. Believing the person who was calling had given up, Supreme sat the phone back on the table. And as soon as he did, his cell phone rang. He looked at his phone, then picked it up from the table. He answered it.

Before he could say hello, Glory's voice shot through his phone.

"Supreme!" she shouted.

"Yeah, Ma! I'm sorry for not comin' home in four days, but I got something to take care of before I can come back to ya," he said.

"Supreme, shut up!" Glory snapped and burst into a sob. "Where, where, you, you, at?" She barely got her words out in between her convulsions.

"I'm at a hotel. Why? What's up? Why you cryin'?" he asked sitting up straight in his chair. His face showed concern.

"They got meee and Paaam!" Glory whined.

Supreme leaped to his feet. His expression exposed worry. "Who got you and Pam?" he asked.

"I 'on knooooow. They got masks ooooon!"

"Fuck!" Supreme cursed, he knew what was going on. He knew Ray and his men were behind this. But he couldn't figure out how they got them.

"I'm sorrrry! Pleaseee forgive me!" Glory begged.

Supreme closed his eyes and took a deep breath. He knew that Glory saying she was sorry meant she had gone to a private dance for Ray and his men. She had promised him she wasn't going to dance for men anymore.

"I did it because I thought 'cha left meeee! I thought I wasn't gon' never see ya again," Glory pleaded.

"I love you, Ma. I couldn't roll out on you if I tried. Now where they got…."

"Hello." A man's voice took the place of Glory's. "You know who this is," Ray said. "I aint' gon' do too much talkin'. If you wanna see your bitch and her friend again, bring ya ass to Eleventh Street in Northwest. It's the blue house with the porch light off. And come by yourself." Ray hung up.

"Fuck! Fuck! Fuck!" Supreme spat angrily. He tossed his cell phone on the bed. He started pacing the room, thinking.

*Man, what the fuck am I gon' do? I know if I go to this house, I aint' gon' make it back out alive. That nigga gon' kill me. But if I don't go, they gon' kill Glory.* He looked at the time on his watch that read 11:50 pm. He contemplated for a brief moment. *Man, I can't let her die*. Supreme grabbed his .357 and his Desert Eagle from under the pillow. Placing them both on the table, he stared at the guns. He grabbed his bulletproof vest and placed it over the black T-shirt he wore.

He was on his way out of the hotel room when something came to his mind. *Man I can't do this shit by myself. I need some back up*. But, the nigga Ray told me to come by myself. Supreme walked to the bed and grabbed his cell phone. *It's time to keep it gangsta and tell Unique what's up*.


**Unique paced the floor in his basement revealing** to PooBear his decision to get out of the game. Although PooBear wasn't very receptive to the idea, Unique knew he couldn't hurt Kim any longer. She'd been so protective of him lately, that she'd quit her job to be with him every second.

PooBear's expression showed his disapproval of Unique's decision. Selfishly, he wanted his boy to continue selling drugs so that his financial situation wouldn't change. Deep down inside he wanted Unique to at least hook him up with Ray before he quit. PooBear's thoughts were interrupted when Unique's cell rang.

"Yo, what's up Unique? This 'Preme." The familiar voice shot through Unique's cell phone.

Unique was shocked. He didn't believe the man who had stolen 40 g's from him and killed his boy would have the audacity to call him, or to greet him in a friendly tone.

"Why, Slim? I know you wasn't broke. Why'd you have to hit Wop?" Unique asked.

Supreme squinted his face up in disbelief. "Yo, I swear to you Son, I didn't kill Wop. That's my word, Kid."

"Nigga, that night I told you to go get that 40 g's from Wop, he was killed and the 40 g's disappeared. Kim had to come pick me up that night when you should have. You tell me what I'm supposed to think!" Unique yelled.

Supreme had not once thought they would have believed he killed Wop, but now he understood why. "Son, I'd like to tell you now what's goin' on and why Wop was killed. But right now your sista's life is in danger."

"What the fuck you mean my sista's life in danger?" Unique snapped putting on his stone face.

"Your man Ray got 'cha sista held hostage," Supreme said.

"Slim, you ain't makin' no sense. Why would Ray have Glory held hostage?" Unique asked.

"That's what I don't have time to tell you."

"Slim, you fuckin' with me right?" Unique smiled to camouflage his nervousness.

"I'm not fuckin' with you. He got 'cha sista and Pam. I need to come over to ya crib so we can go to the spot where they holdin' her. He told me to come by myself, so we gotta think of somethin'," Supreme said.

"You talked to Ray?" Unique asked.

"Yeah, he got 'cha sista to call me on my cell."

"Let me get this straight. Ray want 'cha to come where my sista is, so he can get you. Then he'll let my sista go?" Unique questioned.

"Yeah, I think so."

"So  you're  willin' to trade ya life for my sista's?"

Supreme pondered the question.  He remembered a while back when he told Glory that he loved her so much that he would die for her.  "Yeah, I'll die for ya sista.  I love her Kid," Supreme answered.

"Me and PooBear gon' be waitin' out front of my house," Unique said ending the call.

"What's up, Joe?" PooBear quizzed, still standing in Unique's face.

"I 'on know yet, but Supreme is on his way over here."

"So we gon' kill him, right?" PooBear asked anxiously.

"Slim, slow down.  Some other shit just came up."

"Like what?" PooBear snapped.

"He told me he didn't kill Wop and that my sista is being held hostage.  I'm guessin' by the same nigga that killed Wop.  He said it's Ray who got my sista," Unique revealed.

"What the fuck you talkin' 'bout? You tellin' me Ray, the nigga you get 'cha shit from killed Wop and he got 'cha sista held hostage?" PooBear questioned.

"Yeah."

"That nigga runnin' game on you Slim. He settin' us up, so he can kill us," PooBear said suspiciously.

"He said he gon' tell me what's up when he comes here." Unique stepped around PooBear. "Let's quietly go out front to wait for him so Kim doesn't hear us."

**When Supreme pulled up, he saw PooBear and** Unique standing at the bottom of Unique's driveway. He noticed Kim standing on porch fully clothed. Her arms were folded across her chest as if she were cold. Supreme parked his Navigator, stepped out, and walked up to Unique and PooBear.

Supreme looked at Unique and PooBear. He knew Poo Bear was up to something. Just as he looked away, he felt a hard, right hook land perfectly on the left side of his jaw, sending him to the concrete. PooBear quickly pulled his Glock 9mm from his waist and stood above Supreme pointing it at him. "Nigga, I should light 'cha ass up right here."

Unique grabbed PooBear by his arm and pulled him away from Supreme. "What you doin' Slim?" Unique yelled into PooBear's face.

"That nigga killed Wop," PooBear griped.

"No I didn't!" Supreme protested, making it to his feet. He slid his right hand over his mouth and looked at it. He spat out blood. He wanted to strike PooBear back, but he understood why PooBear hit him. If it were reversed, he would have done the same.

"What's goin' on down here?" Kim said, making her way down to where the three men stood.

"Kim, go back in the house," Unique ordered.

"No! I wanna know what's goin' on," Kim stated, standing her ground. She stared into their faces for an answer.

Unique stepped in front of his woman. "Don't make no scene out here. Go in the house!"

"Noooo!" Kim broke into a sob, throwing herself into Unique's chest. He wrapped his arms around her. "Don't leave meeee!" She cried.

Unique looked back at PooBear and Supreme. "Y'all chill, I'll be back." He marched Kim into the house, and after consoling her, he left.

"Let's go," Unique ordered. "We ridin' in my car. I got my gun in there." Unique led the way to his car with the two men on his tail. The moment they slid into the Mustang, Unique said, "Supreme, tell me where they holdin' my sista and then tell me all about what's goin' on."

Supreme truthfully began to tell them what was going on and why. *He left nothing out.*

# TWENTY-NINE

Unique slowly pulled to the curb, parking his Mustang between two cars a half block away from the blue painted house. The plan was simple. Supreme would go in first. If after fifteen minutes there was no sign of Glory, Unique and PooBear would come to her rescue.

Inside the house with the porch light off, Nut and Sean waited upstairs in the living room where they peeped out from behind a curtain waiting for Supreme. The house was completely dark, except for the basement, where Ray guarded Glory and Pam.

"You think that nigga gon' show up?" Nut quizzed Sean who stood next to him.

"Yeah, he'll be here," Sean said with confidence. "Ray told us that if we kill anybody in here, we gotta burn the house down?"

"Ya know we gon' kill Supreme, whether it's in this house or not," Nut said.

Peeping out the window Sean said, "There's the nigga walkin' from across the street towards the house."

"Where that nigga car at?"

"He probably parked it around the corner or somethin'." Sean pulled his black .357 from his waist, and  stepped over to the front door of the house and opened the door a crack.  He then stepped over to the window with Nut who had pulled his 9mm out from his waist. "When he walks up the steps, we gon' stand on each side of the door so when he come in, we got 'em from both sides," Sean explained.

As soon as Supreme stepped onto the porch, Nut and Sean took their positions. The first thing they heard was the squeaking sound of the storm door being opened, then the main door into the house slowly opened. Nut placed his gun to the left side of Supreme's head.  Then Sean placed his gun to the right side of Supreme's head.

"Take two steps forward and put ya hands above ya head," Nut ordered. He shut the door after Supreme did what he was told. Nut patted Supreme down for weapons.  He didn't find a gun nor did he feel the bullet proof vest Supreme wore.

"Come on!" Nut piped, stepping behind Supreme and grabbing the back of his jacket collar. He pushed him forward in the direction of the kitchen.

Nut guided Supreme through the kitchen. Sean ran upstairs to grab a fold-up chair, and quickly ran back downstairs to assist Nut with Supreme. Standing in front of the door leading into the basement, Nut said to Supreme, "Reach out and open that door."

"I can't see the door knob," Supreme complained.

Sean smiled under his mask.  His opportunity to strike Supreme came faster than he expected. Since he already wanted to make the man that shot him suffer, he balled his right hand into a tight fist, hitting Supreme dead on his cheekbone.  Supreme's legs buckled instantly causing him to collapse to the kitchen floor. Sean pulled Supreme up to his feet by the back of his jacket.  Sean opened the door and led the way down the stairs.

The torture and humiliation of Glory had been in play for nearly two minutes when Glory's eyes focused on Supreme.  Seeing her man for the first time in four days, Glory leaped from her chair and ran up to Supreme.  Throwing her arms around his neck she sobbed and planted kisses on his swollen lips. That's when she noticed his right cheekbone.

"They did this to you?" she murmured, staring up into her man's face.  She ran her fingers over his engorged lips.

Supreme leaned his face down towards Glory's left ear. He whispered, "I'm sorry about all this. I never meant for this to happen. I love you Glory. If I don't make it out of this house alive, all my money is in my truck that's parked in front of ya brotha's cri...."

"All right, that's enough for the lovebirds!" Nut said, forcing Glory, and Supreme to sit down.

Pam, Glory and Supreme sat in a row staring up at the three figures that stood before them. Ray wanted to take off his mask to say what he was about to say, but he didn't. He knew Supreme knew who he was.

"Yo, you got me, let the girls go. They don't have shit to do with this," Supreme begged.

"We are," Ray said as he stepped around Supreme's chair and stood behind him. He placed his chrome .38 behind Supreme's right earlobe. Then he put his left hand on Supreme's shoulder, gripping his leather jacket. "I want you to see somethin' first." Ray nodded toward Nut. Nut tucked his gun back in his waist. He swiftly stepped closely in front of Glory, bent down and seized both of her ankles. With one quick motion, he yanked her body from the chair, causing her butt to hit the carpet with a thud. She yelled out in agony as the pain from hitting the floor unexpectedly shot up her vertebrae.

"Nooooo! Pleeeeease!" Pam bawled, springing to her feet. She watched her friend being dragged along the floor. She took one step forward, motioning as if she was going to help Glory and was met by the butt of Sean's .357 exploding across her forehead. Her body crumbled to the floor as she loss consciousness. As if Pam was nothing, Sean turned around to watch his crony continue to drag Glory along the floor.

Still seated in the aluminum chair with the .38 behind his earlobe, Supreme observed the woman he loved being humiliated. Tears flowed freely down his face. He inhaled deeply and exhaled slowly. Balling up his fists he slammed each one into his thighs, grunting and grating his teeth simultaneously.

"What? You 'on like that nigga?" Ray snapped. "Ain't that what you did to my girl? Huh?" He laughed loudly. Abruptly, Nut stopped dragging Glory. He let go of her ankles and watched them drop clumsily to the carpet. He smiled under his mask as he looked down into her tearful face. He knew the carpet had put burn marks all over her back and arms and maybe her butt that was partly protected by the tight jeans she wore.

"Get up bitch!" he spat.

Glory could see the man that stood above her, but his words didn't register. Her mind was focused on the pain she was feeling from the carpet burns. They stung like hell. Her skin felt like it was on fire. Even the back of her head that had met the carpet a few times while she was being dragged, was on fire. She heard him yell, "Get up bitch!" again, but this time his words registered.

Hearing Nut's order clearly, Glory rose slowly. She glanced over at Supreme who still had a gun pressed behind his earlobe by the man who stood behind him. She saw the helpless look in his eyes. And at that moment she decided to do something that might cost her her life. After all, Supreme did show up knowing he more than likely would be killed, and she knew the only reason he showed up was because he loved her. Any other man, she reasoned, wouldn't have showed up.

"Come on Son, let…let her go!" Supreme said to Ray who he knew was only doing this to Glory out of revenge. "Man she don't deserve to be treated like this."

"Yeah, I know," Ray replied. "My girl didn't either."

Nut kicked at Glory's feet. "Stand up bitch!"

Glory fixed her eyes on Nut's crotch only a foot away since he was standing in front of her, and she made her way to her knees. She stood up and with dazzling speed she threw a right jab at Nut's crotch, causing him to yell out in pain. Glory went to work again, placing both of her hands behind Nut's head and in one motion she kicked him in his face. His body fell to the carpet like a sack of potatoes.

Before Glory could notice the man that lay before her in a fetal position, Sean grabbed her from behind and put her in a chokehold. He applied pressure to her neck, but not enough to put her to sleep. She clawed at his arms. Quickly realizing it didn't help, Glory thought quickly, and swung her hips to her left just enough to allow her right hand to reach back and take firm hold of Sean's crotch.

"Whoa! Aw! Aw! Ahhhhh!" Sean screamed and immediately let go of Glory.

Ray was undecided whether or not to help his men or watch them get taken down by a woman. He watched Glory grab Sean's dick with her left hand as he balanced himself on his toes as if that would relieve some of the pressure.

Ray looked over at Nut who would turn the tables when he got to his feet. So, he covered Supreme's mouth to keep him from warning Glory. Nut hopped to his feet and in two long steps was next to Glory who didn't even notice until it was too late. As quickly as she had earlier rammed his dick, he rammed his fist into her jaw. Her body crashed to the floor and she loss consciousness.

"Yoooo!" Supreme bawled, he leaped to his feet, but was slammed back down into the chair.

"Nigga, if you get up again, I'm gonna kill you now instead of later." Ray said placing his .38 up against the back of Supreme's head.

Nut was on his knees in front of Glory's unconscious body. He bent over to turn her on her back. Unfastening her jeans, everyone knew his intent.

"What 'cha doin', Son?" Supreme quizzed with anger.

"What does it look like I'm doin' nigga?" Nut shot back. "I'm takin' ya bitch's pants off so I can dig in her guts." He struggled with Glory's tight jeans. Finally, he pushed them to her ankles. Nut removed his gun, unbuttoned his pants, and let them drop to his ankles. His skinny, but hard and long dick swerved at attention.

Pam's vision was blurred when she awoke from her comatose state. When she did, she saw Supreme sitting with one of the three men standing behind him. They were looking straight at something. Pam followed their stare and saw Nut standing above Glory with his pants down and stroking his protruding dick. He was talking, but she couldn't make out what he was saying. Then she saw Sean come from the bathroom walking in Glory's direction with his hand on his crotch showing the pain in his face.

Pam watched Nut drop to his knees in front of Glory's feet, sliding her jeans completely off. She glanced over at Supreme whose eyes were closed as tears escaped from them. At that second, she knew what she had to do. She reached into her pants pocket for the .25 automatic. Tears began to tumble off of her face. She thought of what she saw happen to her mother when she was nine years old. She knew if she didn't do something Glory would be violated just as her mother had been. Pam had a gun and she was damn sure going to use it in the name of her mother and to make sure Glory wasn't raped.

Nut smiled under his mask as he spread Glory's legs apart. He looked down at her clean shaved pussy as if it were a piece of meat that he was about to devour. He crawled up between her legs and suddenly, a loud yell rung out, then the sound of Bap! Bap! Bap! Bap! Bap! filled the basement.

The basement went silent. It was as if the gun shots that rang out brought order. No one moved, especially the two bodies that couldn't even if they tried.

"Get off meeeee!" Glory whined hysterically, breaking the silence in the basement. She had just recovered consciousness after the last shot sounded. It had taken her two whole minutes to realize that a limp body lay on top of her. "Pleeeease somebody get him off me!" She tried to push Nut's lifeless body off her, but he was too heavy. His body seemed to grow heavier by the second as she lay under it oblivious to what had happened. She didn't have a clue as to why Nut was on top of her, but she did know that she'd been hit in her jaw.

Sean still gripped his gun tightly. At that moment, Glory didn't realize he had fired one shot that struck Pam in the middle of her forehead and killed her as Pam shot and killed Nut. Sean snapped out of his trance and stepped over Glory and Nut's body to Pam's. "This bitch had a gun all this fuckin' time. I knew I should have searched both of those bitches." Sean bent down and placed Pam's .25 into his pocket. He rolled Nut off of Glory onto his back looking for any sign of life. Dead, Nut had two holes in his neck and one just above his right eye.

Glory quickly got to her feet. And when she did, she immediately noticed she was naked from her waist down. She swiftly covered her private part with her hands. Blood ran from her mouth from the punch she was hit with by Nut.

Ray took his gun away from the back of Supreme's head and pushed him out of the chair. Quickly, he and Sean fled from the basement with plans on burning down the house. Supreme ran to Glory and threw his arms around her tightly. She cried like an infant in his arms as her head rested on his chest.

"Why my pants off?" Glory asked. "Did he rape meee!"

"No," Supreme responded. "No. He didn't get the chance to. Pam shot him."

"They killed her didn't theeeey?"

"Yeah." Supreme knew Glory's sobs would increase so he squeezed her tighter into his arms.

"Paaaamm! Paaaaamm!" She welled. "Paaaammm!"

"Come on Glory be strong," Supreme said while patting her head. "Be strong for Pam because she was strong for you. Come on." He slowly guided her over to her jeans and sneakers. He made sure he used his body to block Pam's dead body from Glory's view. "Come on baby you gotta put ya clothes back on so we can get outta here," Supreme said hearing footsteps coming downstairs.

As Glory slid her jeans on, Supreme's eyes shot towards the steps. He wondered if they'd make it out alive. He wondered what was taking PooBear and Unique so long.

**When Unique and PooBear reached the porch,** they had second thoughts about what they were about to do. Luckily, Ray's men had forgotten to lock the door. They slowly entered the pitch-black house with PooBear leading the way. With their guns drawn, both men looked for anything suspicious.

"Man ain't nobody in this mothafuckin' house," PooBear spat angrily. He and Unique stood at the top of the steps that led to the three bedrooms and bathroom upstairs.

"Supreme came in this house," Unique said.

"Well, the nigga ain't in here now.  Your sista and Pam ain't in here either."

"Hold on," Unique stated, "this house gotta have a basement."

"Man face it.  The nigga ran game on us.  He came in the front door but crept out the back," PooBear said.

"Let's head to the basement.  And if ain't nobody down there, I'll believe somethin' ain't right," Unique uttered.

They both started down the stairs, but stopped in their tracks when they heard a door slam underneath them.

"What was that?" PooBear asked wide eyed.  He gripped his gun tighter.  "It sounds like footsteps comin' our way."

They crept back up the steps and into one of the bedrooms.  They cracked the bedroom door waiting to see who climbed the stairs.

"Shhhh!" Unique hushed PooBear.  "Somebody is coming' up the steps now."

As the footsteps got closer their hearts beat faster.  When they saw the tall dark figure that seemed to be covered in all black from head to toe, Unique almost fainted.  They watched the tall figure hurriedly stride pass the bedroom they were in and enter the bathroom.

"Dawg…that nigga had a mask over his face," PooBear whispered.

"I saw him," Unique replied.  He tried not to show his nervousness. Seeing the man with the mask confirmed that what Supreme told him was indeed true.  Unique opened the bedroom door a little more.  And at that moment, the bathroom light was flicked on.  The light from it shined out into the hall giving their eyes a better view of their surroundings. They crept out into the hall as if they were walking on eggs. Unique led the way with his Tec-9 out in front of him.  They stepped in front of the slightly open bathroom door and stood side by side with their guns extended.

The bathroom door swung open.

"Don't move nigga!" PooBear barked.

Sean stopped in his tracks.  You could tell the sight of the two men in front of him frightened him.  His body jerked.

Unique's eyes went to the gasoline can Sean held in his left hand. "What's up with the can of gasoline?" he asked eyeing Sean's right hand which was still on the doorknob.

Sean's mind raced. He knew Unique and PooBear knew what was going on. He wished he hadn't tucked his gun on his waist, but he had. He knew he had to do something. Sean thought quick by slamming the door shut. He only needed a split second, he thought, to grab his gun from off his waist. He was wrong. Three of PooBear's rounds exploded through the door lodging into Sean's stomach and left shoulder. He dropped the can of gasoline and stumbled backwards landing in the tub. Sean managed to grab his gun from his waist and point it toward the door. Although he was hurting, he wasn't going to let his life be taken without a fight. He knew whoever came through the door first would get it. He had five rounds left in his .357 and he planned on using them.

BOOM!! PooBear rushed into the bathroom after he kicked the door in, but was stopped in his tracks by two of the five .357 bullets that Sean fired. One of the bullets hit PooBear directly in his face, killing him.

Unique was right behind PooBear when he rushed into the bathroom, but when Sean fired his shots, he quickly stepped back. He peeped into the bathroom but was only able to see PooBear's black sneakers. He inhaled deeply and tried to nullify the jitters that took over his body. He was beyond nervous. Unique was scared to death! "PooBear!" he managed to call out, but received no answer. "PooBear!" he said again.

"Nigga, stop callin' him, he's dead!" Sean shouted, still seated in the tub. He dug into his pocket for the .25 automatic he took from Pam. Smiling, he felt good about the one bullet that remained. "Come on in here if you wanna nigga," Sean yelled. He knew if Unique stepped into that bathroom, he would be killed.

Unique's bottom lip started to shake. He held his gun with two hands up against the right side of his face. With glassy eyes he was on the verge of crying out loud.

"Nigga if you ain't gon' come in here, take your scared ass home," Sean spat, thinking about what Ray had told him earlier about Unique being soft.

Sean's words hit a nerve in Unique. He let the words "ya scared ass" roll around in his head. "He thinks I'm soft," Unique said to himself.

"I'm comin' out of this bathroom, so get ready or take ya ass home," Sean uttered, struggling to raise himself out of the tub.

"I'ma kill this nigga,   I'ma kill this nigga," Unique recited psyching himself up.

Sean had managed to climb out of the tub and was now sitting on the rim.   He looked down at PooBear's body.   "Your man's shit is fucked up, Slim." He giggled slightly as pain shot through his body.   He quickly shifted his attention to his bullet wounds. He knew he'd die if he didn't get medical attention soon.   He was losing too much blood.   So he yelled, "I'm comin'out, Slim.   If you wanna live…"

In one step, Unique was inside the bathroom firing away.   He yelled out loudly as if he were possessed.   His first two shots missed his target, but his third, fourth and fifth landed in Sean's chest, killing him instantly.

# THIRTY

In the basement, Ray stood a few feet in front of Supreme and Glory waving two guns at them.

"Which one of y'all wanna die first?" He asked the couple.

"Neither of us!" Glory spat boldly. She jumped in front of Supreme as if to protect him.

Supreme stepped around Glory and stood in front of her. "I thought you said you was gon' let her go. Be a man of your word!"

"Your tomboy ass girl fucked all that up when she started kickin' ass fightin' like she's Lailah Ali and shit. She caused all this extra shit to jump off," Ray explained.

"What? I'm supposed to let 'chall do that stuff to me?" Glory snapped, still standing behind Supreme. She looked over Supreme's shoulder dead into Ray's face.

Ray snatched his mask off and tossed it to the floor, finalizing what his intentions were. "Now I gotta kill you along with your man," Ray boasted.

Glory stepped around Supreme standing back in front of him, but this time, she threw her arms out to her side as if she were nailed to a cross. "Noooo!" She burst out into a piercing sob. "Pleeease!"

Supreme pushed Glory's arms down to her sides and hugged her from behind. "Come on baby be strong," he whispered into her ear.

"Pleeease!" Glory still whined. "Don't kill uuusss!"

Ray looked at the couple. At that very moment, he had great respect for them both. They both were trying to protect one another. But his respect for Glory was much, much greater. Seeing a woman acting this way under the circumstances was almost unbelievable. She had heart and he admired that.

"Come on Dawg, let her go man. That's my word Son, when she leaves out of here she ain't gon' call nobody. Right Glory?" Supreme asked sincerely.

"No!" Glory replied with tears running down her face. "I'm not leavin' without you."

"Come on Ma." Supreme stepped from behind her and stood in front of her. He placed his hands on each side of her hips while gazing down into her face. "I know you love me, but you don't have to die for me," he said.

"You didn't have to come here for me either, but you did."

"Damn Slim, you got yourself a trooper for real," Ray exclaimed, then Sean came to his mind. *What's takin' that nigga so long to get back down here? He thought to himself.*

Just then the basement door opened. All dialogue from Ray, Supreme, and Glory ceased. Their eyes shot towards the steps.

"Nigga, you took long enough!" Ray yelled without seeing a face yet.

By the time Unique made it half way down the steps, they all knew the person wasn't Sean. Reacting swiftly, Ray fired two shots from his .38 into Supreme's back. Before Supreme's body hit the ground, Ray had swooped in on Glory and grabbed her from behind. Clutching Glory's neck with his 9mm in his left hand, Ray pressed against her temple with his .38.

"Glad to see you could join us," Ray said to Unique who had made it down into the basement. He held his Tec-9 out in front of him.

"Glory, you all right?" Unique asked his sister, watching the tears flow from her eyes.

"He just shot Supreeemmme!" She whined, crying heavily.

Unique looked down at the three bodies that lay scattered around the basement's floor.

"Where Sean at nigga?" Ray asked.

"He's dead."

Ray snickered then asked, "Who killed him? I know you didn't."

"Oh yeah" Unique had the look of a killer in his eyes. Something he didn't have prior to taking Sean's life.

Ray pressed his .38 harder into Glory's temple, causing her to squeal. "Nigga drop ya fuckin' gun or I'll put a bullet in ya peoples head!"

"Damn!" Unique mumbled to himself. "Listen Ray, me and you ain't never had no problems. So why don't 'cha let my sista go and all three of us can walk out of this house alive. We ain't gotta tell nobody about this shit. I'm sorry for being down with a nigga that robbed you. I swear I didn't know," Unique pleaded.

"No! Don't put 'cha gun down!" Glory cried. "He gon' kill both of us. He already…"

"Bitch shut the fuck up!" Ray applied pressure to her neck causing Glory to gasp for air. She scratched his forearm.

"OK Slim. I'ma put my gun down." Unique tossed his gun to the floor.

"Who came here with you?" Ray quizzed.

Unique didn't reply right away. He knew he had to say someone was with him, if he didn't Ray would probably kill him and Glory. "I got two nigga upstairs," Unique said.

Ray removed the .38 from Glory's temple and aimed it at Unique. POP! POP! Unique's body dropped to the floor.

"Noooo!" Glory yelled at the top of her lungs. "Uniqueeeee! Nooo!" She tried to break free from Ray's hold but his strength was too much for her.

"Calm ya ass down bitch!" Ray slammed the butt of the .38 down on Glory's head. Not once, but twice, knocking her out. He quickly slid the .38 into his front pocket keeping the 9mm in his right hand. With the strength of a giant, he stood Glory up, turning her around to face him. In one motion, he tossed her over his left shoulder and started heading up the stairs.

He shut the basement door behind him as he entered the dark kitchen. He placed the 9mm to Glory's head. "I got Unique's sista with me!" he yelled out to whoever was in the house. "If you don't let me out of here, I'm gon' kill her!"

The house was soundless. He took two steps, stopped, and listened again. Nothing, not a sound.

"OK, you wanna play games. I can play games, too. I'm gonna count to five, and if you don't' show your face, I'm gonna pop her anyway. One…Two…Three…Four…Five." The house was still void of sound. "Man ain't nobody in this mothafucka!" Ray mumbled and began to walk out the kitchen to the back door of the house.

When he reached the back door, he sat Glory down on the floor with her back up against the wall. She slid down the wall and onto her side, still incoherent. He pointed the 9mm down at Glory aiming at her head, but before he could squeeze the trigger, POP!POP!POP! Three .380 bullets invaded his body, hitting him twice in the back and once in the back of his head, ending his plans of killing Glory and burning the house down.

Glory regained consciousness only after the sound of the gun shots. Her head was spinning. She had an instant headache. But that didn't stop her from staring through the darkness to see the figure that stood before her. She slowly sat up straight, re-focusing to make sure she wasn't seeing things. "Come on Glory, a soft, gentle voice uttered, then the person extended a hand.

# EPILOGUE

Today is January 4th, 2004. Sunday 1:00 pm.

It has taken over a year for my life to get back to normal. Today was a bad day. I thought a lot about Jay, his death, and his funeral. At his funeral I can remember being touched when the flag was given to his mother, and for a split second, I envisioned it was my hands. I know that might sound crazy, but seeing his young girlfriend there deterred me from fully being crushed when I saw him lying in that shiny black casket with his hands across his chest.

When I talked to Jay's mother she told me that his family thought his death was from a drug bust gone bad. She had heard other stories as well, most of them negative. What stood out for me was when she said word on the street was that he was a dirty cop and he got what a dirty cop was supposed to get. Now that I think about it, he did spend a lot; on a cop's salary.

I guess everybody was having problems back then. *I clearly remember the night I stood on my porch watching Unique, PooBear, and Supreme arguing out front. I knew something big was unfolding. So, after Unique walked me back into the house, I started plottin'. Soon as he left our house, I ran up to the bedroom and grabbed my .380 automatic that I had hidden in my closet. Jay gave it to me for protection over five years ago. It only took me a hot second to grab my gun and run back downstairs. I peeped out my window and saw the three men stepping in Unique's Mustang. I pushed my .380 into my pocket and ran out the house hopping into my Benz. Twenty minutes later, I was, four cars behind Unique as he parked his car about half a block from the house they went into. I parked on the opposite side of the street eight cars back far enough to see, but not be seen. The first person I saw step out of the car was Supreme. Then twenty minutes later, I saw my baby and PooBear step out of the car.*

*I watched them go into that house, but decided to wait outside. Ten minutes turned into twenty, twenty minutes turned into thirty, then I heard gun shots. I looked around at other houses on the block to see if bedroom lights were going to flick on after the shots rang out, but they didn't. I was scared to go in there, so I stayed outside. Then one minute after the first shot, I heard more.   I burst into tears. Although my man had gone into that house, I couldn't muster up enough courage to go in after him, so I waited. But, finally, I stepped onto the porch and crept nervously into the dark house.*

*I roamed through the house with my gun held out in front of me the way I was taught when I was a correctional officer. The house was so quiet I couldn't believe I was in the same house I had heard gun shots come from. I saw a door in the kitchen that I thought, at the time, would lead down into the basement but I ignored it. I wanted to go upstairs, so I did. When I made it to the top of the stairs, I saw the bathroom light on, but couldn't see inside the room. So I decided to go in the bathroom first. I did, and stumbled upon a gruesome scene. Blood was everywhere. I thought I was going to vomit. A man lay dead inside the bathtub. I didn't' recognize him, but I did recognize PooBear who lay on the floor face down. I hurried back downstairs. I marched into the living room and cried like a big baby. I just knew Unique was dead somewhere in that house. Then I heard a noise, the sound of a door shutting. Then a male voice called out, "I got Unique's sista with* me." The voice paused them spoke again, "If y'all don't let me out of here, I'm gon' kill her."

I took refuge behind the sofa in the living room and was shaking like a leaf. After hearing him rant and rave for several more minutes about counting and killing someone, I closed my eyes expecting to hear a gun shot, but there wasn't one. Then I heard him walking down the hall towards the back door. I moved from behind the sofa and out into view. That's when I saw him place who I believed was Glory, down on the floor up against the wall. I watched her body slide down the wall and onto its side as I quietly crept closer. He pulled what looked like a gun out and pointed it down at Glory as if he was going to shoot her. I just couldn't let him do that; so I got close up on him from behind and pumped three shots into him.

I guess the sound of my gun going off woke Glory up, because she sat straight up. I extended my hand down to her and she took it. When she got to her feet, she started crying and hugged me tighter than I was ever hugged before. She mumbled to me that Supreme and Unique were dead in the basement. I told her to lead the way to the basement and she did. But when I opened the door, to my surprise Supreme was carrying Unique up the steps.

We all walked out of that house and I took Unique to Howard University's hospital. Supreme said his bullet proof vest kept him from needing medical attention. So, he and Glory stayed behind to clean up the evidence.

The next day, the police stopped by to ask Unique some questions, but nothing came out of it. And two days later, Supreme, Glory, and I went to Wop's funeral. Three days after that, Unique was released from the hospital and mustered up enough energy to attend Pam and PooBear's funeral. PooBear and Pam both had closed caskets because they were burned in the fire that totally destroyed the house.

It took Glory a long time to allow Supreme to set the fire knowing Pam's body was in there. But, in Glory's heart, Supreme knew best. Everything that occurred that night happened because of Supreme's addiction to robbing people. If he hadn't robbed Ray, all those who died would still be here.

*As for me, over the past year, I've started back working even though Unique can take care of me. I work in the security department at the MCI center sitting in front of monitors and watching for suspicious people. I'm also engaged to be married. Unique proposed to me two months ago. I'm 6 weeks pregnant and wearing a phat two carat platinum engagement ring on my finger. We plan on tying the knot before we have our baby. I'm hoping for a girl and Unique hopes it's a boy.*

*Brother Hetep has been dropping hard science on us over the last year. He convinced Unique and Supreme to go into business together. They already own one house and three, 20- unit buildings. He has even convinced Glory to attend Maryland University. Most of all, Brother Hetep has really helped to change Supreme. After going to the Mosque regularly, Supreme promised us all that he would never rob again. He didn't want to ever endanger the people he loved again. He also said that he was now a firm believer in what goes around comes around and that it doesn't really matter if you stopped doing something that was evil, the evil that you did could still come back for you. So, it's best to do good things and let that come back for you. Either way, good or bad, the law of 'karma' will come for you.*

## Words from the Author

Writing and completing this book has been the greatest accomplishment in my life thus far. I've put in hours of work to create a good, believable story. But I wouldn't have been successful without hard work, determination, and commitment. I'm a living testament that no matter what your circumstances are, success can be achieved. Although I'm physically being stagnated, I'm mentally mobilized at the speed of a Benz sittin' on 20's (smile).

On the real though. To all my brothers and sisters incarcerated and in the hoods: Make whatever current misfortune you're in a turning point in your life and strive for the best. Be sure to sign my guestbook, and send me a shot out a www.lifechangingbooks.net.

Until my next joint,

I'm out!

Order Today!

A Life to Remember                 Double Life

## ORDER TODAY
(PHOTO COPY)

Life Changing Books
PO Box 423
Brandywine, MD. 20613

## Purchaser Information:

Please send me the book(s):
**A LIFE TO REMEMBER**

_____ @ 15.00 (U.S.)  =  _____

quantity

Shipping/Handling*        =  _____

Total Enclosed            =  _____

Name —————————————————————————————

Address —————————————————————————————

City ——————————— State ——————————— Zip Code ————————

---

**DOUBLE LIFE**

_____ @ 15.00 (U.S.)  =  _____

quantity

Shipping/Handling*        =  _____

Total Enclosed            =  _____

**PLEASE ATTACH NAME, ADDRESS, TELEPHONE NUMBER (for emergencies)**

**\*Please enclose $3.50 to cover shipping/handling ($6.00 if total more than $30.00)**

Please make checks or money orders payable to Life Changing Books (do not send cash).

Send your payment with the order form to the above address, or order on the web.
Please allow 3-4 weeks for delivery.

WWW.LIFECHANGINGBOOKS.NET